It is the height of the Roaring T[...] enthusiasm for the arts, science, a[...] the past have opened doors to a wider world, and beyond…

And yet, a dark shadow grows over the town of Arkham. Alien entities known as Ancient Ones lurk in the emptiness beyond space and time, writhing at the thresholds between worlds.

Occult rituals must be stopped and alien creatures destroyed before the Ancient Ones make our world their ruined dominion.

Only a handful of brave souls with inquisitive minds and the will to act stand against the horrors threatening to tear this world apart.

Will they prevail?

ALSO AVAILABLE

ARKHAM HORROR

Wrath of N'kai by Josh Reynolds
The Last Ritual by S A Sidor
Mask of Silver by Rosemary Jones
Litany of Dreams by Ari Marmell
The Devourer Below edited by Charlotte Llewelyn-Wells
Dark Origins: The Collected Novellas Vol 1
Cult of the Spider Queen by S A Sidor

DESCENT: LEGENDS OF THE DARK

The Doom of Fallowhearth by Robbie MacNiven
The Shield of Daqan by David Guymer
The Gates of Thelgrim by Robbie MacNiven

KEYFORGE

Tales From the Crucible edited by Charlotte Llewelyn-Wells
The Qubit Zirconium by M Darusha Wehm

LEGEND OF THE FIVE RINGS

Curse of Honor by David Annandale
Poison River by Josh Reynolds
The Night Parade of 100 Demons by Marie Brennan
Death's Kiss by Josh Reynolds
The Great Clans of Rokugan: The Collected Novellas Vol 1
To Chart the Clouds by Evan Dicken

PANDEMIC

Patient Zero by Amanda Bridgeman

TERRAFORMING MARS

In the Shadow of Deimos by Jane Killick

TWILIGHT IMPERIUM

The Fractured Void by Tim Pratt
The Necropolis Empire by Tim Pratt

ZOMBICIDE

Last Resort by Josh Reynolds

ARKHAM HORROR™

GRIM INVESTIGATIONS

∽ THE COLLECTED NOVELLAS VOLUME 2 ∾

JENNIFER BROZEK
RICHARD LEE BYERS
AMANDA DOWNUM

Origin Stories by
ANNIE VANDERMEER
GRAEME DAVIS • A P KLOSKY
JASON MARKER • MALLORY O'MEARA

ACONYTE

This collection first published by Aconyte Books in 2022

ISBN 978 1 83908 130 9

Ebook ISBN 978 1 83908 131 6

Cover art by Anders Finér

Distributed in North America by Simon & Schuster Inc, New York, USA

Printed in the United States of America

9 8 7 6 5 4 3 2 1

ACONYTE BOOKS

An imprint of Asmodee Entertainment Ltd

Mercury House, Shipstones Business Centre

North Gate, Nottingham NG7 7FN, UK

aconytebooks.com // twitter.com/aconytebooks

CONTENTS

To Fight the Black Wind by Jennifer Brozek   7

Blood of Baalshandor by Richard Lee Byers   151

Dark Revelations by Amanda Downum   269

Investigator Origins   393

About the Authors   457

TO FIGHT THE BLACK WIND

JENNIFER BROZEK

CHAPTER 1

There are events and people that change your life forevermore. It is rare, though, that we acknowledge these occurrences. My perspective, my worldview, my life has been so altered I feel I must record what happened. I will always remember this week as a turning point. I will always remember Josephine as the catalyst for that change.

It began as all such things begin – on an ordinary day. I had seen all my regular patients. Then I met my newest patient, Miss Josephine Ruggles. Our first meeting was a study in power dynamics between patients and doctors.

Josephine, heiress to the Ruggles Publishing fortune, sat on the edge of an overstuffed chair, her back straight and chin raised. She had not yet become one of the anonymous unfortunates of the asylum, shuffling to-and-fro with slumped shoulders and vacant eyes. She still wore a fine linen dress of pale yellow that enhanced her warm, tawny-beige skin. Her ebon hair held organized *curls gathered in a bow. A small gold cross adorned her neck.*

At first glance, Josephine was a lovely young woman of good manners and quality breeding. That is, if you ignored the pale blue dressing gown she wore over her linen dress. Ignored the darkness under hollow brown eyes and did not see the slight tremble to hands that clutched at the heavy silken fabric of a robe not usually worn out of the bedroom.

Her malady – nightmares that left her bloody – seemed, at first, to be a common self-harm complex. Then I looked at the wounds. The mind is powerful, but I have never seen the mind create wounds like these.

Little did I know her wounds were just the first of many mysteries I would face while caring for Josephine.

"You do not believe me, Dr Fern." Josephine's voice was a smooth contralto, roughened by fatigue.

It was a challenge designed to bring about a black and white reaction – disbelief brought distrust while belief allowed the patient to manipulate the doctor. I did neither. "We have yet to begin our first session, Miss Ruggles." As Josephine pondered this, I noted which drugs my new patient was taking. All were designed to give blissful, dreamless sleep.

Josephine gestured to the notes in my hands. "You began when you read those, *Doctor*. You do not believe me."

What would I not believe? My patient had nightmares, despite the medication she took to prevent such things, and she harmed herself at night. Something in the way she said "Doctor" made me wonder what kind of encounters she had had with Dr Mintz. Perhaps that was where her aggressive stance stemmed from.

There was nothing specific in her records. Then again, many of his more esoteric experiments were never written about in public files. I kept the distaste from my face as I took a seat in the chair next to Josephine's. "I am listening. Please, tell me what you think I do not believe."

Josephine sighed. "The wounds – the *words* on my back. You do not believe they were caused by things in my dreams. Even when they are in places I cannot reach. Even when they are fresh and lined as if made by a printing press."

None of what Josephine was suggesting was possible, of course. However, in the beginning, I always allow my patients a way out of their fantasies. A way to prove or disprove their statements. "I have not seen your wounds. I cannot judge them."

Josephine stood as if jerked by marionette strings. She turned her back to me and opened her robe. With the almost soundless crumpling of fabric to the floor, the reason for the robe became clear: the back of the linen dress was stained red-brown. The rows of weeping wounds pressed their image into the cloth. It was even and regular. While it was unusual for patients to be so careful with their self-inflicted wounds, it was possible.

"Malachi. He told me once that you might understand. That you had tried to help him."

I twitched from my examination of Josephine's back and the hieroglyphic bloodstains in linen.

"Malachi?" How could she possibly know the name of my murdered patient from Providence Sanatorium? There was no earthly way she could know of him, an itinerant man in another part of the state.

"Yes, Malachi. I used to see him in my dreams. He is gone now. I have not seen him in a long time." The beautiful woman turned in one controlled, smooth motion – another testament to her inner strength and spirit, yet unbroken by the asylum. "Do you understand? Do you believe me?"

I did not. She spoke to Malachi in her dreams? How was that possible? It was not, of course. Josephine could not be speaking of my murdered patient. That would be ludicrous. She had to be speaking of another Malachi. After all, she was speaking of conversations in dreams.

I covered my confusion by taking Josephine's robe and standing. I offered it to her with a gentle smile that hid the turmoil within. "Perhaps we should begin at the beginning. Pretend I know nothing. We will go from there."

Josephine stared at me for a long, timeless moment before she accepted her robe and slid it on. She nodded once. "The beginning then. Such as it is."

The pounding of my heart was loud in my ears as I took my seat once more. I tried to put the very idea of Malachi out of my mind. My patient was before me. She needed my help. If I listened close enough, I would understand her true trauma. I focused the whole of my being upon her.

Five heartbeats later, Josephine joined me, once more the unruffled young woman of high society. Despite her calm demeanor, the mask of her control was cracking: the unconscious flicks of her eyes about my office lingered on the windows and door as if seeking escape. If I did not work quickly, I would lose her to the asylum.

"The beginning. Three weeks ago, I woke up screaming. Even as my maid rushed into my chambers, the nightmare faded. All I remember now is a spiral of symbols and a labyrinth of woods." Josephine paused, glancing at me.

I nodded encouragement, my pen and my voice silent. It was standard fare so far. Images of being lost or out of control. I wondered what had happened three weeks ago to bring this about. I would have to find out what changed in her life.

"In truth, I do not remember these things. I wrote them in my dream journal. I have always been a vivid dreamer. Almost everyone in my family is. My brother, Leland, he dreamed even more than I do. Such lovely dreams." Sadness marred her face for a second, then disappeared back into that studied face of cultured politeness. "Even on the medication, I still dream, but I do not, cannot, remember what I dream of." Her dark eyes flittered over my face, seeking something. "I cannot tell you why the symbols or labyrinth frightened me. I regained my composure and continued my day." Her hand, with its neatly trimmed fingernails, petted the smooth fabric of her dressing gown.

Again, I said nothing, but gestured for her to continue. Silence was ever my ally. It did appear that Josephine had a rich fantasy life. Not too unusual in the grand scheme of things. The fact that her family seemed to encourage the fantasy in both of their children *was* unusual. They had clearly spoken of their dreams to each other.

Josephine's eyes glazed as she looked into the past. "I

thought it was a singular folly. Instead, I woke up screaming the next morning, and the next and the next, for a full week. I did not remember these dreams upon waking. I forced myself to forget them. I did not want to remember." She paused. "Part of me did. But I was too afraid to uncover what made me scream my throat raw each night.

"Two weeks ago, the wounds began to appear on my back. First one symbol – a word, perhaps. Then what I presume was a sentence, to what you just saw: the paragraph carved into my flesh. I chose to come here for help. I chose you to help me after I discovered you worked here."

"How did you discover this?" I noted Josephine had begun to weave me into her narrative. She assumed I believed the wounds to be writing. Alternatively, she was not willing to accept that I did not believe the wounds to be writing.

"Dr Mintz mentioned you in passing to Nurse Heather. I remembered your name from Malachi." Josephine gave me a sly smile. "As I am here voluntarily, I still have a say in who treats me. I suspect the good doctor is unhappy with this turn of events."

Again, I suppressed my distaste at the "good" doctor's experiments. "I would not doubt it. Do you mind, though, if I talk to him about his findings?" I wondered if Josephine had mentioned Malachi – *her* Malachi, not mine – to Dr Mintz. It was a name he would know.

No. It was a coincidence. Nothing more. The name, while not popular, was not unusual. She was not referring to my lost patient.

Josephine shook her head. "No, I do not mind. But I will

not be subject to his experiments. I have seen the results in some of his patients as the poor creatures pass by my room."

"Of course." I considered my words carefully. I did not want to agree or disagree with her. Nor did I want to slam any doors. Trust was still being established. I needed to make certain I understood what she was telling me. A clinical summary would be the baseline for future discussions. "As I understand it, for three weeks you have had nightmares, but no memory of what they are about. Is that correct?"

Josephine took a moment to consider my words before she nodded her agreement.

"Two weeks ago, the wounds began to appear. Were they always on your back?"

"No. The first one was on my side." She touched her left hip. "It was a single mark. After that, they moved to my back."

"Do they heal?" I wanted to write out notes, but writing anything down would throw a barrier between us. I would go from confidant to doctor with a single stroke of the pen. Trust, once broken, is difficult to re-establish. I had to rely upon my memory for now.

"Some. Though they are renewed each night. I fear I will ever carry their scars."

"Has anything new appeared in the last couple of days?" If they had, it would mean her illness was still progressing. If not, it had stabilized… perhaps with the knowledge I would be her new doctor.

Josephine shook her head. "Not that I know of. But my back is so filled with the writing, I would not be able to tell if there were something new. The pain is the same: a single, widespread ache over my entire back, heightened into sharp clarity when fabric is pulled from it."

I held my chin for a moment, considering. As a doctor of the mind, I did not physically examine my patients unless it was absolutely necessary. In this case, I believed it was. I had to see the wounds themselves to mark them and determine their healing progress. It would also give me a better sense of what could have caused them to appear in the first place.

Decided, I stood. "Miss Ruggles, I need to see your wounds. I also need to make a written copy and an impression of them. Will you allow this?"

"What will you do with them?"

"I will not know until I have seen them. It matters how the wounds were made. Looking at them will tell me." I left the door open for Josephine's remarks about her wounds to be true. I also allowed her the dignity to deny me and to protect her fabrications.

While I did not state I thought they were self-inflicted, I watched as disappointment, fear, determination, and acceptance crossed Josephine's face, one after the other. She had decided that I did not believe her, but she felt my examination would vindicate her belief that her dreams caused the marks – that she had not created them herself.

I, on the other hand, expected to see what I have always seen – the torn skin of self-inflicted wounds made by fingernails. It did not matter how neat they were.

Josephine inclined her head. "I will allow this. My maid is waiting outside your office."

Hanna, Josephine's maid, was a lady's maid in every sense. She wore a black dress of good quality and a white apron. Her sepia skin was clear and clean. Her hair – black with gray shot through it – was pulled back into a neat bun. Smile lines graced her face, and she did not have the calluses of a maid of all work. Instead, Josephine appeared to be her singular priority.

The two women were comfortable with each other and their respective roles to the point of a heightened, silent language. They understood each other on a level few reached. Hanna would go to the ends of the earth for her mistress, no doubt. Perhaps I could arrange a meeting between the two of us to see if there was something the servant could tell me that the patient could not.

I locked the office door as Hanna helped Josephine with her dress. It was rare for anyone to interrupt me during a session, but it did happen. I wanted no mistakes.

A hiss behind me caught my attention. Turning, I saw Hanna peel the linen cloth from Josephine's back. The maid reached for a soft cloth from the basket she had carried in with her – another foresight of the young Miss Ruggles, no doubt. I raised a hand and my voice. "Wait. Please. Allow me to look first."

Hanna glanced at Josephine who nodded her permission. "Pardon, ma'am. I usually bind her wounds each morning. Except for this morning."

At first glance, Josephine's back was a bloody mess, then the marks became clear. I peered close, focusing in on one of the wounds. Her skin puckered outward, as if the mark had been pushed *out* of her rather than scratched *into* her.

As I stared, the wound became a glyph before my eyes. Then the rows of marks became sentences. It *was* writing. I felt myself drawn into them. It was familiar and alien at the same time.

"Well?" Josephine asked.

I shook off the train of thought I had followed and focused back on my task. How could I have thought it was writing? They were nothing more than rows of wounds – not glyphs. I needed to determine how the wounds were made. "One moment, please."

When one scratched at a wound over and over, it left a divot. I had patients who had picked their scabs bloody. The edges of those wounds also stood up. However, the edges always morphed with the healing process and the damage caused by the tearing of scab from skin.

These edges were straight and unmarred. I touched a fingertip to Josephine's back, running it over one of the marks. Drying blood rasped against my fingertip, but the flesh beneath was soft. It felt as if this was the first time the wound had been made, even though the lacerations had been there for more than a week. This was not the repeated ripping of skin. This should not be possible.

"If you would, Hanna, clean each wound one at a time. I will copy it down. Then go on to the next one."

"Yes, doctor."

"Miss Ruggles–"

"Call me Josephine. We are… *intimates*… now. Are we not?"

Though the young woman did not turn around, I sensed her smiling at me, or at a private joke. "As you wish.

Josephine. Do the wounds continue to weep throughout the day?" I wondered if she noticed I did not invite the same familiarity of having her call me Carolyn. Whether or not she believed we were friends, we were not. There were boundaries we needed to keep as patient and doctor.

"Sometimes. The more difficult the day, the more the wounds react."

"Thank you." I nodded to Hanna. "Begin, please."

We stood like that, the heiress, her maid, and myself: a tableau of concern. Josephine held her dress to her, preserving her modesty. Hanna cleaned each wound one by one and allowed me the time to copy it down exactly before going on to the next one. A heavy silence filled the air – not awkward, just anticipatory.

As Hanna finished cleaning the blood from the last of the marks, more than half of them had begun to glisten and weep. I pulled one of my clean handkerchiefs from a desk drawer and unfolded it. "We will press this to Josephine's back in a single motion," I instructed the maid, "then pull it away as soon as all of the marks show themselves." It would not take long for the fine white cloth to capture the wounds as a whole.

Together, we covered Josephine's back. I pressed a careful hand to the fabric. The glyphs – the wounds – bled through immediately. With a nod, we pulled the handkerchief away, carrying with it a perfect replica of the writing that appeared to force its way out of Josephine's skin.

Something in the way the blood soaked into the cloth pressed another image into my mind: blood forced through the skin in myriad religious paintings. As Hanna bound her mistress's wounds and helped her dress again, one idea crowded my mind: *stigmata*.

Whatever trauma afflicted Josephine's mind, it was possible, logical even, that her only means of expressing that trauma was the manifestation of stigmata-like symptoms. I smiled, relieved. Somehow, I had a possible answer.

But I would need to consult with the "good" Dr Mintz first.

CHAPTER 2

After my meeting with Josephine, I sought out her former psychologist, Dr Mintz, for any information he would give me. I knew from the start that this would be a challenge. Thus far, I had refused to link my research into hypnotic drugs to his research involving his "dream enhancer". Had I known that his helpfulness was based only on what he could get from me, I might have refused to work at Arkham Sanatorium.

With this between us, my relationship with the "good" doctor was strained at best and adversarial at worst. I had hoped to land somewhere in between in this conversation.

Our meeting went about as well as could be expected.

"Dr Mintz!" I hailed the doctor just before he disappeared into his office. He paused in the doorway and waited – a trim, older man who gazed at me with an air of impatience. He was not a friendly man when you would not give him what he wanted. While he was not outright hostile, his pleasant demeanor was saved for those who were willing to give him something.

"What is it?" He stepped into his office and turned, putting his hands behind his back.

"Miss Josephine Ruggles. You interviewed her several times. I thought I would—"

He scoffed, interrupting me. "That hysterical woman? Have you not already sorted out the fact that she is harming herself for attention? Prescribe her some laudanum and send her home."

I paused, taken aback. "Oh? After a week with Miss Ruggles, that is your only diagnosis?"

Dr Mintz hesitated at my question and the tone of my voice. He *hmphed*. "Well, I must admit, for a woman of her race she is uncommonly well-educated, well-spoken, and well-to-do. She is remarkable in those rare aspects."

I widened my eyes, hiding my annoyance at his old-fashioned sensibilities. "Her race?"

"Yes. You do not often see black heiresses, or even educated black women for that matter."

"That is not exactly true, doctor." I kept my voice light. "I come from a well-to-do family. It was required to afford my education. More than one-fourth of my university class was not white. As for well-to-do, when it comes to the *nouveau riche*, which many of the black elite are, it is the color of your money that matters. At least among the younger generation."

The doctor *hmphed* again. "Be that as it may, Dr Fern, I stand behind my diagnosis of hysteria. Miss Ruggles simply wants attention."

"And her wounds? I have looked at them. They are very regular and the skin around them is–"

"She is talented, I will give her that. Limber enough to scratch all parts of her back. I do not know why she is hurting herself. I did not have enough time to understand that part of her psyche and she would not consent to my treatment." He peered at me, a small, condescending smile playing about his lips. "But, if you cannot solve her issues, I would be happy to consult with you. Perhaps it is time we put our collective research together. It *is* her dreams, she says, that are causing her the distress. If we can get to the root of the problem…"

I shook my head and stepped back. I would find no help here. "No, doctor. I do not believe that will be necessary. I just wanted to see your private notes from the interviews. Her case file was light on information."

"Private notes are just that, doctor. Good day." With that, he closed his office door in my face.

I adjusted my glasses. "Thank you for your help," I muttered at the uncaring door. I should have known better. He would not help me unless it also helped him. No wonder the asylum was a depressing place to be. I would need to go to the records room and see if there was something else to be found. Or, better yet, see if I could talk Nurse Heather into dropping a hint of what Dr Mintz refused to share.

I pulled my suit jacket close. Even here, in the faculty hallway, the permanent chill of the building's stone walls invaded, despite the industrial carpet and the artwork on the walls. It was the only hallway in the entire building to be carpeted. This visual and auditory cue told visitors and patients alike that the top floor of the asylum was not like the rest of it. This was where the doctors had their offices and performed their interviews. Patients in this hallway were always accompanied by asylum staff.

I hurried from the upper hall down the cramped stair-well to the lower floors where Nurse Heather spent most of her time caring for the patients in her own way. The odor of unwashed bodies hit me like a physical blow as I entered the hall. My shoes clacked against the black and white checked floor, stained with dirt and other unmentionable things. Normally, I could ignore the asylum's chill, its smell, and the dim hallway lights that cast unnatural shadows.

I worked here to make it a better place for all – doctors and patients alike. My work was not for the fainthearted, as I had learned during my time at Providence Sanatorium. But I could, and would, continue my work without falling prey to the asylum's air of desperation and damnation. I had to. I seemed to be the only one who would.

It was time to ignore my surroundings and put my task into perspective. This was no different than the first time I walked into a debate or an interview with a recalcitrant patient. It is always the first look that tells me whether or not there will be a problem. Whether it is because I am a woman or younger than whomever I am speaking to, the look is the same. I became an expert at recognizing and ignoring it at the University of Chicago.

Unsettled or not, by the time I reached the first of the patients' halls, I had my pleasant, professional mask on once more. This was one of the open halls where non-violent patients were allowed to roam between their rooms and the day room. Most days, I saw my patients in their rooms. It made them feel more comfortable. As if they had some control of the situation. I acknowledged Theresa, my dancing patient, when she waved at me – she liked to waltz with the figment of her deceased husband – and Victoria, who sat on the couch and rocked back and forth as if she were a machine. She nodded when she caught my eye, but did not cease her rocking.

I found Nurse Heather escorting an unfamiliar patient back from the showers – one of the few locked doors on this hall. I believe I would recognize the nurse's posture anywhere. With wide shoulders, a rectangular core, and short-cropped, graying hair – impossibly stylish in this austere setting – Nurse Heather would look at home in the latest flapper fashions. She always moved with deliberate intensity, like a woman on a mission. In my mind's eye, I could see her marching in a suffrage protest or dancing at a speakeasy with that same intensity.

Right now, Nurse Heather was focused on moving her patient through the chilly asylum hallway. Behind her, an orderly strolled on patrol, glancing into the patients' rooms. I noted that he kept an eye on Nurse Heather and her patient. The patient seemed common enough. Long, wet, black hair hung in the woman's face, and she had the shuffle of a thoroughly drugged patient. I dismissed her from my mind. She was not my patient, thus not my concern. "Nurse Heather, a word, if I may?"

The older woman gave me an automatic, thin-lipped smile. She held the patient by one arm as she halted in the middle of the hallway. "What is it, Dr Fern?"

"It is about Josephine Ruggles. I would like Dr Mintz's files concerning her."

"I'm sure those files were transferred to your office." She gave me a frown and pulled her patient into stillness with an absent gesture. The patient tilted her head toward our conversation.

"Not all of them."

She gave me a look and I worked to keep my breath steady. I could not stop the flush I felt creep up my neck to my cheeks.

"I see. Well then, I guess you need to talk to Dr Mintz."

"I would, but he is just going to tell me to get them from you. We both know how he is."

She raised her chin to look down her nose at me, suspicion plain on her face. "I'll see–"

The patient, who had been tilting her head up to look at me from beneath her wet hair, moved with sudden speed, pulling herself from Nurse Heather's grasp. She grabbed my arm and yanked us both to our knees. I found myself gazing into a single golden-brown eye, bright as it gave me a gimlet stare. The rest of her face was obscured by her hair.

Before I could pull myself from her, she shook her head, violent and distressed. "You must help her. You're the only one who can."

Startled and stunned, I froze where the patient held me. "Help who?" It was the only thing I could think to say. I tried to get a better look at the woman's face, but she shook her head again, hair still hiding her from me. One bright golden-brown eye – lucid despite the drugs in her system – stared back at me.

"It's within her. It was too much for me. Too many things to care for. I couldn't… She needed it… I didn't know what she'd do… the protection failed. You have to help her."

I put my hand on hers, keeping my voice calm. "I do not understand. Whom do I need to help?"

The grip on my arm tightened even as the lucidity in that single eye dimmed and dulled. "Don't make me rip the scales from your eyes. Don't make me. It'll change you forever. It'll change me, too. Please, don't make me do it!"

Then, Nurse Heather had the woman by her shoulders and wrestled her into a standing position. I stood, shaken, and watched the patient. She reached a hand to me. "Help her, please. But don't make me rip the scales from your eyes!" Then, she was in the custody of the orderly. The man wrapped a huge arm about the woman's waist as he bent one of her arms back. He propelled the no-longer-struggling woman before him with ease.

With her free arm, she reached for me, muttering about someone needing help and scales upon eyes. None of it made any sense.

"Put her in her room. Wrap her up until she's calm." Nurse Heather turned and cast an experienced eye up and down me. "Well, that was interesting. She hasn't said that much at one go since she arrived three weeks ago."

I still felt the patient's grip on my arm, still felt the urgency in her voice, still saw her trap me with her gaze. "Who is she?"

"Professor Sati Das. A professor of archaeology from England. Born in Assam, India to a British father and an Assamese woman. She fell into a coma while visiting some place here on the East Coast. She transferred in from Saint Mary's after she woke and would only babble nonsense about shards and tomes."

It made a strange sort of sense. Her British accent had been tinged with a foreigner's timber. "What did she mean by 'rip the scales from my eyes'? Has she said this sort of thing before? And whom does she want people to help?" I held my arm to my body – it still throbbed with the patient's strength of purpose.

"I don't know the answers to your questions. She's never said such to me." The nurse gave my arm a cursory look, manipulating my wrist, then my elbow. "You're fine. You're going to bruise, but that's all." Nurse Heather adjusted her nurse's cap. "It's strange. She's usually so calm."

I rubbed my arm, trying to banish the feel of Sati's cold hand from it. "Probably the malady she suffers from. We have never seen each other before. Who is her doctor?"

"Dr Mintz is in charge of her treatment. She's a possible candidate for his dream enhancer." Nurse Heather gazed at me. "I'll have to tell him of her reaction to you – when I get those records you want."

I nodded, knowing that Dr Mintz would deny the nurse. Or give her copies of the useless information he had already sent over. "Of course."

"Perhaps it's something about you… your hair color or your glasses… that struck such a chord in her." The head nurse continued to peer at me as if I were an interesting bug.

"Perhaps," I agreed, suppressing a shudder. "Thank you for getting those files for me." I gave her a nod and turned on my heel. Nurse Heather did not stop me as I hurried away, although I felt her keen gaze on my back. What else was she going to tell the good doctor about the strange encounter?

Returning to the safety of my office, grateful for the scant warmth within and the familiarity of my books, I was torn between my current case and the encounter with the professor. Why had she reacted so?

Shaking my head to clear it of the patient who was not mine, I turned to my notes of Josephine Ruggles. I peered at the copy I had made of the wounds and compared them with the handkerchief impression. The marks on Josephine's back – they looked so near to writing. Perhaps a cross between Sanskrit and Arabic; something old. A forgotten dialect? Was it possible to have a case of stigmata that resulted in written words on the skin?

I had too many questions and no answers.

In the meantime, I had to consider my treatment of Josephine for her nightmares. Whether the wounds were self-inflicted or stigmata-like symptoms, it was possible, probable even, that she would respond to my hypnotic sessions. The root of her problem was within her mind. I was sure of this.

Ransacking my reference books, I found only one mention of non-Christian-based stigmata – bleeding from the scalp, palms, side, and/or wrists – in a much older, non-medical book from the early 1800s. It was obvious that I would not find such a book in the small asylum reference library; I would need to go to the university library for a chance to find it, or something comparable.

Arkham Horror

It had been a while since I visited the Orne Library. Perhaps it held the key to Josephine's malady.

CHAPTER 3

I grew up moving about the United States. My father was a rail man and traveled from station to station, inspecting, improving, and managing them until they met Union Pacific standards. Then, we moved on. The longest we remained in a single location was two years.

This travel allowed me to discover and fall in love with the University of Chicago. One of the more progressive universities when it came to women, I completed my undergraduate work with distinction – and an open mind that many on the East Coast do not possess.

By the time I was ready for my graduate work, my family had settled down in Boston, Massachusetts. This allowed me to choose Pembroke College for my continued studies. I wanted to be close to my family. Throughout my university years, I had occasion to visit the Orne Library at Miskatonic University in search of research material for my thesis.

The University of Chicago has a wonderful library –

as does Pembroke College – filled to the brim with books.
But it does not have the sensibility, the atmosphere, or
the reverence for books that the Orne Library possesses.
It is the kind of library bibliotaphs dream of, with its
dark woods, huge stacks, and quiet atmosphere.

Entering Miskatonic University's Orne Library was like walking onto hallowed ground. A preternatural hush lay over the large, open room and the scent of old books permeated the air. Even my steps against the marbled floor were muted. I sighed a happy sigh. This library was home.

My feet knew the way to the card catalog. I slipped through the large wooden tables and nodded to the reference librarian, Ms Mayer. If I could not find what I wanted, I would ask her. However, the librarian had taught me that I needed to search on my own first because it was likely I would come across something I had not considered before.

My first round of catalog searching did bear fruit, although I was uncertain if any of it would be useful. I had four books to begin with: *Five Wounds: The First Case of Stigmata* by Davidson, 1720; *The Phenomena of Stigmata, Divine and Diabolic* by Spring and Mayhew, 1895; *Stigmata: An Investigation* by Hunt and Mead, 1901; *The Miracle of Stigmata* by Harrington, 1910. Although none of them were medical in nature, they would begin to give me an idea of whether or not Josephine's marks could be from stigmata.

While I was collecting the four books, I chanced upon one called *Written in Blood* by Sutherlin and Drury-Crusett,

1919. It was new and, at first glance, appeared to be far more analytical than the first four books. I added it to my pile. When I returned to the large wooden tables, I found myself choosing what had once been my usual seat – a table in the back corner that gave me a good view of the rest of the room. One that would limit the number of people walking behind me.

As progressive as both my universities were, that did not stop some of the less enlightened of my peers from "pranking" the women of my class. Twice I had water dumped on me from behind while I was in the library doing research, hours of work ruined. Twice I walked back to my room, soaked and flushed with classmates snickering behind my back. Twice was enough. I learned to sit where I could watch the room, the people, and my back.

Hours later, I had pages of notes on stigmata, but I was not sure if any of it would assist me with Josephine. There were no cases of stigmata appearing while the sufferer slept. There were no cases, or even stories, of the stigmata wounds spelling out words in any language. Not even stories of stigmata making a design within the flesh.

All the research – if you could call it that – was steeped in religious mysticism and always led back to the Christ figure. Even the promising *Written in Blood* book came up empty with the exception of referencing another book, *Anomalistic Thinking in Regards to Miracles* by Avi Zunger, a Jewish scholar. There was no date given for the book and I could not find it in the card catalog.

It was time to see Ms Mayer.

I approached the reference desk with the same quiet

reverence one gives respected professors. A librarian is the caretaker of the books and knows their secrets. Treat both well, and you will be rewarded with knowledge. That was what I needed now.

Ms Mayer was an older woman; her thick hair, held at the nape of her neck in a chignon, was more gray than black. She wore an impeccable polka-dotted dress and a sweater. She also had reading glasses on a long chain about her neck.

Ms Mayer waited until I was at the reference desk to look up. Her eyes brightened with familiarity. "Miss Fern, I saw you come in. Is it 'doctor' now?"

"Doctor," I confirmed.

"Well done."

"Thank you."

"What may I do for you?"

"I am looking for this book." I showed her the book's name and author. "However, it does not seem to be in the card catalog. It was mentioned in another book as reference material for the psychology behind miracles and magical thinking in regards to stigmata."

The librarian looked away for a long, silent moment, consulting her mental card catalog. She nodded to herself. "If we have it, there are a couple of places it could be. I won't be long."

With that, she left me at the reference desk. I knew better than to follow her around like a lost puppy. Instead, I returned the books I pulled to their rightful places within the stacks. I also gathered up my things. Either Ms Mayer would find what I needed, or I would be done here.

By the time I returned to the reference desk, the librarian was waiting for me. She was bent over a large tome of handwritten notes – a ledger, perhaps, or a manifest. I waited quietly until she straightened. "This is an interesting book you've requested. It's in the Rare Book Room."

"I see. Will I be allowed to look at it?" I was not certain. As one of the visiting staff from the asylum, I was permitted some access to the library, but I was not sure what privileges that afforded me.

Ms Mayer nodded. "Yes, but you will be required to stay within the Rare Book Room and to use cotton gloves. I trust you have some?"

"Yes, ma'am. I do." I showed her my gloved hands. I had kept the habit of storing cotton gloves, along with my usual gloves, in my handbag at all times – a holdover from spending many hours working with pen and paper at the university. Of course, I wore gloves outside of the asylum, but such formality was not needed within it.

She wrote something on a note card. "The Rare Book Room is on the second floor to your left at the end of the hallway. Keep that card with you. It is both reference and…" she gave me a knowing smile, "…a permission slip to be in the room. You will find what you seek on the third bookcase, the second shelf. While it isn't particularly old, it is rare and fragile. Do be careful."

I knew the admonishment was automatic. "Of course. Thank you for your help."

"You're welcome. Remember that the library closes at seven tonight, sharp."

"I shall remember." As I turned toward the stairs, I glanced at my watch. It was already just past five. I had been here for hours without realizing how much time had passed. That was the way research was. But my patient list was light, and my duties would continue in the morning. For now, I was on the trail of something that might help my newest patient.

At the end of the second-floor hallway stood an imposing set of double doors. Above the doors, a sign proclaimed this to be the *Ruggles Rare Book Room*. To the side of the closed doors, a gold and black plaque hung at eye level. I approached it with wary curiosity.

Dedicated to Thomas Ruggles (1846–1918)
In honor of his dedication to the printed word and his lifelong commitment to spreading knowledge to one and all. In remembrance of his generous support to the Orne Library. A man faithful to his family, friends, and community. His loss reminds us how important it is for the librarian to guide the novice, transmit culture, and provide information in times of chaos. He will be missed.
In loving memory, Alonzo and Nina Ruggles

I touched the raised bronze letters of the last two names. Alonzo and Nina were the names of Josephine's parents. At first blush, it appeared to be an unbelievable coincidence. Then I remembered that Josephine was the heiress to the Ruggles Publishing fortune. Of course her grandfather – if that was who Thomas Ruggles was – and her parents supported the university and its library.

I opened the doors to the Rare Book Room and took a breath, looking around. Rather than the grays and whites and dark wood of the lower floor, this room was decorated in lighter shades of brown and beige. I turned up the lights. Heavy russet drapes blocked all natural light from the delicate books. The temperature was cool but dry. I closed the doors to preserve the climate.

Ochre bookcases with glass fronts lined the walls with two sets of standing shelves that stood alongside three large tables. Each set of shelves had a brass number on top of it. So much esoteric knowledge. It made my head spin. Even the floor was a mixture of light and dark woods in a spiraling pattern, a striking contrast to the lower level's marble floor.

Knowing that time was of the essence, I moved to the third bookcase and opened the glass doors. Each of them could be locked, it seemed, and I wondered if the librarians locked the shelves or just the Rare Book Room door at night. The unmistakable scent of antique books greeted me like an old friend. Even as I scanned the second shelf for the book I wanted, I noticed that there was no dust. The librarians tended this room, and its valuable contents, well.

My treasure found, I settled in at one of the tables to read.

Anomalistic Thinking in Regards to Miracles by Avi Zunger had been written in Hebrew and translated into English. Most likely, this had been a student's graduate project. Written from back to front, a page of neatly typed English translation had been stuck between the book's pages with marks of corresponding work in the original writing. The student had probably been a linguistic major rather than a philosophy or psychology student.

I dug into the text. Avi Zunger had an interesting way of explaining the mental calisthenics the mind went through to accept the impossible. While a child could accept everything presented, no matter how improbable, Zunger questioned what could cause an adult to do the same. Perhaps there was a bound translation of the book I could order. It would be an expensive indulgence, but this book belonged in my personal library as valuable reference material.

Even as the minutes ticked by and I wrote out notes to consider when approaching Josephine and her wounds, I wondered if I had accepted the idea of stigmata too easily. I rolled this idea over and over in my mind as I gazed at the floor. Something about it was familiar... and alien.

My vision blurred. I'd stopped taking notes, stopped reading the text. The wooden pattern spiraled and undulated as if alive. The darker russet brown shapes morphed and flowed through the wood in a way not dissimilar to the marks on Josephine's back.

I pulled the note of the three symbols I'd scrawled as reference from my handbag and held it up just left of my eyes. As I compared the design of the floor to the symbols, I let my eyes relax. The marks on the floor and my note blurred in the same manner, almost becoming one design.

Was this room somehow related to my patient's malady?

I considered the answer as I put the paper away. Of course Josephine would have seen this room when it was dedicated to her family member. Of course it would have affected her. Was all this a delayed response of grief to her grandfather's passing? I would have to talk to her about this. What *had* her relationship been with Thomas Ruggles? And why would it have taken more than two years for the grief to manifest in such an overt and bloody manner?

Checking my watch, I saw it was already half past six. I needed to clean up and bid Ms Mayer a good evening. Perhaps she would know who the designer of this room was, and I would be able to link the marks on Josephine's back to her grandfather through the designer.

CHAPTER 4

Hypnotic therapy is not for all my patients. Many are too untrusting, temperamental, or are unwilling to relax enough to explore their inner thoughts through the guided technique. For a patient like that, I use a more standard set of psychological tools to get to the heart of their malady – if it is possible.

My hypnotic therapy technique came about after much research and thought. The essence of the matter is that many patients cannot face their trauma in the cold, hard light of day. But, in a relaxed, sleepy, hypnotic state, the inner child (or critic) loosens its hold and allows them to examine their trauma with a more objective mind.

I was fortunate that the chemist at Providence Sanatorium was willing to converse with me and come up with the concoction that I use today. The sedative relaxes both the body and the mind without causing blackouts. It is enough to still the discomfort of those unable to relax and open the mind to suggestion, allowing the patient to be led down difficult paths to examine their own fear and trauma. They remain just conscious enough to be aware of me, my guiding authority, and my representation of safety.

This is what I had decided Josephine needed. I was right.

With the sun high in the sky, Josephine was the last of my patients I was to see today. I pulled the drapes closed as Josephine settled in. She looked as neat as she had yesterday, in a pale blue dress and a sweater, but the hollows beneath her eyes were deeper, darker, and more haunted. She watched me with a curious gaze but said nothing. I had to prompt her into conversation again. "How are you?"

"Did I have the nightmare last night? Yes. Did I bleed again? Yes. Am I in pain? No. No more than usual." The heiress gestured to the room. "The office is set up in a different manner than yesterday."

I knew she referred to the sitting area of the office in specific. Her abrupt manner and immediate change of topic said just how bad last night had been. Weary and wary, Josephine hurt.

"Yes. The setup is new for you, but this is how I arrange things for almost all my hypnotherapy sessions. It is a visual cue for your subconscious as much as it is for comfort and utility."

The two overstuffed armchairs sat across from each other with the coffee table just to the side. The low table held my papers from her file, my examination notes, and the library research. The sedative I liked to use – syringe and drug bottle – sat on top of it all next to my light enhancer.

I sat down across from her. We were very close, with our knees no more than a couple of handbreadths apart. This closeness inspired trust and honesty for some patients like Josephine. Others, I had to sit much farther away. "After some careful thought, I have some ideas about your case. Have you experienced anything tragic in the last couple of years? A loss, perhaps?"

Josephine considered this for a long moment. "I have had losses, yes... though I cannot think of anything I would consider tragic."

"The loss of a family member or a childhood friend?"

She shook her head. "Not in the last couple of years."

Repression was a natural reaction to the pain of losing a loved one. It was not unusual for my patients to be unaware of both their loss and the mark it left on their psyche. "I believe your wounds may be a unique case of stigmata-like symptoms born of grief."

Josephine watched me, waiting for me to elaborate. When I did not, her rigid posture relaxed. "Grief? What am I... who am I grieving for?"

"Grief," I confirmed. "We will speak of that soon."

Her face shifted from confusion to surprise and grateful relief. "You believe me? I didn't... That I did not harm myself?"

"I believe you." Josephine had dismissed the idea she was suffering from grief because I might actually believe her. This relief and gratitude would make her much more amenable to our hypnotherapy session. I would need to use this.

Another note of interest. Until this moment, she had not

used a contraction with me. Perhaps it was a sign of high emotion. I would watch for it and determine its trigger. Unconscious mannerisms rarely lied – even when the patient was guarded. I gave myself a mental note to notice any and all contractions she used.

Josephine closed her eyes. "Thank you."

"You are aware I use hypnotherapy with my patients to get to the roots of their problems."

She nodded.

"I would like to use this technique on you."

"What does it require?" Suspicion returned to her voice and stiffened her posture as she opened her eyes once more. "What will it feel like? It sounds… unusual."

"It *is* unusual. Odd and strange. Some of my colleagues have called me crazy. However, they cannot deny my results or my number of cured patients." I shrugged. "It requires nothing from you except your willingness to proceed. You cannot hypnotize a person who does not wish to be. They must be willing." I gestured to the syringe and bottle of clear liquid. "This is a sedative. Again, it is not required, but it does relax the patient and make them more willing to go on the hypnotic journey."

"If I do this, what will we do?"

"We will journey into your mind. We will find the source of your pain."

Josephine locked eyes with me. "You will be with me?" It was a question, a plea, and on the outside edges, it was a command. She was a woman used to being obeyed.

"I will be with you the entire time. I'll not leave your side."

"My mind is a dangerous place, if my nightmares are any indication."

It was a challenge. I nodded. "That may well be, but I will not leave your side while we are in session. You are safe with me." This was a promise I gave all my patients, and I held my promises dear.

Her smile was brittle. "I do not believe that is true, doctor, but I believe you are sincere." With that, she unbuttoned the cuff of one sleeve and pushed both the sweater and linen fabric up, exposing her forearm. She offered it to me.

I didn't hesitate. I prepared the sedative and administered it. All the while, I spoke: part distraction, part information. "In my research, I came across a scholar who investigated the way the mind reacted when presented with the impossible – miracles, magic, the supernatural. When we are young, we accept these things because we don't know that we shouldn't. The same thing happens in dreams. When we are older and we are presented with such, we reject it until we have no other explanation. In dreams, we revert to a childlike state of acceptance of the impossible because our minds do not let us know it is impossible."

"This is what the hypnotherapy will do?"

"Yes." I pressed a cotton ball to the injection site before covering it with a bandage. I even helped her straighten her sleeve and button her cuff, as if I were a stand-in for Hanna. "If we are expecting something miraculous to occur, it is as if our minds regress to an innocent state of acceptance. Thus, when the event happens, we accept it without question."

I dimmed the lights until one light shone above and

behind Josephine. "This is what I want you to do. I want you to acknowledge and accept every thought that comes to your head as we journey. No matter what you think, you will be safe. I shall be by your side."

"Do you promise?" Josephine's voice already had the soft quality of one relaxed.

I saw her slump against the comfortable chair. Her dark brown eyes watched me from under heavy lids. "I promise. I won't leave your side while we're in session." I picked up the light enhancer from the coffee table – a device I had invented to help my patients go under. It was little more than a wooden frame with a metal disk suspended in the middle by a thin wire. I sat down across from her. "Focus your attention here, on this disk, Josephine." I set the disk rocking back and forth. The moving light played over her face.

Josephine smiled. "No watch?"

"No watch," I confirmed. "This is therapy, not a sideshow act. No need for a flashy watch to catch the eyes of both an audience and a participant. Just this. Just you. Just me. Focus on this light and let your thoughts wander. Let them go where they will. If your eyelids are heavy, let them close."

She closed her eyes, opened them once, and then closed them again.

I kept my voice low and smooth. A consistent monotone was the key until the patient was under. "Remember, you are safe with me."

"Safe." Josephine's voice was soft and asleep. The sedative mixture worked quickly.

I lowered the light enhancer to my lap. "We are going on

a journey. I want you to think about the last three weeks. Think about them as if they happened to someone else. There is a sheer veil between you and the memories. When you remember, it will be as if it happened to someone else. They cannot touch you. Do you understand, Josephine?"

"It cannot touch me." Her chest rose and fell in regular, slow breaths. Calm and serene.

"Go deeper, Josephine. Sleep. Let your thoughts take you where they will." When Josephine did not respond, I waited and counted her slow breaths. On her seventh breath I asked, "Josephine? Can you hear me?"

"Yes." Her answer was an exhale of breath.

"We have begun your journey. Where are you?"

"I'm approaching the Seventy Steps of Light Slumber."

I paused. That was a peculiar turn of phrase I had never heard before. It seemed specific and important to Josephine. "Describe where you are. Tell me about the Seventy Steps of Light Slumber."

"I walk the path of stone toward the stairs. On either side of me is the mist. I can hear things in it."

I watched Josephine's face. She appeared more than just relaxed. She was comfortable with her surroundings. "How do you feel?"

"I feel fine, thank you." The response was automatic. "I know this place. I have been here before." Josephine paused for a long time, her head twitching back and forth. "Where are you?"

"I am right here, Josephine. Right by your side."

"Not there. I need you *here*. You promised. The Stairs are just down the path. I need you *with* me."

My frown matched hers. I didn't understand. I put the light enhancer on the table and reached out to cover one of her hands with my own. "I'm right here, Josephine."

She flipped her hand over and grabbed me by the wrist in a grip stronger than I expected. "There you are. Come. We need to go. There is something I must do."

I winced as the light above Josephine's head shone bright in my face. Then gravity shifted and I was falling through a rainbow of colors. Before I could cry out, my falling body shifted, and I was flying. I could see Josephine's hand on my wrist, but nothing else of her. All around me colored light pulsed and shimmered in undulating waves.

Gravity reasserted itself as my head spun and the world tilted sideways. My body, crouched forward as I had been sitting on the edge of the chair, stumbled forward in an effort to keep me from falling. The chair was gone. Josephine grabbed me by the shoulder. It kept me from tumbling to the ground, but not from banging into the hard wall that hadn't been there moments before.

Dazed, I pulled back from my patient and the wall. I stared. I was not in my office anymore. I didn't know where I was. I hugged myself, blinking and gasping, trying to make sense of what had just happened.

We were in a stone corridor without any windows or doors. The air was fresh with a faint tinge of wetness. It reminded me a little of the asylum, but the smell was wrong – wetter, loamier. I looked for the lights, saw none, and wondered how the hallway was illuminated. The walls were cool and moist to the touch. More importantly, they were solid.

It was impossible. The wet chill, so familiar and so different from the normal atmosphere of the asylum, told me otherwise. All my senses told me I was here, in this new, unfamiliar place.

Josephine stood halfway between me and the darkness at the end of the hallway – a hallway that hadn't been there before. One I didn't recognize. "Where are we?"

She tilted her head and gave me the kind of look you give a particularly slow student when the answer is obvious. "The Dreamlands, of course."

I walked to her, noting that she no longer wore a dress. Instead, she wore the kind of thing a working archaeologist might wear in the field – pants, boots, shirt, gloves, belt with canteen, and a vest. Everything had changed. I was still in my usual work attire – long skirt, blouse, warm suit jacket, stockings, and sensible shoes. I was the same as before. "I don't understand. I, *we*, were in my office."

Josephine let out a slow breath. "We don't have time for this. I have a task to perform."

"What task?" My mind spun, confused. We'd just been in a therapy session in my office. How had we gotten here?

"Once we get down the Stairs." She turned and walked down the corridor.

I rubbed my face and looked again. The stone corridor was still there. I followed her at a slower pace, grappling with this turn of events. Perhaps my foray into anomalous thinking put me into a similar hypnotic state. Perhaps that was what was needed with Josephine's case. I struggled to put myself back into the doctor's state of mind, to regain my equilibrium.

"Josephine, describe what you see."

She stopped and turned to me. "You see what I see. Don't you?"

"You mentioned mist before. I don't see mist."

"Oh. Well, there is a stone path. It is black and worn, but not dusty. All around us is mist and shadows within the mist. Above, there is a purple sky with blue-purple clouds." She gestured to each area as she spoke. "What do you see?"

I took a slow breath, working hard to remain calm – or to at least appear to be calm. I would not panic. I had my patient's mental state to consider. "I see a long stone corridor that leads into darkness." I pointed down the hallway. "It's cool and damp here. I don't know where the light comes from." I watched her with a keen eye to see what her response would be to the fact that I disagreed with what she said was around us.

Her response was not as I expected.

Josephine laughed and clapped her hands together with delight. "That is the Dreamlands. It is a bit different for everyone. Still, you see the same path I do, leading in the same direction. That is enough for now." She turned away and walked toward the darkness.

The farther she went, the more the darkness receded. I could almost see a door at the end of the hall. As I moved to follow her, a small hand touched my arm. Behind me was a child in tan shorts, white shirt, peach tie, and a tan jacket. He also wore black knee socks and black shoes. "What can I do for you?" I asked.

"You understand that you are making a huge mistake,

yes?" The child gave a contemptuous sniff. "That woman is hysterical. If you follow her, you will fall into her delusions."

"Miss Ruggles is my patient, Dr Mintz. I will do what I believe is best. Right now, it is a joint hypnotherapy session." Eying the spoiled child, part of me understood this version of Dr Mintz was my subconscious fighting against the surrealistic turn the therapy session had taken. Dr Mintz was jealous of my skill and my ability to help my patients without torturing them, and so my mind had transformed him into the form of a petulant little boy.

"You will regret this," he warned.

"No, I won't. If you'll excuse me, I'm very busy." I turned from the child and felt the door close behind me. Josephine stood there with a smile.

She gestured before us. "The Seventy Steps of Light Slumber."

Though we had not moved, the corridor was gone. We were on the edge of a cliff at the top of a set of steep stairs. They were wooden and interconnected by stiff wires that kept them still as they hung in the air without a visible means of support. It was a straight line down to an island landing, also suspended in mid-air.

On this landing, there was a huge gate that spanned the width of the rocky platform. Gold-bronze and glimmering, the gate reached skyward and appeared to go on forever, disappearing into a roiling darkness above that reminded me of storm clouds. I looked down and saw the cliff edge we stood on jutted out over nothing. Not darkness. Just nothing. It was all my mind could compare it to. My stomach flip-flopped. I stepped backward.

"Time to go, doctor." Josephine beckoned before she took to those fragile stairs, the only touchstone above the chasm of nothingness.

I looked down to the landing again. This time, I saw two robed figures – one in red and one in black – standing before the gates. Each held a huge weapon at the ready.

CHAPTER 5

I have never been one to refuse a challenge. To show timidity or uncertainty in front of my peers in college was to admit weakness – something I could not afford to do in that competitive world. This has served me well in my professional life. Unexpectedly, this stubbornness and unwillingness to acquiesce assisted me in my efforts to learn how to lucid dream. When faced with an impossible situation, I learned to accept what I saw and to seek out specific cues to my state of being – awake or asleep.

Josephine descended the stairs with a grace and surety born of familiarity. I descended at a slower pace, still thinking about how I got here. If I focused on that, I couldn't fixate on how high up we were and how small each step was. I was still within my office. But, somehow, I was also in a hypnotic state. This wasn't real. It couldn't be. Was I lucid dreaming? I tested this.

Looking down and to the left, I asked, "Am I awake?" I

looked up and around. I was still upon the wooden stairs. I felt awake. I looked at my wristwatch. 3:11. I looked away and at it again. Still 3:11. In dreams, I had never been able to read my watch a second time. Ergo, I was awake. I looked at my blue skirt and thought, *I should be wearing pants. I need pants for an adventure.* Before my eyes, my skirt shimmered into pants. Rather than being startled, I relaxed. I *was* in a hypnotic dream state – both dreaming and awake. It accounted for the conflict of visual clues. My will was strong enough to control it if I could just remember the truth of the reality I was now in.

Movement caught my eye. The robed figures below crossed their weapons before Josephine. How had she gotten so far ahead of me? I promised to stay by her side. Heart racing, I descended the stairs faster than was comfortable, almost stumbling. A fall would be disastrous. There was nothing except an endless chasm below. Even as the robed figures straightened and allowed Josephine to pass, I wondered if it was this fall that made people on the edge of sleep jerk awake.

Pushing the thought away, I hurried down the stairs. "Josephine, wait…"

She paused, a beige-clad black woman on the other side of gold barred gates. "You have not been here before. You must show Nasht and Kaman-Thah that you are strong enough to survive the Seven Hundred Steps of Deeper Slumber." Although she was far away, she didn't yell. I could hear her as if she stood by my side.

"How?" I ran in an uneven gait toward them, keeping my eyes on the landing. I refused to look elsewhere.

"You will know." Josephine turned her back to me and waited.

I slowed as I reached the guardians – for they could be nothing else. They were huge, at least twice as tall and twice as wide as a man. Up close, the robes were identical except for the color. Both had similar beards, but I couldn't see their faces. The beards – brown, long, and evenly trimmed, hung to their chests. The hoods that obscured their faces stood irregular from their heads, as if they wore crowns beneath the fabric. They crossed their weapons, a halberd and a scythe, before the gate and remained silent.

I waited, keeping my own silence.

"Time is of the essence." It was Josephine. The words were whispered in my ear even though she had not turned around.

Mustering my courage, I raised my chin. "I will pass. I have a job to do."

In response, each guardian held out a closed fist. "Which hand revives the dead?" Although neither guardian spoke, the voice was all around me. Both robed figures opened their fists just long enough for me to see a crushed butterfly within before closing them again.

I bowed my head in thought. It was a test. One of mental fortitude. It was a trick as well. It had to be. Some part of my subconscious created this challenge to show me how difficult Josephine's case would be and to prove to her that I was up to the challenge.

I concentrated and held out two closed fists as I raised my head. "These hands revive the dead." With that, I opened my hands and released two butterflies – both very much alive.

The guardians, Nasht and Kaman-Thah, opened empty hands before they straightened their weapons and allowed me access to the gate. Holding my breath, I approached and pulled on the gold bars. The gates didn't move. They seemed rooted deep within the rock. I peered close. Glimmering, gold, and just far enough apart that I should be able to slide through them.

As Josephine said, time was of the essence – perhaps she feared that the longer she spent in the asylum, the more likely Dr Mintz would turn her into one of his experimental subjects. I pushed through the bars. It was tight, but they bowed, allowing me to pass.

Josephine waited at the head of another impossibly steep set of stairs that had no rail and disappeared into the darkness below. They looked exactly like the stairs I'd already traversed. I didn't want to go down another set of stairs like that again. I looked back at the gate. The bars were tightly spaced. I shouldn't have been able to fit through there. My mind gnawed on this.

Josephine touched my arm. "We must go."

"Where?"

She nodded down the stairs that terrified me. "The Seven Hundred Steps of Deeper Slumber. At the bottom, we will reach the Enchanted Wood."

Josephine continued to improve. Her cheeks flushed with exhilaration and the darkness beneath her eyes had all but disappeared. Her speech had returned to its normal formality. "How do you know this?"

Josephine shrugged as she looked around. "I have been here before. This is the beginning of every journey."

"Tell me what you see."

She glanced at my face, searching for something, before she turned to our surroundings. "The stairs spiral down. They are marble. The handrail is wrought iron. All around us the sun shines and puffy clouds drift through. Within the clouds, pupperflies play."

As she spoke, I imagined what she described. Before my eyes, the straight, deeply plunging stairs became a marble spiral with a wrought iron handrail. They reminded me of the marble stairs within the university library. I seized upon this and focused to make the stairs I saw match the stairs I was familiar with. As I did so, the encroaching darkness receded, and fluffy clouds appeared. I didn't see anything playing within the clouds, and I didn't know what "pupperflies" were, thus they weren't important.

What was important was the fact that this was a shared dream-state hallucination – mostly. As long as the two of us agreed upon what we saw, all would be well. It would make for a fascinating research paper in the future. I gestured for her to go ahead. "Lead on. This is your adventure."

Josephine hesitated before beginning her descent. "You believe me? You see what I see?"

"I forced my mind to see as you see. For me, so many stairs feel dangerous. But as you said, you've been here before. I knew they wouldn't seem dangerous to you. I needed to see things the way you see them. Does that make sense?"

I followed her, keeping close behind. The iron railing was a comfort, and I kept my hand on the cool metal. It was not the wood of the university library staircase, but it was a banister and that was worth everything. This control meant I could continue on and help Josephine like I had been unable to help Malachi.

"Is that part of your anomalous thinking?"

"A little. I'm not in a childlike state, but I am willing to entertain what comes to your mind."

We both laughed at that. Our laughter trailed off at a sound. Josephine and I stopped on the stairs and listened. For a long moment, we could only hear our own breath. Then it came again: a cry for help.

Josephine gasped, "Oh no! I forgot. How could I do that? I'm late. Oh, poor kitty."

Without waiting for me, Josephine sprinted down the winding staircase. Whatever was happening was bad. She'd lost control and used contractions again. I ran after her, slower and less sure, but sped up as another cry for help came from below.

I fell just as Josephine disappeared from view.

Tumbling down the stairs, I banged against the railing and rebounded, rolling over and over. My head struck the corner of a marble stair. Lights flashed before me. The pain was enormous. Dazed, I continued to fall. It was too much. I was about to go over the railing. If I did that, I would fall to my death. Or worse, I'd never stop falling.

As I bounced up and over the railing, I shot out a hand and grabbed for whatever I could. I caught one of the balusters and slid down it. My body jerked as I hit the bottom rail and held on. I hung there – partly suspended over nothing and partly over the winding staircase. I could try to climb up or try to swing myself over the stairs below and drop. I wasn't strong enough for the former, and the latter gave me a chance of falling into the abyss.

I looked down. The stairs were so far away. I closed my eyes. "This is a dream. This isn't real. I can fly. I can fly." I swung my legs back and forth and opened my eyes as I flung myself at the stairs. "I can fly!"

I didn't fly.

I didn't fall.

I floated from my hanging spot to the stairs I'd been looking at. As I landed with a soft bump, I collapsed to my knees and shuddered. I was much closer to the bottom than I had been, but I needed to collect myself. I covered my face, shaking, and forced slow, calming breaths.

There was no time for that.

As Josephine's shouts entered the fray from below, I remembered why I was here: I *needed* to be by my patient's side. Josephine would not be another Malachi. She would not die under mysterious circumstances. With a speed and agility born of my sense of duty, I was up and sprinting down the last of the stairs once more. This time, there was no hesitation, no fear. My patient needed me. I would be there for her.

The bottom of the stairs disappeared into the deep, green foliage of oak leaves and trees. I didn't pause. I plunged into, then through, the branches that wound themselves around the stairs. I met the ground with enough give that I was forced to stop and get my bearings. It was the loamy soil of a deep forest, covered in years of fallen leaves that hid gnarled roots and ankle-breaking holes.

I pushed myself to my knees. All around me, glowing

fungi dotted the forest floor. This must be the Enchanted Wood. Things rustled in the underbrush as I looked for Josephine – things I didn't want to see. Some of the oak trees appeared to be fighting vines that threatened to strangle them. As I watched, a vine shifted and slithered around a thick branch as if it were alive, sentient. Shouts broke through my horrified fascination.

Two voices rose above the squeaks and chatter of animals. Josephine shouted, "Get away! Get away from him!" The other voice, higher pitched like a child's, encouraged her. "Get 'em, Josephine! Get 'em!"

I surged to my feet and ran in the direction of the melee. I hurried as fast as I could through the unfamiliar forest. I dodged around oak trees with branches that had exploded out from their trunks like frozen fireworks in wood. I rounded a large tree and stumbled into a glade. In the middle was the largest oak tree I'd ever seen. Josephine, standing on its jutting roots, was dwarfed by the size of them. Above her was an orange cat. Below her was a swarm of creatures I'd never seen before. They looked like a cross between a rat and a weasel, with large, tattered ears, bulbous, goat-like eyes, and a writhing mass of tentacles where their mouths should be.

As they leapt for Josephine with sharp claws and grasping tentacles, they chattered and squeaked to each other. As one, they would leap upon the oaken roots to dart at Josephine's feet. She swung her makeshift weapon, a fallen branch, forcing them back again.

I saw a small contingent of the creatures move with silent steps around the huge tree to the back. They climbed with slow, sinuous motions, flat against the bark. Their target was the orange cat.

I needed a weapon. A good one. One I was familiar with. I saw it in my mind's eye. My father's 1911 Colt .45. Not a decade before, he'd carried it in the Great War. When I started at Providence, he forced me to learn to shoot, and learn I did. I was very good. The pistol now resided in my office desk in the back of one of the drawers. I'd never used it on the job, but I still kept in practice.

Even as I thought about the pistol, I felt its weight in my hand. It was a comfort. I didn't need to look down to know it was there. I braced my arm against a branch and aimed. The shot went wide of the tree. I instinctively knew I shouldn't hurt the creature I'd aimed at. The shot was deafening in the forest and every single creature froze at its sound.

Coming out from behind the tree, I called in a loud, strong voice. "I am very good with this pistol. I didn't hit any of you on purpose. It's time for you to go. Now." I don't know why I spoke to those creatures as I did, but they'd displayed intelligence. I assumed they'd understand me.

They did.

As one, they swarmed toward me – not in malice, but curiosity. A tumble of voices cascaded around me. "Who is she?" "She's new." "She has a weapon. A strong weapon." "A good ally."

I stood my ground. They stopped about ten feet from me in a clump. One of them came forward and peered with those disconcerting, goat-like eyes. "You didn't hurt us. Why?"

I shook my head. "I didn't have to." This close up, I could see their tentacles had suckers on them and wondered how they could eat, and what. I refused to think about what they would've done to the cat.

"You are good and strong. Come. Come with the zoog. We're good allies. Come now. The Enchanted Wood is dangerous. We'll protect you."

Again, I shook my head and sheathed the pistol in the thigh holster I knew was there. "No. I have other duties. Thank you." I glanced up at Josephine. At this point, she was on the ground next to the oak tree with the orange cat wrapped about her shoulders.

The zoog began muttering and chittering among themselves. "As you will. The cats of Ulthar are dangerous. When they betray you, come back here. Come to us. We'll protect you."

I inclined my head once – an acknowledgment, but not an agreement – and said nothing. They looked between us a last time, then scampered off as one into the forest like a moving carpet of fur, tentacles, and claws. As they went, I hurried to Josephine.

"That was brilliant." The words came from the orange cat wrapped about Josephine's shoulders.

"A talking cat. Can this get any weirder?" I shook my head. "Are you all right?"

Josephine smiled at me as she nodded. "Absolutely. It will get much weirder. It *is* the Dreamlands after all. Also, yes, I am well." She pet the cat that snuggled to her. "This is Foolishness, a friend of mine."

"Foolishness. A pleasure." I started to offer a hand, but

I didn't know what the etiquette of meeting a talking cat was. I settled for crossing my arms. "What are you doing out here?"

The cat yawned. "I do what I'm supposed to do. I'm foolish. I walk in the Enchanted Wood alone. I get harried by the zoog. You, or someone like you, rescues me. We all have our parts to play in keeping the Dreamlands as stable as they can be."

I looked around the glade and at the huge oak tree in front of us. The world looked stable enough. Grass peeked up through the fallen leaves. Tiny flowers made of colored paper adorned the winding tree roots that edged the glade. The sun shone overhead. It even looked as if some of the trees were smiling.

Foolishness stood on Josephine's shoulders, stretched, then jumped down. "Come along. I'm sure you wish to speak to Insightful. She'll know what you're doing here." With that he strode off toward a path through the forest I hadn't noticed before.

Josephine linked an arm through mine and led me down the open road. Flowers appeared at our sides as we passed by. "I love that kitty. He is his namesake, but he is an ally."

"You know him?" The trees above us made a natural tunnel of green and gold at the top that morphed into a darkness filled with fungi and scuttling creatures at the bottom. I kept my eyes and attention on the orange cat strutting in front of us with his tail held high.

"Oh, yes. I've rescued him dozens of times."

"Have you ever failed to rescue him?" Josephine didn't respond, but from the look on her face the answer was yes.

Ahead, the forest thinned and ended as tree branches parted, allowing us passage. We stopped at the tree line. Josephine gave a grand gesture as if she were revealing something magnificent. In truth, she was. Across a field, I saw the first buildings of Ulthar.

CHAPTER 6

When you move every couple of years, as I did when I was young, you learn that places are different. Not just strange people and new buildings. It is the landscape itself. The color palette is subtly off until you get used to it. Trees are the wrong shade of green and are shaped differently – rounder instead of triangular. The grass is lighter or longer or stiffer. The buildings are made from yellower rock instead of red. It seemed to me that the farther away from the coast you went, the lighter, yellower, or browner the landscape became. If you were not looking for it, all you would know is that something was "not right" about the new place you were in.

One of the things I would do as a child when we arrived at our new home was pick out exactly what was different – flora, fauna, and colors. I did not know it then, but I was creating coping mechanisms for the loss of my home and friends and all things familiar.

At first, it looked like a small New England village, but the closer we came, the more it looked like what someone *thought* a New England village should look like. Between the meadow and the start of the village was a road that gave Ulthar the perfect border. The rest of the village was displayed like a postcard on the gentle slope of the foothills. The village proper clustered together in a series of business buildings and homes. The rest of the land to either side of the village was farmland as far as the eye could see. Behind it all, the mountain stood as if shepherding its flock below.

It was beautiful and not quite right. It was too neat, too properly quaint for a real village. The central area appeared to be laid out in the shape of a cross with shops on the main street and administrative buildings on the cross street. Snaking out from the sides were several dirt roads that picturesquely wound their way out to numerous farms and small houses. This appeared to be where the bulk of the people of Ulthar lived – if you judged by the people coming and going.

In the center of it all, there was an actual town square. This was where Foolishness led us. Almost every building had some sort of cat motif adorning it in the form of statues, metal silhouettes, and etched glass. People watched the cat lead us toward a door with a sign emblazoned above it: *Einar's Place.*

The cats watched us as well. There were dozens upon dozens of cats in the streets, on porches, in windows, and in the alleys between buildings. All of them looked healthy, well fed, and clean. Several smaller ones, older than kittens but not quite adults, followed us. There were no meows, hisses, yowls, or trills normally associated with cats. Just the soft murmur of voices from humans and felines alike.

Rather than being strange, this felt appropriate. As if it were meant to be. I gave the village and our watchers one last look before I entered Einar's Place after our escort and my patient. Inside, I found myself in a tavern, clean smelling and welcoming. Long tables lined the almost empty room. Two people and three cats turned as we came in.

I froze. One of the people looked like Malachi. Just as I was about to call out to him, he laughed and stood. I was mistaken. That wasn't Malachi. He was too different in stature and tone. I just wanted him to be my dead patient, well again. The man looked over his shoulder, a smile playing about his lips as if he knew he'd fooled me.

Josephine touched my shoulder. "We need to wait."

"Yes," I nodded. I looked from her to the man and found him gone. I shivered, unsettled. "All right."

Foolishness wound himself through our ankles. "I'll find Insightful." The cat disappeared among the legs of the tables and chairs.

Josephine chose a table and sat. "I remember when my brother first brought me here."

"Your brother?" I furrowed my brow. Ah, yes. Leland.

"Sometimes, we would meet in dreams. When he thought I was old enough, he brought me here." She gave me that sly smile of hers. "Our parents did not know. They had a timeline for everything. Sometimes, we skipped the timeline."

"I don't have a brother or any siblings. What was it like?"

Josephine smiled to herself. "It was terrible and lovely

at the same time. Leland was older than me. Sometimes, I think he resented me as the youngest. We fought over so many things. But he was my big brother and he protected me from all who would do me harm."

I glanced at the ceiling with its large, dark wood beams. Leland might be the source of her grief, but I could not remember how he had died. Just that he had passed. "It sounds like a complicated relationship."

"It was. The older I became, the more we understood each other." Her smile disappeared. "Then he left, as all siblings must do in the end." She hugged herself and turned away, ending the conversation.

I sat across from Josephine, watching her and letting the silence grow until she relaxed into that familiar waiting pose. The tavern was like the rest of the village: it looked like a tavern you would see in picture books. The artwork wasn't exactly normal pub fare, however. A framed silhouette of a cat, gold against a black background, hung above the hearth. I gestured to it. "They really like their cats here."

"Of course we do." A heavyset man approached with a couple of tankards. "They're the eyes and ears of the god Ulthar." He gave me a curious look at my obvious lack of knowledge. "Real kitten here, eh, Josephine? Where'd you dig her up?"

Josephine folded her hands. "Good day, Einar. Please meet Dr Carolyn Fern. She is my doctor and a good one at that." Although her tone of voice was smooth and polite, her mild rebuke was plain.

"Pardon, uh, doctor." Einar put the tankards on the

table. "Didn't mean any disrespect. It's just strange here in Ulthar for someone to not know of Ulthar." He glanced at Josephine who nodded her approval. "Ulthar was put on earth to watch the other Elder and Outer Gods. It's said that if things go too wrong, Ulthar will reveal himself and deal with them."

I glanced between Josephine and Einar. "Elder Gods?"

He shook his head. "We don't say their names. Not even here where we're so blessed and protected."

Josephine nodded. "So true. I will explain them later."

"*I* will explain them sooner." This came from a small, long-haired calico cat not much bigger than a loaf of bread. She leapt to the table and sat, wrapping her tail about her paws.

Einar looked uncomfortable. "Anything for you, Insightful?"

The cat shook her head. "No. I have business with these two."

Fascinated, I watched as the cat commanded the room. Her presence was enormous despite her small body. Einar ducked his head and hurried away. Josephine and Foolishness both regarded Insightful with respect.

"Welcome home, Josephine. Welcome, Carolyn."

"Hello."

Sometimes when Insightful spoke, it looked like she actually spoke in words. Sometimes, it looked like she spoke with only her body. "You don't have much time and you have much to do while you are here." Insightful twitched the end of her tail. "But it's dangerous for you to be so naïve to the true ways of the universe."

"You speak of these otherworldly gods?" Just saying those words gave me a shiver. It reminded me of the spiral I'd started to fall into while looking at the marks on Josephine's back. "Who are they?"

"Your world is but one facet of many."

The cat inclined her head toward a ring on the table I hadn't noticed before. I picked it up, shocked at its familiarity. "This is my mother's."

"And will be yours when she passes. I know. I plucked it from your mind. Look at the emerald. The top facet is the world you know, Earth. Do you see the facets to the sides? This one is the Dreamlands. That one is R'lyeh. Each of the others is a different plane of existence, but part of the whole."

As the cat spoke, I found myself not only holding the ring, but standing on top of the emerald itself. I watched the tiny version of me upon the precious jewel. Around me, the tavern persisted, yet became even more unreal.

"Look within the gem. Do you see the other facets? The Elder Gods live here, the Outer Gods there. They want to be on the top."

Both versions of me watched the play of light through the gemstone. "The facets are moving."

"Yes." Insightful walked at my side even as she sat on the table before me. "The facets move. When the edges of the other planes come into contact, beings of that plane can cross over. When all the edges come together…"

"When the stars are aligned…" Josephine walked on my other side.

"The gods travel. When that happens, the order is upset.

We, the cats of Ulthar, watch and wait and try to prevent that from happening. We don't always succeed."

"What happens when you fail?"

"Madness and death."

All at once I was singular again, sitting in the tavern with Josephine and the cat. Insightful lifted her paw and pulled my mother's ring from my hand with a delicate claw. The ring disappeared as she did so. I sat back and pet the black cat that had snuggled into my lap, purring. I don't know when she arrived, but I was grateful for her warmth.

I gazed at Insightful's green eyes, the color of my mother's emerald ring. "I…"

"Ask your questions, Carolyn."

"What are these Elder… Outer… Gods?"

"Beings of great power. Ancient and alien." The cat shook her head. "That is not your question."

I flicked a glance at Josephine. She gazed at her clasped hands. "What does any of this have to do with my… with Josephine? I must help her. These nightmares. The wounds on her back." Josephine raised her head as I spoke her name, but she didn't say anything.

"That is the appropriate question." Insightful flicked her ears about as if listening to something. "The short answer is: everything."

"That isn't helpful." I tried to keep the irritation out of my voice. I failed.

The cat continued as if I hadn't spoken. "The longer answer is this: your journey here is what will help or hinder Josephine. She has a duty. One she's forgotten – for good or ill. You also have a duty. To her. Thus, her burdens are yours.

Both of you will lose something important as soon as you gain what you need from this place. It's not an easy path you must walk. You have already met the one who will help you."

I shook my head. "I don't understand. You didn't answer my question. What do these gods have to do with Josephine's malady?"

"The edges of the planes also meet in a point. A point in time and space. A gate. A portal. These points are rare and dangerous. They have so much power. They are protected in the only way we know how." Insightful turned her attention to Josephine. "You've been gone for too long. You need to return to your childhood. You must remember what you already know."

Josephine pressed her lips together for a moment. "I think I remember the way."

The cat licked her paw then rubbed her cheek. "How you get there is of no consequence, as long as you get there." She turned back to me. "You will help her. In your duty, you will lose something so precious it makes me weep at the thought. But you will gain what you need – what you must have – to continue your own journey. This dream is merely the beginning."

None of this made sense. Not to my logical mind. But there was more here. I could feel it. Dream logic wasn't the same as waking logic. I pushed my frustration away. "Thank you for your… insight." Josephine smiled at me. My returned smile was quick and perfunctory. As interesting and unnerving as the idea of alien gods breaking into my world was, it was still just an idea. Surely they couldn't be actual *gods*.

I shook my discomfort off and pet the cat in my lap again. My patient was before me. She was very real, and she'd said something I could follow up on. I just needed time and privacy with her. "Josephine, I think it's time for us to go."

The black cat in my lap jumped down. I missed her warmth and comfort, but it was time to get to work. The cat rubbed against Josephine's ankle before she looked back at me. In my mind, I heard her say, *"In times of need, think of me."*

In a rush, I realized that the cat's name was Comfort, and she was the reason I'd been taking these most outlandish revelations so well. It was a strange comfort to know that a talking cat kept me from going a little mad. Then again, I understood in all of this there was a journey I needed to take in order to help Josephine. I was willing to do so, no matter how odd or unbelievable.

Josephine and I left the tavern. I realized that neither of us had drunk from the tankards nor paid for the drinks. I wondered if, like in the fairy tales, one should not drink or eat in the Dreamlands. In truth, I wasn't hungry or thirsty, but we'd only just begun.

"Do you know where we're going?" I watched Josephine as much as I watched the beautiful buildings of the village that we passed by. Foolishness continued to escort us even as he took a moment to chase a flock of tiny flying books that scattered like butterflies at his half-hearted swipe.

Josephine frowned. "I… believe so. Insightful said 'back to my childhood' but I believe she actually meant to… to…" She stopped. "The idea is right there. I cannot reach it. There is a veil between my grasping mind and the idea of it."

"Perhaps Insightful meant a place you loved as a child?"

Her head came up. "Perhaps."

I could tell that she wanted to say more, although not here, not in such an open place. As we reached the edge of town, I halted and hunkered next to Foolishness. "Thank you for your help."

"My pleasure. Nice to get away from my duty every once in a while." Foolishness bumped his head against my leg.

I obliged him with a scritch behind the ears. "Do you have any other advice for us?"

"Yes. When you've done what you need to do, return *here*. If not to Ulthar itself, return to the glade where we met. I'm sure we'll meet again."

"Will we need to save you again?"

Foolishness flicked his tail back and forth. "Perhaps. Perhaps I'll do the saving. Just make sure you come back to this place. Don't try to leave through another path."

Josephine stroked his back. "We will."

I stood and looked toward the steep, rocky path we were to traverse. "Our path is before us. One step at a time." I led the way, wanting to put Ulthar and the talking cats behind me. More to the point, I wanted to speak with Josephine about what she wasn't willing to say in front of the cat.

CHAPTER 7

One of the hardest parts about being in the Dreamlands
with Josephine was remembering that I was in a session
with her and keeping that in the forefront of my mind.
I was so very curious about where we were. I could not
resist asking questions. The more I understood about the
Dreamlands, the better I believed I would understand
Josephine's control over it and herself.

With the dirt crunching beneath our feet and a breeze
chilling the air, I began with something trivial. "Is it safe
to eat and drink in the Dreamlands? I noticed you didn't
drink what we were served."

Josephine shrugged, her breath coming in soft pants. "It
depends. Ulthar is a safe place."

Her response sounded like a ritual phrase. I slowed
my pace. I was used to fast walking between patients and
buildings and errands. Josephine was not. When she caught
her breath, I glanced behind to make sure we weren't
followed. "You were saying something about a place you
loved as a child?"

She nodded, walking with slower steps. "I mentioned that I have always been a vivid dreamer. Almost everyone in my family is. We are taught at a young age how to shape our dreams. To combat the nightmares."

This was not what I expected from such a genteel and well-regarded family. It seemed they did more than encourage the fantasy. "You, your brother, your parents, all learned to lucid dream?"

Josephine considered this. "Lucid dream. That is an appropriate term."

"Frederik van Eeden, a Dutch psychiatrist, created the phrase in 1913. I read it in one of his papers. I attempt to practice this from time to time." I glanced at her. "I've been successful here, in this session with you."

"We *are* in the Dreamlands." Josephine spoke with the air of someone stating something obvious. "When I dream, I almost always come here. But not lately. Not since I began having the nightmares. Not that I remember. Perhaps that is my problem. I have forgotten so much about dreaming and the Dreamlands. I don't understand how that could happen."

There was something I was missing. Something important. We were not truly dreaming. Were we? We were in a hypnotic session in my office. This, all this, around us was not real. The fact that Josephine accepted it without question was disturbing. What if I couldn't pull her from her fantasy? "Where do you believe you've been going if not here?"

"My mind. Only within my mind."

"What's within your mind that frightens you?" I wanted

to pull the conversation toward the concept of grief and the dead Thomas Ruggles, but Josephine ignored my question to continue her narrative.

"From a young age, I always had friends here within the Dreamlands. Your patient, Malachi, he was one of them. We would meet at the Red House. He felt safest there." Josephine lowered her voice. "He was afraid of the Darkness that Watches." She raised her voice again to a normal level. "It couldn't see him in the Red House."

As before, my tongue was struck dumb. Those were the words Malachi had used to express his fear before he was murdered. She *had* known him. There was no other explanation. How an itinerant man knew – was friends with – a young woman like Josephine Ruggles could only happen in dreams. I did not want to consider the implications.

Yet, I had to. Josephine knew Malachi. Malachi suffered from nightmares and delusions – delusions that had somehow murdered him with a physical knife. How could dreams manifest in the real world? The answer was before me in the form of my patient. Through the mind. Her dreams were made manifest in her flesh in the form of glyph-like wounds.

Yet the mind couldn't bring a rune-covered knife from dreams into reality. Nor leave it behind in a cooling body. That was impossible.

"This is the place I believe we need to go. It was where I remember being when I was last in the Dreamlands. It is a hidden place. A safe haven. Many of my friends from here meet there."

Josephine had her back to me now. She'd pulled ahead, unaware of my distracted state. I forced myself to focus on her. "How far away is it?"

She paused and looked around. We were high in the mountains now. "I… I don't know. Only some of this is familiar to me."

Josephine stood there, her head turning to-and-fro as if to get her bearings. I didn't understand. There was only one path. As I watched her, something bulged out of her back. It looked like a book pressed against the fabric of her shirt. I stumbled and went to one knee. The pain of striking the hard rock surprised me. When I looked up again, Josephine waited, her head tilted at a quizzical angle. "Your back." It was all I could say.

I pulled myself to my feet as she craned around, trying to see what I saw. I hadn't torn my pant leg or broken the skin. My knee ached. That, in and of itself, upset me. But the blood on Josephine's back upset me more.

"What is it? What's happened?" Her voice was high with panic and fear. She turned around and around, trying to glimpse what had shocked me.

I grasped her by the shoulders. "Wait," I commanded as I shifted to look at the blood. It was on the lower left side of her back where the corner of the book had pressed out of her flesh. I touched it. Dried blood on the fabric scraped against my fingertip. "Does this hurt?"

She shook her head. "No. What's wrong?"

I pushed harder. "Now?"

"No. Please, doctor, is there something wrong?"

"You have a bit of blood on your shirt where my fingers

are." I hesitated. Should I tell her the rest? Yes. I needed to. "There was the impression of something rectangular pushing out of your back against your shirt. It startled me. Did you feel anything?" I shifted to watch her face even as she turned to hide it from me. "Josephine?"

"There is no pain."

"But?" There was more. So much more. I needed her to tell me.

"I felt something within. It *wants* out."

I squeezed her hand, trying to encourage her. "Do you know what it is?"

She shook her head. "No. But I know who would know."

"Who is that?"

Josephine gazed ahead. "We need to go. I think I hear the Black Wind." She headed up the stone path.

I had no choice but to follow. Every conversation with my patient brought more questions. For now, I would ignore the mention of this "Black Wind". It was a delaying tactic. I had to know what she was hiding within. Literally and figuratively, it seemed. I walked alongside her, our pace matching step for step. I was stronger than she was. I could outlast her. I had to. "You know two things you haven't told me. If you want my help, you must trust me to help you."

We walked on in silence for a good minute. It seemed much longer than that. The more we walked, the higher and colder it became. No longer in rocky hills, we were in the mountains, though the path was still clear.

"I was given something to keep safe. I remember that much. I cannot remember exactly what it was. I do know it is important to my friend. She gave it to me and made me promise to keep it safe." Josephine paused on the path, her brow furrowed in concentration. "I was not supposed to look at it. I think … I believe I did."

"Was it a book?"

Josephine blinked her dark eyes, peering into my face. "There are some things man is not meant to know. There are other things that man must be prepared for before they witness it. When your life is as mine is, you need all the protection you can get."

Josephine's true malady took shape. "You learned something you shouldn't have."

She nodded. "I believe I must return what my friend gave me."

"Return to her or give to another?"

"To her. It is my duty to protect it as it protects me." Josephine hugged herself, shivering because of something other than the cold.

"Protect you from what?"

Josephine shook her head. "I dare not say the name again."

Was it this Black Wind she'd mentioned before? Was it more than a distraction? I turned her toward the path again, trying to focus on what was important. "Tell me about your friend? The one who gave you the book?" It was a book. That much was certain. What knowledge it represented was still unknown.

"I …" Josephine's shuddering interrupted her words. With a visible effort, she regained some composure. "She is a child. She is a wise woman."

"I don't understand. She's a child and a wise woman? What's her name?"

"I don't remember. Why can't I remember?" Josephine stopped where she was and hunkered down, burying her face in her hands. Soft sobs escaped her attempt to hide them from me.

I crouched next to her, going to one knee, rubbing her back. "There, there. It's fine. It's fine. You'll remember soon enough." That was when I realized her clothing had shifted from the adventure wear back into the blue linen dress and heavy silken dressing gown. Her admirable control had slipped away. This was the time to push, to get deep into her psyche. "You'll remember. You're afraid of remembering. Why are you afraid?"

Josephine shook her head, still covering her face.

"It's time to stop being a child, Josephine. You need to help me if I am to help you. Tell me what happened. Why are you afraid?"

"The book. I read from the book. I wasn't supposed to. It whispered to me in dreams. I wasn't supposed to read from it. I was supposed to protect it as it protected me!"

She gasped in pain and twisted. Under my hand, the form of a thick book pushed against the fabric of her clothing. I felt the edge of the book dig into my palm. Something whispered to me. I yanked my hand back as if scalded. Josephine surged to her feet and stumbled to the side of the mountain. She leaned against the rough rock, panting. "The book was not meant to be read. Not by me." She gave me a piercing glance. "Not by you."

I stood, uncurling slowly, at a loss for words. The book tried to force itself out of her. I felt it. I could not deny it. But what did that mean? Did it represent something that

Josephine knew, something dangerous? Or was my mind playing tricks on me in this strange place?

Something hovered on the edge of my awareness. Something I did not want to examine. This world. The Dreamlands. They were a figment of Josephine's considerable imagination. Yet I experienced it, too.

Above us came an unearthly cry. I froze. A nightmarish creature assaulted my mind with its alien wrongness. Bulbous eyes protruded from its horse-shaped head and its cry revealed sharpened teeth. The sound of its leathery wings beat the air. It was huge, so huge; the largest creature I'd ever seen. Watching it come with its scales and serpentine tail, I could not look away. Even as I wanted to flee, I did not – could not – move. I watched it come at me with talons outstretched, yet I was rooted to the spot. How could such a monstrosity exist? It was like nothing I'd ever imagined, or even dreamed of in my worst nightmare. Part of me screamed to move. The other part stared at my oncoming death like a deer in a bright light. I closed my eyes.

Something slammed into me. A moment later, I opened my eyes and found myself on the ground, looking at Josephine. She'd pushed me out of the path of the creature's claws.

"Shantak! We must flee. They'll dash us against the rocks." She took my hand and pulled me up behind her.

We ran.

There was still only one path; a winding rocky road butted against the mountain on one side and had a sheer drop off on the other. Behind us the shantak screamed and gave chase. Just as we were hemmed in by the mountain, they were thwarted by it as well.

There were two of them. They darted in from the left side and from behind. They couldn't get close enough to grab either of us. We had rocks to throw and the mountain to keep them at bay, but I didn't know how much longer these would ward them off.

I kept Josephine ahead of me. The danger had paradoxically given her the focus she needed to regain her composure. She was the expert in this realm – whether she remembered everything or not – and she was our best hope for escaping the monsters that pursued us.

In the distance, I could see a stone bridge spanning the chasm. Even though there was plenty of room to flee to the other side, I couldn't see how we'd get across harried by monsters that should not exist. Still, we fled. We had no other choice.

We rounded a sharp bend and hesitated. Not more than one hundred yards before us was the end of our path. Our choice was a rock wall to put our backs to, or the bridge that crossed the chasm. There were no other ways to flee.

Behind us, the shantak screamed again.

CHAPTER 8

I prefer to think about things before I do them. I plot, plan, and consider. I rehearse conversations in my head, research before I write, and decide my route before I travel. I dislike improvisation in uncontrolled circumstances. It is who I am and who I have always been.

However, there are times when I cannot be in control. When I act by instinct, I am usually correct. Usually. I believe appropriate, instinctive actions come from a lifetime of planning and experience. It is only after the fact that I understand what I did and why.

Josephine and I ran until we could go no further without traversing the bridge I'd thought was stone. This close to it, I saw that it was not stone, but ice, and wide enough that two cars could pass each other. My stomach roiled at the thought of crossing that chasm on an icy bridge.

"What do we do?" Josephine stood close at my back.

I looked around for handholds – up or down – for us to climb to safety. There was nothing. Worse, the sky above darkened and swirls of light that looked suspiciously like eyes appeared to watch. The wind picked up and the clouds began to roil as if alive. Lightning lit the clouds from within, followed by the crashing boom of thunder. There was no help there. Even the mountain itself had taken on a malevolent quality, looming over us. Our only escape from the shantak was the bridge of ice.

Then I remembered my father's pistol. It was already in my hand, waiting for me to realize it was there. I checked both the magazine and the chamber. I had six rounds to protect us. Steeling my resolve, I set my stance and took aim. "As soon as I start firing, you get across that bridge. I'll follow." I kept my fear to myself. If I appeared confident, Josephine would trust that I knew what I was doing.

"I am ready." Josephine lifted her robe to make sure she didn't tread on it as she fled.

"Good. Go." I fired my first shot at the closest shantak monster. My shot was true. I hit it in one of its bulbous eyes. My next shot struck it in the neck. Josephine sprinted away, across the icy bridge on nimble feet. I watched as the wounded monster crashed into the mountain and flailed its bat-like wings, keening in pain. The second shantak turned from me to its fallen companion. My hopes for a feral response died in vain.

Instead of attacking and savaging its wounded peer, it landed next to it and licked at the blood. Not to feast, but to clean, to help, to heal. I backed up as the first monster went still and the second gave a cry of rage before launching itself into the air with great flaps of its leathery wings.

I sprinted after Josephine, expecting her to be at the other end of the bridge. To my horror, she stood in the middle of it, staring down at the chasm beneath. "Josephine, run! Run!" The bridge that had seemed so reasonable moments before now seemed impossibly long and thin. My shoes couldn't gain purchase and I skittered across it in an unsteady gait.

As I reached Josephine, the creature above us screamed. Josephine shook her head, mumbling, "The minions of the Black Wind. How do they know I'm here? How can they?"

I aimed a shot at the shantak and fired – more to scare than to harm. "Josephine, go!"

She looked at me with fear-filled eyes. "They know I'm here."

I fired again, keeping the nightmare creature at bay. "We'll deal with it. Now go!"

A deep *crack* resounded through the chasm. It was the sound of breaking bone. It was the sound of the bridge we both stood on cracking beneath our feet. I looked down and realized that it *was* bone. The ice had been its flesh. At the same time, I reached out a hand and pushed Josephine toward the other side of the bridge.

As soon as my hand touched her, propelling her forward, my vision plummeted far below to the raging river I had not known was there. A boat filled with half-man beings seemed to reach up for me. They were men, but they had goat legs with cloven hooves and horns protruded from their heads. More demon than man, they shouted, "The Bride! The Bride is here!" Some with no faces gibbered and jeered in glee. Fear overwhelmed me as bile filled my throat.

Then they were gone, and we were running across the

bridge as it shattered beneath us. Josephine tumbled to her knees as we reached the other side. She disappeared in a shower of falling ice, bone, and stone, screaming.

Plunging my left hand down, I grasped for her. I *could* reach her. And I did. I found and gripped her wrist as hard as I could. She reached up and grabbed my arm with her other hand. I hauled her over the edge, back from the precipice. Josephine sobbed and clutched at me. For the briefest of moments, I hugged her tight. I wanted to fall into the relief of having caught her. I could not. In my other hand was my weapon. Above us, hell screamed its fury.

I aimed another shot, my fifth, and fired. It struck the shantak's tail but didn't appear to slow it down. I surged to my feet and looked for shelter. Not twenty feet away was a door in the wall of the mountain. Framed in dark wood, and as neat as you please, it waited with the patience of a saint. I did not question it. The door looked as if it had been made for us. "There! Go there!"

There was no more time. The shantak was on me. It beat at me with wings of leather as its talons slashed the air. I dodged as best I could. It was not enough. One of its claws caught hold and pierced my shoulder, knocking me to the ground, pinning me there. I screamed my pain and beat at its leg, trying to free myself. My scrabbling hand couldn't get purchase on those slick, hard scales.

Fetid breath assaulted me as the shantak came in to bite. I pistol-whipped it to no avail. The shantak snapped at my face, inches from my nose. I did the only thing I could do. I thrust the pistol into its slavering mouth, pointed up, and pulled the trigger.

For a moment, it continued to flap its wings. Then it went slack and fell, its mouth ripping my father's pistol from my hand, as it hit the ground, half-on and half-off the cliff edge. Its talon tore at my shoulder as the monster's body slid over the edge of the stone. I thought I was going to go with it. Then strong arms wrapped themselves about my waist and pulled me back from the edge. The shantak's talons hung on, tearing flesh and cloth as I screamed. Then the talons, and the monster, were gone.

Pain-dazed and bleeding, all I could do was let those strong, tawny arms – Josephine's – pull me from the cliff edge, through the door in the mountain, and into darkness.

I leaned against a cool stone wall and put my hand to my left shoulder. Pain spiked and my hand came away wet. The sound of a match striking gave scant warning that light was coming. Then the vision of Josephine lighting a lamp came into view.

As did my blood-covered hand.

I was bleeding and in pain. You weren't supposed to feel pain in dreams. I'd never bled in a dream before. I tried to marshal my thoughts, my focus, my will to make the bleeding and the pain stop. Nothing happened. I was still wounded. Still bleeding.

This was real.

"We're in luck. This is a tunnel I know. A little red singing bird of Celephaïs lives here."

I ignored her. I stared at my bloody hand glistening in the lamplight. I touched my torn shoulder again and gasped at the pain.

This *was* real.

This *was* happening.

This *world* was real.

The *Dreamlands* were real. I could die in this place. Josephine could die. I wasn't strong enough to save us both. Worse, I'd lost my father's pistol. No longer did I believe it still lived in my desk drawer. I'd lost my protection, my touchstone. I'd lost...

Malachi sprang to mind, one of our many conversations before a hypnotherapy session.

"You're still suffering from intense nightmares, or bad memories?"

"Well, doctor, those are two things I've got a bit of trouble keeping straight."

"Malachi, let us see what we can do about that..."

He'd been telling the exact truth and I hadn't seen it for what it was. Those nightmares and bad memories had been one and the same. In my mind's eye, his hesitant smile morphed into the relaxed state of hypnotic sleep, then his brow furrowed with fear. I could hear him whispering.

"Shadow figures stood above me, and blood dripped from their fingertips."

I hadn't believed him. I had been so wrong. The ones with curved knives had come for him. Even though he died with one of their knives in his heart, all I could remember were the glyphs drawn in his blood on the wall of his room.

When he told me the shadow figures had taken his last name– *"The Darkness that Watches"* –he'd told me the truth. They'd left one of their knives in his body and I still had not believed. I had been so blind. So arrogant and so blind.

A sound came to me. Someone kept saying the word "no" over and over.

That someone was me.

I couldn't stop myself.

"Shhh. Shhh." Josephine was by my side. "Listen to the singing. Listen. It's a bird of Celephaïs. Listen."

She put her fingertips to my lips.

I wanted to bite them.

The very idea of me biting my patient shocked me into stillness and silence. I listened. There was birdsong. It was sweet. It cascaded over me, relaxing my tense muscles. Pain receded. Although it did not disappear, it cleared my mind of its panic.

I wanted to fight the song's soothing touch, to lose myself to the panic, the fear, and to never have to think of what I'd just realized ever again.

"I need to look for something." Josephine's voice echoed in the tunnel. "I will be back. Listen to the singing. Listen to the bird."

My patient was trying to care for me. She was barely more than a child. I had a duty to her. I had to process what I now knew. For her sake as well as mine.

I leaned my head back with my eyes closed. Birdsong swelled. I fell into its ebb and flow. They say music soothes the savage beast. In this case, it soothed the chaos of panic. I considered my position. Somehow – *Josephine did this*, my mind whispered, *she brought me here* – I was in this place called the Dreamlands. It was filled with monsters and allies. Somewhere in this land was a place Josephine called the Red House. It was a safe haven. There, Josephine would return something she was protecting, and her nightmares would go away, thus, her madness. I would deal with the rest of her mental trauma back in the real world.

I bowed my head. I had been uncommonly deceitful – to Josephine and to myself. This whole time that I'd assured my patient I believed her, I had actually been waiting for the logical explanation to appear. I'd been waiting for Josephine to realize the lie she'd told herself to cover the pain of a trauma she did not want to face. Deep down, I had believed Dr Mintz. I had believed that Josephine Ruggles was merely hysterical and was crying out for attention. That she had not actually needed help.

How many of my other patients in the asylum had I done such a disservice to?

Back in the asylum. Back on Earth.

I was not on Earth. I was in the Dreamlands. I was in another time and place. There was no denying it as blood leaked from my throbbing wounds, in time with my beating heart, to drip down my body and stain my clothes.

The more I accepted the fantastical idea that I was not on Earth, but in another time and space, the rest fell into place. I thought of the cats of Ulthar and of Foolishness. The orange cat had instructed us to return that way to leave. Thus, there was a way to go home. We were not stuck in the Dreamlands forever. Just long enough to do what needed to be done.

If I could be strong enough to accept what was happening.

I would.

I must.

I tried to straighten as the sound of Josephine returning obscured the birdsong. The pain was too great. This was a concrete problem I could deal with. I would have to have her bind my arm to my body. Looking up as my patient and the lamp returned, I was pleased to see she was again in her adventuring clothing. She, too, was fortifying her will once more.

Josephine knelt next to me and revealed a handful of small red feathers. "Feathers from the little red singing bird of Celephaïs. They heal wounds. As its song can heal the mind."

This would be the final proof. As if I needed more proof. I did, though. My rational mind did not want to believe in the irrationality of my situation. If the feathers healed me, I'd have no choice and could admit aloud I was in a different world with different rules that could be bent by an act of will. "What do I need to do? Eat them?"

She shook her head with a smile. "No. They are to be used like a poultice, although they work more quickly." Josephine eyed my torn shirt. "I am sorry. We will get you a new blouse from the trunk up ahead." She pulled a knife from a sheath at her waist and began cutting the shirt off my shoulders, revealing the bloody wounds.

"Where did you get that?" I nodded to the knife in her hand.

"The trunk. I remember now that we keep trunks of useful things in places we travel to for just this sort of emergency. This is something my family started long ago. It was part of our training. This is not the trunk I created, though I have added to it over the years."

"I see." It almost made sense. I put my hand on my thigh, looking for and not finding the sheath to my father's pistol. The pang of its loss hit me again and I closed my eyes.

"This will hurt, but only briefly."

I opened my eyes and watched Josephine lay the small red feathers against my body where the shantak's talons pierced it. I gasped as the feathers stung like needles piercing my skin. Then, the pain disappeared as the feather melted into my flesh. Over and over, Josephine laid the small feathers against my wound to meld with my body. Each one took away more of the pain, closing the wound. As Josephine ran out of feathers, my wounds were fully healed. I noted that even the scratches on my right shoulder and collarbone had healed.

"Well then." I took a breath, let my worldview tilt upon its axis, and accepted it all. "The Dreamlands has some amazing aspects to it. When we return to our world, I'll have to write as much of it down as I can remember." Josephine helped me up. "We will remember what happens here, won't we?"

She looked at me, her dark eyes shining. "You understand. You believe. You finally believe."

I nodded. "I do now." I wondered if we were in two places at once or if, somehow, Josephine had brought our bodies through, too. I kept my questions to myself. One epiphany at a time.

She gave me a brief, fierce hug. "You were supposed to help me. To come with me. I knew it. You are my anchor."

I returned the hug out of duty and took pleasure in it. Josephine had failed on the bridge, but succeeded when

I faltered in body, then in mind. I had not suspected she could, or would, do either until she acted. She walked a strange balancing act of weakness and fear while standing upon a core of willful strength. She was a complex woman. I had more to learn.

As a point, Josephine did not answer my question. That, in and of itself, was an answer. We probably wouldn't remember what happened here. Or, like a dream, would not remember for long. "Where is this trunk?"

"Of course. Of course. My doctor cannot traipse through the Dreamlands in a camisole and a torn blouse."

There was an airy joy in her voice I had not heard before. I wanted to question it. I wanted a shirt more. Goosebumps covered my exposed flesh.

The trunk was there at the opening of a cave. It had all the things you might need for an adventure – rope, light, canteens, clothing – as well as some more esoteric things – a doll, chalk, a mirror, rubber balls, and a mask. There was no food. Then again, I still wasn't hungry.

I chose a functional shirt that would keep me covered and somewhat protected. I was not surprised that it fit well, as if it were made for me. That was the way of things here. Things would work until they weren't supposed to work anymore. There was freedom in the acceptance of my new understanding of the universe – it was so much larger than I had imagined. My point of view had shifted to save my sanity. Already, I worked to incorporate the new knowledge into my worldview and my psychological tool chest.

Josephine snuffed the lamp. I gave her a quizzical look.

"We won't need it. I believe I know the way now. Someone

else will need this in the future." She put the lamp in the trunk and shut it. The trunk locked itself with a *thunk*, the leather belts affixing themselves on their own. Rather than be horrified at the living trunk's action, I was charmed. It would protect its bounty from those who should not have access.

I turned my attention back to Josephine, replaying her words in my mind. I examined her face. Was that contraction from fear or a new level of comfort with me? Or was it merely a contraction?

Josephine stood still with her hands clasped before her as she waited for my word to continue on. Her face held no answers. Not for the moment.

I gave her a professional smile tinted with concern. "Oh, it's good to leave it then. While you lead the way, we will speak of this Black Wind and his minions."

Her face fell. She cast her eyes to the ground.

I touched her shoulder to soften my words. "We're still in session. I'm still your doctor. We have things we must examine."

Josephine nodded, fear plain on her face. "If you wish."

CHAPTER 9

I remember the way Josephine said "doctor" to me at times in our journey. It was akin to the word "savior." I could not be that for her – as much as I wanted to be. I needed to be Josephine's guide, not her hero. This is always a dangerous time in the relationship between a patient and a doctor. The patient gives up all sense of responsibility and hands it, and their life, to the doctor. The power is as intoxicating as it is toxic. Nothing good can come of accepting such a responsibility. It was hard, though. I had grown fond of Josephine. Thus, I needed to coax her into confronting her great fear.

The cave was about the size of an amphitheater with light emanating from an unknown source. Faint colors of blue, purple, and green swirled about us in slow eddies on the cavern walls and floor, making it hard for me to get my bearings. I refused to search out the source of the light and dismissed the impossible. The words "impossible" and "unlikely" no longer had meaning in this place. The rules were different. Logic wasn't king. Physics were an illusion. Dream monsters could hurt, even kill. I needed to be on guard for all of it.

Josephine led the way, picking her path across the cave floor, weaving through stalagmites adorned with jewels and half-covered by creeping moss. As I watched one stalagmite in particular, yellow-green moss surged over a garnet. A heartbeat later, the moss turned the deep red of the gemstone. A touch to one foot alerted me to a spot of creeping moss that had found me interesting. I pulled my foot away and hurried across the cavern to watch Josephine. Behind us, the room filled with the sound of creeping moss covering and consuming whatever it could.

Josephine paced before half a dozen openings in the cave wall. She paused in front of one tunnel and considered a couple of the others. The one before us was rough-hewn with tool marks, having been carved from the mountain. One of the other tunnels had wooden supports. A third had bricked walls.

"Where do these go? To different places?"

Josephine nodded. "There are many places in the Dreamlands. We want to stay in the west."

I refused to ask the question she wanted me to ask. I would not be distracted from our session. I needed to help her in the way I hadn't been able to help Malachi. "Toward the Red House?"

"Yes."

"Which one takes us there?"

Josephine looked between the three tunnels, her face a mask of confusion. "Things have changed."

I stood close behind her. "You can do this. You know this place. Go with your instinct."

"What if I get it wrong?" She leaned back to me.

I let her shoulder touch mine, taking comfort as much as giving it. "Then we will deal with it together. Choose. Time is of the essence."

Josephine glanced at me out of the corner of her eye as I cast her words at her. She pointed to the rough-hewn tunnel. "That one."

I stepped around her and into the tunnel. "Let's go." I gestured for her to walk alongside me.

Josephine hesitated then steeled herself. With a raised chin, she stepped to my side. We walked in. The tunnel, dim, was wide enough for three people to walk abreast. The light neither waxed nor waned. All around us, the rock of the mountain pressed in. I looked back. Darkness swallowed the entrance of the cavern. It was as if we traveled in a bubble of light. I counted fifty steps before casting my opening questions.

"Who is the Black Wind?"

Josephine took a breath. "One of the Outer Gods. He has another name. We do not speak it. If we do, he might hear. He is one of the gods who interacts with humans." She spoke like a child reciting a lesson.

"And his minions? Are they demons?" I suppressed a shudder at the memory of those men with horns and hooves.

"I do not know. They work for him. They hunt for him. I believe that is their purpose."

"They hunt you now?" Josephine nodded. Her hand

sought mine and clasped it for comfort. I squeezed, encouraging her. "Why?"

"I…" Josephine shook her head. "I am special."

I waited for her to continue. She didn't.

We walked in silence, our steps eating ground. It felt as if we were walking a spiral even though the way was straight and narrow. I smelled the faintest breath of fresh air. The tunnel wasn't going to be as long as I thought it would be. "They called you the Bride." Josephine pulled away from me, walking faster. I let her go. I walked a couple steps behind, watching her stiff posture and fear. "Why?"

"I do not want to talk about that." She continued to march ahead. "I cannot. I have another duty. I must focus on it."

Her first duty, the protection of something within her that was killing her slowly. She was correct. We needed to focus on that for the moment. "Yes. You have a point. We can revisit the Black Wind another day. We will do so, soon," I promised, wondering if her fear strengthened her will enough to influence my mind. I shook my head. I could not, would not, think like that.

I shifted back to our previous conversations and the point we broke through. "Do you remember what it was you weren't supposed to know?"

"I read the book." Josephine's voice was a whisper almost lost to our fast steps.

The tunnel wound in a downward direction. "You were not supposed to read the book."

"No."

There were two ways I could approach this. Only one of

them dug into Josephine's motivations. "Why did you read it?" The light grew, tinted red. I could see the opening.

Shadows encroached around us, squeezing us until it was only possible to walk one behind the other. Even as the light brightened the end of the tunnel, promising a sweet relief, part of me would be forever left behind in the shadows that now clung to my arms, my hips, my legs. It was all I could do to keep myself from pushing Josephine forward, faster. But she had to emerge from the darkness on her own. Her confession would be both our salvations.

"I was afraid." Again, Josephine's voice was soft.

It was a weak admission. A red herring. "What were you afraid of? Why did you read the book?" Closer and closer the exit came. I didn't know what was waiting out there for us. I needed to know what she'd intended when she did what she'd been forbidden to do.

"I thought it would protect me." We crossed out of the tunnel and into the light, Josephine ahead with me at her heel. "I thought it would give me the spell to stop…" She hesitated, unwilling to go on in either word or step.

I stopped close behind, careful not to touch her. She had to take this final step on her own. Instead, I gazed at the beauty that lay before us.

It was a gorgeous valley with a forest at its center. Instead of verdant greens, the forest's leaves were the fall colors of browns, yellows, oranges, and – in the center – red. The path led down the hill and passed a babbling stream, winding into that forest. The sun above us shone bright at high noon. Josephine turned her face upward, letting the sun warm her skin. She had her eyes closed.

I lowered my voice and prompted her with her own words. "The spell to stop…?"

"My death at the hands of the Black Wind," Josephine whispered to the uncaring sky.

It seemed that the Black Wind needed to be spoken of sooner rather than later. How could this Black Wind kill her and why? What was within her that could stop something like an Outer God? "I don't understand."

The valley below us flickered. One moment it was lush mountainside, the next it was a roiling ocean with white capped waves. I blinked and shook my head. The gorgeous flora returned.

Josephine turned to me. "I fear I have hastened my end. I read the book, and its madness brings the Black Wind ever closer. I should never have been so foolish. I must rid myself of this burden." She looked over her shoulder at the forest. "And I will. There, in the Red House." She took a step backward.

As she did, the landscape changed again. The valley disappeared and the angry ocean with its violent waves reappeared. Instead of flat ground, we were on slick rock. The wind howled around us. Josephine gasped, slipping and falling. I reached for her. Our fingertips touched and then she was gone, tumbling to the rocks.

Josephine hit the ground of the valley hard. She'd landed on the path that led us into the heart of the forest below. I hunkered, waiting for the land to change again. It did not. I stood and focused on thinking we were in the valley of the Red House, hoping it would keep us stable.

"Josephine?"

For a moment, she did nothing except lie there on her back. She screwed up her face in a way that made me think she was going to laugh. It would've broken the sudden darkness of the situation and deflected her fear and the uncertainty of our surroundings.

She didn't laugh.

Josephine arched with a shriek of pain and turned over. Her back bulged and moved under her shirt. She pulled her tucked blouse out of her pants and craned her neck. We both saw the book-shaped thing press against her skin, its corners cutting through, blood leaking through punctured flesh. Josephine gasped in pain. "Get it out. Help me, doctor! Please!"

Falling to my knees, I pulled the ornate knife from the sheath at her belt, then pressed a hand to her shoulder. The book, a literal book, had to come out of her. "Still, Josephine. Lie still."

"It hurts. Please." Her words were a panic, but her writhing body stilled.

I pushed her blouse up, exposing her back. With a single slash, I cut her flesh from hip to hip. The book, impossibly large, poked out of that slit. I slid my hands under her skin and grasped the book by its sides. It was slick, like the scales of the shantak I'd fought. I refused to let go. Sliding one arm farther under Josephine's skin almost up to my elbow, I caught the corner of the book. I eased it downward and out from under her skin.

The book resisted, catching on something within my patient's body. She gasped in pain and clawed at the ground. "Please," I whispered. I don't know who or what

I begged to help me, but providence heard, and the book acquiesced. My hands found purchase and the book slid out of Josephine's body. At the last moment, it stuck, and I yanked as hard as I could. The book released Josephine with an audible pop that she echoed with a moan of relief.

I rocked backward and hit the ground with a hard thump. The book – that had seemed so big – pressed against my body, the size of a bible but only half as thick. I pulled it away from me, expecting to be covered in blood, but the book and my shirt were clean.

She still lay on the ground, panting, laughing, crying. Her back was unmarked and unmarred from what had just happened. Even though I'd cut her and the knife I'd used lay discarded at her side, her tawny-beige skin was smooth. I couldn't believe it. "Are you well?"

Josephine pushed herself to her knees and brushed the dirt from her clothes in an absent gesture. She twisted around and looked at her back, touching the unblemished skin. Her smile was beatific as she gave another sigh. "I am free. You have freed me."

I looked down at the book in my arms. Its blank cover now revealed a title in that script that was both so familiar and alien. I could almost understand it. Almost.

She touched my shoulder and offered me a hand up. "I knew I needed you on my journey. Thank you for having the strength I did not."

I accepted the hand and the compliment as gracefully as I could. While Josephine seemed much more balanced, I felt off-kilter. As if I stood on an unseen boat. "Now that I've done this, we need to get the book back to its rightful owner." Josephine did not ask for the book – her duty, her responsibility, her burden – and I did not offer it.

Josephine pointed down the path toward the colorful woods. "Perhaps… perhaps this has pushed my doom farther away."

I breathed slow breaths. "As soon as we give this back to its owner, we will speak, you and I, of the Black Wind and why you believe it means your death."

I wanted to talk about the Black Wind, to continue our session, but I couldn't. Not while I held the book. My mind was too full. I glanced at the book's cover again. I could almost understand what it spelled out. In the back of my mind, the book whispered, tempting me to open and read it. To understand. To know. To become one with it. I now understood the real reason Josephine read the book.

I resisted its temptation with years of study instead of play, years of discipline instead of whim, years of refusing immediate gratification in order to gain my heart's future desire. Still, the book called to me even though I knew that path was madness.

I didn't know how long I could resist its whispered pleas. Here, in my hands, was true magic. I was curious. So very curious.

CHAPTER 10

There are moments when action becomes instinct, and instinct becomes action. Without knowing how or why, you intuit what you need to do, and you do it. There is neither thought to consequences nor thought to retribution. There is the obstacle and an epiphany regarding what needs to occur. It is only after the deed is done that you can reflect upon your actions and determine if they were correct or not. For me, these moments are rare. I both adore and loathe them.

Josephine walked with a light step ahead of me. I let her lead the way as I silently recited poems, quotes, and lectures to keep the whispers at bay. All the while, she chattered as if at a social tea. I listened as closely as I could and responded when I could utter the appropriate words. There were only so many things I could do at once.

"This has always been one of my favorite places in the Dreamlands. Ever since I was a little girl. This is where I met Malachi and Luke and Mimi and Playful and so many others. The valley is safe. That is why it exists. The danger comes from traveling to or from it. That is when things happen. At the transitions."

Josephine's voice had taken on an earnest, childlike quality. As if she were regressing to childhood. I worried. Now, I carried her duty and burden because I needed to. Would I be able to get her to take responsibility for herself once more? There was a freedom in handing one's life over to another in authority. Especially after you had experienced the heaviness of duty and adulthood.

Especially one as heavy as the book I carried. I pulled it from me to look at the incomprehensible writing on its front again and was surprised that I could read it. *The Glyphs of the Eltdown Shards and the Binding Language*. There was no author listed. Just the title.

I was learning by osmosis. This realization kept me from opening the book to look for the name of the author. I'd never encountered a book that was dangerous to hold. Then again, I'd never traveled to another world before. It was strange how calm I felt now that I'd accepted the impossible.

Hugging the book once more, I looked to my surroundings. We'd entered the forest, its huge trees towering cathedral-like above us. Leaves crunched underfoot, but the dirt path was clear of debris. It wove its way through the trees toward a building in the distance.

"Is that the Red House?" My heart sped up and hope flooded through me. There was an end to the journey.

"Yes. Mimi should be there."

"Who's Mimi?"

Josephine paused, tilting her head. "Oh! Mimi is my

friend. The one who gave me the book. She will know what to do now."

As one, we hurried our steps, all but running toward the house in the distance. Around one large tree, the path became a straight line, and I could see why the building was called the Red House.

Sitting in the center of a small glade, the house had red walls and white trim around the doors, windows, and eaves. The roof was covered in slate gray tiles that reflected the red-tinted sunlight that shone down upon it through the trees. If the forest were a cathedral, this was its chancel. Was an altar within? Outside, sitting on the wide, white porch, was an old woman. She watched us come without a sound. Only the rocking of her chair told me she was alive.

Josephine ran ahead. "Mimi! Mimi! I made it back."

I slowed my steps to watch Mimi and Josephine meet, not wanting to interrupt. Their voices carried as if I were next to them.

Mimi stood and embraced Josephine. "So you did." She held Josephine at arm's length. "You've grown, girl. But not as much as I had expected."

Josephine touched Mimi's graying hair. "What happened? Why... why are you so old?"

"It's been years... decades... for me here. I've been waiting. Time passes differently in the Dreamlands. You should remember that."

My heart and my feet stuttered to a stop. This was something I hadn't known or considered. How much time had passed back in my world? Josephine's next words soothed my worry.

"But it's only been a couple of weeks. How could it have been so long for you?"

Mimi turned from Josephine to look at me. "You've brought me a guest."

Although her voice was neutral, I recognized the disapproval in it. I wasn't sure why it was there, but I needed to take command of the situation to make sure the book was returned to its rightful owner. I strode up to the porch. "Hello. I am Dr Carolyn Fern. Josephine is my patient. We've come to return something to you."

Mimi stepped down the stairs on unsteady legs. She shuffled over to meet me. Something about her was familiar. As if I had met her before. Perhaps long ago in another dream. She stopped before me and bowed her head.

"I remember you. You didn't listen to me. Why didn't you listen to me? I couldn't save her. I thought I could save you. Now all of us will live and die together. Our fates are intertwined." Her voice was tired and old and damnably familiar.

"I do not understand."

"Must you do this to me? Must you make me rip the scales from your eyes?" She tilted her head up, one golden-brown eye visible through her mass of graying-black hair.

Suddenly, I was back in the asylum, standing before Nurse Heather and Dr Mintz's drugged patient. "Sati Das? How are you here?" I blinked, the image of the patient melding into the old woman before me, transforming her into a young Indian woman with a straight back, bright eyes, and long dark hair. That appeared to be her true form, her true age, despite the years I felt upon her shoulders.

"Mimi?" Josephine stood next to us. This Josephine was no more than ten years old. "What's happening?"

Sati took a breath and let it out in a rush. "I'm sorry, Josie. I'm not in a mood to play." With that, she turned on her heel and strode into the Red House. She closed the door behind her.

"Doctor? What's happening? What's going on?" Josephine took my hand in hers.

I looked down. She was an adorable child. It would be so easy to allow her to remain so. One more step to taking care of her and protecting that aura of innocence I knew was a lie. After all, I held the very book whose whispers she'd succumbed to. But she knew Sati, the woman she named Mimi, better than I did. I would need her insight, if not her support, to convince Sati to take back the book that clamored for my attention. "I'm not sure. But I think you need to grow up again. I may need your help in there."

Josephine shook her head. "I don't wanna."

"There are many things I don't want to do. So, unless you want this book back … ?" I held it out to her. She let go of my hand and stepped away. "I thought not. Grow up and come help me with this." I refused to believe she would deny me.

I raised my chin and faced the Red House. It was going to let me in if I had to tear it down piece by piece. I strode to the front door and tried the doorknob. It turned in my hand without hesitation. I went in, leaving Josephine behind.

All the while, *The Glyphs of the Eltdown Shards and the Binding Language* wordlessly shouted in my head for me to read it.

I walked into a single room with four doors leading off it. All the doors were closed. This was a parlor where you could invite people into the house, but not necessarily into the home. Three overstuffed chairs and a long couch sat in a horseshoe around a low table on bird legs in front of a fireplace. All of it was decorated in rich hues of reds, oranges, and yellows. The occasional adornment in blue broke up the fierce color pattern.

Sati, once more the old woman I saw on the porch, stood next to the fireplace with a straight back and gray hair in a neat bun. She gazed into the fire's flickering flames. Rather than wearing the sari of her native land, she wore the business dress and jacket of a professor. In my mind's eye, the memory of her true form, the drugged woman in the asylum, flickered in and out of existence.

"We are not done, you and I." I moved into the room and took a seat in one of the overstuffed chairs. "This book. It belongs to you."

"And if I refuse to take it?"

"It's killing Josephine." I didn't say that it was currently gnawing on my will in an effort to get into me.

Sati turned. "It appears that Josephine is no longer in danger." She gestured.

I looked and saw Josephine standing by the porch door. She was once more a young woman, but she was also back in her linen dress and dressing gown. I knew what it meant. Sati did not. "Josephine is still in danger. You gave her a duty too much for her. I know exactly what she went through and why she succumbed."

"I *am* standing here in the room with you both. Do not

speak of me as if I were not." Josephine pulled her dressing gown about her in an effort to salvage her dignity.

Sati rolled her eyes. "Then come sit down and be part of the conversation."

"Perhaps I should throw this book into the fire." My statement was met with a fierce reaction from both Sati and Josephine.

"No!" Josephine, in the act of sitting, jerked to her feet again. "You cannot."

"No. We would lose too much." Sati took two steps toward me, revealing what she'd kept hidden thus far.

"I can take it back. I'm strong enough." Josephine reached a hand toward me. "I know better now. Don't throw it into the fire."

I ignored Josephine's hasty, panicked words. I only had eyes for the scroll case in Sati's hands. About a foot long and two inches in diameter, the beige leather was covered in embossed swirls and whirls accented in gold. It was beautiful. It was important. I recognized it in the depths of my soul. It was what I'd been meant to carry all along.

"I see…" I breathed these words, putting my understanding of Sati's burden and the reason she didn't want the book back into the breath, and locked eyes with the professor.

Sati shook her head. "I've already ripped one set of scales from your eyes. Don't make me rip another."

"There is little more you can do to me that has not already been done. Those horses have escaped the barn." It was true. There was no going back to the way I once was. "All experiences shape us."

"It will change more than just you." Sati raised her eyes to Josephine.

"It must be done. You must take this back." I raised the book to her despite the pain I felt at parting it from my body. Sati remained where she was. I put the book on the table between us. "I will take on your burden."

Sati raised the scroll case then lowered it again as she shook her head. "I…" She fell silent.

I was missing something. I focused on the professor. There was guilt and fear in her posture. She'd turned away from Josephine. "Why did you give Josephine the book? Why would you give something so dangerous to a child?"

"It wasn't supposed to hurt her." Sati's eyes begged for forgiveness. "It wasn't awake when I held it."

"What changed?"

Sati shook her head. "I don't know. It never occurred to me that she would read it. It was a barrier, a ward. Something to hide behind. It wasn't awake. I didn't know it *could* wake."

I could feel the book thrumming on the table. It seduced me with its promise of knowledge and power. "It is awake now."

Josephine moved between us and reached for the *Eltdown Shards* book. Her body froze scant inches from it. As she froze, so did we all. Three women in a tableau of need and conflict. I reached for Josephine with one hand and for the scroll case with the other. Sati held the scroll case with both hands, already pressing it toward me. Our conversation whirled about the room in visible thought bubbles as if we were nothing more than characters on a page.

"*I am right here! Neither of you is listening to me. This was my burden. I should never have given it up.*" Filled with determination, Josephine strained toward the book.

Regret tinted Sati's words. "*It was my burden, but I could not handle two duties at once. I was weak. I thought I was doing the right thing.*"

"*I will take the Elder Sign from you. You will take back the book. Josephine will heal in heart and mind. It will change all of us.*"

It was the only logical thing to do. I pressed my intent toward them, willing them to see things my way.

"*Who am I if I do not have a burden to bear?*" Josephine relaxed but did not withdraw. "*My family are ever dreamers. They have been linked to the Dreamlands for generations. This is what we are meant to do.*"

Sati's thought lashed across the tableau, making the room ripple. "*But at what cost, O Bride of the Black Wind?*"

Josephine did not answer. The tears that streamed down her frozen face were enough.

I focused on Sati, cutting Josephine out of the conversation. "*Professor Das, I know you were in a coma. It must have had something to do with the Eltdown Shards.*" I ignored the book as it writhed against me. I didn't know when I had picked it up again. "*This book is your burden. The Elder Sign must be mine. I will do what needs to be done.*"

Sati's image brightened at the use of her title. "*If you do this, your relationship with Josephine may be torn asunder. Is this a risk you are willing to accept? Do you take the Elder Sign knowing you may lose your patient forever?*"

Part of me struggled with this conflict. My patient came

first. More than that, Josephine was a wonderful young woman who had much to give the world. If I took the scroll, I could damage Josephine. But, if I didn't ensure that the book went back to Sati, I would lose Josephine to the nightmares once more. It was a choice between could and would. *"Yes. I will take that risk."*

The world shattered and fell about us. When all resettled once more, the three of us sat about the low table – Josephine in a chair with her hands folded, me in a chair holding the scroll case, and Sati, still in her old woman form, on the couch clasping *The Glyphs of the Eltdown Shards and the Binding Language* to her breast.

Josephine looked at each of us in turn, her face the smooth neutral of a well-bred woman with emotions to hide. "Well, it appears that is that. There is nothing more to do except go home."

"There is one more thing." I put the scroll case, now no bigger than my hand, in a pocket. "Tell me about the Black Wind." I allowed no argument in my tone of voice. She had evaded the subject long enough.

CHAPTER 11

As a Doctor of Psychology, I must be able to determine the difference between an evasion, a false confession, and an admission. As every patient is different, coaxing and guiding them to reveal their great trauma is a delicate act of cajoling and supporting, convincing the patient to let go of what they fear most. Once they do this, they are shattered in a way that they can pick up their own pieces, with expert psychological assistance, until they are whole once more.

Josephine rocked back as if struck. "No. It's not safe to speak his name."

Even as she tried to refuse, I knew she would do as I demanded. "This is a safe place." I glanced at Sati for confirmation. She nodded. "You told me so yourself. It's only in the transitions that things happen. You have avoided this long enough. Tell me." I locked eyes with her and refused to let go.

My patient stared at me for a long time before her face

changed – a hardness and determination I had not seen before coming to the forefront. "If you insist." She gathered her thoughts as she refolded her hands in her lap. "My family has always dreamed. We've always come to the Dreamlands. Even before the pact with the Black Wind. As soon as we start dreaming, our families mentor us to shape, to create here."

She unfolded one hand and held it up. Before our eyes, a bird came into being. Josephine set it aloft. The wren fluttered about the room until she gestured to the window. The wood and glass disappeared, allowing the wren to escape. With another gesture, the window reappeared. "All that we have learned has been in an effort to run, hide, and escape from the Black Wind."

"Why?"

"The pact. My many-times-removed grandfather, Elijah, bargained with the Black Wind. For what, I do not know. The end result is that one of every generation is marked by the Black Wind. What for? Again, I do not know. I am neither engaged to be married nor twenty-one. That is when all of this is explained. I only know as much as I do because of my brother, Leland. He came to me in his dying dream to warn me. He told me about my doom, then he died, leaving me to fend for myself."

Sati and I exchanged a glance. "Dying dream?" I asked.

Josephine pulled herself from the past. "Leland died almost six years ago in the Great War. As he lay dying on the battlefield, he chose to dream his life away. In that dream, he warned me that the Black Wind would mark me. That I was the only one of this generation left. I would be marked until I had children, or I died in the Dreamlands."

"Then why are you called the 'Bride of the Black Wind'?"

She gave me a bitter smile. "I met him. First, at one of father's parties. Then, in my dream that night. A tall Egyptian man with a regal bearing and a piercing gaze. At the party, he was introduced as Rafiq Talhouni, a visiting antiquarian who specialized in books. In my dreams, as he marked me, he revealed his true name…" Josephine shuddered, forcing the name through her unwilling lips, "…Nyarlathotep."

As Josephine spoke, buttons appeared on her blouse. She raised trembling hands to unbutton them, revealing the smooth skin of her collarbones and breast. "I can hide the mark. But there are always those who can see it." Swirling gold marks appeared, covering her upper chest. They writhed upon her skin as if alive. Several of the tentacles shifted to reveal a single malevolent eye.

One that looked about with interest.

One that focused on me.

It could see me, see into my soul, measuring me for God knows what. I felt a tickle in the back of my head. It was the same feeling I had when the Eltdown Shards book begged me to let it in. I shivered in the chill of it, every hair on my body standing on end. It was more than I could bear. I turned away, shaking.

It could still see me, searing into my soul. It picked through my fears, examining them like a woman considering fruit; scenting them, feeling them, cracking them open wide. All the while, I could do nothing to stop the invasion into my uglier imaginings and baser thoughts. I wanted to scream, but I couldn't catch my breath.

"Josephine, that is enough." Sati's voice was a smooth whipcrack through the tension. "This place is safe but inviting the likes of the Black Wind *in* would not be good for anyone."

Josephine did not respond in words.

The invasion within my mind ceased all at once. It left me stunned and trembling. I reached for my salvation – my work, my patient, my desire to cure Josephine.

I took several shaky breaths and forced my mind to push aside the horror of what had just happened. I faced the problem head on, trying to find an answer to help her. "You are the Bride because you're marked. You don't know everything, but according to your brother, you are the chosen one until you have children – who presumably will then become chosen – or die in the Dreamlands." I raised my head and risked a glance at Josephine. "What does the Black Wind get out of you dying?"

Josephine was properly covered once more with her hands folded in her lap. "I do not know. I believe the book protected me as much as I protected it. I… do not know what to do now. The book *anchored* me."

She spoke as if I should understand what she meant by the word *anchor*. I didn't understand. I glanced at Sati again. She shook her head. I wasn't sure if she indicated she didn't know, or she couldn't tell me. "I believe, now that the book is back with its rightful guardian, we need to journey home. The asylum is not safe for one such as you. Not with Dr Mintz's interest."

Josephine frowned. "But I should be well now. No more bleeding nightmares. I can finally go home."

I nodded. "Yes. I can visit you at your home to continue our talks. I suspect it will be needed. No one is cured in one session. Mental trauma will not disappear simply because we have removed the source of the physical trauma."

The heiress bowed her head. "What do I do now? I no longer guard the book. I need a purpose."

"That is something we can talk about in the real world."

Josephine's scowl marred her genteel face. "This world is as real as the next."

I made a calming gesture. "I misspoke. I apologize. I'm still learning. I meant we could speak about it outside the Dreamlands." I felt the need to return home as if it were a physical thing calling to me. The Dreamlands were too real, too alien, too dangerous.

"This is home to me."

"It is a home from time to time." Sati stood, ending what could have become an argument with the motion. "Time is no longer on our side. The Black Wind is now interested in this place. I will not have it. I cannot fight him off. You both must leave. Now. The question is, where will you go?"

She gestured to the front of the room where two doors stood. "The one on the right will lead you back to the Enchanted Forest. The other..." Sati closed her eyes and stretched forth a hand toward the door on the left. "The other is a path to the north... to the Plateau of Leng." She shook her head. "I don't know why that path appeared. It's both within the Dreamlands and outside it... in another space, another time."

Josephine stood and walked to the sinister door. "The

Plateau of Leng. My family knows nothing of it. This could be my new path, my new duty. Investigate the Plateau of Leng." She smiled at me. "Just think of it, doctor, we could discover something new. Something no one else knows of."

I stood, slow and reluctant. This was what I had wanted Josephine to do – take responsibility for her actions – but not here. Not in this world. Not in this way.

She said "we". She wanted me to go with her. Expected me to go, even. I needed to deny her without punishing her for taking the initiative. I could not journey to a place known as the Plateau of Leng. I was barely holding on as it was.

"Such a thing could be exactly what you're meant to do, but I cannot go with you." I continued to speak even as her face fell. "I have other patients to attend to. Also, a job that requires my attention." I was too aware of the pain I caused her. I wanted to take it back. I could not. This was needed – for both of us. I walked over to the right door and examined it.

"But I need you, doctor. I can't… cannot… do it alone." Her voice was soft and pleading. It broke my heart.

I touched the warm wood, letting my fingers dance over the carving of the large tree. I didn't know if it was supposed to be the tree in the glade or not, but in my mind's eye it was. "You can, Josephine. You've spent your whole life visiting the Dreamlands on your own. You don't need me." I glanced at her. "I believe in you. You can take on this task, this journey, *alone*."

I didn't want her to. More than anything, I needed her

to take my hand and to come with me. I wanted to be back in my familiar world – no matter how changed I was. The scales had fallen from my eyes. I would never be the same again. This had consequences I couldn't anticipate or consider right now.

I watched Josephine's profile as she faced the door she wanted to choose. "Or perhaps you can begin your new task another day. After you've prepared for it. Come back with me." I offered her my hand.

She was afraid of being alone. She never was in her real life – I couldn't think of the Dreamlands as real. Not yet. Her face flickered with emotion: fear, longing, stubbornness, need. She turned to her door, touched the stone, and withdrew her hand with a start. "It is cold. Freezing." She rubbed her hands together.

I needed to make a decisive choice. I looked over my shoulder to say farewell to Sati Das. I wasn't surprised to see that she and her Red House were already gone. As was the valley. Once more, we stood on a rocky plain. There were *things* moving in the distance – moving toward us at inhuman speeds.

"Whichever path you choose, we must go now. I am returning to the Enchanted Wood to go home. Go to the Plateau of Leng or come with me. It's your choice, but you must make that choice now." I didn't wait for her response. To hesitate meant death. I threw a hand to her as I grabbed the doorknob and turned it. "Please!" The door swung open, revealing the Enchanted Wood. As I stepped through, Josephine grasped my hand and held on for all she was worth.

I didn't have time to be relieved. The rocky landscape fell away, leaving us deep within the verdant forest that even I recognized. Behind us, the bandits with their horns and hooves jeered their hunting cries, coming ever closer.

CHAPTER 12

No doctor of the mind succeeds one hundred percent of the time. We all fail to help our patients. Some are just too far gone. Some are unwilling to leave their delusions behind. Sometimes, it is the doctor who cannot figure out the path needed to cure our patients of their maladies. It was there, in the Enchanted Wood, where I failed Josephine.

I still do not know what I could have done differently to save her.

Relieved more than I ever thought I would be, Josephine and I ran hand in hand, dodging branches and leaping over roots. The Enchanted Wood didn't seem as welcoming as it had before, but it didn't appear malevolent. Not yet. I focused on finding Foolishness. I had no idea where he was or what he could do against our pursuers – who seemed like both half a dozen and a horde of thousands.

Josephine pulled her hand from mine, and I allowed it to happen. We could run better and faster side by side. "They're gaining."

They were. The minions of the Black Wind were only a few trees behind us. I had no weapon. My father's gun was lost to the chasm. Then I realized that I had no problems speaking or breathing. Had we been back on Earth, I would have been a broken wreck. "I know. Can't you do something? You've trained for this. Create weapons."

An explosion of sound erupted behind us, and a metal spear stabbed itself deep into the tree next to Josephine. We hid behind another tree to look at the weapon. A long line of chain yanked it out of the wood. Josephine's face went neutral. Only the press of her lips into a white line showed her fear and determination. She raised both hands to the trees above her. Their fruit – large, green, bulbous things – pressed themselves to her. She flung these at our pursuers.

They flew unerringly as if birds on the wing and the sound they made upon impact, wet and sizzling, made me wince. Still, we both smiled as the bandits screamed their pain.

"That should make them a bit more hesitant." Josephine threw several more of the dangerous fruit then shook her hands as if they were hot.

"Yes." I gestured for us to go. We took off running. "We need to find Foolishness."

"In the Glade of the Haunted Moon Tree. It's where he's meant to be." Josephine leapt off one protruding tree root up to a high branch. "Come, the branch roads will be faster." Without thinking about what I was doing, I mimicked Josephine's leap. The jump took my breath away. She steadied me as I landed. "We also have a better chance of finding a cat in the branches than on the ground where the zoog will attack him."

I laughed at the joy of being up so high. My laughter died at the first sound of gunfire and splintering of wood. Josephine and I took off running again. I dodged over and around branches that threatened to knock me from my height. I was equally cautious to avoid the glowing fungi and vines when they appeared in our path. Even in my haste, I saw that both were alive and hunting. Could these be used against our pursuers? "Why won't they climb the trees?"

"Two reasons. The first, cloven hooves are not meant to climb trees like these. The second, the trees do not like them."

I had no response. Both reasons made sense. A flash of orange ahead gave my heart hope that we would escape. "There!"

Josephine let out an unladylike whoop of joy and led me through the woven branch roads toward Foolishness. Behind, the bandits called and jeered in an incomprehensible language that hurt just to hear it. I shook my head and forced myself to go on. Josephine paused and faced our pursuers as I reached her. Again, she raised her fists high. This time, at her unspoken command, a wall of thorny vines sprang upward between us and the bandits. They wound themselves around the trees, linking them together in an armored lattice of living flora. The bandits howled their fury and pain as they rebounded off the barrier. The twining, writhing vines grew until they blocked the bandits from sight.

"I didn't know you could do that."

She looked at her hands. "Neither did I."

"The trees, the Enchanted Wood, helped," said Foolishness. He sat on a branch in the distance. "Hurry. Hurry! We don't have much time. You have to get to the Haunted Moon Tree. That's your way out."

Josephine and I sprinted over and through the branches toward him. Leaves slapped at my face and my body. I did my best not to disturb them, but they seemed to leap into my way. Vines snaked out to trip me. Was the forest trying to delay me in order to save Josephine? I pushed the thought out of my head as the madness it surely must be. I ran harder through leaves that blinded me. I would survive. I would make it through.

Then I was falling.

I hit the ground with a hard thump and sprawled there, stunned. Behind me, sounds of pursuit rose as the barrier of thorns and vines fell. I pushed myself to my feet and looked around. We were in the glade where we first saved Foolishness. This time, the glade was huge. It would be like sprinting across the university.

Foolishness twined himself about my ankles. "You must climb the Haunted Moon Tree. It's the only way to escape now."

"Will it send us home?"

Gold-green eyes stared up at me. "Yes. It's your way out of the Dreamlands."

I stared at him, sensing there was more he was trying to tell me. The crack of gunfire as well as the explosion of the spear ballista told me I had no time to interrogate the cat further. "Josephine!"

She stood on the edge of the glade. "I can hold them back."

"No. It's time to go. We've got to go home."

"I can do it." Her hands clenched and her eyes narrowed in fierce determination.

I touched her shoulder. "I know you can, but now is not the time for this fight. We need to go home. Up the Haunted Moon Tree." I squeezed her shoulder, my voice low even as the horned and hoofed bandits came ever closer. "Please, we've got to go. Before it's too late. I believe you. I believe in your power. But now is not the time."

Josephine hesitated a moment longer. Then she nodded. My heart soared. I would save her as I had not saved Malachi. In our world, on Earth, we could plan and fortify ourselves. We needed time. We needed safety.

We sprinted through the impossibly tall, purple grass. It was as if we'd stumbled into a purple cornfield. Yet in front of us stood the Haunted Moon Tree. So huge now, it seemed to rise to the moon above us.

When had it become night?

As before, I leapt for the tree, intending to climb it. Instead, I stumbled and fell flat against the bark of the trunk. It was as if I'd missed a step descending stairs. I stood on the side of the tree, unsteady and confused. Gravity was both beneath and behind me. How?

"Doctor, time is of the essence. We must go." Josephine put a hand to my back and pushed. Then we were running up the tree as if it were on its side. We ran upward, my hair flying behind me. At the same time, we ran forward. Both states of being were possible in this place.

A shot hit the branch in front of me, throwing splinters of wood into my face. I cried out and shielded my eyes. Two more shots. Josephine stumbled.

I turned to her as she got to her feet. Her leg was bleeding. We reached for each other even as the bandits behind-below fired again. This time, it was the spear ballista and it struck true.

Josephine screamed as the spear pierced her through the shoulder. I did not let go. I held both of her hands as she was pushed toward me then pulled backward. "Don't let go."

"I won't," I promised, not knowing I lied despite my sincerity. I saw that the spearhead had a hook to it that prevented it from slipping free of her tortured flesh. I would have to break the spear from behind. "Hold onto me. No matter what happens, hold on."

Josephine nodded, her face gray with pain. "I will. Do what you–"

The rest of her words were lost to the sound of another spear ballista firing. A spearhead punctured Josephine through the chest with an audible breaking of bone and splash of blood. The world froze into flatness and silence. Josephine and I still held both hands in a tight grip. Her mouth opened in the beginnings of a scream that would never come as her body arched with the impact of the spear.

I stared at her, not believing my eyes. Not wanting to believe the death in hers. Unable to make myself move.

Foolishness walked down a branch. He was the only thing moving. "She's dead now. You can let go."

"No. I promised I wouldn't."

"It's fine. I've died many times." The cat cleaned his face with a paw. "At least this was quick for her. She's already dead. She can't feel anything anymore."

"I can't." I stared at Josephine's face frozen in shock and saw that he was correct. There was no life in her eyes. The spear that was still moving toward me had already taken it. "The healing feathers. You must have some. We can save her."

The cat shook his head. "We cannot. The feathers only work on the living."

I watched the spear tip come ever closer to my chest. "I promised her. I can save her body from them. Bring her back from the dead like I did the butterflies?" It was a hopeless question. I already knew the answer.

"You also promised Sati." The cat's tail flicked back and forth, agitated.

I didn't know if I could resurrect Josephine. If I left her, I couldn't for sure. "I can't leave her."

"You can. You must. You have another duty to attend to." The cat reached out a ginger paw to the pocket where the scroll case was. "You can stay here and die with Josephine, or you can return to your world to do what needs to be done. Choose."

I thought of Sati's words and wondered if my taking of the Elder Sign was what cost Josephine her life.

Foolishness answered me even though I didn't ask the question aloud. "Her fate was written in the stars long ago. Yours was not. Do you want to die in vain?"

I shook my head and chose to live. Chose to let Josephine fall. With that decision, the world reasserted itself. I jerked back from the spear before it impaled me as well. Josephine was yanked from my hands even as I let her go. I watched her lifeless body plummet into the waiting arms of the minions of the Black Wind. I didn't know what they'd do with her. I didn't want to know.

I turned and ran. Ran for my life, my sanity, my soul, toward the moon. Its fullness filled me. I ran faster. As I reached it, I found myself slumped in my office chair, the single spotlight above and behind Josephine shining in my face.

Across from me with our knees touching, Josephine lay limp in her seat, her eyes closed, her breath non-existent.

CHAPTER 13

Returning to reality – to Earth, to my office – was both a blessing and a curse. While I knew that I did not know my home at all, I have never been more glad to see familiar surroundings. I thought I was done, free of that place and its frightening truths. I was wrong.

I struggled to a seated position and looked around. The clock on the wall lied to me. No more than fifteen minutes had passed. I couldn't believe it. We'd been in the Dreamlands for hours. I turned from it and reached a hand to Josephine. "Please, God in Heaven, please. Be all right. Be well. Please."

I shook her knee. There was no response. My stomach dropped to the floor. I shook her knee harder before my fingers found her wrist and sought her pulse. It was there. Slow and steady. I wanted to cry. She wasn't dead.

It *had* been a dream after all. I was home. All was going to be well again.

Josephine's eyes fluttered open. She looked around in

a panic. She focused in on me, her eyes burning with loss and anger. "I died and you left me." Her voice was soft and intense as she sat up. "I – died."

I moved away, recognizing the high emotion. "It was a dream... our session... the hypnotherapy. It wasn't real. I'm still here."

"Of course it was real." She stood with slow decorum, a woman using every ounce of will not to scream. She covered her face with her hands. "Did you learn nothing during our time in the Dreamlands? It was a *real* dream. A living, real dream, and I died." She pulled her hands down so they only covered her mouth. A gesture of anguish.

Agony tore at my heart. I should have done something, but I hadn't been able to. I reached a hand to her. "It was a dream. It wasn't real. You're here. Alive."

She turned her back to me. "You do *not* understand. You could *never* understand. I can never go back. The stairs are closed to me. I am exiled from my home, my dreaming home."

I moved forward to put a comforting hand on her shoulder. "You will dream. You will still dream."

Josephine whirled, and with a strength born of grief she struck me across the face. I tumbled backward, falling over the low table. Stunned, I lay on the floor, aching from my hard fall. Something within an inner jacket pocket jabbed my breast. As I gathered my senses, Josephine ripped at her dress.

"If it was just a dream, if I am barred from my Dreamlands home, why am I still marked? Why does His mark still burn my breast?"

I saw her upper chest revealed. Upon it were the glowing, writhing, gold marks, beautiful and terrible against her beige skin. If I kept looking, one of those tentacles would move and reveal the eye of the Black Wind... in this world.

My world.

The real world. I refused to see. I turned my face away, ashamed at my cowardice.

"Why can I feel him looking through me? With my way to the Dreamlands barred, why does His mark still burn my soul?" Josephine flung her arms wide in supplication. "Why do I feel this power within, searching for a way out? Why can I do this?"

For a moment, she posed as if martyred. I stood, something metallic falling from my pocket. I thought to chide her for her dramatics – despite the glowing mark upon her breast – but stopped. The wall nearest her left hand began to warp and melt. I had to remind myself we were no longer in the Dreamlands. Such things did not happen here. "Josephine!" I pointed to the wall. "What's happening?"

My patient turned to the warping wall and tilted her head. It was as if someone had taken a picture of the wall, put it on fabric, and was winding that fabric up from the middle. My bookcase, and all its books, twisted and turned but did not fall from the wall nor the shelf. It was as if they no longer existed in this world. "Josephine, are you doing that?"

Her voice came slow and thoughtful. "Yes. I believe I am. I don't know how. I did not have this power before." Even as she spoke, the glow from her chest intensified. She smiled, wide and mad. "I understand now what happened to me."

I backed away and found myself behind my desk, as far away from the warped reality of my office wall as I could be. With trembling hands, I unlocked the desk and sought my father's gun. I almost collapsed to my knees as I found its cool, solid, metal form. I hadn't lost it in the Dreamlands. It was here. What was happening before me was an impossibility. And yet… "What do you understand?" I left the gun in the unlocked drawer – available but not yet at the ready.

"Why I needed to die in the Dreamlands. What my family's pact with the Black Wind is." Josephine reached a hand toward the swirl in reality and tapped it with a single, elegant fingertip. A tiny hole appeared. It did not reveal the office on the other side of the wall. Instead, a faint eldritch light flickered through the small tear in reality.

"Tell me, Josephine. I need to know." I couldn't take my eyes from the hole that looked onto another place and time. The edges of reality shimmered and undulated in a rainbow of colors that reminded me of what I saw as I was pulled into the Dreamlands.

Josephine turned to look at me with three eyes – hers and the Black Wind's. I froze, pinned like prey in bright light. "I have not lost the Dreamlands. I can journey there again at my whim." Pleasure traveled through her words and over her face. "I have not lost my second home."

Behind her, the gate between worlds widened. Through it, I could see movement. Creatures I recognized – and ones I could not. My mind slid off these other abominations, refusing to give name to their forms. "You can open a way. You have become one of those meeting points."

"Yes."

"Can you close a gate once you've opened it?"

She blinked at me as if I had said the most absurd thing in the world. "Close the gate? Why would I want to close the gate? This is the power I'm meant to have." A manic joy that bordered on madness danced in her eyes.

I realized I wasn't speaking just to Josephine anymore. I had to reach through the thing influencing her to find her core. I pointed to the hole in reality. "If you can go through, back into the Dreamlands, they can come here. Isn't that so?"

Josephine whirled about and stared through the porthole-sized opening at the oncoming mass of monsters. "That cannot be. They do not belong here. This is my world. They are *not* welcome. I will not have it!" The glow upon her chest diminished in her outrage.

"Then I suggest you close the way." I sounded far calmer than I felt.

She looked down at her chest, at the mark of the Black Wind. When she looked at me again, her eyes cleared from madness to fear. "He is inside me. The Black Wind is doing this."

"Then stop him." I used a tone of command with no expectation of failure.

Josephine furrowed her brow and reached a hand toward the tear. She shook her head. "How? I don't know how. Help me."

"How would you have done it in the Dreamlands?"

"We aren't in the Dreamlands."

I pointed to the widening hole in reality with the minions of the Black Wind running ever closer. "We are. Partly. Use what you know. Use what you've always used. *Fight* him."

Josephine turned back to the window-sized gate and held out her hands. She brought her hands together closer. The gate halted its opening. "It works!" Her triumph was short-lived. The mark upon her breast flared and she fell to her knees with a cry of pain.

I rushed to her side and helped her up. The eye of the Black Wind focused on me, glaring, and I felt my soul quake. I was nothing before its glare. It was hungry and I was food. I would be the first consumed when the Outer God's minions arrived.

"It… He is fighting me." Josephine bowed her head.

"All your life, you've learned to fight, to evade, to escape the Black Wind. Use what you know. I believe in you." As I spoke, the first howls and jeers of the bandits came through the portal. I needed to help as much as I could. If Josephine could at least keep the gate from opening any wider, we would have a good chokepoint. It would be the Battle of Thermopylae. Hopefully with a better ending.

I squeezed her shoulders. "You know what to do. Fight him. Fight the Black Wind. Close the portal." I stepped back and left her to do what she could while I went for my father's gun. It was not much, but it was something.

A glint of metal from the floor stopped my steps. I had not lost my father's gun to the chasm, but I had returned to this world with another weapon – one I had chosen to carry. A weapon that could help close the gate.

It could also kill Josephine in the process.

I picked up the scroll case. In this reality it was as long as my palm and twice as thick as my thumb. The end cap came off in my hand as if eager to help. The rolled tube of paper was stiff with rough edges. I could still see pieces of the plant fibers that made the paper. It reminded me of papyrus, but every instinct I had screamed that the paper was not of this world.

I unrolled it with careful fingers. Swirling glyphs filled my mind. I don't know how, but I understood what they said. Not the exact words. Only their true intent. I could not grasp it as a whole. I understood the concepts. I understood that I could use this spell – for that was what it was – to close and seal this breach between our worlds.

I also understood that it might harm, even kill, Josephine. I looked at her back as she struggled with the tear she'd created. It was smaller, yes, but she would not close it in time. If she died, I didn't know what would happen to the gate. My heart feared for her. The bandits might use their ranged weapons to repeat what had happened in the Dreamlands and murder her in the name of their otherworldly god.

And yet, if I used the spell, it might tear her asunder. It was a choice. A choice only I could make. I couldn't ask her if she would sacrifice herself. Could I? Saving the world from the chaos of the Dreamlands might require a sacrifice. Was there really a choice?

Two things answered my unspoken question at the same time. First, a cyclopean abomination appeared upon the horizon so large I could not find anything to compare it to. It stared at me with its writhing tentacles playing over each other as it moved with impossible speed. Second, Josephine cried out, horror plain in her exhausted voice. "He comes! Doctor, help me!"

I straightened and chose the only path I could. "I have the Elder Sign. I'll use it."

Josephine did not answer. She focused on making the portal smaller, but she only managed to keep it the same size, her body trembling with the effort.

If my patient died, her blood was on my hands.

So be it.

I raised the scroll and began to read in that impossible language. Line by line. After the first sentence, Josephine straightened, a strength flowing into her posture. After the second sentence, she echoed my words. After the third, she echoed my words and drew glowing glyphs, clockwise, in front of the portal, ending with a pentagram to seal it.

> "Here on the skin between worlds,
> The dream of pain and exchange awaits.
> Here in the place between death and darkness,
> The threshold spirit lives.
> Tremble at my prayer.
> Tremble as I call.
> Fear this moment in time.
> The threshold spirit denies.
> The way is closed.
> Go.
> The way is denied.
> Go.

The way is sealed,
Forever more.
Go!"

With each line of the spell and Josephine's echoed response, the portal grew smaller. The abominations on the other side of the breach howled their fury. As did the Black Wind. With eldritch might, the Outer God tried to suck Josephine through the portal before it closed, heedless of the damage it would do to her mortal body. A foul wind pulled books and papers from the shelves and my desk. They clattered, fluttered, and thumped to the floor in an unholy cacophony of sound.

I found myself holding Josephine by the waist with one arm and the tatters of the Elder Sign spell in the other hand as we finished closing and sealing the gate together. We yelled the last line, struggling against the grasping wind and the noise that threatened to burst our eardrums.

Then there was nothing.

CHAPTER 14

When patients have momentous breakthroughs in their therapy, it often looks like a catastrophic breakdown. There can be tears, shouts, curses, temper tantrums, and the tearing of clothing. A psychologist learns to identify a breakthrough in and among patients acting out. After the wild release of emotion, the patient's demeanor tells all. Do they watch to see your reaction, or do they turn inward to examine themselves? A breakthrough can be a lovely thing to witness. It can also be destructive and painful. In Josephine's case, her breakthrough saved more than herself.

There was no hole in reality in my office wall. No portal to the Dreamlands. No racing bandits with hooves and horns. No abominations seeking to consume us whole – body and soul.

Josephine and I tumbled to the floor before my unmarred bookcase. My patient sobbed as if her heart were broken. Undoubtedly it was – and would be for a long time to come. Kneeling next to her, I held her tight and rocked her back and forth, grateful she was still alive. I tried to make soothing noises, but my voice was raw from the spell I'd wrought.

Someone shouted at my office door and shook it. The noise of our fight to close the portal had not gone unnoticed. There were at least three voices there, clamoring to get through the locked door. I heard Nurse Heather's strident voice command the rest to move aside.

Still holding and rocking Josephine, I heard the door unlock and watched as it was flung open. Even as the orderlies rushed in with Hanna and Nurse Heather behind, I threw up a hand, warding them all off. "It's fine. Everything is fine here." I tried to muster as much authority as I could from my kneeling position. My face was flushed, my cheek throbbed where Josephine struck me. "We have had… a breakthrough. I believe all will be well now."

Nurse Heather pushed the orderlies aside and gazed at the shambles of my office with a disapproving eye. I could just imagine what she was seeing. I followed her gaze as she visually picked over the books and papers on the floor, the overturned chair – I do not know when that happened – the mess of files and spilled notebooks on my desk. I met her gaze without flinching as she narrowed her eyes at the mark on my cheek.

"This is a new one for you, Dr Fern. Usually your patients are sappy, sleepy, and pliant. What happened?"

I narrowed my own eyes at the question. "That is between me and my patient."

Nurse Heather put her hands on her hips. "I will need to tell Dr Mintz something."

"Tell him that Miss Ruggles, my patient, had a breakthrough. We now understand what has been causing her…" I glanced at the girl in my arms and pushed on with the lie, "…hysteria. That is all he needs to know. He will understand."

She gave a thin smile. "I see. I will leave one of the orderlies–"

"You will leave no one. We are fine. In fact, I need all of you…" I met each of their eyes in turn, "…to leave. Now. Nurse Heather, please lock the door again on your way out."

I saw Josephine twitch a hand in a small, peculiar gesture. Even though she still had her face buried in my chest, it was enough. Hanna stepped from the office without a word. Both orderlies glanced between me and Nurse Heather. Silently, they decided they were no longer part of the power struggle. Both retreated to the hallway, taking themselves out of the fight, although they remained close enough to be of use if needed.

I kept my face neutral and bland as Nurse Heather looked over the scene again. I guessed she catalogued all that she saw for her report to Dr Mintz. I nodded to the door and waited. With that thin smile of disapproval in place, the nurse returned the nod and backed out of the office. She did not take her eyes off me or Josephine until she closed the door between us. I waited until I heard the clack of the lock sliding home before I focused in on Josephine again.

"Can you stand?"

She nodded.

I helped her to her feet. Then left her long enough to

set her chair right before guiding her into it. Once seated, she slumped forward, wiping at her face. I settled into my chair. We still sat close, across from one another, our knees almost touching. When Josephine stopped wiping at her face and began to straighten her clothing, I asked, "May we speak about what just happened?"

Josephine cast a furtive glance at her chest before pulling her collar up to her neck. "Yes. I think we must."

"Before all this, you said you understood why he, the Black Wind, wanted you dead in the Dreamlands. What did you realize?"

"That my ancestor was either selfish or stupid." She gazed about the office, frowning at its disarray. "What kind of a man would allow his children and all their children to be marked by an Outer God, to be murdered within the Dreamlands, only to be given the impossible choice of exile from their second home or to bring ruin to this Earth?" She shook her head. "Selfish stupidity. And cruel. The Black Wind cannot take a child as his portal. As children, we are… we are not strong enough to open a gate. It is only with an adult's mind and understanding of what is lost that gives the strength needed to tear a hole between this world and the Dreamlands."

I let out a slow breath, astonished and pleased by her insight. I was not going to have to rip the Dreamlands from my patient another time. She had seen the truth of it immediately. It was as if the child had grown up in the blink of an eye. But now she saw only the loss and not the gain. "Perhaps, but now you have a new duty; a new thing to protect."

She turned bleak eyes to me. A glint of hope shimmered in the distance. "What do you mean?"

"You will need to speak to your mother and demand the information she has on this pact. While you are neither of age nor engaged, you have gone through hell. It is time for you to know what they know. It could be that you are the first in your family history to discover the consequences of the agreement made by your ancestor. You have knowledge. This is power. You must chronicle it for future generations."

Josephine nodded, slow and thoughtful. "Perhaps you are correct." The hope in her eyes transformed into determination.

"There are two other things you must consider." She gave me a quizzical glance. "First, now that this power has manifested within you, there will be those who will wish to use you to open the way between here and the Dreamlands. You must always be on guard."

Josephine smiled a weary smile. "As an heiress, I must also always be on guard. This is nothing new. What is the second thing I must consider?"

"Your beloved friend, Mimi, is Professor Sati Das. She is a patient here. You are not alone."

Her eyes widened in surprise and joy. "She is? She's here?"

"Didn't you wonder how I knew her in the Dreamlands?"

Josephine waved a dismissive hand. "Dream logic. Such things happen all the time. There was no need to question it." She leaned forward, eager. "I want to see her."

"I shall try. I think she will be pleased to see you in this reality." I half-frowned. "Assuming we can get her out of the clutches of Dr Mintz. That might be difficult. She is a visiting professor who has no family here as far as I can tell."

Josephine sat up straight, raising her chin. "That is where money comes into play. I will have my lawyers get her out of the asylum and bring her to my home." She paused and considered this for a moment, tapping a finger to her lip before folding her hands together once more. "I will need to find out which university sponsored her to study here and on what project. The invitation to host their visiting professor should spur things in motion. No matter. My lawyers will make my wishes known in the appropriately persuasive manner."

I breathed a soft sigh of relief. Josephine would be fine. She no longer looked to me for all the answers. I touched her knee with a gentle hand. "You realize you cannot talk about this with anyone except me and your most trusted people. Only to those who know the reality of your family." From the blank politeness in her eyes, she did not understand what I was trying to say. I opted for bluntness. "You must admit to being hysterical. That you had a bad period, but we found the source of your fear." The stubbornness set in on her face as she thought this over. It cleared when she realized I was correct

"Which is what?" Her voice, both resigned and wary.

I considered for a moment. "How long have your parents been on tour?"

"About two months."

"Have they been on tour since your brother died?"

Josephine shook her head. The light of realization came

into her expression. "I feared for the loss of my parents? When Leland left, he died?"

I nodded. "It was a bout of hysteria brought on by the memory of your brother." I touched her knee again. "We will need to continue our sessions. Though they will be at your home. There is still much you will need to work through."

That determination dimmed. She nodded. "I am exhausted."

"I would like to keep you here for another week. Daily sessions. Then you will go home. It will give your servants enough time to prepare. If I can get you in to see Professor Das, I will. If not..."

"I will allow my lawyers to deal with Dr Mintz."

"Yes. In the meantime, you will have much to consider. I would like to have you off all medication for this week. I want to make certain there are no lingering aftereffects of our journey into the Dreamlands and the removal of the book. I will give your maid sleeping pills to hold. If it appears you still need them or prefer not to dream..."

Her lips tightened into a line of remembered pain before she nodded. "Thank you, doctor... Carolyn. I will try to be strong – for all of us."

It was all I could ask her to do. In return, I needed to be strong for me and my sanity. I wondered what I would dream of this night. Or, if I could, would I return to the Dreamlands on my own? Even now, the remembered whispers of the eldritch book I had held still called to me.

EPILOGUE

Dear Future Carolyn,

I do not know whether you will believe everything I have had to say when you read this in the coming years and consider your past, but I feel I must write what I remember of my time in the Dreamlands and of my patient, Josephine Ruggles.

Three days have passed since the hypnotherapy session with Josephine that changed our lives forever. Josephine's bleeding nightmares are gone, but the reality of her loss is still settling in. There is no question of trust between us. We journeyed through hell together and came out with a bond that can never be broken – whether or not I want it to be. She trusts me. She relies on me. She talks to me. She is so much better. I feel I honor Malachi's memory with every successful turn she makes.

My duty as her doctor is to be there to a point. That

line has blurred with our shared experience. I must tread carefully in our sessions. There will come a point where we discuss the fact that I was unable to save her from the bandits in the Dreamlands – that I chose to leave her body behind – and that resulted in the loss of access to her beloved "dreaming home". Then I will find out if she blames me in any way. I am an easy target, and she still has so much rage and grief within her.

In truth, much of what happened in the Dreamlands has faded from my mind. I find myself referring back to previous notes with wonder and some skepticism – despite the fact that I lived these memories. I know it all happened, but as with dreams, only specific details remain. All else fades, leaving an incoherent string of thoughts and images.

Still, I continue to write down everything I can remember. Every detail of every creature encountered: the zoog, the cats of Ulthar, the shantak, the feathers from the little red bird of Celephaïs, the goat-legged bandits with hooves and horns, the guardians at the gates between the Seventy Steps of Light Slumber and the Seven Hundred Steps of Deeper Slumber, and the Dreamlands themselves.

I admit my fear to writing down anything about the Black Wind. I fear bringing the god's attention to me again after I thwarted the plan to use Josephine as a gateway between our worlds. That hunger I felt will haunt my dreams – waking and sleeping – forevermore. It is why the fading of details does not upset me as much as it could. I know when I look back on these notes and read them with a more experienced and jaded eye, I will read them without the immediacy of memory or fear.

Tell me, future Carolyn, does the nameless dread I feel now in the pit of my soul ever go away? How many more times do we fight the Outer Gods? Or the Elder Gods? What do we lose each time we do?

I am being dramatic. I will move on before the fear grows again.

In other news, Dr Mintz is less than pleased at Miskatonic University's renewed attention to Professor Sati Das. It seems that the university is more than pleased to have piqued the interest of a well-to-do young woman such as Miss Josephine Ruggles and, of course, the Ruggles pocketbook.

Once Sati is ensconced within the Ruggles household, I will be able to speak to her in depth about the Dreamlands. I can only hope she will be able to answer some of my lingering questions. I have some concerns as to her mental well-being now that she carries the awakened book that drove Josephine mad.

Until then, I will care for Josephine as best I can. The next couple of weeks will bring interesting changes. I look forward to them.

This afternoon, I will walk through Arkham with renewed eyes. I wonder which details, that once held no meaning, will come to light and change my perspective of my home? Sati is right. The scales have fallen from my eyes, and I am changed forever. I find myself both eager and afraid to discover what I will see with my newborn sight.

Until next time,
Present day Carolyn

BLOOD OF BAALSHANDOR

RICHARD LEE BYERS

CHAPTER 1
May 1926

"I'd like to look at the *Necronomicon*," Dex said.

Professor Henry Armitage was chief librarian of the Orne Library, also known as the Miskatonic University Library, which put him in charge of the restricted collections. He was a gaunt man in his sixties or perhaps even his seventies, dressed in a suit that, in show business circles, would be considered stodgy and ten years out of style. He smiled a sardonic smile that Dex found less than encouraging. "Might I ask why?"

It was time to trot out the spiel Dex had prepared for the occasion. "I found a loose page of the book when I was overseas, and I've picked up a few more since." That part of the story was true. He opened the briefcase he'd bought thinking it looked scholarly, businesslike, or serious and responsible somehow, brought out several yellowed pages, and handed them across the librarian's desk.

Armitage inspected them casually for a moment and then, his eyes narrowing, more closely. "They really are pages from the John Dee edition of the *Necronomicon*. In poor condition, I might add. Did you fold one of them?"

"Hey," Dex said, "it was torn and burned around the edges when I found it, and you try carrying it around when you're in the Army, moving from place to place. The thing is, reading just this much convinced me the whole book must be full of spooky hokum, and I've been thinking of putting together a new act that leans on that kind of thing. People like those Lon Chaney pictures, and after I read the whole *Necronomicon*, I bet I can serve up something more interesting than the same old ghosts in mirrors and rubber bats."

This was the part of the story that wasn't true, or mostly not. If he hit on a good idea for a trick, he wouldn't turn his back on it, but it wasn't the main reason he was asking.

The librarian grunted. "Yes, Mr Drake, it is at least remotely possible you might end up with something 'interesting'. However, your lack of credentials–"

"Hold on," Dex said, "I've got credentials." He reached back into the briefcase and brought out his scrapbook.

Armitage flipped through it, lingering for a bit on the military commendations before merely glancing at the newspaper clippings. "'Almost as amazing as Houdini,'" he murmured, reading aloud.

Inwardly, Dex winced. He knew it was gauche, since the man had recently died, but he couldn't help it. Variations on "almost as amazing as Houdini" annoyed him every time the reviewers trotted them out. But that was neither here nor there at the moment.

"You see?" he said. "Maybe I haven't played Arkham

yet" –Did they even have a theater in this little New England town?– "but I'm not some nobody."

"I don't mean to imply you are," the librarian said. "But these aren't academic credentials. Did you ever even attend a university?"

"I was a little busy fighting in the Great War, remember?" Really, he'd hit college age years before America entered the conflict and had never wanted to go. He'd been too eager to break into show business. But so far, his military service was the only thing about him that seemed to have impressed Armitage even a little bit, so maybe there was no harm in bending the truth a little.

"Which is to your credit," the librarian said. "Truly. But no one is granted access to the Orne Library without the proper scholarly credentials and a valid research purpose. Certainly not, if you'll forgive my bluntness, some vaudevillian."

"I can post a bond guaranteeing I won't damage the book."

"That's not the issue."

"And if for some reason I don't get the money back–"

Armitage glared. "Mr Drake. Are you attempting to bribe me?"

"What? Never!" Not if you won't take it. "I just meant, universities always need donations, don't they, and maybe I can help."

"Then I recommend speaking to someone in the Administration Department. Our business is done."

"Thanks. I guess." Dex retrieved his pages of the *Necronomicon* and the scrapbook, closed the briefcase, and departed the office with its portrait of one of Armitage's librarian predecessors – judging from the man's long, prim, Puritan face, he'd probably been a killjoy, too – scowling after him.

Molly Maxwell was still lounging in the waiting area where he'd left her. Onstage, as his assistant "the exotic Morgana", she wore a diaphanous sequined gown, a long red wig, and dramatic makeup that made her look like some devil goddess out of the pulps. At the moment, though, she was a modern flapper at the height of fashion with bobbed blonde hair and a hemline not far below her knees.

She took a look at his face and, rising, said, "Spill. From your expression, I'm guessing the professor said no."

"Yeah." Dex took her arm and they started through the public part of the library toward the exit. Somewhere amid the towering bookshelves, a conversation became too boisterous, and someone shushed the speakers.

"Maybe I should have taken you into the office with me," Dex told Molly. "Maybe you could have charmed him into saying yes."

"Or, if he's like the rest of the stuffed shirts we've seen around here, he might have hated me on sight."

"I wouldn't have been any worse off," Dex said, but he had to admit, Molly had a point. Armitage might well be one of those old fogeys who found flapper fashions scandalous. Now that it was too late, it occurred to Dex that his brilliantined pompadour, pencil-thin mustache, and pinstripes might have made a poor impression in their own right.

Dex and Molly stepped out of the library into a sunny

spring afternoon on the university's quad. Students were strolling, sitting on benches reading textbooks, and, in one open area, throwing a baseball around. Someone missed a catch and, smiling, a passing professor with a Santa Claus beard picked up the rolling ball and threw it back to the players before continuing on his way toward Miskatonic's astronomical observatory.

"Give me a cigarette," Molly said. Dex reached into his coat for his silver case and Ronson Wonderlite lighter. "You know, I warned you he wasn't going to let you in. And now here we are, stuck in Arkham, Massachusetts, when we could be having a real vacation."

"I won the coin toss."

"That doesn't mean you should ignore the brains of the operation." She smiled, and he knew from long association that she was about to ease up on him. "Although maybe it would have been worth it if we'd gotten material for a new act."

Dex felt a twinge of guilt that he hadn't told her the real reason he wanted to read the *Necronomicon*, either.

When Molly called herself the brains of the operation, she wasn't wrong. They'd met shortly after the end of the Great War when they were both struggling performers on the bottom of the bill on the Midwest vaudeville circuit. The song-and-dance act of which she was a part was breaking up, and the fact that they were both patriots who'd interrupted their show business careers to volunteer for military service drew them together, even though their paths had never crossed during the War. He'd been on the front lines while she, to her disgust, spent the

War stateside as a file clerk in the Navy. At any rate, they teamed up, and it changed everything for them.

She taught him a lot about showmanship and had good ideas for new illusions and staging the old standards in new ways. They had strong chemistry onstage, too, and with all she brought to the act, they quickly began their rise to stardom. Technically, her role was magician's assistant, but they were true partners, and in time their partnership had deepened from professional to romantic.

Still, as much as he loved her, there was one thing he'd never shared with her. It was just too weird, and he didn't want to risk losing the person who meant everything to him.

"Well," he said, "it's not like we have trouble coming up with new ideas. So, what do you say we catch the next train out of here and start that real vacation?"

"Now you're talking."

"Then let's get back to the hotel and check out. The taxi dropped us right over there." He turned toward Church Street, Arkham's primary business thoroughfare, which ran along the north edge of the campus. Presumably it would be the easiest place to flag down another ride.

He and Molly had only taken a couple steps in that direction, though, before running footsteps came thumping from behind them. He turned to see who was chasing them down.

It was the graduate student who, playing receptionist, had taken Dex in to see Armitage. The young man was pale, skinny, and horse-faced, sweaty and winded even though from the library to Dex's current location wasn't a long dash.

"Mr Smith," said Dex.

The graduate student blinked. "It's Spratt. Emmett Spratt."

"Right, I'm sorry, Mr Spratt. Has Professor Armitage changed his mind?" Dex could think of no reason why the librarian might have, but he also couldn't think of any other reason for Spratt to run after him.

"Uh, no."

It didn't seem fair that Dex should be disappointed twice in such quick succession. "What do you want, then?"

Spratt warily surveyed their surroundings, then nodded toward an old oak that would block the view from the library. "Let's talk over there."

Molly caught Dex's eye and gave her head a tiny shake. She'd already dismissed Spratt as a waste of time, and she was probably right. But Dex was curious, and the graduate student's conspiratorial air amused him.

"It'll just take a second," he murmured to Molly, "and maybe he can direct us to a juice joint."

"Sure," she replied sarcastically. "He looks like a real live wire." But she suffered Spratt to lead her and Dex behind the tree.

Dex took a drag on his cigarette. "OK, Mr Spratt, what do you want to talk about?"

Spratt took another nervous glance around before replying, "You told me why you wanted to see Professor Armitage."

"I know. I was there."

"And he told me he kicked you out after you tried to bribe him." Molly gave Dex a sour look.

"The professor misunderstood me," said Dex. "I'm sorry about that. But what do you want, Mr Spratt?"

"Well... suppose there was going to be an auction. Of items related to the occult. Including books. Maybe not the *Necronomicon*, but books like it. Would you want to go?"

"Where and when?"

"Right here in Arkham, tonight. You're not on the list, but for a price, say, ten dollars, I can get you in. Are you interested?"

"Maybe," Dex replied.

"Mr Spratt," Molly said, "my partner and I should discuss this. Give us a minute, will you?" She took Dex by the arm and hauled him several paces away.

"I guess you think this is a bad idea," he said.

"You know it is. For about a dozen different reasons. For one, your apartment is already full of 'occult' junk."

That was true. Ever since he was a little boy, he'd liked stories of witchcraft and hoodoo. After he became a star performer, he'd had the money to collect articles related to his hobby. The vast majority were simple curiosities that looked interesting sitting on a shelf or hanging on a wall. Only the pages from the *Necronomicon* had proved to be anything more.

"I've got room for a few more things," he said.

"Maybe," she said, "but what are the odds there's a real auction? In New York, London, or San Francisco, maybe, but in this little town? Not a chance!"

"I'm not so sure about that. The Orne Library really does have an extensive collection of rare occult books. That's why we came, remember?"

"Yes, but–"

"My point," he said, "is that maybe Arkham is a logical place for a sale of occult curios."

"That would only be true," she said, "if someone was going to smuggle books out of the Orne Library for the auction."

"Which would explain why Armitage's graduate student assistant is involved. He could be the auction's man on the inside."

"Here's what I think. Spratt knows what you want. He knows you have money because you're a headliner and you tried to bribe Armitage. So, he lures you off somewhere and robs you."

Dex grinned. "Yeah, he looks hard-boiled."

"He might have friends who are."

"Who, a couple boys on the squash team? I fought in the War–"

"I know. I figured it out after you told me your stories ten or twenty times."

"–and I'm pretty sure, if worse comes to worst, I can handle anything this sleepy little town can throw at us. But I don't expect any trouble. So why not go since we're here anyway and it's just a few more hours? We can start our vacation as soon as it's over."

"All right. But you owe me, buster."

"I absolutely do." Dex turned back toward the graduate student, who still looked jittery with the fear that somebody was going to pop up out of nowhere and catch him doing something he shouldn't. "Sorry for the delay, Mr Spratt. Please, tell us more."

CHAPTER 2

"You sure you want me to let you out here?" the cab driver asked.

"Good question," Molly said.

Dex had to admit that it was. What he'd seen of Arkham during the day – the train station, the Excelsior Hotel, the Miskatonic campus, rustic types from out in the countryside driving horse-drawn buggies and wagons past the shops of Church Street – had struck him as pleasant enough in a quaint sort of way. But per Spratt's instructions, the taxi driver had taken them to a shabby part of town along the Miskatonic River. The poorly lit streets and alleys didn't look like a safe place for a stranger to venture at night. Certainly, the double row of dark warehouses illuminated only by the Buick's headlights didn't.

"It's fine," said Spratt. "It's right here." He climbed out of the cab.

Dex scrutinized the shadows between the buildings. As far as he could see, there wasn't an army of hoods – or squash players – lying in wait. He handed the driver his fare and tip and got out. Molly heaved a sigh and, cloche hat on her head and strings of beads swinging around her neck, did likewise. As soon as everyone was clear, the taxi pulled away with a backfire and a burst of exhaust.

"Wait here," said Spratt. He walked to the door of the nearest warehouse and knocked a special knock, two raps, a pause, then three more.

Dex chuckled. "It's like we've gone to a speak."

"I wish," Molly replied.

The door opened partway, and a silhouetted figure was visible through the gap. Spratt and the figure were evidently talking, and after half a minute, it struck Dex that the conversation was taking longer than it should. "Come on," he said.

The figure behind the door turned out to be a small man with the signs of the zodiac emblazoned on his azure tie, a couple of jeweled rings on each hand, and a chrysanthemum dyed a deep blue in his buttonhole. He gave Dex and Molly a look that managed to be unwelcoming but not belligerent. "I was just explaining to our Mr Spratt that the two of you weren't invited."

"It's a sale, isn't it?" Dex replied. "No point turning away paying customers."

"I have a very exclusive clientele."

"You mean celebrities? We are Drake the Great and the exotic Morgana – maybe you've heard of us? And we've got the bankroll to prove it." Sleight of hand made a well-stuffed money clip appear in his fingers and disappear again.

"It isn't just about money. I only sell talismans of power

to those who can be trusted to use them responsibly." The man in the zodiac tie studied Dex through narrowed eyes. "But I see by the hues of your aura that Mr Spratt was not mistaken in you. Come in, then. My name is Bernard Palmer, dealer in the mystical and otherworldly. Welcome to the sale."

With that, Palmer ushered the newcomers inside. It looked like a warehouse, one that, with its stacks of dusty, cobwebbed boxes, had sat unused for a while except by rats and bugs. But somebody had cleaned up the middle portion of the space for the auction, sweeping the floor, setting up chairs, and laying out the objects for sale on a couple of long tables placed end to end under lights. Half a dozen people – the invited customers, presumably – were milling around inspecting the merchandise. One of them beckoned imperiously to Palmer, who hurried to attend him. Spratt scurried after.

"Well," Molly asked, "are you impressed?"

Dex laughed. "By the rings with the paste gems, the zodiac necktie, or the way Palmer acted like he didn't want to let us into the party? Oldest trick in the book. You pretend you don't want to do business, and the sucker wants what you're selling all the more."

"So you see Palmer's a confidence man."

"Or maybe just a good salesman. I've met some funny birds since I started collecting this kind of thing. Just because Palmer's odd doesn't mean his merchandise isn't the real McCoy."

"Says you. What does 'real' even mean when all this occult stuff is just a bunch of bunk? Oh, never mind. We're here now, and I know we're not leaving until you at least take a look."

"Absolutely. Shall we?"

As they approached the tables, Dex took in the other customers. Their suits and dresses revealed they all had money, which didn't keep them from looking a little screwy or at least eccentric, each in his or her own particular fashion.

To get a good look at some of Palmer's "talismans of power", he had to step close to a pudgy middle-aged man. The stout man was wearing a derby and bundled up in a Chesterfield overcoat with upturned velvet collar and kid gloves even though the warehouse wasn't chilly. He recoiled when Dex came near.

Dex gave him a smile. "Easy, fella. I don't bite. I'm Dexter Drake." He offered his hand, and the man in the Chesterfield flinched back another step.

"It's nothing personal," drawled a hoarse alto voice. Dex turned to behold a tall, gaunt woman in a turban. She held a cigarette in a long jade holder poised near lips painted bright red. "Mr Hogarth is worried someone will filch a hair, a loose flake of skin, or some often worn item from his person and use it to lay a curse on him. Isn't that right, Charles?"

"It happened in Chicago," Hogarth replied. "You go among people with the requisite knowledge, and you need to take precautions."

Dex grinned. "I thought Palmer inspected all our auras for evil intentions."

Hogarth grunted. "A true adept might be able to fool him."

Molly offered her hand to the woman in the turban. "Molly Maxwell."

"Olivia Duquesne. Of the Richmond Duquesnes." She scrutinized Molly as she briefly took her hand. "You're a Capricorn." Her tone had become accusatory.

"Sorry, Taurus."

Miss Duquesne didn't miss a beat. "But with the moon in Capricorn, surely. At any rate, I don't do well with earth signs." She turned and headed toward a third table along the wall where, Dex now noticed, a couple of bottles and a number of tumblers awaited. Maybe Palmer had found his customers bid higher when half under.

"This is swell," Molly said. "Everybody's so friendly."

"Well," said Dex, "they are all rivals. Competitors trying to get their hands on the same stuff."

"And what nifty stuff it is."

Now that Hogarth and Miss Duquesne had moved out of the way, Dex silently acknowledged that Molly had a point. Most of the items in the nearest part of the display – a crystal ball, a shriveled "Hand of Glory", a wavy-bladed ritual dagger – didn't impress him. In many cases, he already owned their counterparts and had eventually learned a number of those counterparts were fakes. Without bothering to read the cards that purported to explain the nearer articles' provenance, he looked down the length of the two tables for the books Spratt had promised. They were there in the center of everything else, the place of honor, he supposed, and the objects of the remaining bidders' attention. He headed for them with Molly in tow.

Most of the books, like *The Lesser Key of Solomon*, *The Grand Albert*, and *The Sixth and Seventh Books of Moses*, were familiar to him, but there were three he hadn't seen before, the ones, he suspected, Spratt had sneaked out of the Orne Library, and it was these that were of the greatest interest to the other collectors. Dex gave them the same friendly greeting he'd tried on Hogarth.

It worked a little better this time. Nobody served up a big smile in return, but most of the others were polite enough to introduce themselves and engage in a little chitchat. Over the course of the next couple minutes, Dex met Randall, a shaven-headed fellow who dressed like a Catholic priest but declared himself a "hierophant of the Qliphoth", the petite Madame Lemaitre, whose voice dropped an octave whenever Magister Randor, her "spirit guide", allegedly spoke through her, and Troughton, a silver-haired limey who limped with the aid of a cane and alluded to his affiliation with the Hermetic Order of the Golden Dawn every other sentence. Only a tall, broad-shouldered man with pince-nez glasses ignored Dex while continuing to peruse a comparatively small volume with a worn red leather cover.

Dex turned his own attention to the ragged-edged, musty-smelling books Spratt had stolen. There was something about them, something that made Dex's skin crawl to handle them. Maybe it was just that they were old, or his fellow bidders' fervent belief in the supernatural was working on his imagination, but there was no denying they intrigued him.

Still, none of the books were the *Necronomicon*. Not

unless it was the one in the hands of the man who'd ignored Dex's greeting. Given its size, that seemed unlikely. The loose pages in his possession had come from a larger volume. But maybe the red book was the pocket edition or something.

"Hey, fella," he said. "Sorry, but I didn't catch your name."

The big man raised his eyes from the book. They were a lustrous brown with motes of red speckling the irises. "Carlyle."

"And I'm Dexter Drake, in case you missed it. Mind letting me take a look at that?"

"If you insist." Carlyle closed the book and handed it over.

As Dex had expected, this wasn't the *Necronomicon*, either. According to the title page, it was *The Blood of Baalshandor*. He skimmed the first couple pages and couldn't make much out of them. But he had the same sense of hidden meanings squirreled away under the surface that had come to him when he first examined the loose pages from the *Necronomicon*, and after several readings, for better or worse, those meanings had indeed revealed themselves. He closed the book, started to put it on the table, and Carlyle held out his hand. Dex returned it to him, and, without a word of thanks, the big man resumed his own examination.

"You're welcome," Molly said. "Are you done looking, Dex? Because I have to go see a man about a dog."

Dex grinned. "Not a bad idea." They headed for the table with the hooch and glasses.

What they found was disappointing. This close to

Canada, there must be some quality whiskey available, but the bottles had no labels. He assumed some local bootlegger had distilled the contents.

"I see Palmer's not one to splurge on the good stuff," Molly said. "Big surprise. But any port in a storm."

"Don't drink that stuff," said Dex. "You'll go blind." He brought out his hip flask. "The bellhop at the hotel fixed me up with some nice Cuban rum."

"I knew there was a reason I put up with you." Molly took a swig from the flask. "So. We're still not leaving?"

"A couple of the books are interesting."

"They're in foreign languages. What good are books you can't read? Do you think the little bit of French you picked up to sweet talk the mademoiselles 'over there' is going to get you through Dee Velma's Misery or whatever it is?"

"They'd still be nice to have in my collection, and the red one, *The Blood of Baalshandor*, is in English."

"What about the fact they're stolen?"

"We don't know for sure that they came from the Orne Library."

"Baloney!"

"Even if they did, they shouldn't be locked away where nobody–"

"Not 'nobody'. You."

"–ever gets to read them. That goes against the whole point of a book, and a library."

"So really, you'd be striking a blow for knowledge. Got it. OK, here's the deal. You can bid on the book you can read. I'd kind of enjoy seeing you disappoint Mr Funny Eyes there. But don't waste your money on any of the others."

"Fair enough. It looks like everybody's done inspecting the goods. Palmer's going to start the auction pretty soon."

But he didn't start it yet. First, he and Spratt had a conversation in the corner. At the end, the graduate student slipped out the door, possibly to run an errand of some sort although he didn't look particularly happy about it. It was then that Palmer asked the bidders, most of them with freshly filled glasses of the local liquor in hand, to take their seats.

The bidding was lively even on the items Dex was pretty sure were fake, which didn't speak well for anybody's claim to real knowledge in the esoteric wisdom department. He noticed, though, that Carlyle made only a few low bids and failed to acquire any items. Maybe he was saving his dough for *The Blood of Baalshandor*. Dex braced himself for a fight.

He got one, too, but not from the quarter he expected. Despite the interest he'd displayed previously, Carlyle didn't bid any higher on the red book than he had on any other item, maybe because he just didn't have the cash. It was Randall who ran the price up to a hefty one hundred dollars before dropping out.

"That wasn't as much fun as I hoped it would be," Molly murmured, "and you really are an idiot to spend that much. But oh well. Can we pay up and go?"

"That comes at the end," Dex replied. "It shouldn't be long. There are only a couple more items."

Palmer auctioned those articles, the two remaining books stolen from the university, and then brought out a cashbox and materials for writing out bills of sale while the bidders readied the satchels and wrappings they'd brought along to transport their newly acquired prizes. From the subtle taunts that jabbed back and forth, Dex gathered that in some cases, frustrating a rival's desire to acquire an especially coveted item contributed significantly to the satisfaction of buying it for oneself.

Troughton handed over money to Randall and slipped a gold ring set with an opal on his pinky finger, the only one where it fit. "The ring of Cagliostro!" he said, and, perhaps expecting it to have hypnotic properties, waved it at Miss Duquesne. Unfazed, she blew a blue plume of cigarette smoke back in his direction.

"Huh," Troughton said.

"The ring will attune itself to your psyche over a period of weeks," Palmer said. "Who would like to settle up next?"

The Englishman grunted and doubled over. The walking stick slipped from his grip to clatter on the floor, and he thumped his hand down on the tabletop to support himself. It wasn't enough, though. His legs buckled under him, and he fell down shaking.

Dex knelt beside him. "Troughton? Troughton!"

Troughton didn't answer. His eyes had rolled back in his head, and his body was throwing off a feverish heat.

"He needs an ambulance," said Dex. "Where's the nearest phone?"

Palmer and the other collectors stared back at him. "Calling for help might prove awkward," the auctioneer said.

"Nobody has to know about your damn stolen books," Molly said.

Meanwhile, Troughton stopped shuddering. Dex put

his hand in front of the stricken man's nostrils and lips. Troughton was still breathing, but for how much longer was anybody's guess.

Palmer's eyes opened wide in surprise. He made several choking sounds and then flopped forward in his chair. His trembling upper body sprawled across the papers he'd brought out to finalize the sales.

Hogarth backed away from the tables and his fellow collectors. "One of you cursed them!" he shrilled. "But you're not getting me!"

Miss Duquesne sneered. "Don't be ridiculous."

"That's just what the sorceress who cast the spells would say!" The man in the derby and overcoat kept backpedaling until he reached the point where the cleared and lighted area gave way to heaps of boxes and shadow. Then he, too, staggered and collapsed.

Randall fell down moments after that, then Miss Duquesne, and then Madame Lemaitre. "It's the bootleg!" Molly said. "Has to be!"

"How perceptive," Carlyle said.

Dex looked around. The big man was still on his feet and not showing any signs of distress. But he did have a .45 Colt automatic in his hand.

Dex stood up. Slowly, so as not to provoke a shot. "You slipped something into the liquor," he said. "That's why you didn't try to buy anything. You expected that at the end, with everybody out of commission, you could just take what you wanted."

"I'm not wealthy enough to be certain of outbidding all these others."

"Are they going to die?"

Carlyle smiled. "Define 'die.'"

Dex didn't know what to make of that but hoped it meant the poisoning victims could still be saved. "Take whatever you want and scram. Molly and I won't talk to the police, and nobody else will, either. We all came here to buy stolen books."

"Sadly," Carlyle said, "under the circumstances, I don't trust you to keep your word, and even if I did, there are other considerations. I'm afraid you and your lady friend will each have to drink from the tainted whiskey like the others. So, get moving." He punctuated the command by jabbing the Colt an inch farther forward. Dex turned and headed for the table by the wall, once again proceeding slowly to give himself time to think. Molly walked along beside him.

"You mentioned you aren't all that wealthy," said Dex. "If this is about money—"

"It isn't," Carlyle replied. "Keep moving."

Dex reached the table and positioned himself in such a way that he was blocking Carlyle's view of the bottles and glasses. Hoping Molly was paying attention, he filled a glass with the contaminated whiskey and palmed one of the extras in his other hand.

He turned back around with the full glass on prominent display. "You know, Mr Carlyle, it occurs to me that if I'm going to die anyway, a bullet might be an easier way to go."

Carlyle shrugged. "If you prefer."

"No, on second thought, cheers." Dex brought the glass to his lips. The whiskey tasted like ordinary moonshine on his tongue. Well, it would, wouldn't it? Had it tasted funny, the others wouldn't have drunk it.

Molly screamed, "You're a monster!"

As usual, her timing was impeccable, and Carlyle's gaze automatically shifted to her. While he was distracted, Dex spat the poisoned liquor back into the glass, set it down behind him on the table, and shifted the empty glass from one hand to the other. When Carlyle looked back at him, he had the empty to his lips.

"Very good," said the man with the pistol, "and now, miss, it's your turn."

It had taken a while for the poison to hit the others. Dex was afraid that if he pretended it had affected him immediately, Carlyle would be suspicious. But he couldn't allow the bastard to force Molly to drink. He groaned an anguished-sounding groan, doubled over, and fell down shaking, much as Troughton had.

Carlyle peered down at him. "Hmm. You were very susceptible, weren't you? I suspect you're going to make–"

Right on cue once again, Molly bolted for the cover of the stacks of boxes. Carlyle pivoted and fired after her but missed. She vanished into the gloom.

As he scrambled up, Dex threw the tumbler. It clipped Carlyle on the temple but glanced away without stunning him, and the poisoner swung the Colt back in Dex's direction. He ran for the piles of boxes that rose beyond his end of the table.

The automatic barked twice, but neither shot hit him. He kept moving, swinging around one pile of crates and then another, changing direction to throw Carlyle off his trail.

He hoped the gunman would come after him. Molly was on the opposite side of the warehouse, and that was where the door was. She could make her escape and get the cops while he played hide-and-seek with Carlyle.

Carlyle shouted. Dex could make out a thudding cadence and even rhymes but no actual words, just noises that had too many consonants and too few vowels.

The recitation was chilling in a way that reminded him of his pages from the *Necronomicon*. But, he told himself, the important thing was that the direction of the snarling and rasping indicated Carlyle hadn't moved away from the liquor table. If the occultist wasn't chasing either Molly or Dex, surely she could get outside. Maybe even he could.

The darkness deepened and churned around him, or perhaps he was reeling off balance. He couldn't tell. He had a sense of the walls receding, the interior of the warehouse expanding around him, even as he lost all sense of where he was relative to anything beyond the piles of boxes immediately around him.

Evidently Carlyle knew how to cast real magic spells. If it weren't for Dex's experience with the *Necronomicon*, the shock of it and the disorientation the spell had produced might have panicked him. As it was, he was now as afraid of the poisoner's occult powers as he was of the Colt, and he could only hope that Molly hadn't fallen prey to a crippling terror.

Maybe she hadn't. She was tough. Still, if she was as disoriented as he'd become, neither of them was likely to reach the door anytime soon. And if Carlyle wasn't disoriented, he might be able to catch up to them while they were groping around.

So, keep moving! Cover was cover whether Dex was lost or not, and the stacks of boxes would cut Carlyle's sight lines.

Turning frequently, he skulked on until there came a flash and a bang. The bullet thunked into a pile of boxes to his left. He ducked behind it and scurried onward.

The close call made his unnatural fear and confusion worse. It was like the shifting shadows were inside his head as well as outside, addling his thoughts. Without meaning to or knowing it was coming, he let out a tiny whimper.

He breathed slowly and deeply. It quelled the fear a little, as did the reflection that, whatever else Carlyle was, he hadn't proven to be a crack shot. Still, assuming he had enough rounds, he was bound to hit the target eventually. If Dex was to save himself, he had to do better than just blundering around.

The central portion of the warehouse, where Palmer had set up the auction, had lights. Everything looked dark now, but surely that area wasn't as dark? If Dex looked for an area of lesser gloom, perhaps he could find it.

Maybe that was it over that way? Still remembering to change course every so often, he headed in what he thought was the general direction of the center of the warehouse. It seemed to take an unreasonably long time to get there, another suggestion that the interior was somehow larger than before.

The lights Palmer had used to illuminate the auction items and the proceedings in general were still on, so it made no sense that the area was as murky as it was. The lamps had dwindled to dots of feeble glow that only barely revealed the tables, the objects on top of them, the chairs, and the bodies slumped on the floor.

Dex resolved not to let this new bit of strangeness distract him from practicalities. What mattered was that he needed to cross the open space without getting shot. He dashed for the other side.

Once across, he ran on into new stacks of boxes and deeper darkness. In one of the aisles between the stacks, a shadow appeared, and he started to lunge for cover in the desperate hope of reaching it before Carlyle could fire at close range. The shadow wheeled to flee from him, and he heard clinking. It was the sound of loops of beads swinging and knocking together.

"Molly!" he said. "It's me!"

She turned back around. "You didn't look like yourself."

"For a second, I didn't recognize you, either."

"I don't understand what's happening."

"Me neither." That wasn't completely true, but now wasn't the time for an explanation that, even if she believed it, might only alarm her further. "But I've got my bearings now." He hoped. The open area was behind him; he was on the south side of the warehouse, and that meant the door he and Molly had come through ought to be ahead and to the right. "Give me your hand."

He led her through the lanes of boxes, still taking an indirect route to throw off Carlyle and hoping he wasn't confusing himself in the process. After what seemed a long time, they reached the door they'd come through, beside the big roll-down loading doors. As Dex reached for the knob, he felt a sudden dread that whatever had changed the inside of the warehouse had changed the outside, too. That the world he knew would be gone and something ghastly would be in its place. But when he opened the door, it wasn't so. Warehouses stood in rows in the moonlight just as they had before. Traffic noises – the rumble of somebody's flivver and the clop-clop of hooves – sounded from elsewhere in town, and the cool breeze carried the smell of the nearby river.

He and Molly slipped out the door, and when they closed it silently behind them, he took a long breath. His heartbeat slowed, and much of his fear fell away. In its place bloomed anger.

"Wait here," he said. "I'll just be another second."

"What are you talking about?"

"Carlyle wants the *Baalshandor* book most of all. He could hardly stand to let go of it before the auction started, and it was still lying on the auction table when he tried to make us drink the poison hooch and started chasing us around. I'm going to get it."

"Don't be a sap!"

"If he wants it, he can't have it." Dex smiled. "Besides, it's mine. I won the auction fair and square."

"What about Palmer, Hogarth, and all those others? Maybe somebody could still save them."

"We will. Just give me a minute. If I haven't come out again, beat it and get help."

"If you insist on going back in, I'm going with you!"

"I need you out here. If I get turned around, I'll yell, you answer, and the sound will lead me back to the door." He turned and reentered the warehouse.

As soon as he did, feelings of disorientation and dread gnawed at him anew. I know the way, he insisted to himself. I know the way. He sneaked toward where the open space and the auction items ought to be.

They were. He hurried on toward the point where the two tables met, and where the books were still reposed along with the upper portion of Palmer's motionless body.

He considered taking all three volumes, but *De Vermis Mysteriis* and *Cthaat Aquadingen* were as bulky as dictionaries and not conducive to sneaking around. Better to content himself with *The Blood of Baalshandor*. He picked it up and returned the way he'd come.

He was halfway back to the boxes and the area of deeper gloom when a dark figure appeared between two of the piles ahead. Carlyle had at some point crossed over into the part of the warehouse nearest the exit.

Dex sprinted for the cover the boxes afforded. Carlyle's .45 flashed twice, and he felt a bullet streak past right beside his ear, but neither round caught him. He ran down the aisles between piles of boxes, turning and turning again to confuse the gunman.

The changes of direction deepened his feeling of disorientation and the fear that came with it. Once again, the warehouse felt like a maze so vast no one could ever find its end.

"Molly!" he called.

"This way!" she answered. The sound came from the left. He ran in that direction, and the door was suddenly before him. As he scrambled through, a shot cracked into the panel.

He glanced back. Carlyle was just a couple steps behind him. Molly grabbed hold of the door, and when Carlyle's rushing footsteps sounded right on the other side, she shoved it hard.

The bang and jolt as the door slammed into Dex's pursuer showed she'd timed the attack correctly, and it was immediately followed by a bumping sound that suggested Carlyle had fallen back into a stack of boxes and knocked them over.

Dex ran on with Molly now dashing at his side. They made it around the corner of the next warehouse in line without any more gunfire at their backs.

With a grin, Dex brandished *The Blood of Baalshandor*. "Got it!"

"Whoopee," she answered sourly. "Now can we get the cops?"

Keeping to the shadows, they headed for a part of town where more lights were shining and from which the traffic noises were coming. Until, glancing backward, Dex saw a figure step out into the dirt road that ran along the front facings of the warehouses. He pulled Molly behind the cover of a building, and they both peeked around the corner.

He expected to see only Carlyle, and the big man was indeed the first to appear, holding the Colt in one hand and pressing a handkerchief to his forehead with the other. But others followed. It was easy to identify Hogarth in his overcoat, stick-insect-thin Miss Duquesne, and Troughton, still limping albeit without the use of his cane. The other trio of shadows must be Palmer, Randall, and the diminutive Madame Lemaitre.

"Thank God they didn't die," Molly whispered. "But now he's taken them hostage."

"I don't think so," Dex replied, "not in the way you mean." Carlyle wasn't making any effort to stand where he could threaten everyone with the Colt at once. In fact, he wasn't pointing it at anybody. Instead, judging from his gestures, he was organizing a search party, and once he finished giving directions, the cluster of figures spread out in pairs and one group of three.

"What the hell?" Molly said.

"Come on," said Dex. "It's dark, and we've got a good lead on them. If we're careful, they won't catch us."

CHAPTER 3

In the course of their progress away from the warehouse and their pursuers, Dex and Molly had to pass a church with an old graveyard. After what he'd already experienced, proximity to the crumbling tombs and markers scraped at Dex's nerves. But they made it by without anything else alarming happening, and in due course reached a more brightly lit and busier part of town. A cab was dropping off a couple at the curb, and they ran to catch it before it could drive away again.

The taxi driver gave the magician and Molly a smile as they scrambled into the backseat. "You're lucky. I almost didn't see you. Where to?"

"Just drive!" Dex replied.

Still twisted around in the front seat to face his new fares, the cab driver asked, "Who are you, Nick Carter?"

"Get moving!" Molly said. "Please! We'll tell you where we're headed in a minute."

"Whatever you say." The cabbie put the taxi in gear.

Keeping her voice low, Molly asked Dex, "Aren't we going to the cops?"

"I'm thinking about it," Dex replied, "but what would we tell them? That Carlyle poisoned half a dozen people? Who are all up walking around and on his side now? Even the doctored whiskey has probably gone down a drain."

"We can say he tried to shoot us."

"Again, our word against his with six other people backing him up. And how much of the story do you want to tell? That we went to the warehouse to buy stolen property? That it felt like we went crazy while we were inside? That'll convince the bulls we're on the up and up."

She frowned. "Tell me it isn't that you don't want to go to the police because you don't want to give back the *Baalshandor* book."

"That's not it." At least, not mostly. "I just don't see it doing any good, and if the story hits the papers, we could end up looking crazy and ruin our reputations. Maybe theaters would stop booking us, or people would stop coming to the shows."

"So, what do you want to do?"

"Pretty much what we meant to do anyway. Hide out in the hotel for the rest of the night and catch the first train out of Arkham in the morning."

"All right." Molly raised her voice. "We figured it out, driver. Please take us to the Excelsior."

The façade and lobby of the hotel were brightly lit and reassuringly devoid of lurking gunmen and their accomplices. Mr Trombly, the concierge, greeted them as they came in. Still, even though everything seemed normal, Dex didn't feel entirely secure until he locked the door to his and Molly's room.

He pulled his suitcase out of the old oak wardrobe as Molly sat down on the edge of the bed. "Start packing tonight and we won't have it all to do in the morning."

"Hold on," Molly said.

He turned to look at her. Until now, she'd comported herself like the tough, brave woman she was, but now that they were safe, her eyes were wide, and her face was pale. She was feeling the heebie-jeebies, and who could blame her?

Dex brought out the hip flask and sat down beside her. "Have another drink."

"No," she said, "that isn't what I need. What happened back there… we didn't drink the whiskey, so we weren't drugged. No hypnotist I ever heard of could do what Carlyle did to us in the way he did it. You're the magician. Explain it to me."

Dex didn't know what to say. What he should say.

She seemed to take his hesitation as meaning he was at a loss for an explanation. "Look, I know we create illusions for a living. We're the last people who ought to fall for them. So don't you razz me! But do you think there could be such a thing as real magic, and we just ran into it?"

Now that she'd asked straight out, he didn't have it in him to lie. "Yes. Because it wasn't the first time for me."

Her eyes narrowed. "What do you mean?"

"Well, you know I've liked stories about witches and ghosts and such ever since I was a kid."

"Sure, you've told me. That's part of what made you want to be a stage magician."

"Yeah, well, in the Rhineland, right after the War ended,

I saw a street magician. He got into a quarrel with some of my buddies, and it seemed like he made the night get darker to scare them off. I told myself it had to be the power of suggestion, or a trick so good I couldn't figure out how he did it. But I guess I didn't convince myself completely. Anyway, it woke up my old interests and got me looking for books and other relics of real magic. Or at least what people once believed was real magic.

"Later on," Dex continued, "while I was still in Europe, I heard about a deserted castle called Chateau-Sancille. Supposedly, in its day, there'd been midnight gatherings like witches' Sabbaths, hauntings, and people disappearing. I decided to pay it a visit and poke around.

"It was peculiar there. The manor house wasn't locked or anything, but none of the locals had looted the furnishings even though they looked like they were worth a lot of money. Anyway, I looked around the library and found a loose piece of paper before noises down in the basement – or dungeon, if that's what you call it in a castle – spooked me and convinced me it was time to leave. When I got to Paris, an expert on rare books told me what I had was a page from a book of sorcery called the *Necronomicon*.

"I was intrigued and even got hold of a few other loose pages afterward in a funny little hole-in-the-wall place in San Francisco but never the whole book. And I've looked. To tell you the truth, this isn't even my first trip to Arkham. I heard a rumor that the woman who runs the magic shop here might have a *Necronomicon*, but if she does, she wasn't willing to sell it to me."

"I've seen your collection of spell books, witches'

broomsticks, and all that. But I don't remember ever seeing these pages you're talking about."

"Because right from the start, they seemed… strange, strange enough that I was leery of other people looking at them even though I told myself that was silly. The other stuff looked creepy, but it didn't feel like anything. It was all just props like we use onstage. The papers were different. They had, I don't know, a weight to them. They itched the inside of my head when I read them over."

"Which is why you wanted to come here and read the whole *Necronomicon*. Even though, if you weren't a dope, it's the last thing you'd want to do."

"Yes, but there's more to it. Remember three years ago when we took some time off and you went back to Philadelphia to visit your parents?"

"Yes."

"While you were gone, I went out to a couple speakeasies and got a little drunk. After I came home, I read over the *Necronomicon* pages again. By then, I'd studied them enough to more or less understand them, and I thought it would be fun to try to work one of the spells, an incantation that was supposed to summon a spirit to answer questions.

"Of course, I didn't really think anything would happen. I was just playing around. But something came when I called."

"'Something,'" Molly said.

Dex shivered at the memory. "I don't know what to call it. A spirit, I guess. It was scary, like what happened tonight, only worse. There wasn't anything to see, it was just a… a wrongness in the air. It attacked my mind, and I think I might have gone crazy or worse if I hadn't managed to send it away fast before it really got a chance to go to work on me. At least, I think I sent it away. It didn't jump me when I ran out of the protective circle and the apartment, and it wasn't there when I worked up the nerve to come back two days later. After I was back, I vowed to burn the pages."

"Like any sensible person would. Except I'm guessing you didn't follow through."

"No," Dex said, "I didn't. What happened to me was dangerous but fascinating, too. My whole life, I wanted to find real magic even though I believed there was no such thing. Now it turned out there was. Mind you, it was nothing like what I'd imagined. It was so awful that for a while I wasn't sure I even wanted to do stage magic anymore, even though it's not remotely the same thing.

"Still," he continued, "magic was real, and after craving it my whole life, in the end, I couldn't just burn up the proof. I settled for locking the pages away and didn't look at them again until recently. But finally, well, I just did. I needed to find out more, even if I was never going to try casting a spell again myself, and decided to give the Orne Library a try. By that time, I'd pretty much given up on ever buying a complete *Necronomicon*, but I thought maybe I could at least read one."

Molly considered that for several seconds. When she spoke again, her voice had an angry snap to it. "You lied to me."

"I just never told you. It's not the same thing." Or at least that was how he'd rationalized it to himself. When he said it out loud, it seemed like a shabby, flimsy excuse.

"It's close enough. You had this big secret. Something that was important to you. And you hid it from me."

"I didn't know how to tell you without sounding insane. I was scared you'd leave me."

"And because I didn't know what you knew, I walked into that nightmare in the warehouse completely unprepared."

"I didn't know what was going to happen. How could I?"

"Maybe you couldn't," Molly said, standing up from the bed, "but I don't want to look at you right now. I'm going to walk around and think things over."

"You shouldn't–"

"Leave the hotel? I know. I'm not the stupid one in this partnership." She marched out the door and closed it firmly behind her. It wasn't quite a slam, but it was close enough.

CHAPTER 4

Dex stared at the door. He wanted to run after Molly but didn't know what to say to patch things up. She had every right to be angry, and he had no right to pester her if she wanted to mull things over in peace.

He wondered how to pass the time until she came back, and he could try to start making amends – if that was even possible. Packing had lost what little appeal it initially possessed. Eventually he swigged rum from the flask, turned on a reading lamp, and flopped down in an easy chair with *The Blood of Baalshandor*.

The small book felt odd in his hands, greasy at certain moments, prickly at others, as if the crumbling leather cover was scattered with stiff little hairs. At first the wording seemed odd and oblique enough that Dex couldn't make anything out of the initial pages. He simply got the sense there was meaning to be had.

Gradually, though, he gleaned that, in its opening section at least, *The Blood of Baalshandor* was less a collection of spells like his pages from the *Necronomicon* and more an explication of theology, like the Bible. What it had to say about the nature of the divine, though, had nothing in common with what he'd absorbed attending church as a little boy back in Kansas City, even when Reverend Sullivan preached about the Devil.

If you believed the book, the universe was haunted, or infested, with godlike but horrible ancient beings. Baalshandor was one of them and, by the reckoning of the author of the book, the greatest, although that didn't make sense because apparently another such being had managed to kill it. Or forced it into some sort of prison? Dex had the feeling it all should have been clearer than it was.

But it was hard to focus on the book. His vision blurred, and he kept looking away without meaning to or reading the same sentence multiple times instead of proceeding to the next one. A feeling that he was being watched ratcheted his nerves tighter and tighter even though there was manifestly no one else in the suite. Suddenly he felt queasy and rushed into the bathroom to vomit. He was rinsing his mouth at the sink when someone rapped on the door.

The knock probably signaled something innocuous. Still, caution made him slip *The Blood of Baalshandor* under the mattress of the bed.

"Dex!" Molly called. "Open up! I forgot my key!"

Relieved she was back, he hurried to the door, ushered her inside, and closed and locked it again. He then moved to hug her, but the coldness in her expression stopped him.

"You're still mad," he said. He certainly didn't blame her.

"Damn right I am. But I have to sleep somewhere." She looked around the room. "Where's your precious book?"

He pulled it out from under the mattress. "Here. I stashed it before I knew who was at the door."

"We should finish packing." She retrieved the larger of her two bags and opened it on what had come to be her side of the bed.

"Whatever you say." He opened a dresser drawer, removed the underwear, socks, and spare decks of cards and other minor magical implements he carried around to entertain fans who recognized him on the street, and carried them to his bag where it lay atop the quilt. He and Molly continued like that for a while, each moving back and forth across the room as they readied their luggage for departure. Drawers squeaked, hangers clinked, and cloth rustled.

Dex had his back to the wardrobe and dresser, which meant that when Molly went to collect another armload, she went behind him. Every time she came back into view again, he had the stupid hope that she'd be different, less stiff and silent, but of course she wasn't. He racked his brain for the right words to say to express how sorry he was and maybe incline her to forgive him, but everything that came to him seemed trite and inadequate.

Then it dawned on him that she'd been behind him for a while, and he wasn't hearing the tiny gathering-her-belongings noises anymore.

It was pure, stupid paranoia, anxiety left over from the warehouse and studying the book, that the silence made him nervous. But on the other hand, it wouldn't do any harm to turn around.

He pivoted and felt a jolt of fear. Molly was right behind

him with the wavy-bladed dagger from the auction raised icepick-fashion in her hand.

He recoiled but could only go a couple inches before the edge of the bed caught him across the back of the thighs. He threw himself backward and rolled across his open suitcase to fall off the opposite side of the bed. That was good because the wide piece of furniture was now between him and her. It was bad because he'd stuck himself in one corner of the room, and she was almost certain to intercept him if he tried a dash for the door.

"I don't understand," he said. "You can't be this angry."

The truth was that he did understand a tiny bit. Something else unnatural was happening, something as uncanny and awful as the worst of what had led up to this moment. But if he could get her talking, that might be a first step toward stopping it.

She didn't answer back, though. Instead, her gaze flicked to *The Blood of Baalshandor* where it lay atop the quilt among other articles Dex had yet to pack. She'd asked about it, and maybe, for some reason, she wanted it now. Maybe if he let her have it, she'd stop trying to knife him and leave.

But even if it was true, he mustn't let her leave. He had to help her, snap her out of her trance or whatever this was. And it was dawning on him that the red book might be too important, possibly too dangerous, to allow it to fall into the wrong hands. Maybe he belatedly understood Professor Armitage's attitude.

He faked a move in the direction of the door. When Molly reflexively moved to head him off, he lunged across the mattress and grabbed the book.

Molly had only taken a single step in the wrong direction and sprang back close enough to attack. As Dex scrambled backward, the dagger stabbed down repeatedly, missing him by inches as it pierced the covers and the mattress beneath. He floundered back off the bed and out of range.

But only for a second. By the time he was standing upright again, Molly had jumped up on the bed and was charging after him. She sprang at him, and they fell down together, Dex bumping his head on the wall in the process. Crouched on top of him in the narrow space, she raised the knife, and he grabbed for her wrist and missed. She stabbed at his chest but stopped with the blade point an inch short of his body.

"Oh, God," she said, clambering off him. "Oh, God."

CHAPTER 5

Panting, trembling, his heart pounding, he stood up after her when he had room. "Are you all right now?" he asked.

"No," Molly said. "I woke up and fought it. I took control back. But it's still in me, and I think it's getting stronger. In a few more minutes, it might be stronger than I am."

"What is it? What's happened to you?"

"I was wandering around the hotel like I said I was going to. I guess they don't have a lot of business because the sleeping floors are quiet. Quiet enough that when I ran into Carlyle and his new friends, they could jump me without anybody coming along and seeing what was going on."

"Oh, shit." Now that it was too late, he realized it would have been easy enough for Carlyle and the others to figure out where he and Molly were staying. They'd given their names at the auction, and how many hotels did Arkham have, anyway? The shame he'd felt when she learned he'd kept a secret from her was nothing compared to the guilt he felt now that she'd come to harm. "What happened next?"

"They force-fed me more of the same poisoned hooch Palmer and the others drank."

"What does it do? What exactly?"

Now she looked ashamed, like there was something unclean or disgusting about her. "It feels like it puts something inside you, like a tapeworm, only it's in your mind. Then the thing, I don't know, shares your mind. You start to want what it wants, even if what it wants is to kill. I think it especially makes you want to do whatever Carlyle tells you to do. I even have a feeling the moment comes when it is you.

"Anyway," she continued, "Carlyle was on his way to the room to break in and take the book, but after he ran into me, he figured it might be better to send me instead. You'd open the door willingly, I could take you by surprise, kill you quietly with the dagger, and if anything went wrong, he wouldn't be on the scene when the cops showed up."

"This is my fault," said Dex, "and I'm so sorry. But we're going to fix you."

"I'm all for it," she said. "But how? We haven't got long, and I don't think a doctor's going to do me any good."

"You're probably right," he said. "The problem's magical, a curse or possession or something. The poisoned whiskey was just a way to get the magic inside you. But maybe our magic book tells us how to get it out again." He hesitated. "You'll warn me if you feel yourself losing control again?"

She dredged up a crooked smile. "You'll be the first to know. Get reading."

He did. Perhaps a degree of familiarity helped him withstand the text's disorienting and anxiety-inducing effects, or maybe it was simple desperation, but in any event, it made somewhat more sense this time. He picked up that Baalshandor was an entity associated with disease and that it was indeed imprisoned somewhere, not dead in any normal sense of the word. He even found some spells after the opening section. But they all seemed to be for the purpose of causing sickness. He found nothing that appeared to offer a cure for Molly's affliction.

But there was an incantation in his *Necronomicon* pages for "purging noxious influences and vile presences". He didn't know if it would neutralize the effect of Carlyle's particular poison, but it sounded like it might.

Assuming Dex had the nerve to cast it. He'd wanted to read the occult volumes in the Orne Library to learn more about real magic, but now that the moment was at hand, actually working more would be something else. He felt cold as he remembered what had happened the last time he'd recited a spell from the *Necronomicon*'s pages. But maybe this one would be different. In any case, with Molly's life at stake and no more time to puzzle over *The Blood of Baalshandor*, there was no other choice.

He fetched the papers from the *Necronomicon* and reread the section he needed. He'd forgotten how much preparation the "magus" was supposed to do before actually casting the spell. He should have personally manufactured and "consecrated" a whole assortment of vestments and special tools. Too bad there was no time or opportunity for any of that.

He wished he had the tails and top hat he wore onstage. They might have felt a little like vestments, but they were in New York. In their absence, he made sure his pockets were well stocked with the tools for minor tricks. You never knew, that might help a little, and the shiv Molly had tried to stick in him might substitute for the sword the *Necronomicon* suggested, and perhaps something from Molly's cosmetics case could fill in for the "chalk of angel's bone", whatever that was. As for the rest of the props and stage dressing, he'd just have to hope they weren't really necessary.

"I know what to do," he said, "but I need to borrow your lipstick."

"Help yourself," Molly said.

He knelt and drew the geometric designs and wrote the words around and inside them on the hardwood floor according to the illustration in the papers. Meanwhile, he chanted the necessary rhymes.

So far, he didn't feel anything in particular – no sensation he couldn't attribute to a simple case of nerves, anyway – and certainly nothing like the force that had assailed him when he cast the other spell last year. It could mean he wasn't drawing the signs correctly. Or that this particular spell was a dud that wouldn't work, no matter what. But he refused to believe the latter because it would mean there was no way of helping Molly, and that prospect was unbearable.

When he finished her part of the design, he said, "You stand inside there. Don't leave the center whatever happens. The lines and words protect you."

"Got it," she replied, taking her place.

He then drew the concentric circles where he was supposed to stand, and lastly the lines connecting one design with the other. According to the *Necronomicon*, they were the pathway that would permit the power he raised to flow through him and into her.

After that, he was ready to begin. Careful not to step on and smudge any of the lines or writing he'd just set down, he moved into the center of his design with the wavy-bladed knife in his left hand and the pages from the *Necronomicon* in his right. Confidence might be necessary, but he had no intention of botching the incantation because he hadn't recited it precisely. He was going to read from the script.

"Heart of the endless flame," he began. "Soul of the sun. Creator of the dancers of light. Spirit of drought and conflagration. Maker of ash. I beg you, heed me now!"

As he read onward, and the text swung back and forth between old-fashioned English and a language he didn't know, with words like sjorkala and ystitok, he began to feel something akin to the sense of being watched that he'd experienced when reading *The Blood of Baalshandor*. Now, however, it was a hundred times more intense, and with it came a blighting sense of contempt and disgust. He was bothering something that very much resented being pestered for a favor by a creature like himself.

That was frightening, but even worse was the way in which the entity's perception of him supplanted his perception of himself. Why should the deity want to help him? It was vast and he was tiny, a dust mote, an atom. It was eternal and he was ephemeral, here and gone in an instant, a flicker too fleeting for anything that mattered to even notice. It was made of heat and light and other pure essences he was too stupid to even discern, let alone comprehend, and he was a damp, filthy mass of protoplasm, a thing that sweated, salivated, and otherwise excreted.

He wanted to fall down and weep with shame for being

the unworthy, revolting thing he was. No, what he really wanted was to drive the dagger in his hand into his own heart.

But he didn't because there was some part of him that knew these feelings weren't really his. They were being imposed upon him, and even if he truly was a loathsome thing, Molly wasn't. She was wonderful, he loved her, and she needed him to press on with the incantation.

"Maker and ender of worlds. At thy will, the dust births stars, and at thy word, the stars come into full flower and obliterate the children who dance around them. Great one, I ask for a measure of thy power."

As he continued, the feeling of contempt gave way to something different. He would never have presumed to say the entity had come to respect his stubbornness or approve of him, but maybe he'd roused its interest or amused it. At any rate, it decided it was willing to give him what he'd asked for.

A fierce heat poured over and into his body. Molly gasped, and he saw that his hands and arms, his whole body presumably, now wore a corona of blue and yellow flame.

The fire should have burned his clothing and flesh. It should at least have been agonizing. But it wasn't. It was exhilarating, and with the exhilaration came temptation.

At this moment, he'd tapped into the might and majesty of a god. He could use that communion to transform himself into something nearly divine, a transcendent being fit to rule over the common wretched run of humanity for centuries to come.

But once again, he recognized that he, the real Dex,

had never wanted to be anything other than human, and certainly not a tyrant controlling other people, not when he was in his right mind, anyway. He only wanted to help Molly. He suppressed the alien urge as best he could.

"Lord, my sister has a canker inside her. I beg thee to kill it. Burn it with thy flame that annihilates all!"

He felt a shift in his shroud of flame. Before, it had simply waited for him to give it a purpose. Now, somehow, it oriented on Molly like a dog eager for the command to go and fetch the animal its master had shot.

But did he dare let it go? It was fire. How could he be sure it would do what he wanted and not burn Molly to death? Maybe that was why the entity had responded to the incantation. Maybe that was the joke that would amuse it.

No. He mustn't doubt himself now, not when this was Molly's only chance. He released the fire and, abandoning his body, it roared down the channel that connected his part of the design on the floor to hers. The flames engulfed her, and she fell down convulsing.

Horrified, he started toward her to smother the fire, but it winked out of existence before he reached her.

CHAPTER 6

Molly sat up and peered at Dex. "Lord! You look like that hit you harder than it hit me. Should you have just rushed out of your part of the design like that?"

"Probably not, but I think it's OK." He could no longer sense the presence of the entity he'd invoked or magical forces at play. The danger seemed to be over. "I mean, things are OK if you're OK."

"I think I am." She started to rise, and he helped her to her feet. "Who would have thought you could actually make that mumbo jumbo..." Her face twisted. "Oh, no."

"What is it?"

"I still feel the thing squirming around inside me."

Dex tried to hide his dismay. "Maybe it just needs to finish dying."

Molly hesitated and then said, "I don't think so. The magic you did slapped it around. Made it smaller and weaker. But I can already feel it growing again. My hands go numb for a second when it tries to take control, and its hate, its frustration, its determination are bleeding into my thoughts." She shook her head. "I can't believe this stuff is real. That this is happening to me. Except that I have to."

"Molly, you're the strongest person I know. That's how you were able to resist the compulsion to knife me. So can't you, I don't know, just squeeze out what's left of the thing?"

She scowled. "It's not constipation, you sap. Can you perform the ceremony again?"

Inwardly, he flinched at the prospect of subjecting himself to the ordeal again immediately. But he would have done it anyway, except that, as he told her, "I don't think repeating it would do anything more. I also don't think Carlyle and his stooges would keep their distance long enough for another run-through."

"Well, at least you bought us some time," Molly said. "We'll use it to put distance between us. I'll run in one direction. You take the book, or better yet, destroy it and run in the other."

"You mean, leave you behind? I'm not going to do that."

"You have to unless you want me trying to murder you again."

"No. We're going to fix you."

"I don't want to change or have you run away from me. But if your magic can't fix me, what can?"

"Carlyle's magic. What he did, he should be able to undo, and he wants the damn book, doesn't he? That's what this is all about."

"Yeah. After the auction, he made off with *De Verm*… whatever and *Cat Aquadingus*, but just because they were there for the taking. It's *The Blood of Baalshandor* he was really after."

"Then we'll trade it in exchange for having you cured or exorcised or whatever the right word is."

Molly shook her head. "God, I wish we could, but we can't. Carlyle didn't tell me what he wants the book for. But from what he did say, I could tell he wants the book to do something bad."

"As far as I'm concerned, it can't be as bad as letting you lose your mind."

She frowned. "Yes. It can. Think about what you saw in the War. All the dead men on the ground after Blanc Mont Ridge. I'm talking about something as bad as that. Or worse."

"But you don't know–"

"Trust me, it was pretty clear."

Dex took a long breath. "OK. Carlyle can't have the book. But you're not losing your mind, either."

"That's nice to hear, but do you have any kind of plan? Other than destroying the book right here and now?"

"I'm not going to destroy it. As long as we have it, we have leverage. As for a plan…" He snapped his fingers. "Spratt!"

"What about him?"

"You didn't see him working for Carlyle, did you? That means he left the auction early without ever drinking any of the bootleg. So, he's still in his right mind, he's Armitage's student, and he was involved with the sale from the beginning. Maybe he knows something that can help us."

Molly shrugged. "It sounds like a long shot, but maybe. Do you have any idea where to look for him?"

"The one place other than the warehouse where we've seen him."

"Another long shot, but I guess it's worth a try."

CHAPTER 7

By day, the Orne Library hadn't impressed Dex as anything more than, well, a library, a building that pretty much fit in with the other mostly old-fashioned buildings surrounding the quad. In the dark, though, the three stories of gray granite took on a creepier aspect. The gargoyles that seemed quaint and amusing in the sun turned into ominous shadowy shapes, and the padlocked gate in the wrought-iron fence added to the impression of forbiddance.

Dex shook off the apprehension that had stolen over him as he regarded the place. It was closed, that was all. Apparently Miskatonic University didn't think students needed access in the middle of the night, and in fact, the quad was mostly deserted and the classroom buildings dark. Still, the cool night breeze carried the faint sounds of laughter and a recording of "King Porter Stomp" from a party at one of the houses on Fraternity and Sorority Row.

Molly studied the library with a dubious expression on her face. "Do you think Spratt's in there?" She didn't wait for an answer. "I guess there's only one way to find out." She started forward.

Dex took hold of her forearm. "Hang on." He studied the terrain before him as he'd learned to do in the War.

After a moment, a four-legged form padded around the side of the building. It lifted its leg to urinate on a bush and then, taking its time, continued its circuit of the yard and eventually padded out of sight.

"A watchdog," Molly said. "That's not good."

"We can get past it," Dex replied. He put his finger in his mouth to moisten it and raised it to check the breeze. It was blowing in the right direction to keep the dog from smelling them. "We just have to be fast and quiet."

He and Molly hurried to the gate, and he attacked the padlock with his escape artist's lockpicks until it clicked open. Dex ushered Molly through the gate, locked it after them, and they hurried on toward the wide stone steps and the double doors at the top. Until, halfway across the fenced-in yard, Molly gasped and stumbled to a halt.

"What's wrong?" Dex whispered.

"The thing inside me," she replied, her voice rasping with strain. "It's trying to take control, and it hurts my head. But don't worry about that! Get us inside before the dog comes back around!"

He took her by the arm and helped her up the steps, then started probing and prying the lock securing the double doors. It was as old as the heavy oak panels containing it and only took a moment to give way. He and Molly ducked inside, and he was marginally reassured that she moved without assistance.

"Is it all right now?" he asked.

"Copacetic."

He didn't like the bitter edge in her voice. "You're sure?"

"For now. I'll hold it down as long as I can."

"It'll be long enough. I promise."

At this time of night, there were no lamps burning in the front section of the library, but just enough light leaked in the arched windows to reveal the forms of card catalogs, bookshelves, tables, chairs, desks, and carrels. Dex and Molly managed to grope their way to the restricted collections without bumping into anything. Here, a trace of light shone under the door that was the final barrier protecting the rare, valuable, and, as it turned out, dangerous volumes. He twisted the doorknob slightly, testing it, and found that the person on the other side – please, let it be Spratt – hadn't bothered to lock it behind him.

Dex and Molly crept through the door and onward. Shining somewhere deeper in the space, the light grew gradually brighter as they approached it, and they heard the sounds of someone moving around. Finally, they caught sight of Spratt. He was pulling books from the shelves and packing them in a pair of valises sitting open on a table.

Dex skulked forward and made it most of the way to Spratt before the student happened to look in his direction. Spratt's mouth fell open, and he whirled and bolted.

Dex followed suit and lost sight of Spratt for a moment when he vanished behind a bookshelf but saw him again upon rounding the same corner. The graduate student was only a few strides in the lead. The magician put on a final burst of speed and brought him down with a tackle.

Spratt squawked and flailed in an ineffectual struggle to escape. Dex reached under his jacket, pulled the wavy-bladed shiv out of his belt, and stuck it in front of the graduate student's face. Goggling at the blade, Spratt froze.

"I don't want to hurt you," Dex told him, "but by God, you're going to answer some questions." He hauled Spratt to his feet and shoved him back in the direction of the light.

Molly was at the table inspecting the books Spratt had put in the bags. "*The House of Seven Gables*," she said. "*Leaves of Grass. Moby Dick*. No hoodoo books as far as I can see."

"Just first editions he could sell for a lot of scratch," Dex replied. "Our friend here was getting ready to take it on the lam, weren't you, Emmett?"

"I don't have any choice!" Spratt's face took on a crafty look. "I could cut you in."

"Sorry," said Dex. "What we need is someone to give us the goods on Palmer and Carlyle."

"I don't know anything that could help anybody."

"Just spill. How did you get involved with Palmer?"

"He found me. He must have looked into who's who at the library and found out I was Professor Armitage's assistant."

"With access to the restricted collections."

"Yes. See, Palmer was just what he said, a dealer in occult items but mostly or maybe all fakes. His customers were getting on to him. So, he wanted to have an auction that featured 'forbidden volumes' from the Orne."

Molly nodded. "And you wanted a cut of that money for yourself."

Spratt gave her a resentful look as though to rebuke her for impugning his character. "I needed it. I… play cards. I owe people."

"OK," said Dex, "so you and Palmer made your deal, he contacted his wealthiest clients, and I'll bet Carlyle said he'd come to the auction if one of the stolen books was *The Blood of Baalshandor*."

"That's what Palmer told me."

"Did he know why Carlyle wanted that particular one?"

"I don't think so. If he did, he didn't pass it on to me."

"So," said Dex, "Palmer sets up the auction, on the day, you seize the chance to rope in another big spender – me – you sneak the books out of the library at the end of the afternoon, you get me and Molly to the warehouse that evening, and Palmer sends you away again. Why?"

Spratt frowned. "He said he needed me to go out to the main road and keep an eye out for the police."

"But you didn't believe him."

"No."

Dex grinned. "That's the first smart thing you've said. My hunch is, Palmer wanted you out of the way so he could double-cross you and scram with all the money."

"That's what I decided, too. So, I sneaked back and saw everybody collapse from the poison. I saw Carlyle pull out the gun and threaten the two of you. At that point, I ran away and tried to figure out what to do next."

"Because you couldn't call the cops when you were a thief, especially, as they would see it, a thief implicated in several deaths. You didn't have your share of the cash. You were scared and decided your best move was to beat it after grabbing some other valuable books to sell."

"Yes! And now I've told you everything I know about everything. Please, just let me go!"

Dex supposed there was no reason they shouldn't, but it was frustrating. Spratt had explained his part in the events leading up to this moment, but nothing he'd revealed pointed to a cure for Molly.

"Hold him down," Molly said, "and give me the knife."

Spratt squawked and tried to make a run for it. Dex grabbed him, gave him a shake to quiet him, and then looked around at Molly. She had a cruel smirk on her lips.

"I don't think he knows anything else," Dex told her.

"Says you," she replied. "He just needs encouragement."

"Stop and take a look at yourself. This isn't you."

She faltered, and the eager malice on her face crumpled into shame. "You're right. It's the thing tugging on the puppet strings."

"What matters is you resisted."

"This time. I'm sorry, Emmett. You lured us into a terrible situation, but I'm sorry anyway. Dex, we should let him go."

"With two bags of stolen books?" Dex asked.

"We've got bigger things to worry about."

"Indeed you do," a new voice said.

CHAPTER 8

Dex spun around. While he, Molly, and Spratt had been occupied with one another, Carlyle and the servants he'd created at the warehouse had stolen up out of the gloom.

Carlyle had a satisfied smile on his face and the .45 automatic in his hand. Even in the dim light, the red flecks in the irises of his brown eyes glinted like tiny rubies.

Palmer, Troughton, Madame Lemaitre, and the other stooges all looked sick. Their pale faces gleamed with sheens of perspiration, their clothing was stained and stank of sweat, and every few seconds, one of them twitched. Yet paradoxically, they also seemed keenly alert and poised to pounce, as eager to do violence as Molly had been moments ago.

"Hello again," said Dex. "How did you guys get past the watchdog?" He didn't care, but if he could get Carlyle talking, it bought him time to try to figure a way out of this.

Madame Lemaitre tittered, and Hogarth chuckled. Looking at them more closely, Dex realized that not all the stains on their clothing were sweat stains and that they had traces of blood on their fingers and mouths as well.

"It seems to me," he said, still addressing Carlyle, "that your hopped-up friends aren't hitting on all sixes."

"They're of the blood of Baalshandor now," Carlyle replied. "As is your lady friend. Why aren't you doing as instructed, Miss Maxwell?"

Molly sneered. "I have a strong constitution."

"You may," Carlyle said, "but that doesn't explain your resistance. I can feel the god's blood at work in you as it lives in all of us. It's how I tracked you here. Blood calls to blood." His scarlet-speckled eyes shifted back to Dex. "Back in the warehouse, you displayed a warlock's resistance to the spell of confusion. Did you slow Miss Maxwell's transformation?"

"Not me," said Dex, following Molly's lead. "Now if you want a lady sawed in half, I'm your man."

"I think you're lying," Carlyle said, "but at the moment, it scarcely matters. Drop the dagger and give me *The Blood of Baalshandor*."

"I'll put down the shiv." Dex set it behind him on the table with the valises where he could snatch it up quickly again. Not as quickly as Carlyle could pull the trigger, but he needed to maximize his chances however slim. "I don't have the book on me."

"We've been to your hotel room. It isn't there."

"You're right. I stashed it somewhere else." Come on, Dex, think of something!

"You're new to Arkham, and it's the middle of the night. I don't believe you."

"I'm Drake the Great, pal. I'm good at hiding things. So how about this? I'll take you to the book if you'll let us live and take the jinx off Molly."

"You're stalling," Carlyle said, "and hoping that as you lead us across town, there'll be a chance to signal a policeman or effect your escape in some other way. But I don't need to play your game. My companions and I are going to search you and Miss Maxwell. If neither of you is carrying the book, we'll torture you until one of you tells us where to find it."

"Please!" Spratt exploded. "I'm not any part of this! They took the book from you, not me! Just let me go!"

"Not yet," Carlyle said. "You might have an attack of conscience and run to the authorities. But if you cooperate, you can live through this. You all can. It's only the book I care about."

The assurance the warlock had just given was as unconvincing a lie as Dex had ever heard. As he'd made clear back in the warehouse, Carlyle wasn't the kind to leave loose ends. But maybe it didn't matter, because Dex finally had an idea. A desperate one, but better than nothing.

When his captors' gazes shifted back to him, he had *The Blood of Baalshandor* in his hands. "Such a little book," he said, "to cause so much trouble."

"Hogarth," Carlyle said, "go get it." The man in the Chesterfield started forward.

"Hold it!" Dex snapped. "One step closer and I'll burn it to ash! Then you'll never get it!"

Carlyle made a spitting sound. "You're bluffing. You don't even have a match or a lighter in your hand."

"Watch and learn, pal. There's more than one kind of magic."

Dazzling in the dim light, flame blazed on the cover of the book, and those who were unprepared flinched and blinked at the flash. At once, Dex threw *The Blood of Baalshandor* high enough to clear the nearest bookshelves and land somewhere beyond.

"If you hurry," he said, "you might find it before it's all burned up."

"Go!" Carlyle snarled. His stooges rushed to look for the book, and he scrambled after them. Apparently, the threat of the volume's destruction trumped all other concerns, including keeping control of the prisoners.

Grabbing the dagger, Dex told Molly, "Run!" When Spratt was slow to move, he gave him a shove. "You, too!"

Carlyle and all his stooges had followed the book to the left. Dex, Molly, and Spratt fled right, sprinting for the door to the rest of the library. They were partway there when Miss Duquesne cried, "Got it!"

Dex swore silently. They weren't supposed to find the book this quickly.

"Catch them!" Carlyle shouted.

Dex reached the door, yanked it open, and he and Molly scrambled through. They ran several strides farther before he realized Spratt wasn't with them anymore. Dex turned around to see what had become of him.

Spratt lurched into the doorway. He was still all right. He'd just fallen behind. Dex started to wave him on, and then a second shape rushed up behind him.

It was presumably Madame Lemaitre. Though Spratt's

body all but concealed her petite form, Dex could make out a skirt and the hint of other female attire. But she was different.

The arms that whipped around Spratt's torso seemed too long and too flexible. So did the fingers. Spratt screamed as the fingertips pressed into him. Then something like a tube or enormous sock arched up behind him and slid down over his head, covering it all the way to the shoulders. For an instant, it muffled his shrieks, until they stopped, and his legs buckled beneath him. Madame Lemaitre – if Spratt's attacker was really her – hauled him back through the doorway and out of sight.

Shaking off the shock of what he'd witnessed, Dex started forward. Then the sock thing reared higher with Spratt's head still inside. His decapitated body fell to the floor.

Dex turned again, and he and Molly raced on toward the library exit. Running footsteps drummed behind them.

In the gloom, Dex missed spotting a table until he ran right into it. It hurt his thighs, but there was no time to nurse the pain. He straightened up, and he and Molly kept running.

Until she said, "Over here!" She ducked under a table, and, realizing what she had in mind, he followed her lead. In the darkness, they heard more than saw their pursuers charge past, still heading for the front doors.

Dex and Molly emerged from their hiding place and sneaked at a right angle to their previous course. They just had to get one of the ground-floor windows open.

He smiled as an arched shape of lesser darkness, with trees, another campus building, and the moon framed inside it, swam into view. He and Molly quickened their steps, and then something sprang into their way to cut off their escape.

Madame Lemaitre, he realized. Because she'd lagged behind to deal with Spratt, she hadn't rushed by with Carlyle and her fellow slaves. As a result, she'd detected Molly and him moving on their new course. Except that she wasn't exactly Madame Lemaitre anymore.

Her prim, modest dress and jacket were stretched tight over the bulbous, misshapen torso beneath. Her legs were more or less as they'd been before, but her arms and hands had elongated and seemed as boneless as an octopus's tentacles while also developing patches of stinking gangrene. The fingertips were pulsing maws ringed with multiple circles of fangs.

The most horrible feature of all, though, was her head, if it could even still be called a head. It had become the tube-like thing that slid over Spratt's head, and like Madame Lemaitre's fingertips, it had multiple rings of fangs inside the opening at the end and reminded Dex of a lamprey. It swayed from side to side and expanded and contracted like a beating heart as the creature advanced on her prey. Dex recoiled and heard himself whimper. A part of him struggled to believe what was happening, assuring him instead that he must be dreaming or delirious. He'd pressed on through all the torments the restorative spell from the *Necronomicon* had thrown at him. He'd faced Carlyle's pistol, twice. But the horror before him was too much.

The Madame Lemaitre creature pointed her lamprey head at the ceiling and gave a hissing shriek like the shrilling of a teakettle. Voices exclaimed in the direction of the double doors.

Dex realized it didn't matter how scared he was. He and Molly had to get past Madame Lemaitre, and fast. Otherwise, Carlyle and the other stooges were going to come up behind their quarries, and the two of them would be surrounded.

Dex raised the wavy-bladed knife and advanced to meet his adversary. Molly darted to the side, and he lost sight of her. He didn't dare take his eyes off the Madame Lemaitre creature to see where she'd gone.

The eel thing rushed him with hands and head all poised to seize him. He held his ground until the last possible moment, sidestepped, and slashed.

The blade caught the lamprey head midway between maw and shoulders. It was a stroke that would have opened the carotid artery in the side of a human being's neck and ended the fight, but it only inflicted a shallow gash in the creature's hide and caught one of the pockets of rot therein. Pus and dark scraps of decay spilled out, and the cloud of sickening stench surrounding her thickened.

The lamprey thing whirled and came at him again. The hands snatched and grasped while the head struck repeatedly like a serpent. As Dex backpedaled, he cut at one of the hands. Maybe it would balk Madame Lemaitre if he sliced off a couple of fingertips.

The creature jerked her hand back, and the slash fell short. Before Dex could recover, she grabbed his forearm, her elongated fingers wrapping around and around it. In another moment, the fangs would bite.

Then something thudded, and the lamprey thing staggered. The noise came again, and Dex saw that Molly had come up behind Madame Lemaitre and was bashing her with a chair.

The eel creature started to flounder around to strike back at her new foe. Her half-stunned condition, however, weakened her grip on Dex sufficiently for him to wrench his arm free. He stabbed for the heart, or where a human heart would be, and Madame Lemaitre fell.

Terror and loathing made him want to keep attacking, but Molly grabbed him, shook him, and said "Come on!" Her voice took the edge off his hysteria, and he realized she was right. They had to keep moving. Carlyle and his other slaves were surely on the brink of catching up with them.

Dex stuck the dagger back in his belt and took the chair from Molly. He swung it, smashed the window, and Molly clambered through the opening. When he followed, he fell several feet, but the shrubbery at the bottom cushioned the jolt.

CHAPTER 9

"Are you all right?" Molly asked.

"Yeah. You?"

"Yes, but that thing–"

"Don't think about it." He looked across the quad. It was as deserted as before, without a passing police car or any other means of salvation conveniently to hand. "Maybe we can hide in one of the other buildings."

"No. Carlyle said I'm 'of the blood of Baalshandor' now. He said he can track me by the poison inside me."

She was right. But if they couldn't hide, what could they do? As Dex tried to think, he heard the strains of "Swingin' Down the Lane" in the distance.

"We'll put ourselves in the middle of a crowd," he said. "Carlyle won't try anything there. We just have to make it."

He helped her over the wrought-iron fence, clambered over himself, and they ran toward Fraternity and Sorority Row. Glass broke behind them as one of their pursuers cleared the remaining scraps of window out of the frame or possibly got caught and cut on one. Without wasting time looking back, Dex hoped it was the latter.

As the Greek letters over the door revealed, the Theta Omega Pi fraternity was hosting the party. The music – currently "The Charleston"– played, people laughed, and light shone through the lower story windows.

Dex straightened his tie and his jacket, making sure the latter draped properly to hide the dagger he'd returned to the back of his pants, and ran a comb through his hair. Meanwhile, Molly attended to her own appearance. When she finished, she looked like she was dolled up for a good time, not a woman who'd just been fighting and running for her life, and, he trusted, he looked reasonably spiffy himself. He offered her his arm, and they climbed the steps and entered the frat house.

Inside, in one room that had been cleared of furniture and had the rug rolled up against the wall, young men and women were dancing. People trying to talk over the music of the phonograph bent close to one another or simply raised their voices.

The red liquid in the punch bowl was perhaps supposed to pass for something non-alcoholic, but the empty bootleg bottles on the floor demonstrated it had been spiked, as did the tipsy condition of some of those who'd been drinking it. Hazy with cigarette smoke, the warm air smelled of that, sweat, and the coeds' perfume.

Once in the midst of the throng, Dex finally felt safe. For a few seconds. Then belated reaction to recent events, the fear and revulsion he hadn't allowed himself to experience fully before lest they paralyze him, hit him hard, and he started to tremble.

But Drake the Great, of all people, mustn't have shaking

hands. He took a long, steadying breath and gave Molly a grin. He gestured to the merriment around them, leaned near to her, and said, "Maybe I should have gone to college."

Judging from Molly's pallor, she might have been suffering her own sudden attack of the heebie-jeebies, but if so, she pulled herself together and answered his flippant comment with one of her own. "What makes you think they would have let in a goof like you?"

He laughed and indicated the punch bowl. "I think we deserve a drink." God knew, he still felt like he needed one.

The spiked punch was too cherry-sweet for his taste, but what mattered was that it had a kick. As he was taking a second drink from his cup, two strapping frat brothers, one blond, one brown-haired, both quite possibly on one athletic team or another, pushed through the other students hovering near the alcohol. "What are you doing here?" the blond one asked.

Dex offered a friendly smile. "Just enjoying the party."

Both the flush on the yellow-haired frat brother's beefy face and the smell of his breath as he stepped up close suggested he'd already consumed plenty of the punch. "It's a frat party. Do you even go to school here? I've never seen you."

"He's too old," said the brown-haired one. "If just anybody can come in here, the school will shut the party down."

It was getting more difficult, but Dex kept his smile in place. "Too old? Now that hurts. I didn't go to school when I was your age because I fought in the War, and it took me a while to get back where I need to be." The line hadn't worked on Armitage, but maybe it would here.

But no such luck. "Baloney," Blondie said. "Beat it before we toss you out."

For a split second, Dex was ready to fight them all. Because he couldn't let them throw him out into the dark where Carlyle and his slaves were. He'd use the dagger if he had to!

But that was his still-jangled nerves trying to betray him into a course of action that could only end badly. He mustn't attempt violence when he was outnumbered and surrounded. Besides, the college boys weren't even Carlyle's stooges, just half-under and misguided.

"Hold on," he said. "Before you do that, you've got something in your nose." The frat boys hesitated, and Dex seemingly produced a five-dollar bill out of Blondie's nostril. "Funny place to keep your dough. You should get a wallet. But anyway, let it go for the evening's refreshments." He handed it to one of the other students, who accepted it reflexively.

Blondie looked bewildered. "What are you doing?"

"I told you," Dex said, "trying to get you squared away before the roughhouse starts. You should probably wipe that nose." He made a bright yellow handkerchief appear, gave it to Blondie, and turned to a coed who ventured close to find out what was going on. "And you should have a flower to go with that pretty dress." He handed her a red paper carnation.

By now, people were catching on that they were watching a magic act. "Hey," said a skinny boy in horn-rimmed spectacles, "this fella's pretty good."

"He's better than good," Molly said. "He's Drake the Great. We're the evening's entertainment."

The idea met with general approval. Even the blond frat brother appeared to accept that a scuffle was no longer on the program.

The partygoers shut down the dancing temporarily to provide a space for the show and spread the word it was about to begin. Without his more elaborate equipment and a stage prepared to his specifications, Dex couldn't do anything as spectacular as the act he performed for paying customers. But he could offer card tricks and other close-up magic supplemented with a little pickpocketing and, just for the hell of it, a blindfolded mind-reading routine he and Molly hadn't bothered with in years, and his audience's applause, surprised exclamations, and laughter indicated they liked what they got.

After an encore, he and Molly accepted congratulations and fresh drinks and were eventually allowed a moment to themselves. Dex twitched aside a curtain and peered out the window. Except for the partygoers loitering on the porch and in the yard, he couldn't see anything moving in the night. Which didn't mean Carlyle, his slaves, and the creatures the slaves could turn into weren't there.

"That was fun," Molly said.

"Yeah."

"I'm glad we got to perform together one last time."

Dex scowled. "What's that supposed to mean?"

"You know what it means. I'm changing."

"You beat it again in the library."

"I can't beat it forever."

"You won't have to."

"In the library, I ran automatically when you did, and since I helped you get by Madame Lemaitre, I'm glad. But there wasn't really any point. Before long I'm going to turn into a monster just like her, a thing that switches back and forth between human and creature until finally it's a creature all the time. I can feel it."

"Please don't talk like that."

"I wish you'd destroyed the book when I wanted you to. At least you finally burned up part of it. Who knows, maybe it was the part Carlyle needed. Maybe, in the morning, you can get away from him, Arkham, and me, go back to living your life, and nothing else horrible will happen."

Dex winced. After fleeing the Orne Library, he'd been like a shell shock case, too rattled by what he'd seen to think about anything but finding a refuge where Carlyle and his servants wouldn't follow. But now Molly was forcing him to face the fact that they hadn't solved any of their long-term problems and things were actually worse than before. But then again, if what he was about to tell her convinced her they couldn't just give up, maybe that was good.

"The book's fine," he said.

"What?"

"I figured you knew. Carlyle was right. I really couldn't have set the damn thing on fire before he put a bullet in me. What I could do was set off some flash paper to make him think it was on fire and throw it into the dark to make him and his stooges chase it."

"God damn you! That means he won everything! Killed me – no, worse than killed me – and he gets to do whatever awful thing he's planning, too!" She balled her fist and pounded Dex in the chest.

"Ow!"

For an instant, she looked like she was going to hit him again, but then she didn't. "I guess you felt like it was our only move, but God damn it."

He set his cup on the windowsill and put his hands on her shoulders. "Look, Carlyle scored a couple runs, but the game's not over yet. We're still going to fix you, get the book back, and make that son of a bitch sorry he ever met us."

"I want that, of course, but how? What more can we do?" One thing. He was just scared to death to try it.

"We still need information," he continued. "Spratt couldn't give us nearly enough. But like I told you, the *Necronomicon* has a spell to call a spirit that's supposed to be able to tell the magus anything he wants to know."

Molly stared. "You mean the spirit that almost ripped your mind apart the first time you called it."

Dex put on a grin. "Yeah, but I was blotto and didn't know what I was doing. Now I'm an expert sorcerer."

"Because you managed to cast one other spell that only halfway worked?"

"OK. Maybe it's a little dangerous. But I don't see a choice. Even if we didn't still need to save you, you're the one who said Carlyle absolutely has to be stopped before he does something terrible with the book."

Molly scowled. "OK. We have to keep trying. But you're not going to cast the spell half-assed. That could be why it went bad the first time. Let me see it."

He brought the several folded parchment pages out of

an inside pocket of his jacket and found the two containing the incantation and the instructions that went with it. Molly put them under a lamp to read them. Her lips moved silently as she grappled with John Dee's archaic spelling and phrasing.

Reading over her shoulder, Dex said, "You can see, it's like the other spell. We're supposed to have a bunch of equipment we don't."

"Pipe down," she said. "Let me concentrate." She read for another minute and then looked up. "'Perform the ritual where the realm of men and the underworld meet'. Did you do that?"

"I tried. Sort of. I figured 'the underworld' meant the world of the dead, and I had a skull that was supposedly used in a Black Mass in my collection. I put it on a table beside me."

"Seriously."

"I told you I was drunk and just playing around. Anyway, maybe that wasn't good enough. I could try in a graveyard. We passed one when we were running away from the warehouse."

"Maybe that would work," Molly said, "but the *Necronomicon* doesn't say the spirit is a ghost. It says it's a 'chthonic sprite'." She looked around the room and oriented on a student whose spectacles gave him an owlish appearance. "Fella! You look smart! What does 'chthonic' mean?"

The student beamed as though he lived for chances to show off his erudition. "'Chthonic' means something lives or belongs underground. The ancient Greeks–"

"Thanks," Molly said. She turned back to Dex. "There you go. A basement, maybe?"

"Or, probably better, someplace natural, the mouth of a cave if we can find one." Dex turned to the owlish student. "One more thing. Is there a cave, or someplace like a cave, in town or just outside?"

The student looked bemused by the question, but he answered. "They call it Black Cave. It's along the river."

"Thanks again." Dex smiled at Molly. "That's where we go."

"Give me a kiss first," she replied. "For luck, and just in case."

Just in case it was their last chance.

Dex took her in his arms. Her mouth was feverishly hot under his, and it twitched in a spasm before he let her go.

CHAPTER 10

Dex and Molly found the door that led from the fraternity house's kitchen to the backyard. He peered out the window. He didn't see Carlyle or any of his slaves waiting outside. Which, as he'd already decided, meant damn little. "Ready?" he asked Molly.

"I better be. I'm running out of time."

"Well, if we spot any of them, we just run back inside, and everything's Jake." He wished he believed it could be that easy.

Heart thumping, he slipped out the door, and she followed. They crept across the backyard and down an alley. At one point, laughter brayed through the window of a different house and made him jump. But he and Molly reached the cross street where the fraternity and sorority houses gave way to other structures without anyone or anything shooting or jumping them. Dex sighed, and his shoulders slumped with relief undercut by a sense of anticlimax.

Her voice angry, Molly said what he was thinking. "Carlyle and his flunkies just left!"

Dex grinned. "That's a funny thing to get mad about."

"Once he had the book and we made it away from the library, he decided we weren't even worth bothering with!"

"And won't he be unhappy when he finds out he was wrong. Come on, let's get a wiggle on." They could walk faster now that they weren't trying to go unseen. Dex lit a cigarette for each of them, trying not to think this was just in case it was their last chance to enjoy a cigarette as well.

He was trying to navigate their way back to Church Street, as it seemed the likeliest place to find a taxi. But when he and Molly found themselves on a lane lined with dormitories, a cab had just dropped off several coeds. Judging from the sound of their giggling, they might have spent the evening at one of the local gin mills. Dex and Molly waved down the taxi as it approached.

The driver was a sallow, scrawny man. He tried to speak but broke into a coughing fit instead.

Dex felt a jolt of alarm because Baalshandor was a spirit of disease. But people got sick naturally, Carlyle's minions hadn't coughed, and the odds that the sorcerer had transformed this particular cab driver were laughably slim.

Telling himself to keep his jitters under control, Dex opened the Chevy's door, and Molly climbed into the back seat. As he got in after her, he asked, "What's your name, pal?"

"Tom." Tom coughed again.

"Nice to meet you, Tom. I'm Dex, this is Molly, and we're having a busy evening. We don't know yet where it's going to take us, but we don't want to waste time looking for a new ride every time we need to go from one spot to the next." Dex took out his money clip and extracted several bills. "Is this enough to keep you with us until morning?"

Tom counted the money and then looked at Dex with something like amazement in his eyes. "It's plenty! Where do you want to go first?"

"You know a place called Black Cave?"

"Yeah. But I wouldn't go there after dark. It has a funny reputation."

Dex laughed and realized it sounded a little crazy. "Sounds perfect. Get us there as fast as you can."

"You're the boss." Coughing, Tom put the Chevy in gear.

CHAPTER 11

The way to Black Cave ran through the warehouse district Dex and Molly had fled just hours before. "Makes me a little nervous being back here," he said.

Her left eye twitched. "That's the least of our problems."

Tom stopped the taxi at a spot where the ground sloped away on one side of the road and the black rippling length of the Miskatonic River was visible through the gaps in the trees that grew on the riverbank. "It's down there," he said.

"Wait here," said Dex. "I'll be back soon." He hoped.

"Hold it!" Molly snapped. "What do you mean, you'll be back soon?"

"It only takes one person to recite the spell, so there's no reason for both of us to be in danger. You and Tom can drive away if anything happens."

"We already are in danger, and you might need me for something." She opened the door on her side of the taxi and hopped out. Dex got out after her.

Perhaps because the slope was fairly steep, there were no buildings on this stretch of the riverbank, and once he and Molly left the streetlamps and the glow of the taxi's headlights behind, the world was very dark, with the branches tangling overhead blocking even the light of the stars. Dex had no reason to believe Carlyle and his servants were lying in wait, but even so, his mouth was dry, and time after time he feared one of the murky shapes in front of him was a creature like Madame Lemaitre had become before discerning an instant later that it was only a bush. When Molly gasped, he spun in her direction.

"What?" he asked.

She pointed to three diagonal lines carved in the trunk of a tree. "Magic?" she asked.

He shook his head. "Hobo sign."

Molly smiled. "Good." She continued down the riverbank before Dex could tell her the sign meant "stay away".

Tom had done a good job of navigating, and Dex and Molly only had to look around for a minute before they found the cave, gaping in the side of the slope like a mouth waiting to swallow anyone foolish enough to step inside. It almost seemed to breathe, giving off a smell of earth and stone that mingled with that of the river flowing close at hand.

"Well," said Dex, "at least there's a flat, clear space right inside. We've got a decent place to work."

"Yes," said Molly, "but it's even darker inside than it is out here."

"There's nothing hiding in there." He hoped.

"What I'm saying is, this is a two-person job. You need me to hold a light while you draw your circles and symbols and things."

"Or you could draw them, and I could hold the light."

"Get down on my knees in the dirt and ruin my clothes? Forget it! What you're supposed to say is, 'As usual, darling, you were right, and I was wrong.'"

He laughed. "As usual, darling, you were right, and I was wrong."

"Attaboy. Now let's get to it. Give me your lighter."

He handed her his Wonderlite, she struck a flame, and they entered the mouth of the cave. He brought out the dagger and started drawing the designs and writing the words from the *Necronomicon* in the earth.

He finished scratching in the dirt, stood up, and dusted off the knees of his trousers. He then took his place in the circle where the sorcerer was supposed to stand, and Molly came to stand beside him.

"Well, here goes nothing." He took a deep breath and started to recite: "Sage. Wise one. Keeper of secrets. I summon thee."

The shadows beyond the glow of the lighter churned. The motion made him feel queasy.

"Thou who knelt before the throne at the center of all things. Thou who have heard the eternal piping. I summon thee."

Shapes congealed from the shifting darkness. Past experience told him he shouldn't look at them. Better to recite with his eyes closed. Except that he tried to shut them and found he couldn't.

It was still night, but not quite as dark as before because he was now under an open sky where the occasional star showed through the drifting smoke. The trench reeked of the latrine nearby and decaying meat. The chatter of machine guns and the boom of artillery indicated a battle was underway.

Dex looked around. Molly was gone, and so, more or less, were Blythe, Warren, and Leibowitz, his best friends. It looked like a shell had come down and blown them to barely recognizable pieces.

For a second, he froze in shock and horror, and then some part of him, the magus part, perhaps, told him to think. Warren and Leibowitz had made it back from the War alive. So, this couldn't be real. Except that wasn't entirely true. Instinct told Dex it was potentially real, that he could be stuck here to be slaughtered in his turn if he didn't press on with the incantation. For the next couple words, he could feel his mouth moving but couldn't hear himself. Then the sound of his voice returned, soft as a whisper at first but growing louder with each syllable as though someone were turning the volume knob on a radio. The battlefield faded away. "Thou who walked with the Pharaoh of Night through a thousand thousand worlds. Thou who bear witness to his works of desolation. I summon thee."

Something shrieked. Dex's head snapped around.

Molly had lost the fight with the poison working inside her. She clutched him, and the fanged tube that had been her head curled in the air to writhe down over his own.

He started to break free, to recoil out of the protective circle enclosing the two of them, and then realized that to grab him with both hands, she had to have dropped the lighter. How, then, was he seeing her so clearly? Just like the trench, this wasn't real, or at least no realer than he permitted it to be. He forced himself to stand fast and continue the incantation.

"Apprentice to the maker of abominations." Molly's lamprey mouth slithered over Dex's head, covering his eyes and blinding him. The rubbery interior was coated with slime that burned, and the rings of gnashing fangs stung him. "Herald to blasphemies made flesh." Now he could see, and Molly was herself again, albeit pungent with sweat and shaking. Apparently, she was experiencing something awful, too. "I summon thee."

Dex was back onstage in some fancy theater. But his throat was dry with thirst and his stomach was hollow with hunger. He and his ragged tuxedo were filthy, and the sores on his ankle burned. The shackle that had rubbed him raw was connected to a long chain that ran backstage.

He was performing his most thrilling illusions, except that they weren't illusions anymore, just murder. A man's corpse floated in a tube filled with water and sealed by a metal hatch and valve wheel. A dead woman lay in two pieces atop the table where he'd sawed her in half. Her tear-streaked face visible through the little window at the top, the living woman inside the Torture Cabinet begged him to stop.

But Dex couldn't stop. Not if he wanted to drink and eat. Not if he wanted to avoid whippings and worse torments. And should he suffer them, he'd break down and do what his keepers wanted anyway. After all these years, he knew how it worked. He picked up the first sword to thrust through the cabinet, and his audience, things like the

Madame Lemaitre creature one and all, howled and hissed in anticipation.

It wasn't real, though! It never had been, and he wouldn't let it become so! He dropped the sword to clank on the stage and snarled the next words of the spell. As before, he couldn't hear them at first, but then they gradually grew louder.

"Oracle. Savant to the masked and unnamable master. Thou who casts two shadows on the book of truth and madness. By all thy affinities and all the ancient pacts, I summon thee and command thee to do my bidding and refrain from any harm. Yaztaroth, attend me!"

The theater vanished. Dex was back in the cave with Molly. Her voice tremulous, she asked, "Is it over?"

"The incantation, yeah."

"I know that, goof. I meant, is the bad part over?"

"Sorry," he panted. "The bad part's only getting started."

The darkness churned again, and the flame of the Wonderlite went out. There came a repeated scratching noise as Molly tried in vain to strike a new one. But then, as though gathering itself to help its maker, the magic in the designs and writing at their feet imbued the lines with amber phosphorescence. Or maybe it was Yaztaroth who willed them to glow so the humans would miss none of what was to come.

Though the luminous sigils remained, the cave floor, along with its walls and ceiling, had disappeared. The darkness itself had curdled, though. It felt more substantial now, a palpable thing, not merely the absence of light, and Dex and Molly were suspended in a bubble of it like prisoners in a cell.

The darkness took on texture and complexity as faces formed and dissolved in it. Some were human or funhouse-mirror distortions of human, all either twisted and open-mouthed with anguish or leering with gloating cruelty. The rest were reptile, insect, or visages so strange that Dex's eyes involuntarily closed, his head turned away, and his brain refused to hold an image of whatever he'd glimpsed.

But the faces weren't the worst of it. He was losing his sense of where they floated in relation to one another. Was the ant face above or below the old man with his eyes torn out? Was the Cyclops face taking form to the right or the left of the five-horned bestial skull? Was Dex seeing faces that were behind him?

Molly drew in a ragged breath. He found her hot, sweaty hand, more by groping than by looking, but he had it, and for the moment at least, that spatial relationship was defined and anchored. "Don't let it get to you," he said. "It's just a really good illusion."

The hovering faces laughed. The sound fluctuated from one pulse to the next, from shrill to deep, from lilting mirth to roars and snarls. "Is it?" Yaztaroth said. Its speech, too, was a fractured thing, one syllable bass and the next soprano, one clear and the next a growl. "Is it indeed?"

"Yes," said Dex. "Now, I called you here to answer questions."

"No," the entity said, "you called me here to feast, and you even brought dessert."

"Don't bet on it," Molly said.

"Wouldn't it be merciful?" Yaztaroth asked. "Do you want to complete your transformation and kill your lover?"

"Enough," said Dex. "I know your name. You have to tell me what I want to know. It's what you're for, and I can force it out of you if I have to. Why not make it easy on yourself?"

"Why not make it easy on yourselves? Break the circle and I'll be quick."

"Daemon-sultan! Crawling Chaos! Mother and father of iniquities! Faceless king crowned with seven stars! I pray thee, rebuke the faithless spirit who flouts the sacred oaths!"

A shudder ran through the darkness surrounding Dex and Molly, as if they were inside a soap bubble disturbed by a puff of air, and all the floating faces contorted in pain.

When the convulsions were done, Dex said, "There's more where that came from. I can start speaking the actual names if need be. Even the final one."

Yaztaroth sneered. "Ask your questions, human. It won't matter in the end."

Dex strained to remember what he'd decided were the essential questions and what was the best order in which to present them. He'd figured it all out beforehand, but the ongoing confusion of right and left, up and down, in front and behind, was grinding away at his concentration.

"What's Carlyle planning to do with *The Blood of Baalshandor*?" he asked.

"Baalshandor was one of the Ancient Ones," Yaztaroth said. "Long before the rise of Man, he quarreled with another Great Old One, Cthugha, the Living Flame, and in their final battle, Cthugha burned him away.

"But not entirely," the hovering faces continued. "A trace of Baalshandor endured in a lesser realm. There, it seeks to regain its strength and force its way back into this universe. It does so by spreading disease."

"Get to the point!" Molly said, her voice harsh and strained.

Dex gave her hand a squeeze. "How does disease help Baalshandor?"

"When someone is gravely ill," Yaztaroth said, "the sickness can sometimes change into Baalshandor's seed. Generally, the sick person then becomes a creature like those you have encountered. Like you are fated to become, Molly Maxwell."

"The hell she is," said Dex.

"After a week or two," Yaztaroth said, "the form you deem monstrous becomes the only form, and then, eventually, the creature rots away to nothing."

For a moment, there was silence, and in that silence, Dex realized he was losing all sense of distance as he'd previously lost the certainty of where one thing was in relation to another. The bubble of darkness was expanding and contracting like an irregular heartbeat. No, worse, the overall configuration of it was changing, one part growing nearer at the same time that a different section was receding.

He finally managed to close his eyes only to discover it didn't help. Somehow, he could still perceive the distortion just like before. He shuddered and fought the urge to bolt. If you leave the circle, he told himself, you die! Molly turns into a monster! You have to finish this the right way!

"Go on," he gritted. "How does making monsters help Baalshandor?"

"Haven't I said enough for you to infer the rest?" Yaztaroth asked. "Sometimes I forget how limited your kind is, the primitive way your minds reason and comprehend. As you wish, then. Baalshandor draws a bit of strength every time one of its progeny drinks blood. But more importantly, prophecy has it that on the day when enough of its creatures gather in the world at the same time, the god will fuse their bodies together to make a new one for itself and through that vessel reemerge into this reality." Once again, Yaztaroth stopped as though it had said all that need be said.

Had it? Dex had the feeling it hadn't but couldn't think what might be missing.

"You asked about Carlyle," Molly said. "It hasn't said a word about Carlyle."

"That's right!" said Dex. "Tell us."

"Of course," Yaztaroth said, "if still more is required. I said that generally the humans Baalshandor infects become like Madame Lemaitre and you, Molly Maxwell. But once in a great while, like maggots growing into flies, they continue to change into something like Edward Carlyle. A higher order of being conscious of the connection to Baalshandor and intentionally seeking the Ancient One's rebirth. They then work to spread plague and foil those who seek to end it. They study arcane secrets like the brewing of the poison that creates lesser progeny and binds them to their will."

The erosion of distance grew worse. One second, certain of the hovering faces seemed miles away, even though Dex could somehow still see them as clearly as ever, while others were close enough to bite him. A couple seemed to approach and recede simultaneously. Then three of them overlapped his body. It was ghastly, and he cried out.

Apparently experiencing the same phenomenon, Molly yelled, "Stop it!"

Yes, Dex thought, it was past time to put a stop to this. He drew breath to punish Yaztaroth, but the entity spoke first.

"Save your curses, Dexter Drake. I've done nothing to harm either of you."

"I don't believe you," said Dex.

"How do you think I can know so much? It's because my native sphere is a deeper, truer level of reality than yours. The ephemera you call space and time are mere shadows cast by the forces at play there."

"So what?"

"When you call me here, space and time crumble around me, and you need them like fish need water. I suggest you release me before your mind and Molly Maxwell's break."

Dex would have considered it excellent advice except that he and Molly still needed what Yaztaroth could tell them. "Answer my damn questions."

"If that's your choice. Sadly, from their perspective, sorcerer-priests like Edward Carlyle can't use the transforming poison to create lesser progeny in sufficient numbers to bring Baalshandor back. The ingredients are too rare, and the distillation process too difficult. But Edward Carlyle recently discovered an even greater secret." The spirit paused.

"Which is?" Dex gritted. The maw of an insect-thing was overlapping his own mouth, hindering speech like a dentist's Novocain. He could even taste the nasty acidic tang of it.

"The book called *The Blood of Baalshandor* contains a ritual for sacrificing several lesser progeny to infuse a crop ripening in a field with magic akin to the poison that will infect all who partake. That's the secret to resurrecting Baalshandor, and once Edward Carlyle learned as much and received word of Bernard Palmer's auction, he requested that *The Blood of Baalshandor* be one of the volumes stolen. Now that he has it, he intends to perform the sacrifice at the Kensico Reservoir."

"Jesus Christ!" said Dex. "That supplies water to all of New York City!"

"I don't get it," Molly said. "Why would anybody want–" She faltered.

The tempo and spacing of her words were wrong. Sometimes she was speaking faster than any person should be able. Other times, it took too long to articulate the syllables, and the gaps between them yawned. She and Dex had already lost space in any comprehensible sense and now, as Yaztaroth had warned, they were losing time.

Molly forced out the rest of the question: "–anybody want Baalshandor to make a comeback?"

"You're assuming Edward Carlyle has a choice," Yaztaroth said.

"Right," said Dex, "he's possessed, too. How…"

His words weren't coming out right either, only it was worse with him than it had been with Molly. Maybe he'd said what he wanted to say already. Maybe he hadn't even started. Maybe he'd always been asking this question and always would be.

No! However things seemed, he was the sorcerer. Reality

was what he willed it to be. He pressed on, "How do we stop Carlyle and cure Molly?"

"With magic and death."

"Explain." Short statements were marginally easier. Easier to say and easier to believe he was saying them here and now. Assuming here and now still meant anything.

"Baalshandor's influence runs through Edward Carlyle. The proper spell will destroy him and purge those he poisoned if their transformations haven't gone too far."

"Teach me the ritual."

Yaztaroth laughed. "Most sorcery is ritual," he began, at which point the words became incomprehensible. Dex couldn't tell what order they were in. He was afraid he didn't know what order was. He was absence, a soldier in the trenches, an old man in a wheelchair, absence again, a child, and a baby, in flickering succession or perhaps all at once. Molly was gone, an eel thing all but rotted away to nothing, herself, a little girl, and an eel thing merely spotted with gangrene, the lamprey head pivoting this way and that as though in search of prey.

It was too much. Yaztaroth was right, human consciousness couldn't work without space and time. Dex felt his mind giving way, and a part of him welcomed the release.

Among Molly's other selves, an old woman flashed into being and disappeared.

Dex bellowed as soldiers had when going over the top, to drive fear and doubt out of his head. If there was an elderly human Molly in the mix, even just a glimmer of one, surely that meant she could be saved, and if so, he had to hang on.

He concentrated hard, and while the sense that Yaztaroth's words were scrambled remained, he was able to wring sense out of them. It seemed he'd only missed a few.

"–there is an incantation that may serve the purpose."

"What do I say?"

"Za'al Cthugha. N'zarra st'gax wga'al."

Dex repeated the phrase in his head, fixing it in his memory, stops and all.

"Last question: where do I find Carlyle?"

Yaztaroth laughed. "He's boarding the early train out of Arkham at this very moment."

Dex felt a jolt of horror. "That can't be! I remember the schedule. The first train isn't for hours yet."

The spirit laughed.

CHAPTER 12

Dex wanted to believe what Yaztaroth had said was impossible, but he had a terrible feeling that it wasn't. Not if time had come unstuck, and bad luck or, as he suspected, the spirit's malice had made the ritual last much longer than he'd realized.

He had to get to the train station! It took an effort of will to put that urgency aside and recite the dismissal with the proper focus and cadence.

"Savant, return to thine own realm, doing no harm as thou go and abiding there until I summon thee again. By the Blind One, by the Haunter of the Dark, by the Womb and Seed of Filth, by the Feaster from Afar, be gone, be gone, be gone!"

For a dreadful moment, nothing changed, but then the bubble of darkness frayed apart, the glow in the symbols and writing at Dex and Molly's feet faded, and so, too, did the hovering faces, laughing as they withered. The distortions in space and time disappeared, and Black Cave reverted to normal.

Dex felt a visceral relief as the assault on his reason ended, but he was also frantic with the need to catch the train. And check on Molly! As best he could tell in the gloom, she was physically her normal self again, but she was staring at nothing. Had she come through without her mind disintegrating?

He put himself in front of her, took her by the shoulders, and gave her a gentle shake. "Molly! Molly! Are you all right?"

She drew a ragged breath. "That was all kinds of fun. But my brain didn't go blooey. So come on, we've got to go!"

As they scrambled back up the riverbank, Dex had the terrible thought that Tom might not have waited all this time. But the taxi was where he and Molly had seen it last, only now with the lights and motor off.

Tom himself was wide awake and had already been peering in their direction. As they reached the taxi, he said, "I was wondering if I should come looking for you. Or get a cop."

Dex yanked open the door, and he and Molly piled inside. "We need to get to the train station, fast!"

Tom put the Chevy in gear. "Why?' He coughed several times and wiped his mouth on his sleeve. "What happened down there?"

"It's too hard to explain," said Dex. "Just please, fast!"

"OK," the driver said. The bemused undertone in his voice was that of someone humoring an eccentric or a drunk. "You paid for it."

"What time is it?" Molly asked.

Dex checked his watch. "About five." Assuming he could

still trust the timepiece after what he and it had been through.

"And what time does the train pull out?"

"I don't remember exactly, just that a southbound one leaves Arkham around now." He tried to summon up an air of confidence. "But don't worry. We'll make it."

"I know we will," she replied. "We didn't come this far, didn't face down Yaztaroth, just to fail at the end."

Desperate as the situation was, her words brought something home to him. The encounter in Black Cave had been a nightmare, but in the end, he had forced the "chthonic sprite" to do his bidding. He'd worked sorcery so successfully that he doubted even a screwy half-human cultist like Carlyle could have done any better.

Molly frowned at whatever she saw on his face. "Did your brain break back there? You almost look happy."

Dex put on a sober expression. "Hell, no. It's just like I said. I believe we're going to win."

"We…" Molly grunted, and her eyes rolled back in her head. She slumped against the door on the side of the seat and started shaking.

"St. Mary's Hospital!" said Tom. Even though he was driving, he'd registered something was wrong.

"No!" Dex said. "Doctors can't help her! The train station!" He turned to try to rouse Molly. Her body was throwing off a fierce fever heat. He could feel it even before he touched her.

She reared up and reached for him as well. Her face was blank as a sleepwalker's, the eyes still rolled back, but her hands were the elongated hands of a lamprey thing complete with little fanged openings in the fingertips, and she snatched for his throat with the suddenness of a cat pouncing on a mouse.

Dex caught her wrists, and she struggled to break his grip. The Chevy bounced them around and made it that much harder to hold her off. Once again, Tom must have glimpsed what was going on behind him, and shock made him lose control and the taxi swerve.

"Molly!" cried Dex. "Molly! Wake up!" It was all he knew to do. This time, it was enough. She blinked, and her eyes returned to normal. So did her hands, shrinking back to their normal dimensions over the course of several seconds. "Dex?" she croaked. "Yeah." He took her in his arms. She was still shuddering and still too hot.

"Get out of the cab!" cried Tom. Dex realized the driver had regained control, brought the Chevy to a stop, and twisted around in his seat to glower at his fares.

"Take it easy," said Dex.

"No! Go to hell! I saw what happened! I saw it!"

"You're right," Molly said. She turned to Dex. "I need to get out. I can't help with the last part. I'm too close to changing completely. We can't let New York turn into Monster Town because I jumped you."

"But–" Dex began.

"When you get rid of Carlyle, come back. If we're lucky, I'll be me again." She looked at Tom. "If I do get out, will you take Dex on to the train station? He'll pay extra."

"Yeah. OK. If you get out right now."

She did, and Tom sped onward, perhaps because he was eager to put distance between himself and his former passenger. Dex looked back at Molly, but it only took a moment for the dark to swallow her.

He faced forward and told himself he'd be with her again soon, and then everything would be all right. He practiced the incantation in his head in rather the same way that, during his Army training, he'd gone over the actions involved in aiming and firing a rifle in his head when he wasn't actually on the range. Za'al Cthugha. N'zarra st'gax wga'al. Za'al Cthugha. N'zarra st'gax wga'al. Until Tom made a final turn, at which point Dex cursed in dismay.

The early train out of Arkham had already pulled away from the station and was accelerating down the track.

CHAPTER 13

Sorry," said Tom, braking to a stop. "I guess you'll have to settle for the next one."

"Chase it!" Dex replied.

"Are you kidding me?"

"No! Go, before it gets too far away!"

"There's no road alongside the track. I'll wreck the car."

"I'll buy you a new one!"

"It's not just the car. If you're thinking what I think you're thinking, you're going to kill yourself."

"Let me worry about that!"

"No. I won't help you commit suicide. I brought you where you wanted. Now get out of the cab."

For a second, Dex didn't know what else to say. Then he remembered all the coughing. He put it together with Tom's sickly appearance and the fact that the two of them were about the same age.

"Your lungs," he said. "Gas attack?"

Tom blinked. "Uh, yeah. Belleau Wood."

"I fought, too. The Meuse-Argonne Offensive. Blanc

Mont Ridge. And I give you my word, if I don't get aboard that train, terrible things will happen."

"Or maybe you just came home with shell shock." Tom paused. "But I saw your lady friend's hands. So, OK." OK, but then he turned the taxi away from the track.

"What are you doing?" Dex cried.

"Can't follow it across the trestle. We'll have to cross the river a different way and pick it up on the other side."

Dex seethed with impatience as the train disappeared from view and the taxi shot across a bridge and looped around. After a few minutes that felt considerably longer, he and Tom reached a place where central Arkham gave way to houses set well back from the road and one another. Tom sent the cab racing up somebody's rutted drive, then crashing through brush and around trees that seemed to spring up in an instant. The train appeared ahead and to their left.

Tom spun the steering wheel and gave chase. The ground here was even rougher and bumpier than before. The jolting shook Dex and clacked his teeth together. Once, it bounced him up to bang his head on the roof of the car.

"We can't keep this up!" Tom shouted.

"We just have to get even with the back end!"

Gradually, they closed the distance. Dex opened his door and climbed out on the running board. When they caught up with the open platform at the end of the last car, Tom veered closer to put him within arm's reach.

That was good, but dear God, the shaking! In his mind's eye, Dex saw himself losing his grip, falling, and breaking his neck.

Still, he had to try. He stretched out his hand and gripped one of the uprights of the ladder that ran up to the roof of the car. At the same moment, some unevenness in the ground, or the start of some mechanical breakdown in the taxi, made the Chevy lurch farther away from the train.

Feeling as if he were about to be yanked apart, Dex let go of the car door and dropped to dangle one-handed from the ladder. His feet bumped along the ends of the railroad ties, the dragging threatening to knock him loose. With a grunt of effort, he grabbed the ladder with his other hand and heaved himself onto the platform.

For a moment, all he could do was hold fast to the railing, catch his breath, and watch the taxi – two headlights shining from a shadow shape – come to a stop in the night. When he felt able, he turned and peered through the window set in the door that led to the car's interior. The rearmost coach was empty, perhaps because it was so early, and the train's route began in little Arkham. The cars would fill up as it made its stops in Cambridge and Boston.

He tried the door handle, and, when it wouldn't move, he popped the lock with his escape artist tools, vowing to never again leave home without a set of lockpicks in his pocket.

As he stepped inside, he glimpsed something at the periphery of his vision. Tucked away inconspicuously in a corner behind the final row of wooden benches was a toolbox, possibly containing items the conductor used to make minor repairs inside the train.

It was worth taking a moment to look inside it. He still had the knife, but if he could find a second weapon, so much the better. He appropriated a wrench and stuck it in the back of his trousers beside the dagger.

He then moved toward the front of the train and onto the platform of the next passenger car. It wasn't empty. When he peeked through the window in the door, Palmer was there, and he was striding up the aisle in Dex's direction.

Dex jerked himself away from the window, raised the wrench, and waited for Palmer to come out after him. He didn't.

After several seconds, he risked another peek. Palmer was now marching in the opposite direction. Evidently, he didn't know Dex was between the cars. He was simply pacing up and down the length of his coach like a restless – or hungry – tiger in a cage.

Hoping to put him out of commission while his back was turned, Dex eased the door open and stalked after him. He believed he was moving silently, but within three paces Palmer sensed him anyway and turned around.

"Good morning," said Dex, letting the wrench dangle inconspicuously at his side. It might work. After all, Palmer wasn't expecting to see him here on the train. Surely, Carlyle and all his slaves thought they had left Dex behind hours ago.

The pretense bought Dex another couple steps. Then the little confidence artist in the zodiac tie grinned the widest grin Dex had ever seen. He extended his hand, and the fingers curled as if they had no bones inside them. "Ka'ljzak ystak," he said. "Zol Baalshador p'kok."

The world spun, and Dex's legs went rubbery. Feeling like he was about to throw up, he collapsed in the aisle. His vision blurry, he looked at his hands. Pustules were rising on the skin, bursting, and leaking pus even as new ones formed.

Damn it, this wasn't fair! Palmer was supposed to be a fraud who didn't believe in the magic he sold, not someone who could cast real spells. But now that he was a creature of Baalshandor, apparently he could draw on what he'd learned previously while conning suckers to cast an actual curse.

And Dex had little doubt the spell would kill or at least incapacitate him if he let Palmer go on chanting. He had to shut him up immediately, but the way he felt, jumping up and rushing Carlyle's slave was out of the question. With a snarl of effort, he heaved himself to his knees and threw the wrench.

The tool caught Palmer in the gut. The con man grunted, faltered in his recitation, and the sickness that had afflicted Dex came to a sudden end. He scrambled up and charged Palmer.

Dex wanted to reach his foe before Palmer could do anything else, but the smaller man's mouth and the head containing it writhed into different shapes as Palmer rushed forward to meet him.

Dex punched at Palmer's face, but his adversary blocked the blow with one elongating, looping arm and snatched for Dex's face with the other hand.

Dex twisted away, and Carlyle's slave fumbled his hold though the fangs in the ends of his fingertips pricked and nicked the illusionist's skin. Now, after reflexively dodging, Dex found he'd shifted out of the center aisle and into the narrow space between one bench and the next. With the window at his back, he was boxed in, and, to make matters worse, he no longer had the wrench.

Dex snatched for the knife under the tail of his jacket, but Palmer looped his fingers around his arm and immobilized it before he could grab the weapon. The creature dragged him forward, and, fully formed now, the lamprey maw arced to engulf his head.

Dex used his free arm to try to hold back the head and brought his knee up into Palmer's groin. He froze long enough for Dex to pull free, push past him, and grab the wrench off the floor. As Palmer reached for him again, Dex smashed repeatedly at what its head had become. Maybe there was still a brain in there somewhere.

It was a good guess, and luck was with him. One of the savage swings connected with a vulnerable spot, and Palmer collapsed.

As best he was able, Dex stuffed Palmer's monstrous form under one of the benches. That accomplished, he gripped the wrench anew and pressed on.

With the wheels of the train clattering and rumbling under the adjacent platforms, Dex peeked into the next coach. It was different, a closed compartment car. The corridor that had been running down the middle of the train jogged left to proceed along the side and maximize the size of the private enclosures.

Dex frowned. It seemed likely that Carlyle had opted for this more comfortable mode of train travel. But even if he was in this particular coach, the only way to find him would be to work one's way down the line and check each compartment in turn.

Dex knocked at each door, waited, and cracked open the doors if no one answered. No one did, until the third one. There, a male voice said, "Yes?"

Dex thought it was Hogarth's voice but wasn't sure. Afraid the plump man who'd had such a fear of being hexed – and had fallen victim to it anyway – might recognize his voice, he didn't answer except to rap again.

"Damn it," Hogarth – if it was Hogarth – said. Footsteps sounded on the other side of the door. Dex's fingers tightened on the wrench as he wondered who or what would momentarily appear, some innocent or one of Carlyle's slaves.

It was Hogarth, now with sores dotting his mouth and pus dribbling down his chin to stain the front of the Chesterfield overcoat. As soon as Dex saw him, he clubbed the shorter man in the head. Hogarth fell backward. Dex watched him for a moment to make sure he was out, then closed the compartment door, turned, and found himself looking Carlyle right in his red-speckled eyes.

Dex dodged into the compartment where Hogarth lay bloody-headed and unconscious. Carlyle's gun banged a split second later. Dex turned the lock, dropped to the floor, and did his best to curl up under the left-hand bench. The door handle clacked as Carlyle tried to open it. Then the door itself banged as, presumably, he sought to kick it in. "Za'al Cthugha," Dex began.

Out in the corridor, the automatic roared repeatedly, and the .45 slugs punched holes in the partition. Dex flinched and stumbled over the remaining words of the spell.

How could anyone be expected to recite this gibberish

correctly under these conditions? Magic be damned! He would have given anything for his old Springfield.

But that was exactly what he shouldn't be thinking. He had to believe in the power of the spell and his ability to cast it. He cleared his mind and started again.

"Za'al–"

The Colt banged, and the locking mechanism flew out of the door in pieces. Carlyle pushed the door open, spotted Dex huddled under the bench, grinned, and aimed the pistol at him. Over his shoulder stretched a lamprey maw. Another of his creatures had joined the party just in case its master needed backup.

"–Cthugha. N'zarra st'gax wga'al!"

Dex felt a sensation of effort as if he'd heaved something heavy over his head. Coronas of dazzling blue flame engulfed Carlyle and the thing at his back, and both reeled and staggered before collapsing. The fires winked out. Dex noticed there was no smoke in the air, and nothing had burned except the bodies themselves.

Dex crawled out from under the bench and looked at what the magic had done. Carlyle's body was charred black, the eyes like fried eggs. But the eel thing was still feebly gnashing the fangs in its lamprey maw. It was Troughton. Dex could tell from the ring of Cagliostro encircling one of the elongated fingers.

Happily, after another moment, that wasn't the only way to recognize the self-proclaimed initiate of the Hermetic Order of the Golden Dawn. The hideous body began to revert to human.

Dex grinned. He remained certain Yaztaroth had wished

him nothing but ill, but damned if the spell hadn't worked exactly as advertised.

In the aftermath, he felt like he'd run several miles, either because working the magic had tired him, or it was a natural reaction to nearly getting killed – again – or a combination of the two. But he couldn't just stand here. He still had things to do.

The door wouldn't lock anymore, but it would pull shut to conceal what lay inside. Someone might still spot the bullet holes in the partition, but there was nothing to be done about that. Dex closed the door and moved on to the compartment from which Carlyle had emerged.

The Blood of Baalshandor, *Cthaat Aquadingen*, and *De Vermis Mysteriis* were sitting out in plain view. Maybe Carlyle had been studying them in preparation for the big ceremony at the Kensico Reservoir. The big ceremony that would never happen.

Dex moved to collect the beat-up old books – volumes more dangerous than land mines, he now understood – then faltered when a tearing sound rasped down the corridor outside.

CHAPTER 14

"No," Dex thought. The danger was over. It had to be.

It wasn't, though. His heart thumping and his mouth dry, he slipped back down the corridor, cracked open the door to the compartment where Hogarth, Carlyle, and Troughton lay, and looked in.

The Englishman had completed the transition back to human and, like Hogarth, still sprawled motionless. Carlyle's body, however, had bloated throughout the torso, splitting apart what remained of his burned jacket and shirt in the process, and the bloat was squirming and heaving as something ripped it from within. The cracking noise was the sound of flesh fried crisp as bacon giving way.

Carlyle's abdomen tore open wide, and then, hissing and chittering, reeking of decay, something started crawling out. It had a head like an eyeless lamprey together with a long, sinuous body lined with legs resembling a centipede. It was bigger than a man's leg, impossibly big, especially considering that more were now emerging.

Dex reached for the fallen Colt automatic on the floor.

Two of the creatures struck at his arm, and he snatched the limb back just in time.

Magic, then. It was supposed to be magic anyway, wasn't it, and it had worked before. He just had to finish the job.

He ran out of the compartment and down to the rear of the car. There, he turned, cleared his mind, and waited for the lamprey creatures to scuttle out into the corridor after him. As they did a moment later, half a dozen jostling and climbing over one another in their eagerness to run him down.

"Za'al Cthugha. N'zarra st'gax wga'al."

This time, it felt like the weight he was lifting was even heavier, heavy enough that it hurt getting it over his head. But blue flame erupted around the bodies of the lamprey things and, shrilling, they convulsed. He grinned through the pain until the blaze flickered out more quickly than before, and, seemingly unharmed, Baalshandor's creatures resumed their scrambling toward him.

Christ, they were fast! Fast enough to close the distance before he'd be able to recite the spell again. He bolted through the door onto the platform, shut it, rushed through the chair car from which he'd come a couple minutes before, closed that door, and retreated down the length of the coach.

He didn't expect doors to delay the lamprey creatures for long, and they didn't. The door at the front end of the chair coach crashed inward as the centipede things broke through in a screeching, rasping chorus.

"Za'al Cthugha. N'zarra st'gax wga'al."

This time, reciting the spell was like taking a punch.

It stunned Dex for a second, and when he shook off the shock, he saw the fire hadn't come at all. He was apparently out of magic, willpower, or something, and Baalshandor's spawn were halfway down the car.

Closing doors behind him as he went, he fled into the last car and onto its platform.

The sky had turned from black to gray, and the feeble predawn light revealed the train was now speeding along, likely at sixty miles an hour or even faster. Still, Dex might survive a jump from it. It was more likely than surviving the bites of the lamprey things. He climbed down the steps, then hesitated.

Suppose he simply fled, and the eel things were still capable of commanding the slaves and performing the sacrificial ritual at Kensico Reservoir. Hell, suppose they were able to join together and become Carlyle again the way thousands of lesser progeny were supposed to fuse together and become Baalshandor. After everything Dex had been through, he couldn't rule it out, which meant he needed to finish what he'd started.

He climbed back up the steps and then up the ladder onto the roof. If the lamprey things assumed he'd kept retreating from coach to coach, they'd waste time hunting him down the length of the train, giving him a chance to recover his magical strength. If that was how it actually worked. If he'd ever had enough strength to deal with a half-human high priest like Carlyle in the first place.

Crouching low in the smoky air blowing back from the steam engine to keep the wind and the rocking of the train from throwing him off, Dex crawled and then risked a jump onto the roof of the next car forward. If he was guessing right about where the creatures would climb up after him, the move would give him a little more warning of their arrival.

The hills of the countryside south of Arkham roughened the terrain to either side. Woods and scrub, mostly, with not much farmland and just the rare shack visible in the distance. It would be a strange and lonely place for Drake the Great, who'd not long ago played Broadway, given an interview to Vaudeville News, and headlined at the Cotton Club, to die.

Below him, the carriage door banged open, and his pursuers hissed and chittered. Then the door to the last coach did the same, and the hideous sounds receded. Dex breathed a sigh of relief even though his respite was only temporary. The creatures were going to look for him on top of the train eventually, and if they didn't, he was going to have to go looking for them.

It turned out to be the former. In what felt like far too short a time – Dex still ached on the inside, still felt winded – the lamprey things climbed onto the roof of the rearmost car. Evidently spotting him, they scuttled forward with an agility that ensured they didn't have to worry about falling off the top of a speeding train.

Frightened though he was, instinct told Dex to wait for the lamprey things to get closer before casting the spell. If the sorcery failed again, it wouldn't matter anyway. Keeping his eyes on the onrushing creatures, he crawled backward until one foot slid into open space, warning him he'd reached the end of the roof on which he was making his final stand.

Baalshandor's creatures sprang across the gap between cars and charged within a few feet of him, near enough to make out the slime coating the gnashing fangs and lining the pulsing maws, near enough to smell the carrion stink of them. Then, with a sliver of red sun showing above a hill to the east, he shouted the incantation:

"Za'al Cthugha! N'zarra st'gax wga'al!"

Once again, pain hammered him. But blue flame exploded around the lamprey things. Screaming, four tumbled off the train to burn alongside the tracks. Two remained on the roof, however, until the fire reduced them to ash and the wind swept the gray powder away.

Dex laughed and cried at the same time. The magic worked! It finally worked, and he was going to live!

Shakily, feeling like he'd used up all the stamina and luck he had coming, he clambered down the ladder and checked on Hogarth and Troughton. Both were still unconscious but breathing. Dex then dropped the stolen books into the valise Carlyle had evidently used to carry them and brought them onto one of the platforms. When the train slowed to make a turn, he jumped. He landed hard on gravel but came through with nothing worse than additional scrapes and bruises.

CHAPTER 15

Dex rushed into the lobby of the Excelsior with its Neoclassical tables, chairs, and sofas, and other old-fashioned Victorian furnishings. It had taken all day to get back to Arkham. He'd had to find a road winding through the wooded hills to the south, hitch a ride, and the battered old flivver that picked him up had sputtered along at a leisurely pace. It had been little comfort to reflect that, in this part of New England, it could just as easily have been a horse and wagon.

On top of all that, he didn't even know if Molly would be in the hotel. It was just the logical place to start looking.

She was here, though, with her eyes fixed on the door, and she sprang to her feet the instant he came in. He rushed to her and wanted to embrace her but settled for asking, "Are you OK?"

"Yes," she said. She glanced around and then lowered her voice sufficiently that nobody else in the lobby was likely to overhear. "I felt the thing inside me disappear. It was like it was burning up, only the heat didn't hurt me. So, I knew you got Carlyle. But I couldn't be sure he didn't get you, too, until you walked in the door. You took your time about it! Is everything really all right?"

Dex nodded. "I'm pretty sure it is."

He didn't even expect any trouble over anything he'd done. Among the living, only Molly, Tom, and Carlyle's surviving slaves knew anything about what had happened in the warehouse, the library, and on the train, and none of them were going to spill.

"Good! I checked the train schedule while I was waiting. There's one this evening. If we hurry, we can catch it and finally get the hell out of Arkham."

He hesitated. "What?" she asked.

He didn't want to say. Not yet. Not when he sensed the possibility that things could maybe be all right between them again. "I still have to track down Tom and give him the rest of his dough."

Her green eyes narrowed, and she stepped back. "But there's more. What aren't you telling me?"

Apparently, there was no putting this off, and though the prospect of revealing his intentions scared him, he supposed this moment was as it should be. He should have learned by now that keeping secrets from her was wrong. "On the ride back, I was thinking. Am I really done? Is this really over?"

"Why wouldn't it be?"

"Sure, we slammed the door on Baalshandor. But I'm worried that other beings want to come to Earth and take over. A different one imprisoned it, after all."

"But that's just a guess, isn't it?"

"Not completely. Not if I understand what I've read."

"Well, OK. Maybe you're right. But what does that mean right here and now for you and me?"

"Not many people know what we just learned the hard way. Not many people can do real magic, either. But I know. And I can. Maybe I have a responsibility to learn more, and even do more if it turns out to be necessary. Maybe that means I'll have to come back to Arkham from time to time."

"I–"

"I don't blame you if you don't want any part of it. Bad as I had it this past night, you had it a hundred times worse with that thing eating away at you from the inside. So, I don't expect you to ever come back here with me." He took a deep breath. "As far as that goes, I understand if you want to leave me and go your own way. If only because we can't be sure that something horrible won't follow me home or ride home inside me someday."

"Besides being a liar," she said, "you're an idiot. Shut up and let me talk."

He blinked. "Uh… sure."

"I don't know if it can ever be like it was between us. Time will tell. But that's no reason to break up the act, and I didn't say I'd never come back to Arkham, much as I hate the place. Yeah, it was awful feeling that thing squirming around inside me and filling my head with nasty urges. But at the end of it all, we won, and if you're right that somebody's got to go on plugging up the holes when the monsters try to crawl out, well… I can't do real magic, yet, but I do know what you know. Maybe that makes it my responsibility just as much as it is yours."

"Are you sure?"

"Yes, and if I were you, I wouldn't try to talk me out of it. You wouldn't stand a chance without me."

"No," he smiled. "I probably wouldn't."

DARK REVELATIONS

Amanda Downum

CHAPTER 1

I read to the end.

I don't know if I spoke the final words aloud. I felt my tongue shape them but could hear nothing over the roar of blood in my ears. Or was that the roar of the storm? Thunder shook the house and branches lashed the windows as the wind surged.

My vision swam, washed with red and ringed with darkness. A pale figure stood in front of me – only after I rubbed my eyes, did I realize it was Rachel.

My beloved Rachel, tears tracking her chalk-white cheeks, her hair an auburn storm across her shoulders. She clutched a knife, her knuckles bloodless against the hilt. She trembled such that I feared she would cut herself.

Realization swept over me. She had meant to stop me from finishing the book, however she could. She had known what must be done, but at the last moment love had stayed her hand.

The book fell from my nerveless fingers. An instant later, the knife fell from hers. We embraced, sobbing. I had failed to stop the book. She had failed to stop me. At least we would be together at the end.

Our tears slowed, and we looked at one another with renewed determination. We would face the end together.

Hand in hand, we turned to the open casement and gazed upon the sky.

The sky roiled.

The sky writhed.

Red clouds parted and swept aside to lay bare the firmament beyond. The stars glowed brighter, hotter, until the blackness around them scorched and peeled away like melting celluloid. From point to point, the sky opened along an invisible seam. There ought to be darkness behind the stars, but instead, red light bled through the opening, illuminating…

Illuminating what?

Gloria Goldberg sighed and leaned back in her chair, flexing her fingers against the ache of long typing. This particular image – the devouring sky – had haunted her for days, burned in her mind whenever she woke. But when she tried to exorcise it onto the page, every effort was unsatisfactory.

In her dreams, she saw it all so clearly. Dreaming, she knew with a terrible certainty what lay beyond that unseamed sky. Waking, it receded to a jumble of images and dread.

How do you describe the end of the world?

She straightened her shoulders, wincing as her neck cracked. She wasn't supposed to be writing about a cataclysm in the heavens. The latest book she had proposed to her publishers was a much simpler story, a more confined and personal horror. But the dreams wouldn't leave her in peace.

She pushed back her chair and blinked. Night had fallen while she worked; only her desk lamp burned against the gloom. From down the hall, she could make out her neighbors shouting at one another. Not in anger – Mrs Singer was half-deaf and refused to admit it, so every conversation with her husband rose to a bellow. Upstairs, Mr Zebrowski was practicing his clarinet again, though he'd been asked several times not to do so after the dinner hour.

Everything around her was as it ought to be. So why did she feel so strange, so disconnected? Had she eaten anything since lunch today? Possibly not. Perhaps that would solve it.

She turned toward the kitchen, but a queer flicker of light drew her attention to the window instead.

A crimson maelstrom roared outside.

She stumbled forward in shock and drew up again with a start. Her apartment was gone – rather than white walls and molded ceilings, the familiar city street through the window, the view instead stretched into a wide expanse of angry red sky. She stood on a wooden balcony, only a precarious railing between her and empty air. Wind tugged at her, charnel and metallic, threatening her balance.

Clouds seethed, the color of scabs. Soon they would peel back to reveal the horrors that waited beyond the skin of the sky. A dark ribbon spiraled down, shifting and shredding like smoke. Bats, or birds – vultures. No, something larger.

"You knew."

A man stood beside her, a young man with sad, shadowed eyes. She recognized him, but the sudden shock left her too scattered to speak his name.

"You knew," he said again, stretching out a hand. Blood dripped from his fingers, welling fresh from fine cuts across his palm.

Gloria flinched away, catching her hip against the balcony. Wood creaked and shifted.

"You knew this was coming, and you did nothing. Why wouldn't you help me?"

Above their heads, the clouds parted with a wet, tearing sound. A crimson torrent fell, splattering Gloria's upturned face, choking her with the stench of an abattoir.

"I've started something," the man said, his words all but drowned under the roar of the deluge. "I need you to finish it for me."

The balcony gave; Gloria reached for his hand, blood or no. For an instant, she touched cold skin. Then he was gone, her fingers closing on empty air. The wooden railing disintegrated, and she fell with a cry –

She landed with a painful thud on her own parquet floor. Her outstretched hands were unstained. Her heart pounded in her ears, and a throbbing ache spread through her hip.

She groped for the windowsill and levered herself up. With a breath caught in her throat, she flung back the curtains.

A heartbeat later, she let out that breath, her chest hollowing with the force of her exhalation. Outside, the familiar skyline of her neighborhood rose against the charcoal darkness of a Manhattan night. She threw open the window, letting the sound of voices and vehicles wash over her. The night was humid, but the air held the promise of autumn. She sagged against the window ledge, drawing the commingled scents of asphalt and motor oil and cooking spices deep into her lungs.

"Jamie," she whispered, turning back to the empty room. James Galbraith, writer and poet. She had met him when he was still unpublished, a young man trying hard to disguise his nerves as he lingered on the edges of a holiday party one of her editors had thrown. They had maintained a correspondence, but she hadn't seen him in person in over a year.

You knew. Why didn't you help me?

"I couldn't," she said. "I couldn't help you."

Fiction might be, as some claimed, the art of constructing elaborate lies, but she had never been much good at lying to herself.

She had been thinking of Jamie earlier this evening, before she sat down to write. A premonition? No, nothing so melodramatic. Simply a nagging reminder from the recesses of her mind.

A stack of mail spilled across her small kitchen table, several days' worth. Nothing pressing – the odd bill, a royalty statement, a thick envelope that was sure to contain reviews of her last book, clipped from various publications and forwarded to her by her cousin Edith. Gloria had been unable to politely convince her cousin that such a service was unnecessary or even desired. There – amid all the usual postal detritus, a familiar handwriting.

James Galbraith
25 Noyes Street
Arkham, Massachusetts

She had planned to read Jamie's letter when she finished her latest chapter – which ought to have happened two days ago, but the right scene had never come to her. Her hands shook as she opened the envelope, and the paper sliced into the side of her finger. It left only a painful red line beside her knuckle, but she still shuddered at the lingering image of Jamie's bloody palm.

> *Gloria,*
> *I –*

After that several lines were furiously scratched out. Ink smeared the paper. Nothing like the neat correspondence she was used to.

> *I've started something. I started my book, but it's something else now. Something too big for me. There are things you and I don't speak of, but I think we must face them now. I need your help. I've started something. I need you to finish it. Please come to Arkham.*
> *Your friend,*
> *Jamie*

Gloria stared at the page, sucking absently on her stinging finger. Nothing about it made sense – not just the sentences themselves, but also the idea that Jamie would or could have written such a thing. Curt and confused was the antithesis of his usual style.

The letter distracted her from the terror of her vision; her heart had nearly slowed its mad rhythm when the telephone rang. Gloria startled so completely her feet left the floor. The letter fell from her hand and fluttered gently to the ground. Laughing at her own foolishness, she crossed the room and reached for the receiver.

"Gloria? It's Ellen." Her agent's voice was tinny and hollow through the line. "I'm sorry to call so late, but I suspected you'd still be awake." She continued before Gloria could respond, "I've just spoken to Judith at Scribner & Sons. It was an odd conversation, and she has an odder request for you." She paused, more for dramatic effect than for the need to breathe. "Do you remember James Galbraith?"

CHAPTER 2

In my dream, a grave-gray fog rolled off the Miskatonic River. It coiled through the streets, clinging to eaves and rubbing chill against windowpanes. It hung about the sloping gambrel roofs, turning them into hulking shadows, the shoulders of crouching giants. The streets were silent, lonely – but in a town as haunted as Arkham, no dark alley might ever be truly empty.

A woman with fox-red hair walked carefully through the mist. I recognized her hair at once, as I recognized her straight spine and lifted chin. How often had my heart turned over to watch her moving through a crowd? But now she didn't turn to me with a smile. I watched, but could not speak, and she was oblivious to my presence. The hand that clutched her stole tight at her throat trembled faintly, knuckles white with tension. She never glanced over her shoulder, but she moved like one who knew herself observed.

From the clouded darkness, a whippoorwill called out, then another, swelling into a haunting chorus. A familiar sound – nightjars crowded the trees outside my house, until I heard *them singing in my dreams. Now, though, in this dream, the sound filled me with dread.*

A shadow followed Rachel – no distinct shape, nothing I could see, but rather a formless darkness, a nebulous attention.

I had left her alone, and now she was in danger. The idea horrified me so much that I fought against the dream, and it began to lose its clarity. I regretted it instantly, but too late.

I woke in a strange bed, clammy sweat pasting my nightshirt to my skin. I nearly leapt to my feet to begin packing, but eventually my breathing calmed, and sense returned. It was only a dream. Even if it weren't, it would take me days to return to America. I would reach my destination tomorrow. My business would be concluded quickly, and then I could race for home.

Gloria blinked out of a daze. Her head lolled, resting against the cold window of her taxicab. She straightened and rolled her neck. Fog pressed close against the car, filming the glass with moisture.

It was nearly midnight, and Gloria felt wrung out and hollow. She was no stranger to odd hours, but the journey from New York had been a wretched confluence of delays, repairs, and poor planning. She had left the train station in Boston to catch the very last bus, which eventually deposited her in Arkham. If she hadn't managed to find the single taxi circling that lonely block, she might still be haunting the empty station.

She wanted to give Jamie a piece of her mind for dragging her out here. The knowledge that she couldn't did nothing to help her mood.

He fell, they said – her agent Ellen and Charles Emerson,

Jamie's uncle. Fell from the balcony in his rented room in Arkham. The little hitch in their voices before the verb spoke volumes.

She had meant to refuse when she first heard Jamie's request. He had come to Arkham to work on a book – his first, after years of publishing short fiction and poetry. His death had left an unfinished manuscript and ample notes; he wanted Gloria to collect his literary affairs. It was a morbid undertaking, and one she had no taste for. Going through her husband's things after his death had been hard enough. With Benjamin, at least, she had already shared intimacy – death was only a new facet of that. She had been fond of Jamie, counted him as a friend, but they were hardly lovers or kin.

Refusal, however, had never really been an option. Charles Emerson was an editor at Scribner & Sons – one of long standing and no little clout, as Ellen had been quick to remind Gloria. It wouldn't do any harm to help the family in a time of grief.

Gloria had a few choice words about that – some of which she'd shared with Ellen – but in the end, she'd acquiesced. If nothing else, this ought to earn her a little leeway with her next deadline.

Jamie's last letter – his penultimate letter – had reached her months ago, after he settled in Arkham. Before his arrival here, Gloria's only knowledge of Arkham came from a review in the *Arkham Advertiser* – sent courtesy of Cousin Edith – calling her latest novel "purple and overwrought". Jamie described the town as full of character, but secretive.

It is, as so many tucked-away parts of New England, haunted by the ghosts of dead Puritans. I mean that figuratively, of course, but one hears rumors that suggest the ghosts may also be more literal. It's a lovely, picturesque town, but I have stumbled into places that are downright sinister. And not always where one might expect them to be.

My dreams have been quite vivid of late. You would recognize some of them, I think. I wish I could tell you more, but I respect your wishes on the matter.

If he had told her more, she would have set the letter aside with a sigh. Now she wished he had.

Critics who championed her work – those not currently writing for the *Advertiser* – claimed she wrote allegories of the horrors of war, or stories of human alienation and despair, viewed through the lens of the fantastic. It sounded very serious and clever when they said it.

Dr Gladstone, the alienist she'd seen as a child, would have recognized her "allegories" from the recurring nightmares that had plagued her youth. Nightmares when she was lucky – daylight visions when she wasn't. She had been so certain those terrors were real. Other doctors would have locked her up in a madhouse, but Dr Gladstone had convinced her they were only the product of a fevered imagination, and that she could harness her overactive subconscious into some creative process. He encouraged her toward painting, but it never took.

The technique had worked, for the most part. Years of careful journals had turned the dreams into something to be explored. It took longer to learn to fit those images into proper stories, with plots and characters and clever phrasing, as well as the thematic resonance that lent itself to the allegorical. She had published her first several pieces under a pseudonym, at her mother's insistence. After her parents' death, the charade had been too much work to maintain.

Over the years, a few readers had approached her, in person or in writing, to ask – some with careful circumlocution, others with alarming bluntness – if the things she wrote about were real. They all claimed identical visions. Some were obviously mad, others desperately searching for some connection. One such, however, a polite young man with haunted eyes, had described the details she had never written of, nightmares she had never shared.

She had spoken to Ben about her dreams early in their courtship, but it was clear the things she saw disturbed him. She told no one of the visions she saw waking. Long practice left her with a repertoire of excuses for starts and stumbles and moments of abstraction – some bordering on fugue. Writers were expected to have their quirks, after all.

She avoided such discussions with readers. She had grown adroit at deflecting questions over the years and walking away if that failed. Ellen had learned to recognize the worst offenders at public events and see them quietly escorted elsewhere. Jamie, however, had been well-spoken and self-deprecating, hardly a candidate for the madhouse. After the first few changes of subject, he accepted her refusal with good grace. He mentioned things from time to time, but never pressed her to acknowledge them.

The similarity of their visions was chilling, and sometimes it had taken all her resolve not to speak of it. But it was difficult enough to be taken seriously as a writer of weird fiction, let alone a woman. She had spent years cultivating a dry, pragmatic public persona, someone who didn't wake trembling in the dark, a cry stuck in her throat. Who never saw shadows move, or strange shapes stalking unseen through crowds. Who never saw the sky tear open.

The car turned a corner and red light bled through the fog. *Not again*, Gloria thought as her pulse leapt.

"Velma's." The taxi driver's rough voice startled her out of a panic. He was of the taciturn rather than the loquacious variety of cabbie and hadn't spoken a word since he'd tossed her luggage into the trunk. He nodded toward the light, a crimson neon sign glowing in the haze.

"A diner?" Gloria guessed. The sign and the sleek lines of the building stood in sharp contrast to the aging brick architecture around it.

"Ayuh. Good coffee. Good pie. Lots a' cops, sometimes, but they mostly leave you be."

Gloria raised her eyebrows. "That's nice to know. Not that I was expecting to be shaken down by the law."

"Well, never can tell, with that case you're hauling around. A typewriter? A real one, I mean, not the Chicago style."

Gloria laughed. Her Corona No. 3 in its battered case sat beside her on the seat, the one piece of luggage she never entrusted to cabbies or porters.

"Just a real typewriter, I'm afraid. I thought Tommy guns were usually carried in violin cases."

"Sure. Everybody thinks that, so you'd want something different. It don't pay to underestimate folks. Especially… ladies." She cocked an eyebrow at that pause. She suspected that it held an elided "old".

"I'll have to hire you if I ever need muscle. Or a getaway driver."

"You a writer?"

Gloria suppressed a sigh, sorting through the list of answers she held ready against that question. Whenever her profession came to light, she was inevitably subjected to queries about her progress and process, and at least one armchair intellectual would tell her all about the novel, or memoir, or history that they planned to write, if only they could find the time.

"Yes–" She had steeled herself to give the cabbie the benefit of the doubt when a flicker of motion caught her eye through the window. She broke off as the car drew closer.

A shadowy figure stood in the glow of a streetlamp, on the border of a broad, grassy square. Tall and thin, wrapped in a long coat, there was something disconcerting about the dimension of the shape, the way the person's head swiveled as the car passed. Gloria glanced away, suddenly unnerved by the thought of making eye contact. When she looked back, the figure had vanished into the fog.

The cabbie's eyes gleamed in the mirror, marking her gaze. "Arkham's got plenty to write about, that's for sure. Better to take a cab than walk 'round here at night. Better still, wait until morning."

Gloria forced a frown off her face and kept her voice light.

"I thought you just said it doesn't pay to underestimate people like me."

"Sure, sure. But it don't pay to underestimate a danger, neither. Especially in Arkham."

With that cryptic pronouncement, he lapsed back into silence.

The fog thinned as they traveled north through Easttown, away from the river. The streets opened, dilapidated brickwork giving way to trees and houses. Autumn was slow in coming to New York, but here it was in full swing. Leaves blanketed lawns and piled in drifts along the sidewalks. Night dulled their colors, but Gloria imagined the trees would blaze crimson and gold in the daylight.

"Here you go," the driver said, turning onto a cross street. "Noyes Street." He slowed as they passed several dark houses and eventually pulled over. "This look like the place?"

Gloria craned her neck to look out the fogged window. *I've never been here before*, she almost replied, but Jamie had described the house.

Severson House rose behind a screen of trees, its sharply pointed gables piercing the leaves. It was taller than its neighbors, older and more striking in its architecture. A Georgian Revival, like something out of Hawthorne, perhaps a century old.

"Yes," she said, "I believe this is it."

The strap of her typewriter case bit into her shoulder as she climbed out of the cab – a discomfort so familiar it had become a comfort all its own. Gloria shivered as the night air enfolded her. Tendrils of fog eddied through the cone of the headlights; over the growl of the idling engine, she heard the tap and whisper of leaves drifting to the ground.

The cabbie got out and opened the trunk to remove her bags – more gently than he'd loaded them in. He looked up at the lightless facade, and even in the dark she could see his frown. "You sure anybody's home?"

"They know I'm coming, but I was supposed to arrive hours ago."

"I'll wait a minute, just in case."

The steps were dished from decades of feet and settled into the earth. Leaves and acorns crunched underfoot as she climbed. Gloria winced at the sound, so loud against the heavy stillness of the night.

A chill snaked down her spine as she approached the tall double doors. She felt *watched*, as though someone or something very close had turned its attention toward her. This was nothing like the transportive, transcendent terror of her dreams – this was visceral.

A cry rose from the trees above her, high and mournful. A sharp note, followed by a haunting warble. Another answered it, then another.

Nightjars. Only the nightjars singing.

Foolish as Orpheus, she glanced behind her and at the branches overhead – nothing but shadows and fog. The birds were invisible in the darkness. The feeling didn't lessen.

She kept walking, trying to chide herself out of her nerves. Part of her wanted to turn back to the waiting cab and find a hotel, but she squared her shoulders and kept going. She could read the reviews already: *Horror Writer Afraid of the Dark.*

As she raised her hand to knock, one half of the door swung open. A light clicked on, silhouetting the person in the doorway.

Gloria blinked away the dazzles swimming across her eyes, and the shadow resolved into a woman. Dark-skinned and dark-eyed, wearing a headscarf and an embroidered housecoat. A stern expression softened as she studied Gloria.

"Mrs Goldberg?"

"Yes." She held out her already-lifted hand. "I'm sorry to wake you. I ought to have called ahead from Boston, but I didn't have the number."

The woman returned the handshake with a strong, work-callused grip. "That's all right. I'm Nora Addison, the caretaker for Severson House." She glanced past Gloria to the waiting cab. "I'm glad you made it in all right at this hour."

The driver carried Gloria's bags up the steps. After he collected his fare, he pulled a creased business card out of his jacket pocket. Gloria tilted it to the light to catch his name.

"Jasper Best."

He touched his cap, his rough, broken-nosed face rearranging in a grin. "Best in town. Easy to remember, ain't it?" As he turned back to his car, he called over his shoulder, "You ever need a getaway driver, just give me a ring." The headlights and growl of the engine faded down the street, leaving the night heavier than before.

As she crossed the threshold of Severson House, the uneasy sense of being observed faded. Gloria suppressed a relieved sigh; at least it wasn't the house itself that unsettled her so. The single electric lamp in the front room gleamed on polished wooden furniture and the heavy banister of the staircase. It also caught the barrel of the shotgun propped inconspicuously near the door frame. Answering the door in the middle of the night wasn't something the caretaker took lightly, it seemed.

"Mr Galbraith's family sent you," Ms Addison said, not quite a question. When Gloria nodded, she sighed. "Let's get you settled in for the night. I'll explain what I can in the morning."

A board creaked on the landing above them. Gloria looked up, and all the blood in her body froze.

A woman stood at the top of the stairs. Wild dark hair tumbled over her shoulders, and her eyes were dark holes in a pale oval face. Blood stained her cheek, her hands, the front of her white gown.

Gloria stared – a cold shudder moving through her from crown to feet – and waited for the bloody specter to vanish. This one, however, remained. Ms Addison followed Gloria's gaze and clucked her tongue.

"Miss Westmacott, you're frightening our guest. I ought to hide all your red paint."

The woman on the stairs laughed, a thoroughly flesh-and-blood sound. "Like the Canterville Ghost? And I, like poor Virginia, would be unable to paint any sunsets." She looked down at herself. "I do take your meaning, however." She lifted her hair with one hand, and with the other reached up to untie her painter's smock – not the gown Gloria had first taken it for. Beneath it, she wore a threadbare crocheted jumper and pajama trousers.

"I beg your pardon," the woman said, descending the stairs. "Though in all fairness, I wasn't expecting visitors at this hour. Er, what hour is it, precisely?"

"Half past midnight, I imagine," Gloria said, rallying her composure. "Which wasn't when I'd expected to arrive, either." She extended her hand. "Gloria Goldberg."

"Ruth Westmacott." The other woman scrubbed her fingers against her smock before accepting the handshake. "Don't worry, it's dried by now. I was just going to make a cup of tea."

"Don't go leaving any paintbrushes in the good china," Ms Addison said. Her voice was stern, but Gloria caught the shadow of a smile at the corner of the caretaker's mouth.

Ruth sighed dramatically. "It was only the once," she mock-whispered to Gloria, "but she'll never let me hear the end of it."

"And don't stay up until dawn for a change."

"Yes, Mother." Ruth winked at Gloria. "She'll do this to you, too, if you let her. Welcome to Severson House."

Ms Addison shook her head, but the smile won out. "Some people's children." She schooled her expression again and picked up Gloria's suitcase. "This way, ma'am."

Ms Addison led her up the wide staircase. "That's Miss Westmacott's room," she said, gesturing left, "and that's the door to the attic stairs. Washroom is here." She continued to the end of the landing, where she unlocked a door. "And here you are. The Cerulean Room."

Gloria lifted her eyebrows. "That sounds terribly fancy. Should I be worried about touching anything?"

Another wry smile curled the caretaker's mouth. "All it means, ma'am, is that no one ever got around to replacing the original wallpaper. The name makes it sound like something we're doing on purpose. And *cerulean* sounds fancier than *blue*."

The room was indeed blue. Cerulean was only one of the shades Gloria identified when she switched on the lamps. Alice, cobalt, and navy patterns striped the wallpaper. The bed clothes and knotted rugs were *bleu pervenche*, and even the woodwork was painted a misty French Gray. She remembered this fashion from her grandmother's home. A pretty combination, if more wintry than she would have chosen on her own.

Chilly or not, she was content. She'd had the terrible notion that she might be asked to sleep in Jamie's room. She'd thought herself well inured to the macabre after years of writing it, but it turned out some things could still give her a thoroughly unpleasant shiver.

She set her bags down with a sigh. The entirety of a very long day settled onto her shoulders.

Ms Addison shot her a sympathetic glance. "Do you have everything you need?"

"I believe so, thank you."

"Then I'll see you in the morning. Goodnight, ma'am."

Gloria meant to unpack her things, but she was too tired for that. She set her typewriter on the escritoire and laid her notebook and pen on the bedside table. Normally, she liked to take notes after a day of travel, but that would have to wait for morning. She changed out of her travel-grimed clothes and into her nightdress, crawling between the cold sheets. With any luck, she would be too exhausted to dream.

CHAPTER 3

I knew when I set sail for France that I would see the wounds of war. I didn't realize, however, how raw those wounds would still be. During my travels, I witnessed the scars of trenches carved in the earth, trees shattered, and ground cratered by explosives. Gas still poisoned the land, like the breath of some dreadful wyrm. Those battlegrounds not treacherous with ordnance had become graveyards.

Here, though, in the remote countryside surrounding Sanjeanne, the War might never have been.

I could find no cause for my disquiet as I walked the final mile from the train station. No cause save perhaps my recent dreams. The afternoon was clear and pleasant – warm in the sun, crisp in the dappled shade, a certain scent in the air that heralded the coming of autumn. Green hills enclosed the village, and to the west, cloud shadows rippled over golden grain fields. Compared to the muggy heat of Arkham's summer, or the cacophony of sound and smells in New York, this was an idyll. Spending a week here under any circumstance should have been a delight, let alone a visit with the potential of an inheritance.

Still, that lingering unease. The panic that had woken me

the previous night had faded with the dawn, but I couldn't entirely shake my concern. Rachel was surely safe as houses in my absence; she was the calmer of the two of us, quiet and competent during any crisis. I, wandering the world on my own, was likely in greater peril. I had reminded myself of that often since I sailed; surely the certainty would take root eventually.

I crested a rise in the packed dirt road and looked down at the village. Stone and half-timber buildings lined narrow cobbled streets. Flowers bloomed in window boxes, and ivy clung to old bricks. A cathedral spire rose above the pointed roofs.

As I stood taking in the view, shifting my weary grip on my luggage, church bells tolled the hour. A shadow moved in the clouds – I glimpsed a broad sweep of wings before it vanished again.

Gloria woke with a vertiginous start. Golden light filled the room, making her eyes water. A shadow hung above her, framed in the glow, wings spread wide –

No. The light was only the sun streaming through the curtains. The winged shape was just the shadow of fabric and a trick of her blurred vision. Somewhere in the distance, a clock chimed the hour.

After a few moments, she sighed and sat up.

A weight slid off her chest onto the mattress. Her notebook, which she'd placed on the bedside table last night. Her Conklin fountain pen – her last anniversary gift from Benjamin – lay on her stomach, uncapped. A blot of ink feathered across the fabric of her nightdress.

More ink stained her fingers, blue-black soaking the cuticles of her right thumb and forefinger, seeping through the fine lines in her skin. Her wrist ached.

She opened her notebook and frowned. Notes she'd taken the previous week should have been the last entry, but now three more pages had been filled in. She recognized her handwriting, the spiky, uneven script that meant she had written in a rush.

She had sleepwalked briefly as a child, but she had never sleep-written before.

She studied the scrawl, trying to decipher it. Something about angels and a door into heaven. Had she been recording a dream? It would have to wait. Right now, she had to face the day and her task in Arkham.

By the time she washed and dressed, it was nearly eleven. The house was quiet when she went downstairs – that particular morning stillness that seemed silent at first but was underlaid with the soft creaking of an old house, the wind in the trees, and the distant murmur of automobiles. She hadn't properly experienced it since taking her apartment in the city.

Daylight revealed the Victorian furnishings lamplight had only hinted at – elaborate woodwork and tasseled upholstery. Jamie had told her something of the house's history in his letters. The previous owner had died in the typhus outbreak of 1905. His widow had been reluctant to sell, but neither could she stand to live with the memories – she finally compromised by turning the home into a boarding house and moving across the country.

Gloria found the kitchen at the back of the house, and Ruth in it. The artist sat at the table, a cup of coffee in front of her. She still wore the jumper and pajamas of the night before, but she'd pinned up her hair and cleaned the paint off her fingers. Gloria imagined they both often felt like Lady Macbeth.

"Good morning," Ruth said, lifting her cup in greeting. The late morning light caught glints of auburn in her hair. "Ms Addison saved some toast for you, and I just made a fresh pot of coffee."

"Angels of mercy, the both of you." Gloria found the covered plate of buttered toast and poured herself coffee before settling across from Ruth at the narrow table. She cradled her cup in both hands, letting the heat soak into flesh and bone.

Ruth studied Gloria through ribbons of steam, and her mouth quirked in a smile. "Did you take me for a vengeful spirit last night?"

"You were very convincing. Although not the ghost I expected to find."

Ruth's humor drained away, settling her face in serious lines. "You mean Jamie."

"I'm sorry. That was in poor taste."

The other woman waved the apology aside. "Jamie wouldn't have minced around the subject if it had been someone else. Why should we for him?"

"Why indeed? You knew him, then."

"I moved into Severson House six months before he did. We joked about turning the place into a Bohemian retreat. The neighbors would have spit frogs."

"You're a painter, I take it?"

"Professionally, I'm an illustrator. R M West, purveyor of kittens and bunnies and badgers in waistcoats, and other treacly nonsense, at your service. You may have

seen my work in the pages of *Mister Wiggins & Friends*."
She slumped back in her seat, adopting a particularly
louche and disaffected posture. "Imagine the scandal if the
children knew."

"Oh. Goodness." Gloria pressed a finger to her lips to
hold back a laugh. She remembered seeing the adventures
of a rotund hedgehog and a particularly nervous fox in a
bookshop a few years ago and feeling grateful that her
children were already grown. She doubted she could have
read such a thing out loud without inserting sharp editorial
commentary.

"Your depictions of Mister Wiggins and Flossie are very
well executed," she said, as tactfully as she could. "The
books do seem to be popular."

"They keep body and soul together, and let me spend
time on my own art."

Gloria nodded. "Nice work if you can get it. I tried
writing ad copy when I was younger, but it never stuck."

"Oh, that's right. You're a writer, too. Jamie loaned me a
magazine with one of your stories. 'The Gray Gentleman', I
think it was. Eerie stuff." Ruth gave an approving nod.

"Thank you." Gloria sipped her coffee, trying to think of
something light to say to keep the conversation going, but
for an instant the enormity of the situation returned to her.

Silence filled the kitchen, until finally Ruth leaned
forward on her elbows, dark eyes serious. "You want to ask
me something. Don't worry about my delicate sensibilities."

"All right," Gloria agreed with a wry smile. "If you
promise not to worry about mine." She took a breath and
screwed her courage to the sticking place.

"Did Jamie fall, or did he jump?"

Ruth closed her eyes. "I don't know. The railing really did crack. I would think it was a horrid accident, if—" She broke off and drew a fortifying breath of her own. "Jamie had been terribly erratic lately. Hardly sleeping, skipping meals. He looked ghastly, like he'd come down with pneumonia. Nora – Ms Addison – kept pushing soup at him, and tea, even whiskey and egg. I'd hear him in his room, pacing and muttering to himself, or crying out in his sleep."

"Were the two of you—"

Ruth arched an eyebrow. "Lovers? No. I'm not sure Jamie had any inclinations toward romance. Certainly not recently – all he thought of was his work. I myself am… otherwise inclined."

She shot Gloria a sidelong glance, waiting for a response. As a confidence, it seemed to warrant one.

"I imagine that makes living as an artist much simpler," Gloria said, after weighing her options.

Ruth let out a startled laugh. "I'm certain that it does." She nodded toward Gloria's left hand. "You're married." Her inflection lifted slightly, not quite a question.

"My husband died a few years ago." She touched her ring. "This is a reminder, and habit."

"Oh. I'm sorry."

"He was a lovely man, and I miss him. But, if we're being indelicate, the simplicity of life as a widow is sometimes refreshing."

"I'm quite looking forward to my life as a spinster," Ruth said. "Although, between you, me, and the lamppost, I'm really old enough to be a thornback by now."

Gloria chuckled, but once again, the forced humor gave way and Ruth's bantering tone faded. "Why are you here?" the artist asked. "Nora could easily have packed up Jamie's things. Or the family's solicitor might have. Are you a relation?"

"No, just a colleague, and a friend. Jamie's family sent me to collect his literary effects. Apparently, Jamie asked for me specifically."

At least she had only to gather his notes and writing. The body had already been shipped back to his family in New York.

"Asked for you? When?"

"He posted letters several days… before. One to me, and one to his family. They reached us after he died."

"If he wrote a letter, that implies that he knew what was going to happen."

"It does," Gloria admitted. "It was vague, though. No goodbyes or recriminations or anything of that sort."

The recriminations had come otherwise. *You knew.*

Ruth leaned forward, that inquisitive eyebrow raised again. "That doesn't answer why."

"Jamie… confided in me. Years ago. Or he tried to. I did not want to listen. He suffered from dreams, nightmares, and wanted to make sense of what he saw. I… possess a similar affliction. But talking about chimeras, phantasms—" She shook her head. "He thought it would help, but what could we have done but reinforce each other's horrors?"

Ruth frowned at her coffee. "Sometimes merely knowing that one isn't alone in the world can do wonders. I've met people saved by that knowledge and seen those who died for the lack of it." She looked up in time to catch Gloria's expression, and her already fair complexion blanched further.

"I didn't mean – That is to say, I'm not blaming you. Whatever happened to Jamie couldn't possibly be your fault." Her voice wavered on the last words, sounding not at all certain.

Gloria didn't feel very certain, either.

"I'm sorry," Ruth continued, but Gloria waved the apology aside.

"You gave me an honest answer. One I should have heard some time ago, it seems."

Ruth sighed and threw back the last of her coffee with a grimace. "Here it is not even noon and I'm already making a hash of things. Usually I can get by until teatime. I am sorry. I'll just slink back to my studio now and try not to stick my foot in it for another hour or two."

She pushed her chair from the table with a scrape and set her cup in the sink. She paused in the doorway, hugging her arms beneath her chest.

"If you do see Jamie's ghost, give him what for on my behalf. This whole ordeal has been terrible on Ms Addison, and whoever lets the room next will likely be less agreeable to me."

Gloria sat at the table until the light changed, and shadows moved across the wall. Ruth's words chased their tails in circles inside her head.

Was it really that simple? If she had shared her visions with Jamie, would it have saved him somehow? It seemed the worst sort of hubris to imagine so. Life wasn't a carefully plotted narrative, with all the characters neatly woven together. Imagining she could have prevented Jamie's death was as ridiculous as blaming herself for it.

All she needed to do was convince herself of that.

By the time she collected herself, her coffee was long cold. She drank the dregs like bitter medicine. The toast tasted of ashes and scraped down her throat. When she finished the last penitent bite, she swept the crumbs off the table and washed the coffee dishes.

With cups and saucers drying in the rack, she could no longer postpone the inevitable.

The attic steps were narrow and dim, and creaked beneath her as she climbed. Gray light waited for her at the top – the morning's sunlight had given way to a dull, overcast day.

The space smelled of wood, in the manner of attics, and slightly of damp. A chill pervaded the air, the insidious sort that crept into everything, down to the bones. Gloria shivered, less from the cold itself than from the thought of paper curling in the humidity, and how her hands would ache from typing in this weather.

Faded rugs were scattered over the floorboards, and an unmade bed lay against one slanting wall. A desk stood near the balcony – a drafty spot, but one with the best light. Jamie's typewriter – a newer Remington model – sat in the center, surrounded by drifts and mountains of paper. A battered chaise, a pair of trunks, and a mismatched series of shelves lined with books comprised the rest of the furnishings. Her own novels were on those shelves, their spines well-creased; grief unfolded in her chest, thorny and bittersweet.

The balcony doors were firmly shut. Through the grimy glass, Gloria saw that fateful broken railing.

It was only an accident. Only an accident. Did she believe that? His family didn't seem to. Ruth didn't, quite. *Only* – what an innocuous adverb for a fatal event.

Which was worse, in the end? That uncaring happenstance had claimed a young man's life? Or that his own demons had driven him to end it?

Gloria dragged her gaze away from the window and back to the desk. The sooner she completed the task at hand, the better. Sitting down in front of a typewriter had certainly been a daunting prospect a time or two, but never like this.

The upper layer of papers was chaos, but the further she excavated, the more order she uncovered. She found the first several chapters of a manuscript tucked neatly into a drawer – the beginning of Jamie's novel. It followed a young man returning from abroad, weary not from the war itself, but from witnessing the scars it left in the world. A dark family secret had brought him to Europe and haunted him on the journey home.

The voyage across the cold waters of the Atlantic was a smooth one. When the sight of so much wide, hungry water palled my spirits, I amused myself with books and writing. I began letters to Rachel. One I even finished and posted when I arrived in Le Havre. Most remained incomplete, musings that more properly belonged in a journal. Some things were easier to articulate when I imagined her standing beside me.

This inheritance, if it existed, was our chance at a life of, if not leisure, at least less scraping by. That was part of the reason I had come. The other part was simple curiosity. I had no knowledge of these relatives in France, yet they had bothered to keep track of my immigrant ancestors. Why had my grandparents never mentioned the family they left behind? And why had this great-uncle, whom I'd never met, chosen to include me in his will? Even unwed and childless, he must have had friends on the continent. Anyone closer than a stranger in America.

What that secret was the text did not reveal. Gloria felt the narrative was being too coy, but she still wanted to read on. She recognized Jamie's favorite imagery from his poems and short fiction.

After those chapters, his work grew scattered. She found the next chapter started three different ways, each apparently discarded. New characters appeared seemingly from nowhere. Scattered scene fragments – typed and handwritten – lay all over the desk, in no discernable order.

One sheet of paper contained a list of scribbled names and dates. At the bottom, Jamie had written CONFIRM WITH MALDEFAUNT in strong capitals, and underlined it.

She wasn't sure how long she sat there – long enough for the overcast shadows to creep across the floor and the distant sounds of the neighborhood to change. She straightened her shoulders. She was too old to slouch so. Bright young things like Ruth and Jamie could loll about, louche and languid, but at her age, poor posture left one hunched as a vulture.

She rose from the unforgiving wooden chair, still holding the last few pages she'd been reading, and sank onto the nearby chaise instead. Wisps of stuffing escaped the upholstery, and one leg had been replaced by a block of wood and an unlucky book. It faced away from the window and its morbid view. Gloria sat back with a weary sigh, scrubbing a hand over her face. She could collect Jamie's papers – possibly even arrange them in some semblance of order, though she was no archivist – but to finish his work? Ridiculous. Presumptuous, even if he had asked it of her. Presumptuous of him, to impose on their friendship so.

When her parents died, when Ben died, she'd known exactly what to do. The traditions had been laid out – keriah and Kaddish, shiva and *sholoshim*. Rabbis and relations were there to walk her through all the steps of mourning. As a daughter, as a widow, her role had been clear, even if those traditions had brought her little comfort. None of that could guide her now.

I stood on the fading dirt path, staring up at the abbey. Time had weathered the arches, eaten the roofs from the towers, and left the great gates sagging on their hinges. A low, leaden sky enclosed the abbey and the rolling hills beyond; silence lay thick against the walls. The walk from the village had warmed me, but as I stared at the gates, the chill of the day crept through the seams of my clothing, insinuating itself inside collar and cuffs.

"Is it haunted?" The question fell from my lips before I realized what I meant to say. Schoolboy foolishness, but my companion considered it with all seriousness.

"I do not know." M Duchesne frowned and folded his hands over his walking stick. "If you mean by spectral monks carrying lanterns, I think not. But I have sometimes felt… not alone, when I stood within the walls. These stones remember something, I'm sure of that."

I had the letters from my great-uncle and his solicitor. M Duchesne had his memories of youthful exploration. If there was anything left in the ruin to be found here, we had as good a chance as any.

Would I find answers, or only ghosts?

Gloria set the papers in her lap and leaned against the cushions. Grief and poor sleep settled around her temples in an iron band. Just a moment's rest, and then she would get back to work…

The breeze swayed the trees, and shadows drifted across the room. A dog barked somewhere in the distance. Gloria drowsed, her eyes half-open.

She sank slowly toward sleep, but something stopped her at the threshold. A sense of anticipation grew in her chest, bordering on dread. *Something* was there in the room with her. Watching her.

She tried to wake up, but she couldn't move. All her limbs were too heavy – even her eyes would neither open nor close. Frozen between sleep and waking, with the weight of a night hag pressing on her chest.

The clear sound of footsteps moved across the room. Through half-lidded eyes, Gloria watched Jamie come into view. He stopped beside the desk, staring down at her. His face was tinged with gray, his eyes sad and sunken. Blood stained his hands. His mouth opened, but no sound emerged. After several silent sentences, he raised a hand to his throat, as if searching for his absent voice. He shook his head and gestured toward the typewriter.

He studied Gloria for another moment, lips twisted in a rueful half-smile. Then he walked toward her – walked past her – and vanished through the balcony doors.

Gloria fought against paralysis again, and this time she won. She sat upright with a gasp, the papers in her lap spilling over the floor. Her pulse raced; all she could hear was the roar of her own heart.

Only a dream. A hallucination. Dr Gladstone had assured her that such episodes were not the work of demons as the superstitious claimed, but merely some product of the somnolent brain.

She leapt to her feet, ignoring the fallen pages, and turned in the direction Jamie had vanished. The balcony doors were still shut. The platform beyond them was empty.

Before she could talk herself out of it, Gloria pulled the door open and stepped onto the balcony.

A gnarled oak tree stood behind the house, denuded branches rustling in the breeze. In the summer, the light must fall in dappled waves through the leaves, warm and green. In the winter, the branches would rattle against the walls like bony fingers.

She looked down at last, because she had to. She was too

late to help Jamie, if she ever could have; the least she could do now was bear witness, and not flinch.

A small courtyard lay below the window, enclosed by trees. No silent specters waited there. The stones were clean, free of grisly reminders. Had Ms Addison scrubbed them? Leaves drifted in lazy spirals, landing with a whisper.

Gloria turned away. As she latched the door firmly behind her, a noise drew her attention. A shadow moved at the corner of her vision, and she recoiled with a gasp.

Ruth stood at the top of the stairs, her eyes wide. "I saw you standing there and–" She shook her head, wrapping her arms tightly around her. "I didn't dare say anything, for fear of startling you."

Gloria pressed a hand to her chest. Her pulse leapt under her skin, and all her nerves felt scalded. "Given how easy it was to do, I appreciate your restraint."

"Have you made any progress?"

"Some. I don't really understand what I'm meant to accomplish."

"And have you seen any ghosts?" Ruth's voice was light, but her eyes held Gloria's.

"I – don't know. I saw something," she admitted, before she could think better of it. "But just because I write about ghosts and ghouls doesn't mean I believe in them."

Ruth gave an indelicate snort. "And I don't believe in talking badgers with pocket watches. Ghosts, on the other hand–"

"I've attended a few seances," Gloria said. "Herr Mesmer and his hypnotism are fascinating, but none of the self-professed mediums I've met have ever convinced me."

There was always something a touch too convenient about spirit summonings. Given any large enough gathering of people, after all, who didn't have a dead loved one who might be waiting on the other side?

"Oh, sure," Ruth said. "The usual table-tapping and ectoplasm – cheesecloth or seaweed. Spirit guides and vague proclamations and fleecing the grieving out of their inheritance. I've seen all that. But I've seen other things, too." She shook her head. "Ghosts aren't what worry me right now, though. Come with me, please. I have something I'd like you to see."

"All right." Gloria paused long enough to collect the last handful of pages she'd been reading and tuck them into an unused composition book on Jamie's desk. With that under her arm, she followed Ruth down the stairs.

Ruth's room was appointed in the same style as Gloria's, but in warmer tones. A pair of easels stood in the center, and stacks of canvases leaned against the walls. The vanity overflowed with Bohemian detritus – jewelry and cosmetic pots and stray stockings. All the other surfaces were covered with art supplies. The ghost of Chanel perfume hung in the air, along with the harsher sting of turpentine.

Ruth stopped just before the easels. She still hugged herself, hands on opposite elbows, and Gloria fought not to mirror her pose.

"A few months ago," the artist said, "Jamie asked me to illustrate the book he was working on. He paid what he could, and since Mr Wiggins hadn't any pressing deadlines, I took the job. At first, it was a pleasant diversion. He described such strange, lovely images – they were a joy to create. But he grew more and more distracted in the past few weeks. He stopped asking for illustrations – then he came to me with a stack of scribbled notes. His handwriting was near indecipherable, and he wasn't much more coherent when he explained what he'd written. I tried to sketch what he described, but hardly any of them turned out. And the ones that did–"

She broke off, rubbing her arms. Her smile, when she drew it on, was strained. "Do you believe I had nightmares about them? Of these terrible winged creatures chasing Mr Wiggins and Flossie. That was just as laughable as it sounds, but then the creatures came for me."

"Winged creatures?"

"Here." Ruth opened a large portfolio and drew out a handful of papers. "These are my first sketches."

Part bird, part beast – some almost insectile, but not like any insect she could name. Some had barbed tails like a scorpion, others webbed and taloned feet. All of them were winged. Almost like gargoyles, but instead of stone, they seemed cobbled together from leather and chitin and bone. Most of the sketches depicted them flying, some against a background of stars, but some showed them standing upright, wings folded. In the dark – in a fog – one might mistake them for a person.

"Good Lord," Gloria whispered.

"This is one that I finished properly." Ruth held up an inked page: the scene showed a building in the countryside – a church, perhaps, or something medieval. Above its towers, the sky unfolded, and a cloud of winged shapes emerged. Like a host of angels.

An uneasy chill moved through Gloria, waking flashes of near-forgotten dreams. Ruth was already turning away.

"But that's not what I wanted to show you." Ruth touched the draped canvas on one easel but didn't remove the cover.

"I've been having terrible dreams for days now. Before Jamie. The kind that leave images branded inside you, so vivid you can't tell them from reality, sometimes even after waking. Do you know what I mean?"

"I think I do," Gloria said dryly.

"A proper nightmare once in a while can be inspiring. But these, every night… My point, though, is that I began this series a week ago."

She removed the cloth and stepped back.

Gloria stood in front of the canvas. A night scene, blacks and grays and browns layered so thick the paint dried in ridges. It showed a window, looking in from outside. Warm yellow light filled the opening, spilling out to line tree branches. Inside that bright room, a woman sat, leaning over a desk. At first Gloria thought she was reading, but as she looked closer at the shapes, she saw a typewriter instead. The woman's face had only the suggestion of features, but the shape of her hair, cropped in a graying bob, the line of her neck as she hunched forward… Gloria rolled her shoulders as a sympathetic twinge flared between her shoulder blades.

The resemblance was enough to make Gloria's skin crawl. Worse still was the way the shadows gathered behind that figure, looming in the suggestion of a terrible wave about to fall. Another canvas on the floor showed the same woman, holding a book in hands stained dark and gangrenous – Gloria hoped that discoloration was meant to be ink. Beside it was a painting of a different woman, this one young and red-headed, glancing over her shoulder as she moved down a foggy street.

"Jamie mentioned you several times, but he never once described you to me." Ruth fixed Gloria with a steady gaze. "Are you going to tell me this is all a coincidence?"

Gloria swallowed, her mouth abruptly gone dry. "I–" *Jamie is dead*, a harsh voice in the back of her mind reminded her. *Dead, and you never once told him the truth. Denying it will do you no good.*

She took a breath and tried again. "I don't know," she admitted. "It doesn't feel that way. But what else could it be?"

Ruth frowned. "What are we going to do?"

Gloria shook her head, turning away. Chimeras. Phantasms. How could you face such things? "I don't know that either."

CHAPTER 4

When Gloria went back downstairs, the morning's stillness had left Severson House. Jazz played on a gramophone in the front room, and Ms Addison drifted to-and-fro, dusting and straightening. She hummed as she worked, and her hips swayed in time with the music. A stair creaked under Gloria's weight, and the caretaker immediately composed herself.

Her brows pinched when she looked at Gloria. "You look pale, ma'am. Did you sleep all right?"

"As well as can be expected, I think, considering the circumstances. By the time you get to my age, you either learn to sleep anywhere you can, or learn to do without. Please, no need for ma'am – Gloria is fine."

Ms Addison's gaze fell on the composition book. "You've been to the attic already."

"I've begun going through his papers. I don't really understand what I'm to do."

"I said I'd answer any questions. If I can. These things happen – I'm not sure anyone can ever explain it."

"Ruth told me some of it. About the balcony, about Jamie's behavior. Did you … find him?"

The caretaker closed her eyes. "I did."

"I'm sorry–"

"No, it's all right." She shook off the memory. "I found him. I've seen the dead before, ma'am. That part… well, I can handle it. He looked so frightened, though. And his poor hands–" Her voice broke.

Frightened. Did that mean it truly was an accident? Or that he'd had time, in that endless falling instant, to regret his decision?

Then the woman's final words caught up with her. "His hands?"

"He cut his hands, the day before – no, two days before. I found him in the washroom, bleeding in the sink and trying to bandage himself. Paper cuts, he said, but his palms were so torn up – I don't know what kind of paper could have done that. I helped him clean up and put the bandages on. I thought it might keep him from writing for a time. Lord knows he needed a break. But I heard the typewriter keys clacking again only an hour later."

Gloria's own hands clenched in sympathy.

"I still think I'll run into him on the stairs," Ms Addison continued with a shake of her head, "or find him in the kitchen."

I saw him in the attic. The words wouldn't travel the distance from her brain to her tongue. "When I was a girl, my old cat died. For weeks after, I swore I felt her weight at the foot of my bed when I woke up every morning." She could still recall the sensation, so many years later, the bittersweet poignancy of comfort and loss. Not at all the feeling her vision of Jamie had left her with.

"I think I'd like to step out for a bit," Gloria said, changing the subject gracelessly. "Clear my head. I saw a diner on the way in last night. How far is it?"

"Velma's? About two miles. I can ring a cab for you."

"Oh, no, thank you. I could use a walk."

"All right. Just head south down Noyes, and then turn west before you hit the tracks. You can't miss the sign, even in daylight."

The exercise did clear her head. The day was cool and gray, with a light breeze sighing through the trees. The leaves were every bit as bright as she'd imagined the night before. Despite Jamie's papers tucked into her purse, for the moment she could pretend she was simply enjoying a brief holiday.

The trees thinned the farther south she walked, giving way to fewer houses and more businesses. She passed the open area Jasper had driven past last night. By daylight, it was green and pleasant, scattered with drifts of leaves. Children chased a ball back and forth while their parents sat nearby, smoking and chatting. Nothing sinister.

She couldn't pretend that something strange wasn't happening at Severson House, but not everything had to be as terrible as her imagination insisted.

The neighborhood to the south was less idyllic, but the atmosphere was a wholly mundane sort of decay. The streets were rougher there, pitted with missing cobbles. The mournful cry of a train carried through the air, and a dark cloud of smoke unraveled over the rooftops near the river. Ash and grime settled into the walls and darkened the doorsteps. Several police cars prowled past as she walked, and she remembered Jasper's warning.

Velma's neon sign wasn't quite as eye-searing by day, but the diner was still easy to spot. Gloria wondered how the neighbors had reacted to the encroachment of modernity into what seemed a sleepy sort of town.

Inside, the diner smelled delightfully of coffee, grease, and sugar. The promised pies waited in a glass case. Though it was long past noon, the counter was full with a late lunching crowd. Sure enough, she counted several uniformed police, and a few who had the look of plainclothesmen. None of them glanced at her twice; her facade of respectability was holding. A trio of smartly dressed young women chatted in one booth. In the next, a young couple slouched over a very belated breakfast; both looked as though they would have preferred the hair of the dog that bit them.

A waitress waved Gloria toward a booth in the back and took her order. There had been times while her children were young that she would have given anything for a place as silent as Severson House in which to work. Today, however, the background noise of voices and clattering dishes and traffic from the street soothed her. She stared abstractedly out the window at the cars and passersby.

One figure caught her eye over the heads of the crowd. A tall, pale man in black loitered on the far side of the street, checking his pocket watch. An umbrella hung from one arm, though no one else seemed worried about rain. He glanced up at the diner, and Gloria glimpsed a wide smile below the shadow of his hat.

The arrival of her coffee and pie distracted her. When Gloria looked again, he was gone.

Gloria worked through a piece of cherry pie – silently

promising her mother's outraged ghost that she would eat a proper meal later – and her first cup of coffee before laying out Jamie's notes.

Some pages had dates and clear handwriting. Others were scrawled and smeared with haste. Those reminded Gloria of last night's automatic writing.

Parts of the story were fragmented. Some involved a man – the novel's still unnamed protagonist – wandering through a ruined church, searching for a lost inheritance. A woman, perhaps his fiancée, waited in Arkham, being followed by some unseen presence. Other pages were comprised of what seemed to be a series of ominous portents. On the thirtieth of May, Jamie had written:

> *Calves born with bloody eyes. Or was it birds' eggs filled with blood?*
> *The birds are not right.*
> *It begins with the sky. It ends with the sky.*
> **Ask Maldefaunt for suggestions??*

That name again. Had someone been helping Jamie with research?

A woman sat in the inn's breakfast room the next morning, the only other occupant. She looked up when I entered the room, and her gaze met mine with an unnerving certainty. "Ah. The young relation, the American." Her English was accented but assured.

For an instant, her apparent clairvoyance confounded me. Then I realized that, in a town the

size of Sanjeanne, any new face would be noticed, and
she could easily have learned my identity from the
concierge.

"I am he," I said, inclining my head. "I'm afraid you
have the better of me, madame."

"Esther Duchesne. I was a friend of your great-uncle,
however many times removed. He asked me to assist you
when you arrived."

"I'm sorry I didn't learn of our connection until it was
too late." At her gesture of invitation, I sat down. "My
family's history here is sadly lost to me."

She lifted her demitasse, studying me over the rim.
Her sensibly bobbed hair was shot with gray, the hand
holding her cup was lean and sharp-boned. The lines on
her face spoke of concentration, and her dark eyes were
clear and sharp. I felt myself weighed and measured
under her gaze.

She cradled her cup in both hands. "I can tell you
some of that history," she said at last. "Though it may
not hold much comfort."

This was a more recent entry, dated only a day or two
before Jamie's final letter had been posted. A revision –
Esther replaced Andre Duchesne, the historian and friend
of the narrator's great-uncle. Her mannerisms and physical
description raised Gloria's eyebrows. She had already
wondered if the character of Rachel was modeled on Ruth.
Now she was certain that more than one character in the
story were based on people Jamie knew.

If Esther came to a bad end, she would –

Gloria sighed and pinched the bridge of her nose against the sudden prickling heat of unshed tears. She would do nothing. Nothing but keep reading.

The next page, undated, contained the beginning of a different scene.

Rachel stood before the open window, a cigarette smoldering in one hand. The breeze lifted strands of her hair and fluttered the hem of her dressing gown. The morning light was dim, metallic, a strange shade of pink. She could have captured that color in paint; I, with only words at my disposal, could not find the best comparison. The air smelled of storms.

"What time is it?" I asked. My voice cracked with sleep.

Rachel turned. The delicate crease between her brows – too common, of late – softened as she looked at me. "Dawn."

Thunder snarled – an ugly sound, like something wet tearing. Rachel flinched and nearly burned herself with her cigarette ember. She dropped it in a stray cup on the side table, her hands shaking.

I rose to join her and laid a gentle hand on her shoulder. "What is it?"

"I don't like this storm," she murmured.

The pink light caught Gloria's attention. She could picture it easily – the strange metallic light that preceded a storm, the way the clouds massed and darkened, holding dawn at bay. The scene was only a fragment, but the bones of something larger were here. If she were to write such a thing, how would she go about it? She tapped her pen against her lip for a moment, then unscrewed the cap.

We stood together in front of the window, the wind on our faces. It smelled of rain and distant lightning, and something else. Something raw and metallic.

The sharp sound of breaking glass dragged her attention back to the world around her.

Gloria laid down her pen and reached for her coffee but found only a quarter inch of cold sludge at the bottom of the mug. She couldn't properly recall what she'd been writing, but her fingertips were stained with ink, and her hand cramped. Her ears rang with a low noise like bird-chatter.

She looked up, rubbing her eyes with her left hand, intending to flag down the waitress. A flat, sour taste coated her teeth.

The sound she heard was voices – the voices of the other diners, crowded against the door and windows. Voices low with disbelief, sharp with shock and fright. The waitress turned away, leaning against the counter, one shaking hand making the sign of the cross. A patron stood beside her, his hand on her elbow. The coffee carafe lay shattered near their feet. Light gleamed on broken glass and pooling liquid – a queer light, dull and ruddy.

Gloria extricated herself from the booth. The clock above the counter said it was quarter to four. Nearly an hour had gone by.

"What is it?" she asked, her voice cracking.

A woman sobbed in response. A man put his arm around her, his own face gray, and turned her away from the window. Gloria inserted herself into the space they left.

The sky over Arkham was the color of scabs, the color of a wound. Clouds slid low across the rooftops, suffocating the afternoon light. Onlookers gathered under an awning across the street, pointing and clutching one another.

Gloria leaned against the door; the draft through the gap smelled raw, metallic, charnel.

Thunder growled and the clouds opened.

Gloria gasped as the first drops struck the glass. One landed on her hand, warm and red, and she recoiled. Someone shrieked. Across the street, a man left the shelter of the awning, an umbrella open against the sanguine rain. Gloria had only a glimpse of his pallid face before he turned a corner.

"Don't look," a man beside her murmured to his companion. "Just don't look."

A wave of *déjà vu* swept through her, so strong her knees nearly buckled. She backed away from the door, scrubbing her hand on her skirt as she retreated to her table. This was the sort of horror she had learned to ignore – but everyone around her saw this, too.

She looked down at the open notebook and the words scrawled there. Her pen had run dry. The last several lines were nothing but indentions in the paper.

"Don't look," I murmured, drawing Rachel back from the window. "Just don't look." She trembled against me when I turned her face into my shoulder. Such advice

is easier to give than to follow – I continued to stare
through the red-streaked glass.

Gloria shut the notebook so forcefully that dishes
bounced on the table.

She saw the horrors she described, but always *before* she
recorded them. She wrote to exorcise her visions, not to
make them real.

A moment later, thunder shook the diner, rattling all the
windows. Someone yelped. Rain fell in a crimson torrent.
An instant later, however, the clouds faded from red to gray.
The deluge continued, paling from ruby to rust to clear
water. Soon, a real rain sluiced across the glass.

The diner patrons sat in near silence, watching the
downpour. Some prayed under their breaths; others wept.
No one spoke. What was there to say in the face of such a
thing?

Half an hour later, the rain slacked to a drizzle and
eventually ceased. The clouds broke apart, and wan autumn
light gleamed on wet pavement.

When Gloria finally stepped outside, a faint metallic
scent still hung in the air. Beneath the dripping eaves, a
rusty pink puddle slowly drained away.

Gloria returned to Severson House to find Ruth and
Ms Addison in the kitchen, leaning together. The smell of
coffee filled the room; when she moved closer, she smelled
brandy, too. A half-empty decanter sat on the table.

"Thank goodness." Ruth straightened when Gloria walked
in, dropping her hand from Ms Addison's shoulder. "You
were out in that. I didn't know what might have happened–"

"I'm all right. I was inside Velma's. It's passed now. I don't suppose–" She gestured toward the bottle of brandy. When Ruth nodded, Gloria poured a healthy slug into a cup. She considered adding coffee, but decided her nerves were frazzled enough already. The first sip burned her sinuses, and sweet warmth burst over her tongue and palate.

Gloria turned away from the kitchen windows. "Jamie described Arkham as haunted. I thought he was being poetic, but after today..." She shuddered.

"I've been in Arkham for a year and a half," Ruth said, "and I don't think Jamie was being poetic. But there's a difference between getting the heebie-jeebies walking past a graveyard and seeing a rain of blood with your own eyes. Unless you think it was only red dust from the Sahara."

Gloria snorted; she had also read Charles Fort's *The Book of the Damned*. "I do not agree with Mr Fort's conclusions about many things," she said dryly, "but on this we are aligned – that was not red sand."

"What was it he said?" Ruth asked. "'If gushes of blood should fall from the sky upon New York City, business would go on as usual.'"

Ms Addison laughed shakily. "I can just imagine that."

"So can I," Gloria agreed. "Arkham, it seems, is less metropolitan about such things."

"There's many would say that Arkham has always been strange," Ms Addison said. "I've heard stories..." She shook her head. "Only stories, my mother always said. Superstition and nonsense. But things have taken an especially queer turn in the past few months."

"How so?"

"Just little things, maybe. First I heard of was the Prentice's cow birthed a calf with no eyes. Poor thing didn't last but a day. After that, Eb Crampley's chickens laid, and the eggs were full of nothing but blood. These things happen – but then the starlings started acting queerly. An old preacher from Kingsport got real worked up about it, but he's that sort, so nobody paid it too much mind. Josephine Manley swore up and down she saw an angel in her garden at night. But again, she takes turns that way."

Birds' eggs filled with blood. The birds are not right.

"Jamie mentioned things like that in his notes," Gloria said. "Was his book based on Arkham's oddities?"

Ruth and Ms Addison exchanged a glance. "Possibly," Ruth said. "He was working on a novel ever since he arrived – or trying to. He talked to me a bit about false starts and slow progress. He finally found some inspiration... in May, it must have been. I remember him enthusing about it, but I had a deadline for Mister Wiggins at the time, so I'm afraid I didn't pay much attention."

"He came across something in a bookshop," Ms Addison said. "Some bit of history that had him all lit up. I heard him typing at all hours after that, wandering in for breakfast after noon, his face smudged with ink, stumbling into the furniture." She shook her head with a soft chuckle. "He acted like he was in love."

A fleeting smile crossed Gloria's face. She remembered that feeling. Beginning her first novel had felt much like her courtship with Ben. If one were lucky, the affection remained after that first dizzy blush faded into familiarity.

"But that was well before the Crampley chickens," Ms

Addison continued. "That happened sometime in the summer."

Had Jamie written those portents *before* they occurred? The suspicion lingered in the back of Gloria's mind, too ridiculous to voice. But she had written a rain of blood before it fell. Ruth had painted her before she ever came to Arkham.

"Does the name Maldefaunt mean anything to either of you?" she asked. "I came across it in Jamie's notes more than once."

The other women looked at one another again. Ruth lifted her shoulders in a shrug. "Not a name you hear every day," the artist said. "It sounds familiar, but I can't tell you where I heard it." She cocked an eyebrow. "Do you think it's important?"

A glib dismissal slid into Gloria's mouth, but she choked it back. She had spent years trying to prove her sanity to the world; where was the sanity in denying the things they had all seen?

"It might be," she admitted. "Something strange is happening, and it seems to be connected to Jamie's book. To your paintings."

Ms Addison's eyebrows drew together, and she glanced from Gloria to Ruth and back again, as if trying to decide which of them were crazier.

Ruth, however, leaned forward, elbows on the table. "How can we help?"

An hour later, the three of them sat around the long dining room table, stacks of Jamie's papers and composition books spread out under the electric lights. Outside, the early autumn evening deepened into real night. Ms Addison had brewed a fresh pot of coffee and added a medicinal slug of brandy to all their cups.

Ruth surveyed the clutter. "And I thought I was poorly organized. I admit, I imagined something more along the lines of daring sleuthing, not filing."

"The life of a writer is rarely daring," Gloria said dryly. She had done a bit of unwise snooping in the name of research in her younger days, mostly sneaking through abandoned buildings looking for 'ambience'. She was lucky she hadn't contracted tetanus.

"How do you want these organized?" Ms Addison asked. She might not share Ruth and Gloria's "heebie-jeebies", but she hadn't hesitated to help when given a practical task.

Gloria spread her hands in a shrug. "I'm not certain. For now, let's separate typed from handwritten, and put anything with a date on it in order."

They worked in silence for a while, moving papers from one stack to another, leaning close to consult on particularly impenetrable bits of Jamie's handwriting. When the soft shuffling of pages had nearly grown soporific, Ms Addison began to hum under her breath.

"*Well, who's that writin'? Who's that writin'? The book of the seven seals.*" She caught herself singing and broke off abruptly.

Ruth ducked her head, failing to conceal her smile. "She sings beautifully," she whispered to Gloria *sotto voce*, "but only when she thinks no one is listening."

The caretaker snorted delicately and kept sorting papers.

"Are you from New York?" Gloria asked Ms Addison later, when Ruth had stepped out to the powder room. "It sounded as though you know the city."

"I lived in Harlem for a while when I was younger. Nearly married a musician there." Her face softened in a brief, wistful smile. "I'm sure that would have been a terrible idea."

"How long have you worked at Severson House?"

"Five years now. My mother worked for Mrs Severson since before the typhus and kept up the place after she moved out west. Mrs Severson offered me the position when my mother died, and I came back here." She shook her head. "Did the responsible thing." She let out a quiet sigh.

"You miss the city."

"Most days," the other woman admitted. "I loved Harlem, loved the people there. If you'd told me six years ago that I'd ever come back to Arkham, I'd have called you crazy. It's not so bad, though, just quiet. The work is easy, and this town has some interesting history of its own, ma'am."

"Please, do call me Gloria."

"All right then." She smiled, brighter this time. "If you call me Nora."

An awkward silence filled the room until Nora lifted another volume off a stack of composition books. This was an older journal, leather bound and well-worn with time and handling. She flipped it open and paused. "Oh. Speaking of history–" She held it out for Gloria to read the bookplate.

"Dorian Lefevre?" She flipped through the journal, but it was entirely in French, in an antiquated handwriting she couldn't easily parse.

"The Lefevres came over a few generations ago – which everyone knew, because they'd tell you about their history in the Old World every chance they got. They had a big house on French Hill, threw fancy parties. Not that I ever saw them, of course, but my mother and their gardener were friends from way back when. Helene Lefevre lived there when I was a little girl – she'd already married Frederick Griswold by then. They fell on hard times, though, and Mr Griswold fell on hard debts. Their two sons died in the War. Mr Griswold died not long after – grief, they said, but I suspect the bottle helped. Poor Mrs Griswold had to sell the whole estate a year or two ago."

"It's amazing, isn't it?" Ruth said, pausing in the doorway. "I can barely remember the names of people I've met more than twice, and she can tell you the life story of everyone in this town."

"I listen, that's all. It's important to pay attention to people – it makes them feel good when you remember things they say, and it warns you about whose company to avoid."

Ruth propped her hip against the table. "Flappers and Bohemians and wastrel artists like me, you mean?"

Nora snorted, far less delicately this time. "As if I could avoid you if I tried."

Ruth's cheeks held more color than usual, and Nora's shoulders had lost their usual rigid set. Gloria wondered how much of that brandy they'd gone through before she returned.

Ruth picked up another notebook and flipped through it. "Rachel," she said, rolling her eyes. "Jamie decided to use me as a muse."

"I noticed that," Gloria said.

"In the original draft, she was the narrator's fiancée, you know. I gave Jamie a bit of lip over that – I've never seen him blush so much. I accused him of being too conventional. He promised he'd turn her into a sister when he revised. Somehow, a lady fox and gentleman hedgehog can simply be friends without scandalizing the children, but when humans are involved, that's just beyond the pale."

Her voice cracked on the last words, and Ruth scrubbed the heel of one hand over her eyes. Stricken, no doubt, as Gloria had been, with the knowledge that those revisions would never come.

"Oh." A slip of paper drifted free of the notebook, and Ruth held it up. "Here's your Maldefaunt."

A sales receipt, dated from April. Maldefaunt and Co Rare Booksellers, on College Street.

As Gloria tilted the receipt to better light, a shadow in the doorway caught her eye. Jamie stood there, pale and silent. He held her gaze and shook his head in a grim expression she couldn't decipher.

Then he was gone, leaving Gloria breathless and frozen.

"What is it?" Ruth asked.

"I – Eye strain, is all," she said, her voice steady. She had too much practice with such questions. She rubbed her eyes and pinched the bridge of her nose. Perhaps that really was the culprit. Fatigue, strain, guilt. That was a much more plausible option – a pity she couldn't convince herself.

"This is our best lead so far. We should visit this bookseller tomorrow. And just to be safe, perhaps neither of us should write or paint anything until we do."

Both women stared at her, and Gloria realized how ridiculous she sounded. *This is why*, she thought angrily, unsure if she was addressing herself or Jamie.

Finally, Ruth nodded. "All right. That might not be a bad idea. I'm going to make myself a nightcap. Would either of you like one?"

"A toddy does sound just the thing," Gloria admitted, pushing her chair back. Her speakeasy days had passed well before Prohibition was effected, but it still felt good to thumb one's nose at the Volstead Act from time to time. And it was awfully nice brandy.

"I feel strongly that toddies are for whiskey," Ruth said, "and a waste of good Cognac. But Cognac is all I have, and these are desperate times."

No other specters confronted her in the halls, and the warm, honeyed brandy took the edge off the day. By the time she was ready for bed, Gloria's neck had finally relaxed, and the tension in her temples had eased. She wouldn't have minded a dose of barbitone to see her through the night, but this might suffice.

She made sure her notebook and pen were on the escritoire – far from her bedside table – and latched the Corona's traveling case. Just to be safe.

CHAPTER 5

Within, the ruined abbey was even more desolate than without. Cobwebs hung in tatters, and dust lay thick as snow in the corners. It was not entirely uninhabited, as evidenced by empty bird's nests and the smell of mice, but at the moment, nothing moved but we intruders. Our footsteps broke the heavy stillness as my companion and I moved down a shadowed corridor.

The dread I had felt in my nightmares returned to me now, icing my blood and tightening my stomach. If answers did await me among these broken stones, did I truly want to find them?

As we neared the end of the hall, Esther paused, her hand closing on my arm. She spoke my name, and the sound echoed off the stones.

I tried to answer, but I could not. I felt unmoored, caught in some gray place between life and death, waking and sleep. I remembered my dream of Rachel, of the force that had stolen my voice when I tried to call to her. That same force bound me again now.

Mute, I gestured to the arched doorway ahead of us. We had to go forward – of that I was certain.

At last, Esther took my hand and nodded.

The door stood open – through it lay a scriptorium where a monk sat at a table, his pen moving steadily over parchment. Ink stained his fingers, his lips, his eyelids. Three candles had melted, winding sheets of long-cooled wax spilling from the candelabrum. Beyond the single open window, a leaden sky paled with the coming daybreak.

Bells tolled the hour.

The monk stirred, as if shaking off a trance. His pen stilled; robbed of its familiar movements, his hand trembled. He might have been ancient of years, hunched and palsied. Or perhaps he was a young man, driven to exhaustion.

The bells fell silent. Sandaled footsteps approached. Esther and I turned in the doorway to see another monk walking toward us. His eyes passed over us, passed through us. He walked through us altogether, without so much as a chill to mark his passage. Whether he was the ghost or we were, I couldn't say.

He paused just inside the room, hands clutched nervously at his waist. "Brother, you have missed prayers again, matins and laud."

The scribe raised his head, blinking wearily. For an instant, his eyes seemed to mark us, but they settled at last on the other monk. "Forgive me, brother," he said, his voice cracking with disuse. "My work got the better of me."

"The others are concerned about you, Aurelien. I am concerned. This work consumes you. No good can come of it. We should never have opened our gates to that trader."

"Deny hospitality to one in need, just because you dislike his face?"

"It's not his face I dislike – well, not only that. He wore it like a mask. And his smile..." He raised his hand to trace the stations of the cross. "He said all the right pious things when he accepted our hospitality, but I saw his smile when you took those books."

Aurelien waved his hand, still holding his quill. "It is my own heresy, I know, but I do not believe in turning away knowledge just because it comes in a strange form. I will never accept the sanctity of ignorance. Though the knowledge here comforts me not at all."

The second monk moved closer, curiosity overcoming his reluctance. "Have you translated the text, then?"

"Oh, I translated it days ago. It is a fragment of the Liber Omnium Finium: The Book of All Endings. It is a book of prophecy."

"Brother, this is heresy. You must stop. If the abbot sees this..."

Aurelien looked up, and the hollow expression in his eyes sent a shiver through me. "I don't think I can stop. I've started this, and I believe I must see it through. As I said, what the trader gave me was only a fragment. But now that I've translated it, it continues to reveal itself to me. I must know how it ends." He turned toward the window. "It begins with the sky."

Gloria woke with a start, a cry stillborn in her throat. Vertigo seized her and spun the room around in wild angles. She flung out a hand, expecting to catch the bedclothes. Instead, she struck something cool and solid. Her balance abandoned her, and she fell sideways, toppling the chair in which she sat.

The impact knocked the wind out of her. She lay on the floor, staring at the room, trying to make sense of what had happened.

Her hip and elbow throbbed; her head swam; her hands cramped so badly she gasped out loud.

She had fallen from the chair by the escritoire. Her typewriter sat uncovered on the desk, a sheet of paper fed around the roller.

Gloria levered herself carefully to her feet, cradling her hands against her chest. The page was nearly filled with type; more sheets spilled over the corner of the desk.

What time was it? Dawn? The light outside was a strange ruddy shade. She stumbled to the window and threw open the curtains. The sky was the same scabbed color as the storm over the diner yesterday.

It begins with the sky.

Gloria cast a horrified glance at the pages by her typewriter but didn't waste time reading them. Instead, she raced down the hall to Ruth's room.

"It's happening again!"

She tried the knob, and the door opened. The queer light washed the artist's room with shades of rust and garnet.

"Ruth, wake up."

Ruth's bed was empty – an instant later, Gloria found her standing in the center of her easels, a brush in her hand. Crimson paint stained her fingers, splattered one cheek. Her eyes were unfocused, blind; her mouth hung slack, a single smear of red on her lower lip. The canvas in front of her was a roiling mass of red and black.

"Ruth! Stop!"

The other woman gave no sign she heard. The brush slashed across the canvas. A sound that wasn't precisely thunder vibrated through the house.

Gloria lunged, knocking over a stack of paintings. She grabbed Ruth's wrist and tore the brush from her grip. It bounced across the floor, leaving a bloody smear behind.

"Wake up!"

Ruth gasped like a drowning man breaking the surface, and a violent shudder wracked her. Her eyes focused and she cried out, throwing off Gloria's grip with a start. Both women stumbled away from each other; Gloria fetched up against an easel, and Ruth against the foot of her bed.

Ruth stared, her face chalky behind a wild fall of hair. Her eyes were black pools. "What's happening?"

"Look outside," Gloria said breathlessly. Her heart leapt against her ribs.

Ruth turned to a window and moaned when she saw the sky. The color was already lessening, though, giving way to a saner red-gold dawn.

The artist looked down at her hands. "I was painting?"

"In your sleep, yes. I was typing in mine. I only woke a moment ago, to find the sky that way." She traced a hand through the air, from the window to the sanguine canvas.

Ruth let out a choked sound. "I've always said I'd be more productive if I didn't need to sleep." The joke fell flat. "What are we going to do?"

"I still only have the one plan. We're going to find that bookseller."

A different driver answered their call for a taxi. Gloria and Ruth sat in silence in the backseat – or rather, Gloria was silent, while Ruth deflected the cabbie's attempt at conversation with single syllables. The artist looked very different, dressed in a smart olive walking suit, her hair pinned up under a cloche. Careful cosmetics disguised the sleepless shadows beneath her eyes. Gloria no longer bothered with such artifice; she liked to tell herself that the dignity of age was armor enough against the world.

Gloria half-expected to discover the shop closed or empty, mysteriously vanished, but they found the address on College Street easily enough. Maldefaunt and Co Rare Booksellers was a narrow space wedged into a row of more academic bookshops near Miskatonic University. The windows were gray with dust, obscured by shelves and fading handbills for theatre events and various student activities.

The sidewalks were full of students – some laughing and carousing, others glumly burdened with books. Across the street, a soda shop swallowed and disgorged a steady stream of customers. Leaves mixed with stray bits of paper skittered on the pavement in the breeze. Starlings and pigeons fluttered along the rooftops and telephone lines. Another cloudy day. Gloria nearly missed the sun, but a gray sky was vastly preferable to other options.

"You want me to wait?" the driver asked.

"No," Gloria said absently, staring at the shopfront. "We may be a while."

A chime rang as they entered, fading into silence when the door closed behind them. Gloria caught her shoulder blades creeping toward her ears and forced herself to relax. Behind her, Ruth drew a deep breath and let it out slowly.

The sound was too loud for the muffled stillness. The noise of the street had vanished.

The draft stirred dust motes and sent them dancing through the wan fall of daylight. Worn carpet swallowed their footsteps, and tall shelves flanked the door, leading into a maze of books. The air was heavy with the scent of old paper and leather, mothballs and the grassy musk of decay just shy of mildew. Gloria knew many writers who waxed romantic over the smell of old bookshops, but mostly they just made her nose itch.

Gloria tried to call out, but the words caught in her throat. A soft scuff carried from further in. Rallying her resolve, she stepped forward, rounding a bookcase. Another corner, then another. Finally, they reached a more open space, where a man stood behind a desk, his back to them as he sorted through a filing cabinet.

Ruth squared her shoulders and cleared her throat. "Excuse me."

The man turned, and Gloria was chilled but not at all surprised to recognize his gaunt silhouette, the pallor of his face above his dusty black coat. His smile stretched across his narrow face and creased the corners of his eyes. Gloria had a profound sense of *déjà vu*, as though remembering a dream or something she had read long ago.

"Hello, hello. Welcome to Maldefaunt's. Feel free to browse – the best discoveries happen that way. But if you're looking for something in particular, I do have a catalogue."

"Are you the proprietor?" Gloria asked, though she was certain she knew the answer.

"I am. Gaston Maldefaunt, at your service." He gave a

theatrical bow, barely avoiding toppling a stack of books with his outstretched hand. "What may I help you find?"

"Information, as it happens. We wondered if you might recall a customer of yours from some months back. James Galbraith."

Maldefaunt cocked his head. "Galbraith. Galbraith. Ah, of course. The young writer. Yes, I remember him. He hasn't stopped by in months. He told me he would let me know when he finished his novel."

"I'm afraid he won't," Gloria said, "finish the book or tell you of it. He died recently."

"Oh." Maldefaunt pressed a hand to his chest, his long face rearranging itself into an expression somewhere between sorrow and surprise. It was a perfectly correct expression for such news, but Gloria couldn't help but feel that she was watching an elaborate mask. "How terrible."

"Yes. Yes, it is. Excuse my manners. I'm–"

"Gloria Goldberg. The novelist."

Gloria blinked. She was occasionally recognized by readers in the wild, but she was hardly as well-known as some in the New York set. Recognition was sometimes flattering, but more often disconcerting – this was definitely an instance of the latter.

"I'm sorry," she managed, "have we met?"

"No, I've never had the pleasure. I've heard you read, though."

Gloria was certain she would have remembered Maldefaunt had she seen him before. The thought of him lurking unseen at the edge of an audience gave her an unpleasant shiver.

Good manners suggested she offer him her hand to shake. She braced for a cold or clammy touch, but in fact his grip was cool and dry and perfectly normal. His hands were long and ink-stained, but otherwise neatly groomed. He smiled when he saw the similar stains on her fingers; she hadn't remembered her gloves.

"Professional hazard, I suppose," he said. "But yours are from creating words. Mine are merely from the words of others."

"This is Ruth Westmacott," Gloria continued. Her reserves of polite small talk were empty. "We're in the process of collecting Mr Galbraith's writings and organizing them. I understand he found research for his novel here."

"He came here seeking a spark, yes. I don't look the part of a muse, it's true, but my greatest joy in this world is to provide some breath of inspiration to an artist."

To a horror writer, someone like Maldefaunt was all too inspiring. Gloria had enough tact to keep that to herself, at least.

"What did he find?"

"Let me see." He folded himself into the chair behind the desk and began opening drawers. "I keep records, fortunately. Provenance is so important."

He produced a receipt book and flipped through it. She had a sharp image of his hands moving over organ keys in the vault of a decaying church.

She pinched herself surreptitiously. The man was trying to help them, and she was letting her morbid imagination run wild.

"Here." The bookseller produced a thin sheet of paper

and studied it. "Mr Galbraith visited my shop in February, and again in April. The second time, he purchased a collection that came from an estate sale. Old journals, mostly in French. Obscure family histories."

"Do you know their provenance, too?"

"Of course." His smile widened, which Gloria hadn't imagined possible. "It's a fascinating story. Sit down, please. Would you care for tea?"

"No, thank you," Gloria said, biting back an automatic polite acceptance. "Just the story, please." She settled into a cracked leather chair near the desk. After a brief hesitation, Ruth found a seat as well.

Maldefaunt stood, paced a tight circle behind his desk, then leaned against the edge. "I could regale you with the origin of Sanjeanne, France, and the abbey there, but most of that is irrelevant. There was a town, as quaint as you might imagine. There was an abbey, full of monks, praying and chanting and doing all the things monks did. The great conflicts and scandals of the time passed their little valley by."

His voice took on a soothing rhythm as he spoke, and his hands moved with a subtle, almost hypnotic gesticulation. He might have been handsome, Gloria supposed, in a shabby, Romantic sort of way, but all his various parts didn't quite fit together properly.

"Then, one day, the abbey was simply… empty. No one knows precisely when it happened. The brothers didn't come to the village for supplies on their usual day. Nor the next. Eventually, the villagers climbed the road and knocked on the gates, but no one answered. When they finally gained access, they found the entire place deserted. Food molded on plates in the dining hall. Floors were half-scrubbed, dishes half-washed. The donkeys had kicked open their pens. It seemed as though, all at once, every brother had stopped what they were doing and walked away – but the gate had been locked behind them. Only one body remained – broken on the stones beneath a high window. Long dead and picked over by carrion birds.

"The townsfolk were unsettled, as you might imagine. Then they found the only witness – aside from the donkeys. A young shepherd turned up far from his flock, shaken nearly out of his wits. He claimed that he had watched the sky above the abbey unfold itself, and a host of angels descend and carry all the brothers bodily into a blazing heaven. Beyond that, he could tell them nothing, except to murmur over and over about the terrible glory of the angels."

Gloria had a clear image of the scene – because, she realized an instant later, Ruth had sketched it.

"The town couldn't decide if the abbey had been the scene of a miracle or some great evil," Maldefaunt continued. "They barred the gates again and left it to crumble. It stood that way for over a century, until the story was nothing but a legend and no longer enough to overcome the potential of forgotten treasures. The building was eventually scoured from roof to cellar, and anything of value carted away. Including the contents of the scriptorium. Those ended up in the possession of the Le Marquand family, who had become the Lefevres by the time they came to America. I found the papers at an estate sale, and so Mr Galbraith in turn came upon them. The legend of the abbey seemed to provide the inspiration he needed for his work."

His words conjured memories of a dream. A dream, something she'd written, something Jamie had written? It was becoming impossible to tell the difference. "There was a book – a manuscript, in the abbey. A monk translated it."

Ruth turned to her with a puzzled frown. Maldefaunt merely raised an eyebrow, showing no surprise at all at the statement.

"Yes. Yes, there was. Only a fragment of a larger work, however. It has gone by many names, but to that monk it was the *Liber Omnium Finium: The Book of All Endings*. The collectors of obscure and esoteric tomes have heard many theories about its beginnings. Some say it came from Egypt, from the court of some ancient pharaoh. Others, that it survived the fall of a lost city – Atlantis, Lemuria, Ys, and so forth – no one can ever decide which one. I doubt anyone truly knows its origin. Save perhaps some insightful few who have read it."

"It was a book of prophecy?" Gloria asked.

"Of sorts. It foretold countless disasters and cataclysms. From plagues and floods and volcanoes to… far more permanent fates. It was, supposedly, destroyed centuries ago. But pages are believed to survive."

"And one such page came to the Abbey Sanjeanne," Gloria said, "where it was translated. And everyone died."

Maldefaunt shrugged, a disturbing articulation of narrow shoulders. "Who's to say they died? Perhaps it really was a miracle, and they were transported bodily to heaven. As far as the accounts know, only one of the monks died."

A soft scratching sound caught Gloria's attention. She glanced at Ruth and flinched. The artist had produced a stray piece of paper and a pencil stub, and was sketching abstractedly, gazing not at her work but into the middle distance.

"Ruth!" She leapt to her feet so abruptly that she overset her chair. It rocked into a stack of books and sent the precarious tower crashing down. Dust blossomed through the air.

Gloria's hand closed hard on Ruth's shoulder, and the artist flinched as she came back to herself. She stared at the sketch for a heartbeat, then flung it away. The pencil bounced against the dusty carpet as she scrubbed her lead-smudged fingers against her skirt.

"Not again," Ruth whispered.

"I'm terribly sorry," Gloria began, turning to the bookseller. Maldefaunt showed no interest in the fallen books, but instead studied Ruth. For an instant, Gloria thought he was smiling, but then his expression shifted into concern.

"Are you all right?"

He wore it like a mask. And his smile –

Gloria shuddered. She took a step back and caught Ruth's sleeve. "Yes, quite all right. We should be going now. Thank you for your assistance. I am sorry about the mess."

Maldefaunt dismissed the apology with a wave of his hand. "It's nothing. I am curious about the book, however. Do let me know how it turns out."

"What did you draw?" Gloria hissed as they reached the door.

"I'm not sure. I only got a glimpse of it when you shook me. Something with wings."

CHAPTER 6

Stepping back into the noise of the city felt like waking from an unexpected dream. The scene had changed in the brief time they had spent in the bookshop. The pale gray sky was sullen and lowering, and the wind ripped handbills off the walls and tugged at Gloria's hat and coat. The birds on the wires had doubled in number, hopping and shrieking and beating their wings against the air, while passersby eyed them uneasily.

"Now what?" Ruth asked, pinning her hat in place with one hand. Tendrils of hair whipped around her face.

"That estate sale he mentioned–" Gloria frowned. "A French family. Nora mentioned something similar. I need to find a telephone."

Squinting against the wind, they hurried down the street toward a telephone booth. A tattered ribbon of starlings and grackles circled overhead. Both women crowded into the booth for cover while Gloria searched for a coin in her handbag. Her hand tightened on the receiver as she waited for the operator to connect her to Severson House.

Nora answered on the third ring.

"It's Gloria," she said. "I need your help. You mentioned the Lefevre family last night. The last of them, the widow, is she still in Arkham?"

Gloria's breath echoed through the line as Nora considered. "I think so," she said. "She moved into Uptown, I heard. She teaches classes there and goes by her maiden name these days."

"Thank you."

"Have you learned anything?"

"The more we discover, the more questions I have. We'll fill you in when we get back."

"A lead?" Ruth asked when Gloria hung up.

"I hope so. We need to get to Uptown."

"That's just a few blocks over. We can ankle it."

Gloria eyed the sky. It didn't feel like rain, but she didn't trust the weather in Arkham.

A yellow cab slowed, and the driver whistled. Ruth turned with a glare, but Gloria laid a hand on her arm.

"It's all right," she said. "It's my getaway driver."

Jasper touched the brim of his hat as they slid into the backseat. "I heard Frank picked up a couple ladies off Noyes – I thought you might have gone to knock over a bank without me."

"Not yet. We don't mind a ride, though."

"Some weather this week," he agreed, deadpan. "Where to?"

"Uptown. We're looking for a Helene Lefevre. I'm afraid I don't know the address."

"Oh, Madame Lefevre, sure. I know the place."

"How long have you been in Arkham?" Gloria asked.

"Three years," Jasper said, "almost four. I have family in Kingsport. They wanted me closer after the War, and the taxi business is less cutthroat here than in New York."

Gloria studied his reflection in the rear-view mirror. In better light, he was younger than she had first imagined. Were the lumps and scars on his face the product of combat, or just a rough life? Her own sons were safely living their lives in Boston. If they had gone to the front, would they be as battered now? Would they have returned at all?

She shook off that line of thought. "Do you see a lot of the city?"

"About all there is to see. People need rides anywhere."

"And do you see any of the … stranger things that happen in Arkham?"

"Hunh." His eyebrows lifted in the shadow of his cap. "You mean like this weather?"

"Like that, yes. Or anything else that's happened in the past six months."

"Is this for something you're writing?"

"I'm not sure yet," Gloria lied.

Jasper hadn't heard the same stories Nora had, about calves and chickens, but a few of his passengers had told of strange things glimpsed at night, the sound of wings in the dark. More than one of the local indigents claimed to have seen angels, or winged demons. Ruth and Gloria exchanged a glance. How many of those "angels", Gloria wondered, looked like the figures in Ruth's sketches?

Uptown – the south side of Arkham, which seemed contradictory to Gloria when she pictured a map – was green and well-maintained. The nicest area she had seen so far. Jasper finally pulled up across from a shingle style cottage with bright trim and a sloping gambrel roof. *Madame Lefevre's*, read the tasteful sign by the front step. *Deportment, Elocution, Etiquette.*

If she hadn't been a writer, what skills would she have had to fall back on when Ben died? Would she have ended up living with Jacob or Michael and their families? She should be grateful, she knew, that her children were alive and able to support her; she was still fiercely glad that she didn't need them to.

A young woman answered the door – around sixteen, freckled and large-eyed, with hair perfectly set and skirt pleats sharp enough to slice. She led them inside to a sitting room and politely offered refreshment – which they politely declined – before going in search of Madame Lefevre.

Everything was bright and polished and perfectly angled; Gloria tucked her ink-stained hands in her lap and tried not to touch anything. A gramophone played in a farther room, and the sound of heeled shoes punctuated the music.

"Posture, Miss March," a woman called. "Chin up."

Gloria straightened her shoulders automatically and caught Ruth doing the same. A moment later, the speaker entered the room.

She was around Gloria's age, with long, iron-gray hair swept up in an old-fashioned Gibson Girl. The style matched her high collar and ankle-length skirt. Most women so attired would have looked like the worst sort of Mrs Grundy – but her poise made it seem that everyone else was terribly out of fashion.

"Good morning," she said. "I'm Helene Lefevre. How may I help you?" She fixed each of them in turn with a gimlet eye. "It's not too late to do something about that slouch."

Gloria couldn't stop a chuckle. "I'm afraid my days in a health corset are long over. I'm Gloria Goldberg, and this is Ruth Westmacott. You were Helene Griswold, weren't you?"

Madame Lefevre arched one dark eyebrow. "You don't look like most of my late husband's creditors, but if you are, I'll use you as a lesson to my girls in how to be rid of unwanted guests."

"We are not," Gloria promised. "We would like to ask you some questions, though, about some items that came from your estate."

Helene's chin lifted. "If this is about that wretched china set my husband claimed was an antique–"

"No, no. This is about some of your family's records. Are you acquainted with a man called Gaston Maldefaunt?"

Beneath her careful layer of ivory face powder, Helene blanched. She drew a deep breath. "Maldefaunt. That's a name I haven't heard in some time."

"So, you do know him?" Ruth asked.

The woman's sharp gaze settled on them again. At last, she nodded. She cocked her head toward the hall: the music still played, but the footsteps had stilled.

"Let's discuss this elsewhere, shall we?"

Helene led them into the house, through a bright room where a handful of neatly dressed girls were suddenly absorbed in anything else but eavesdropping. "Miss Upton," she said, gesturing toward a small pianoforte, "perhaps you should practice your scales. Everyone else, continue your posture exercises."

Gloria and Ruth followed her past the kitchen onto a covered patio overlooking a small garden. Past the neighboring rooftops, trees rose blazing against the gray sky. A pair of grackles perched on an empty clothesline.

Helene removed a cigarette case and an ivory holder from her pocket, then muttered a particularly unladylike word under her breath.

"Do either of you have a light?"

Ruth produced a box of matches from her handbag and traded it for one of Helene's Chesterfields.

Helene exhaled a careful plume of smoke. She didn't precisely relax – the architecture of her clothing precluded that – but her gaze softened, settling into the middle distance toward the trees.

"Maldefaunt was a friend of my father's, when I was a girl. Or at least an acquaintance. They would talk for hours about history – books and battles and the Old World. He always admired Father's library. There was a particular set of books that caught his interest – old family journals. He inquired about buying them several times. Obliquely, at first, but Father would always deflect or ignore the question. Eventually, he asked outright, and Father refused. They were family history, he said, for his children to inherit, and he wouldn't part with them. Their friendship grew strained after that, and Maldefaunt stopped dropping by."

She drew another lungful of smoke; it trickled slowly from her nostrils when she spoke. "He came back years later, after Father died. I was already married then and pregnant with my oldest son. Maldefaunt offered his condolences and his regrets at not maintaining the friendship with the family. He seemed sincere, but… I don't know what it was. I simply wasn't comfortable. It struck me how little he had aged, though at least fifteen years had passed.

"I had learned – or so I thought – the root of his interest in my family's history. The journals were written by my great-grandfather Dorian Lefevre, but they recount the history of an older ancestor, Etienne le Marquand. Etienne was an explorer, which seems to be a more glamorous way of saying a treasure hunter or someone who looted old buildings. Not a noble profession, perhaps, but it caught the interest of an adolescent with dreams of seeing more of the world than Arkham.

"Etienne was one of the first to search the ruins of the Abbey Sanjeanne, which had been abandoned long before his time and was purportedly haunted. He found little of material value but did discover a collection of books and scrolls sealed in a vault. He claimed he saw no ghosts in the abbey, although was plagued by strange dreams for weeks after.

"He wrote of an antiquities dealer who was especially interested in what he found." Here Helene took a drag of her cigarette for a dramatic pause. "A man called Maldefaunt. Etienne sold some of the books, but not all of them. Maldefaunt was insistent that he purchase the entirety of the Sanjeanne library, but by that time, Etienne had run afoul of some local magistrate or another and left the area in haste."

Gloria frowned. "So Maldefaunt – or his ancestor," she added quickly, realizing how ludicrous it sounded otherwise, "had some connection to your forebear and wanted to complete the collection?"

"So I assumed," Helene said. "Sure enough, on that visit, he asked about the books again. Money was already tighter than it had been, and I was tempted. I suspect, had Frederick been home, that he might have suggested I sell. But the books were my inheritance. I remembered Father's refusal, and I thought of my own children to come. I didn't know if they would have any interest in the affairs of our ancestors but felt I should give them the option all the same." Her lips tightened for a second, before she carefully smoothed her expression again. "Not to mention, I found the request distasteful, under the circumstances. So I, too, refused.

"He took it with good grace, but I remember thinking – I don't know what I saw in his face, but I remember thinking he was terribly angry under his composure. It frightened me, and I was grateful when he took his leave."

She shook her head, careful Gibson curls brushing her cheek. "That... may have been the last I ever saw of him. *Must* have been."

"May have been?" Gloria prompted.

"After Frederick died, and we had to sell the estate..." She soothed away another frown. "I was there the first day. I couldn't stand it, though, watching strangers walk through our house and touch all our things. I was so furious. Before I left, I saw someone heading toward the library. Tall and gaunt and pale – he looked just like Maldefaunt. Even the way he moved. But it couldn't have been him. I knew him when I was just a girl, and he was thirty then if he was a day. He would be a much older man by now."

Ruth and Gloria exchanged a long glance.

"Perhaps he is," Gloria said at last. "But someone using that name certainly acquired those papers from your estate and passed them on to a friend of ours."

Helene looked at them, and her gaze sharpened. "Passed them on? Strange that he would, since he was always so keen to have them. Why the interest, if I may ask? The idea of my family history finally falling into his hands – or whoever is using the name – doesn't please me, but he did acquire them legally."

"Our friend–" Gloria pressed her tongue against her teeth, trying to craft an explanation. "The person to whom Maldefaunt gave the journals died recently. Under circumstances we don't understand. We're concerned that something or someone may have had an… unhealthy influence on his state of mind." Not the cleverest response, but Gloria had always found her ideas better with ample time for revision.

"I see," Helene said, with a raised eyebrow that implied she most certainly did not. "I'm sorry I can't be of more help to you."

"You've given us more than we had before. Thank you for your time." Gloria paused. "Would you like them back, the journals, if we can locate them?"

This time, Helene allowed herself a frown, or at least a delicate crease along her brow. "No," she said at last. "Thank you, but there's no need. I won't read them again.

And my sons saw as much of the old country as they ever will. There's nothing left for me in that past. I've made a new life for myself, as you can see."

Having said their farewells, Ruth and Gloria lingered for a moment on the front steps of the cottage. Jasper waited for them across the street, leaning on the hood of the car with a cigarette. A line of birds had settled on the nearest phone line, chattering and jostling each other. Another flock swept in, tracing spirals in the air before they landed on roofs and fences. The sky was dark and low, clouds nearly scraping the spire of a nearby church.

Ruth abandoned her futile struggle to pin up a stray lock of hair. "So, if Maldefaunt – but it can't possibly be the same man – was so determined to get those books, why sell them to Jamie for a song?"

We never should have opened our gates to that trader. Who had said that? Had Gloria read it in Jamie's manuscript, or heard it in a dream? *I saw his smile when you took those books.*

Pages are believed to survive.

And one such page came to the Abbey Sanjeanne…

"I think…" Gloria paused. It sounded absolutely mad. But what didn't, lately? "I think he gave those journals to Jamie on purpose. That book of prophecy he spoke of. *The Book of Endings*. He wanted Jamie to find it. I think he knew what would happen."

Ruth shot her an incredulous glance. "You mean – he wanted Jamie to write the end of the world? I know something strange is going on, but–"

Gloria's awkward attempt at a reply was cut off by a shout from the street. A bird had dived at Jasper, knocking the cigarette from his hand. Another followed, then another. The murmuration of starlings lifted into the sky, tracing wild spirals through the air.

"I think it's time to go," Gloria said instead. Ruth didn't argue.

Wings beat against Gloria's face and upflung arm as they dashed for the car. Talons caught on her sleeve – fabric tore. A pair of birds snatched Ruth's cloche off her head, screeching as they fought over it.

Jasper threw the door open, and the two women tumbled into the backseat in a tangle of elbows and curses. As the door swung shut behind them, he shouted and stumbled back. Gloria pushed herself up in time to see a cloud of wings and flashing beaks engulf his head.

For an instant, all she could do was stare, frozen. Then instinct took over, and she flung herself over the front seat, bashing ribs and knees as she reached for the door handle. Jasper lunged in her direction when she called his name, clipping his shoulder on the door. Blood streaked his face. One tenacious starling clung to his collar, wings beating furiously as it struck over and over at his eyes.

Gloria seized the bird with both hands and yanked. Soft and prickling at once, like grabbing a feather pillow, except for the heat of flesh and blood. It thrashed and a talon gouged her skin. She squeezed without thinking and felt with awful clarity as slender bones cracked. With a cry of horror and disgust, she threw the bird outside.

Jasper slammed the door shut. Half his face was a mask of blood; Gloria's stomach clenched as she glimpsed torn flesh hanging from his left eyelid. He pressed one hand over his ruined eye, fumbling for the keys with the other. They fell to the floorboard, and he cursed.

"You can't drive," Gloria said, her voice far too calm. But then, she had plenty of experience in ignoring horrible sights. Feathered bodies struck the windows, talons scraping against the roof. "But I can't either."

"I can," Ruth said. "Slide over."

Gloria dragged Jasper across the seat despite his protests. She found a handkerchief in her handbag and helped him press it against the wound. Red seeped through white fabric.

Ruth squirmed into the front seat and took the keys. The engine turned over and she settled herself, hands white-knuckled on the wheel. Another bird hit the windshield, and she stepped on the accelerator.

Gloria's shoulder slammed into the door as they swung around a corner. Another sharp turn left her clinging to the seat cushions. The birds kept pace for a block, but finally a space formed between the taxi and the shrieking flock.

Other cars honked as the cab sped out of Uptown and past the university; students on crosswalks leapt out of their way. It wasn't until they reached the bridge and crossed the dark water of the Miskatonic that the avian menace finally gave up the chase.

As if they were being herded back toward Severson House. And the waiting book.

CHAPTER 7

Gloria wanted to take Jasper to the hospital, but his mistrust of authority extended beyond the police. After a quarter-hour of arguing, she and Ruth finally gave in and delivered him to the rear entrance of an unprepossessing doctor's office near the railroad tracks.

"Take the cab," Jasper said with a grimace, while a nurse with suspicious eyes and sure hands taped a bandage across his forehead. "I'll send someone to collect it. I won't be getaway driving for a while. Try to stay out of trouble for a few days."

"I'll do my best," Gloria said.

"We'll return the car in the morning," Ruth added. She and Gloria exchanged a glance. Neither of them sounded convinced, or convincing.

Gloria shut the bolt behind them when she and Ruth returned to Severson House. If her fears were true, the worst danger was in the house with them, but the solid thunk of the deadbolt was comforting all the same.

Nora emerged from the back of the house, and her eyes widened. "What happened to you?"

Stray feathers still clung to Gloria and Ruth. The talons that had stolen Ruth's hat had also grazed her face; blood dried in a dark line across one temple.

"We found Madame Lefevre," Gloria said. Her pulse had finally slowed, but she was still cold and shaky with shock. As she caught her breath, anger built inside her, forcing out the fright. "Then something else found us."

"Did you learn anything?"

"I think we've learned enough." Gloria strode into the dining room where Jamie's papers were still stacked and seized the chapters of his book. If Maldefaunt had told the truth, a single page had started this, but she didn't feel like sorting through the entire manuscript to find it.

She carried the stack back to the front room where a fire burned in the hearth. Her hands tightened on the pages; the idea of destroying any writing, let alone a friend's, filled her with nausea. "No," she muttered to herself. "I should have done this already." With that, she flung the manuscript into the hearth.

Ruth and Nora moved closer to watch the flames lick at the scattered pages. The three of them held their breaths in unison.

An instant later, Ruth cried out.

The hem of her skirt had begun to smolder. Sparks fell to the floor, and nascent flames licked the cloth – and Ruth's skin.

Nora gave a shout and rushed to Ruth's aid. Gloria stood frozen – the other woman had been nowhere near the hearth, nowhere a stray spark could have caught her – a terrible understanding unfolded. When Ruth's cry of shock turned to one of pain, Gloria broke her paralysis and fell to her knees by the fireplace. She plunged her hands into the flames and retrieved the manuscript.

The fire surrendered the offering easily, almost eagerly. A few of the pages were brown and crisp along the edges, but nothing had ignited.

A moment later, Ruth was safely put out. Her olive skirt was beyond saving, and angry red welts spotted her knee and thigh. Gloria's own knees throbbed; she had bloodied them on the hearthstones.

Nora broke the stunned silence, ushering Ruth upstairs to the washroom and retrieving ointment for her burns. Ruth shook off the doctoring halfway through and ran toward her room, a wild light in her eyes. Gloria and Nora followed.

"To hell with this," Ruth said, snatching a palette knife off her dresser. With a wordless yell, she slashed the red canvas she had painted that morning. The knife skidded off the surface, no more than nicking the top layer of paint.

An instant later, Gloria let out a yelp of her own as pain blazed along her forearm. She looked down to see blood welling from torn skin.

Half an hour later, bandaged and shaken, the three of them had once again retreated to the tenuous safety of the kitchen and the swiftly emptying bottle of Cognac. The first glass of brandy finally dissolved Gloria's reluctance. Over the course of her second, she told Ruth and Nora everything – her visions and Jamie's, her dreams in Arkham, her fears about Maldefaunt and the nature of the book. This time, there were no sidelong glances, no incredulous expressions.

"What can we do?" Ruth asked. Her voice shook, as if on the verge of tears. "We can't stop it."

Gloria had been asking herself that same question, and still had no answer. She raised her glass, then set it down before she dropped it.

In the doorway, behind Ruth and Nora, Jamie stood watching her. He lifted a hand to his throat, shaking his head in frustration.

Ruth, staring into her glass, noticed nothing. Nora caught Gloria's wide-eyed stare, but by the time she turned around, the specter had vanished.

"Oh," Gloria breathed. The book was using them. How many times had she heard some young writer say such a thing? *I don't know where the inspiration comes from. The story just takes me…* More romantic a notion than groveling one's way through trial and error, indecision and revision, years spent honing a craft. Like many romantic notions, Gloria had always considered it pure applesauce. If she were right…

"What we create becomes real," she said. "But what if we can keep control of the story?"

"How, though?" Ruth demanded. "It just… takes us, without warning."

"We have plenty of warning by now. Come with me – I have an idea."

In the blue room, Gloria sat down at her typewriter and flexed her hands. Her bandaged arm still smarted, but the slice was shallow. Only a warning – the book needed her, after all. Whatever terrible power it possessed, it could not write itself.

"Watch me," she said. "If I start to slip. If something happens, stop me."

Where to start, though? The story had always lured her in – she would have to find a way to slip past its defenses. A memory nagged at her… There.

I watched but could not speak; she was oblivious to my presence.

She slid a fresh sheet of paper into the machine and hit the carriage return. The satisfying clunk grounded her. Her fingers settled on the keys.

I watched but could not speak. I fought against the silence, forcing words through the barrier that bound my tongue. The weight built and built, until something had to give – I could not tell whether that something would be me or the compulsion.

As she typed the words, Gloria felt that weight herself. Her hands were a stranger's; her fingers moved toward different keys against her will. The words in her mind grew muddled, disconnected.

She drew a deep breath and forced herself to focus. The words were hers, not the book's.

My lips parted, air filled my lungs, and Rachel's name flew from me to shatter the stillness. She stopped with a start, scanning the night around her. Then at last her eyes found me, and I was made real again.

"That took you long enough."

Gloria didn't flinch at the voice – she was past surprise. Ruth, however, spun with a little shriek and hurled the glass she held. Gloria watched it sail through the air toward Jamie and pass through him to shatter against the wall.

Jamie glanced behind him, then offered Ruth an apologetic shrug. "Sorry. I'm sure I deserved that."

"You–" Ruth pressed her hands over her mouth as all the color drained from her face. "You–"

"You certainly did," Gloria said crisply, giving the other woman a chance to recover. "I'm told you inconvenienced Nora terribly."

Jamie flinched, then laughed. The sound was like the wind through dry grass, but still familiar. Still her friend.

"I am sorry for that," he said, inclining his head toward Nora. "I'm sorry for all of this."

"What *happened*?" Ruth cried, clenching her hands at her sides. Nora put a steadying arm around her. The caretaker's lips were pinched, her eyes wide, but otherwise her composure held firm.

Jamie shook his head. His skin was bloodless, nearly translucent. "I'm not sure. The book had me, and I knew it. I tried to fight, but nothing worked. No matter what I did, I just kept writing. Writing what it wanted me to.

"The only way I could think to stop it was by taking my own life, though the idea terrified me. That was how the last poor soul tried to escape, and not even that was enough. I wrote to Gloria in desperation – I wonder now how much of that idea was truly mine, and how much was the book searching for a new victim in case I succeeded.

"That last night was terrible. I couldn't stop writing. The words burned in my mind, until the only release from the pain was to set them free in the world. I looked outside and saw the sky grow red, roiling and seething. I ran to the balcony–" His face twisted with the memory. "I don't know any more if I meant to jump or not. I'm not sure I knew in that moment. The balcony began to give, and I had this instant of terror and relief, all twisted together."

"You're skipping over some important exposition," Gloria said, to distract all of them from that awful image. "How did this happen in the first place?"

Jamie gave her a lopsided smile. "I never do know where to start, do I? I'd been struggling with a novel for months. Everything I began felt like rubbish. Then I found the history of the Sanjeanne Abbey in Maldefaunt's shop. The story of its rapture. It caught my interest immediately, the inspiration I'd searched for. Tucked in among the journals was a single sheet of parchment, old and thick and scraped into a palimpsest. I could just make out a few faded lines. The first was: *It begins with the sky.*"

"*The Book of Endings.*"

Jamie nodded. "The Lefevre journals call it *Le Livre des Fins*. To the translator in the abbey, it was the *Liber Omnium Finium: The Book of All Endings.*"

"I dreamed of it. Of the abbey and monk. Maldefaunt knew about it."

Colorless lips thinned. "Oh, yes, he knows it."

"Did he … create it?"

"I don't think so. Something greater than him must have done that. He's only a servant. A messenger. A plague carrier."

"The trader at the abbey."

"Yes. The trader, the bookseller – I imagine he's had a hundred guises throughout the years. Scattering pages all over the world. Waiting for them to find their prey. I don't properly understand it. Aurelien has a better sense of it."

"The monk? You've… spoken to him?"

"He exists, trapped in the book. Like me."

"Will he speak to us?"

"I think so. But you'll need to pull him out, as you did me. The book protects itself and its secrets."

"How do we draw him out?"

"With words, like you just did." He turned toward Ruth. "Or, perhaps, literally."

The artist stared at her dead friend, looking half a ghost herself. Then her jaw firmed, and her chin lifted.

"I'll get a sketchbook."

Still pale but no longer shaking, Ruth hurried to her room and returned with a sketchbook and charcoal pencil. She sank cross-legged onto the floor beside Gloria's desk, pulling her hair back in a clumsy chignon.

"All right. Describe the scene."

Gloria closed her eyes, conjuring the images of a dream.

The door stood open – through it lay a scriptorium, where a monk sat at a table, his pen moving steadily over parchment. Ink stained his fingers, his lips, his eyelids. Three candles had melted, winding sheets of long-cooled wax spilling from the candelabrum. Beyond the single open window, a leaden sky paled with the coming daybreak.

Bells tolled the hour.

The monk stirred, as if shaking off a trance. His pen stilled;

robbed of its familiar movements, his hand trembled. Pale hair drifted around a narrow face. He might have been ancient of years, hunched and palsied. Or perhaps he was a young man, driven to exhaustion.

The bells fell silent. The prime bells. He had missed matins and laud. He had worked through the night.

Footsteps approached. A man and woman paused in the doorway, staring at the monk. A gulf of time separated them. Was he the ghost, or were they?

The scribe raised his head, blinking wearily. After an instant, his gaze settled on the intruders, and his eyes widened.

"What phantoms are you?" he asked, his voice cracking with disuse. "You are not from this place. Or from my book."

"No," the woman answered, "but you are from ours." The monk was not, she realized, truly speaking English. But the logic of dreams translated his words from some ancient dialect of French into something she understood. It seemed to provide the same courtesy to him in return.

The man held out his hand. "Come, brother. Leave this prison for a moment and speak with us."

The pen fell from the monk's fingers. "I know you, do I not?"

"Yes. We've met before. We're both prisoners here."

With halting steps, the monk crossed the scriptorium to stand at arm's length before them. His gaze took in their foreign clothes and the woman's cropped hair, before lingering on her face. "You I have not seen before."

"No, we haven't met. My name is Esther Gloria. Will you come and speak with us, friar?" She held out her hand as well. Together, she and her companion took hold of the scribe's bony wrist and pulled him gently over the threshold.

"Slow down," Ruth called from the floor. "I can't sketch as fast as you can type." She looked up and flinched. "For Heaven's sake, stop that!"

Gloria and Jamie stood in the center of the room. In front of them stood a gaunt, stooped man wearing a much-mended robe. Hair as colorless as a cobweb floated around his narrow jaw, and his hands and face were stained with ink. He stared around the room and made a soft, wondering sound.

His eyes focused at last on Jamie. "James, it's you." Thank goodness the translation of the dream had come to life with him, Gloria thought, or this would be an awkward conversation indeed. "This is not the book."

"I'm afraid it is," Jamie said grimly, "or will be soon. The poison spreads. It has infected my friends now. We must find a way to stop it, before it finally completes itself."

Aurelien shook his head. "I tried. I damned myself to stop it, and it continues all the same. Now you have joined me in damnation to no greater avail."

Gloria cleared her throat loudly. "Before anyone joins anyone else in damnation, perhaps introductions are in order. Followed by explanations."

"Excuse me," Jamie said with a wry smile. "Gloria Goldberg, Ruth Westmacott, Nora Addison, this is Brother Aurelien, of the Abbey Sanjeanne. I began dreaming of Aurelien shortly after I found the page, but we didn't properly meet until… the end."

Ruth unfolded herself from the floor, swiping a strand of hair out of her eyes; the motion left charcoal smeared across her forehead. "Why are you damned?"

Aurelien's gaze swept the room again, settling nowhere.

"I took my own life. But it began before that ..." He blinked and collected himself with a shudder. Bony arms folded across his chest, hugging himself tight.

"I was a scribe, a translator. One of the most skilled in my order in the craft of language. Pride was my sin then, though I tried to attribute all my works to the glory of God. A trader came to us one day, not an uncommon thing. He sought shelter from the elements and offered in return a selection of manuscripts he had collected abroad. He spoke softly and said all the right words, but several of my brothers distrusted him. I told myself I was above such unfounded judgment, but perhaps it was only that he flattered my work and praised my love of learning.

"I took the manuscripts he offered – none of them strange or scandalous. Among them, I found what seemed a blank page, a palimpsest. I could make out the impression of a few lines in Latin. *Ex caelo incipit*, read the first. It begins with the sky." He glanced up, as if seeing that sky again beyond ceiling and roof.

"I traced that line with my pen, and another followed, then another. Visions began to unfold to me – first in dreams, then waking, some so strong I was stricken to my knees with them. My brothers feared for my health, then my sanity, and eventually my soul. I worked day and night recording the images I saw – I neither ate nor slept nor prayed. I had realized by then that something was terribly wrong, but no matter how I tried, I could not stop.

"I tried to control the words. I wrote of the glory of the Lord, of the saints and prophets. I wrote of the heavenly hosts, but the will of the pages corrupted everything.

Blasphemy piled upon blasphemy. My brothers tried to intervene – they tore the quill from my hand, wrenched the pages from my grasp, locked me in my cell. All too late. I wrote in dust and blood, carved stone with stone. I looked out my window and saw the sky begin to open, and knew the end was upon us all. The heavens opened and a host poured forth, but these were not the angels of scripture.

"Only one course remained to me that I could see. I had not yet written the end. I must not, but I knew my will was too weak, and prayer was no longer a respite. I watched those winged shapes descend, and took the only action left to me. I accepted my damnation and threw myself from the window."

Silence filled the room. Gloria was acutely aware of the sound of her breathing, and of Ruth and Nora's. Neither Jamie nor the monk drew breath.

"What then?" Nora finally prompted.

Aurelien blinked. "I lay broken on the stones, trying to pray. I watched as the false angels closed like locusts over the abbey and carried my brothers away. They bore them up to that shining breach in the sky, into some strange heaven like none we had been promised. The sky closed after them, and the end did not come. I believed I had succeeded. I had died unshriven, in mortal sin, but perhaps God would forgive me anyway. That thought was with me as my eyes closed."

Gaunt fingers trembled as he held himself. "I knew better, of course. I woke again to neither heaven nor hell, but to a sort of purgatory – my soul now dwelled inside the book. Not just the page that I had stumbled upon, but the entire book. *Liber Omnium Finium: The Book of All Endings.* I dwell there even now."

"Well," Ruth said, her voice bright and brittle, "I'm not throwing myself out of any windows. Clearly that solution hasn't been much use, so perhaps we should try something else."

Jamie shrugged. "Burning it is no use, as you learned. I tried to tear the wretched thing, but only sliced my hands." He spread his palms; the stigmata no longer dripped blood, but red lines remained. "But I can't accept that this is our only fate."

"I could not find any way of defeating the book," Aurelien said, "but I set myself against it, nonetheless. All my visions, all that terrible prophecy – I could feel it pressing against me, searching for a release. The book wants to be written and works its will on the world until it finds some unwitting vessel. I met others there in that liminal place, others like me. Poor damned souls who had become the scribes of their own destruction. Human, many of them, but some… I do not know what they were, but they were not made in the image of God. Unless God wore stranger faces than my brethren could ever conceive." He smiled sadly. "Even now, I am a heretic."

It was a fascinating line of thought, but this was not the hour for it. "You set yourself against the book," Gloria prompted.

"Ah, yes. I cannot properly explain it. I put myself between that weight of prophecy and its unwritten ending. I set my will against it in an attempt to keep it from ensnaring some other poor soul. For a time, I think, it worked. But it wore on me. All I could think of eventually were my brothers, carried to heaven, and how much I missed them. If the end came at last, would we be reunited? Would I finally have the chance to beg their forgiveness? And so my will eroded, like stone beneath the elements, until finally–"

"Until finally I found the page," Jamie said.

Movement caught Gloria's attention. Ruth still held her charcoal pencil, turning it absently between her fingers. Her sketchbook lay safely out of reach, but her free hand slid closer to the escritoire and the paper there.

"Ruth!"

Ruth looked at her outstretched hand as though it were a stranger's. "I'm sorry – It just creeps in. I'm so tired. It's hard to concentrate."

As soon as she heard the word *tired*, Gloria felt all the fatigue that dragged at her, weighing on her bones and scraping inside her eyelids.

"We have to rest. We can't do anything like this."

"How can we, though? As soon as we sleep the book will move us around like puppets again."

"I have an idea," Nora said.

Three quarters of an hour later, the caretaker had collected Ruth's art supplies and Gloria's notebook and typewriter and locked them in the attic with Jamie's things, and scoured the Cerulean Room for any stray pens, pencils, or lipsticks. Ruth's room was off limits; it would take days to remove all the paints and cosmetics squirreled away in every drawer.

Nora had escorted Ruth to her room to find a change of clothes. Aurelien had faded back into whatever strange netherworld he inhabited, leaving Gloria alone with Jamie.

"Gloria." Jamie reached out as though he might touch her arm, pulled back again. "Before you sleep, can we talk?"

She looked up at him and swallowed, her throat gone abruptly dry. "Yes. Yes, I think we ought. I'm sorry," she said, before he could speak. "So profoundly sorry. You reached out to me, and I put you off, time and again. It was cowardice. If I had only been braver–"

"Things would have been different?" He gave her a sad, sideways smile. "We can't know that. I might have ended up here all the same. Or the book would only have snared someone else. I won't deny it hurt me, all the evasions and refusals. But I can't blame you for this."

"You were right," she said. "The things you saw, the things you dreamed. I saw them, too. I've seen them since I was a child."

Jamie nodded. "My parents didn't know what to do with my night terrors and wild stories," he said. "Doctors and tinctures and all manner of things to calm the mind. I was lucky they didn't believe in ice baths and straitjackets. It got better, thank goodness, as I got older. I learned what to say and what not to say, and stopped frightening everyone around me. When I started reading ghost stories and weird fiction, at first I was excited to learn about other people's terrors, and then disappointed when their imaginings seemed so bland compared to the things I saw. I remember the first time I found one of your stories: 'The Alchemist's Legacy'. The things you described, Clarissa's visions of the vast library on a dying world. I knew that place! Nearly as well as I knew the little bookshop near my parents' house." He shook his head. "It was like I'd been struck by lightning. I knew in that instant I wasn't mad. Or, at least, I wasn't alone."

Gloria stood in silence for several heartbeats. A weight

filled her chest and caught in her throat. "I never had anyone to listen to my visions," she said at last. "Not my parents, or friends, or even my husband. It was always too much, too strange, too far beyond anything they understood. So, I turned them into fictions. By the time I met you, I couldn't admit they were anything else. I didn't think of what it must have been like for you."

She swallowed past that pressure in her throat. "I had a chance to help someone the way no one helped me, and I was too afraid to take it. I'm sorry I wasn't there for you."

Once more, he reached for her and pulled away. "We all have to survive as best we can. Gloria–" His chest swelled as if he still drew breath. "If you and I share these dreams, others must, too."

She nodded slowly. "They're not merely dreams. If Maldefaunt and this terrible book exist, what other horrors also exist beyond the waking world?"

"I always wanted to know," he said with a grimace, "and now look at me. I'm glad you finally spoke to Ruth and Nora, at least."

"It wasn't easy," she admitted. "Even when they saw the same terrors I did, I still feared they would turn away."

"If I'd thought to talk to them, perhaps I would be more corporeal now."

"We can't know," she echoed. "And between the two of us, we've certainly put them in danger. At least together, we may have a chance of stopping this."

The midnight chimes had faded when Ruth and Gloria lay down. Nora tied a length of twine between their hands and another from Ruth's ankle to the foot board. If either woman sleepwalked, or tried to leave, the other would be alerted.

"I heard a story about two sisters who lived in a lighthouse," she said as she tied the knots firmly. "One of them would sleepwalk, so this was how they kept her from drowning."

"Did it work?" Ruth asked.

"I hope so." She stared at both of them, her brown eyes pinched with concern. "Get some rest. I'll be outside the door." She turned the lamp down as she left, leaving the two women alone in the dark.

"I can't admit it in front of her," Ruth whispered, "but I'm frightened."

Gloria let out a sound that wasn't quite a laugh. "I should damned well hope so. I'm terrified!"

"Thank goodness. You're so... calm."

"Long years of practice. I assure you, it's all a facade."

They laughed together, and Gloria pretended she didn't hear the hitch in Ruth's breath. No, she thought an instant later – she'd done enough pretending. She reached out for Ruth's hand and held it tight.

Sleep came in waves, ebb and flow. Every time Gloria sank below, some noise or image startled her awake again. After a terrifying instant of falling upward into a maw in the sky, she opened her eyes to the shadowed ceiling. Her heart kicked against her ribs and sweat stuck her nightdress to her chest.

Ruth shifted beside her, breath changing. "You, too?" she whispered.

"Me, too," Gloria replied. The quality of the darkness had changed, the depth of the stillness outside the windows.

"What are we going to do?"

"I don't know. There must be something. I refuse to accept this future is set in stone."

"I never believed in fate or predestination. But this… All my life I've fought to make my own future. To never feel helpless or pushed around by the whims of the world. And here I am."

"And here we are." The pressure of unshed tears filled Gloria's skull. She couldn't remember when last she'd cried. When Ben died, surely…

Silence filled the space between them for a time.

"What Aurelien said," Gloria murmured, more to herself than to Ruth, "about setting himself against the book. Guarding the world from the ending…"

"But he failed," Ruth said. "In the end, he failed."

"Everything fails in the end, doesn't it? He succeeded for decades. Centuries. Five hundred years can hardly count as a failure. If one of us could hold out that long, I'd call it quite a success."

As she spoke the words aloud, her fears coalesced, transforming into a cold, grim determination. Gloria sat up and reached for the knotted cord. "We're not sleeping tonight. Come on. It's time for a council of war."

CHAPTER 8

They gathered in the kitchen – three women and two ghosts – while Nora put on a pot of coffee. Gloria had always considered herself fairly staid compared to New York's bright young things, but she doubted even the Fitzgeralds or the Vicious Circle ever found themselves in company quite like this.

Gloria accepted coffee with a grateful nod. She cradled the cup, letting the warmth soak into her bones. As the silence stretched, she looked up to find everyone watching her expectantly.

She breathed slowly and rolled her shoulders, settling her nerves the way she did before a reading. "We have to set a new guardian against the book," she said. "I think everyone can agree that holding out a few hundred more years is preferable to an immediate cataclysm."

Brother Aurelien recoiled; Ruth and Jamie opened their mouths to speak simultaneously. Gloria kept going. "I'll do it," she said, forcing the words out. "You've already sacrificed enough in this attempt, Jamie."

"Don't be ridiculous!" Jamie made an angry sweeping gesture, which would have struck Nora had he been corporeal. Instead, his hand passed through her shoulder, earning him a narrow sidelong glare. "I'm already dead! If I can be of more use in death than life, by God I will. Those of us among the living shouldn't be so quick to waste that opportunity." His voice softened, and he leaned forward. "You have the chance to act on all those visions you've ignored. A chance to help someone else like you and me. Don't throw that away."

Gloria leaned back in her chair, swallowing arguments. That thought was as daunting as the idea of sacrificing her life, if not more so. But he was right. "How, though? How do you become the guardian? Can you explain it, Aurelien?"

The monk lifted his hands in a shrug. "No better than I have. I was there, inside the world of the book. I saw an opening and wedged myself into it. Despite my folly and pride, I had years of training in prayer and meditation. That, I think, was what let me endure as long as I did." He tilted his head, fixing her with an unsettling bright stare. "You speak of replacing me. Do you understand what that means? I died unshriven, with a mortal sin staining my soul. I am *damned*. Only the influence of the book granted me a reprieve from an eternity of worse torment. If you remove me as its guardian, I will no longer be spared."

Gloria met his gaze and saw the strength of his certainty and fear. A facile response about Heaven's mercy rose to her tongue, but she bit it back in time. Her mother's orthodoxy had been just as strong, if different in its application.

"But the book still claims you," Jamie said gently. "You

haven't truly been its guardian since it sank its hooks into me, yet here you are. Why do you fear being set free now?"

The monk glanced aside for an instant. "I may have failed in my appointed role," he said after a pause, "but I have not yet been replaced. If you supplant me... I accepted my fate when I chose the fall but having been granted even this purgatorial reprieve–" He swallowed. "I am still the guardian – if you wish to stop the book, help me regain my strength, and I will continue to stand against it."

From the corner of her eye, Gloria saw Ruth shift her weight, unease flashing across her face. She exchanged a glance with Jamie and saw the same misgivings reflected there.

Nora's eyes narrowed, then softened. "I was raised to believe in the same things, friar. Salvation and damnation. I understand, believe me. But you've stood long enough. The burden has passed to someone else." She lifted one hand, palm up to encompass the entire room. "To all of us. No one can face something like this alone. We have to help each other. We do our best, and trust in mercy. That's all we can do."

"Mercy." Aurelien shook his head. "Of all the heresies to have tempted me, that is surely the sweetest. And the one in which I can never trust." He drifted back from the table, his entire outline flickering for an instant. "What makes you think you might succeed where I failed?"

"We *can* affect the book," Ruth said. "Gloria summoned Jamie and let him speak. We conjured you up, friar."

Aurelien shook his head again, a sharp jerk of frustration. "I tried to write anything other than what it showed me, but I could not. It corrupted every word."

Gloria looked from Ruth to Jamie. Goosebumps roughened her arms as an idea took hold. "You were a scribe. A translator. I mean no slight to your abilities, brother, but those are not the same as being a *writer*."

A muscle leapt along Aurelien's jaw. His hands clenched on his sleeves. "I don't know. I don't–" He flickered again, then vanished entirely.

Silence held the room until Gloria swallowed. "Jamie – are you sure you want to do this?"

He turned away from the empty space the monk had occupied and met her eyes. "I don't *want* to, but I'm certain it's the best choice. I'm willing to take the risk."

They climbed the attic stairs at just past three in the morning, carrying every lantern Nora could find in the house. The light painted the room with gold and threw their shadows long and liquid across the walls. Gloria's typewriter sat next to Jamie's on the desk; Ruth maneuvered her easels nearby, laying out paint and charcoal in neat rows. When she finished, she rolled back the rugs to bare the warped floorboards.

"What are you doing?" Gloria asked.

"Making a circle." Ruth held up a stick of white chalk. "To keep out… whatever's out there. While we work. Or maybe to keep whatever's in here with us from getting out."

"Will it help?"

Ruth shot her a narrow glance. "Can it hurt?"

Gloria raised her hands in acquiescence.

Ruth crouched on the floor and began to draw. The circle was round and even – Gloria could hardly have done it so well with a compass. After the thick chalk line, she made another loop, this time tracing strange symbols or letters inside.

"Where did you learn to do this?" Gloria asked.

"I told you I've seen more than table-tapping. This is the first time I've done it myself, though."

When the circle was nearly complete, she paused and looked up. "Nora, come inside." Jamie and Gloria were already within its confines.

The caretaker shook her head. The shotgun rested easily on her shoulder. "You do what you have to in there. I'll wait here. You may need more than words and chalk."

An expression passed over Ruth's face that Gloria would have needed an hour of revisions to properly describe. She filed it away for future reference. If there was a future.

"There is a future," she whispered to herself. Speaking the words out loud to make them real. *Future irrealis*.

"Wait."

Gloria glanced up to see Aurelien outside the unfinished boundary. His face was composed, smooth as a mask. "This is madness, but I don't know what isn't anymore. May I join you?"

Ruth hesitated for an instant before lifting a hand in invitation. The monk drifted through the opening, never touching the floor. Ruth drew the last symbol, and the circle was sealed. Even if it had no tangible effects, the act was powerful all the same.

The wind gusted outside, rattling tree branches against the roof and shaking the patio doors. Flames swayed on lamp wicks and shadows danced along the walls and ceiling.

Gloria sat down at the desk. Her chest and stomach were cold; her hands trembled.

"Jamie, we can try something else. You don't have to do this."

"This is quite likely our only chance. I won't waste it with cowardice. Besides, what else would I do with this existence? Haunt you and whisper all my stories until you wrote them down?"

Gloria laughed in spite of everything. "You could haunt Hemingway instead. Or the Fitzgeralds. I don't think poor Scott's nerves could take that, though."

The wind blew harder. A dim reddish cast crept over the black velvet sky, but dawn was still hours away. A haunting cry pierced the darkness outside – the high trill of whippoorwills. Beneath that, a lower, steadier rhythm rose; in the center of the circle, Aurelian chanted under his breath, hands clasped and head bowed.

"All right," said Ruth, loading the last colors onto a palette. "How shall we do this?"

"The book needs a guardian. We're going to turn Jamie into one."

Jamie laughed, light and hollow. "And my mother worried that I would waste my life being a poet."

"Gloria!"

She flinched at Ruth's sharp cry, then looked down. Her hands had settled on the typewriter keys without her noticing. Pressure already moved through tendon and bone, ready to spell out the end of the world.

"The longer we hesitate, the more it corrupts our will," Jamie said. "Write."

"Where do I start?" Mountains and drifts of paper rose around her, a scattered mosaic of scenes and ideas.

The end. Write the ending. Spell it out.

Pain lanced through her skull like a knife prying between her eyes. Her hands cramped with the effort of resisting.

Finish it.

Fine, she shot back. *I will.*

She rifled through the pages, searching for the last scene Jamie had written. The shifting light made her squint; she might need reading glasses soon. That was a problem she would welcome, under the circumstances.

"Hurry, please!" Ruth called. "It's telling me what to paint!"

Gloria found the sheet. Her fingers settled on the keys again, this time with purpose.

I had read to the end.

I don't know if I spoke the final words aloud. I felt my tongue shape them but could hear nothing over the roar of blood in my ears. Or was that the roar of the storm? Thunder shook the house and branches lashed the windows as the wind surged.

A sound – that growl that wasn't quite thunder – shivered through the house. The reverberation mingled with the cadence of Aurelien's chant.

My vision swam, washed with red and ringed with darkness. A pale figure stood in front of me – only after I rubbed my eyes did I realize it was Rachel.

My beloved Rachel, tears tracking her chalk-white cheeks, her hair an auburn storm across her shoulders. She clutched a knife, her knuckles bloodless against the hilt. She trembled such that I feared she would cut herself.

A sense of momentum surged through Gloria, hot and sweet. That brilliant rush she always felt when the end of a story came together. But this was a trap – this was the book, reveling in its victory. She shook her head, searching for grim, cold clarity instead.

Esther stood behind her, a fountain pen like a dagger in her hand. Realization swept over me. They had meant to stop me from finishing the book, however they had to. They had known what must be done. But at the last moment, love had stayed their hands.

The book fell from my nerveless fingers. An instant later, the knife fell from Rachel's. We embraced, sobbing. I had failed to stop the book. She had failed to stop me. At least we would be together at the end.

"This isn't over yet," Esther said.

Isn't it? Doubt closed iron bands around her chest, shattering her momentum as it stole her breath. The storm had taken on a steady rhythm, mingling with the monk's prayers, with her own heartbeat.

"*Confice,*" Aurelien murmured.

"Don't stop," Jamie said, his voice thin and faint.

"*Isn't it?*" *Hand in hand, Rachel and I turned to the open casement and gazed upon the sky.*

Red-black clouds roiled, pressing low against the roofs and treetops. Scarlet light seethed within, more sinuous than lightning. Every flicker illuminated the winged shapes waiting above us. The nightjars sang, a chorus of the damned.

Gloria swayed in her chair, fighting a wave of dizziness. The cry of the whippoorwills deafened her.

"The sky!" Ruth called out. Her hair had fallen free

of its pins and spilled wild around her shoulders. Tears glistened gold in the lantern light. The canvas in front of her was a writhing mess of red and black brushstrokes.

The sky was once more the color of scabs. Already, a seam was forming in the clouds.

They would part and sweep aside to lay bare the firmament beyond. I could feel the waiting stars.

Gloria shuddered, clenching her fists until they ached. It was no use. The ending was written. All she was doing was spelling out their fate. She had seen this coming her entire life, had ignored a hundred warnings about the horrors hiding beneath the skin of the world. She had built a life of clever lies and misdirection, and wasted every chance to *do* anything –

Confice.

She glanced at Aurelien and caught him staring at her from beneath his cowl. In its shadow, his eyes were black. A ghastly smile bisected his narrow face.

"Don't stop now," he said, lifting one long, ink-stained hand. The gesture was fluid and disjointed all at once – a marionette's motion. His voice was smoother, coldly amused. "You're so close. *Confice.* Finish it."

Jamie swung around, eyes widening. "No!" He lunged, closing his hands in the front of Aurelien's robes. His touch might pass through the living, but it struck a fellow ghost solidly enough. The monk staggered and slumped, catching at Jamie's wrists to keep from falling.

"What are you doing?" Jamie cried, shaking the other man sharply.

"I'm sorry," Aurelien said. "He whispers to me

unceasingly. He will cast me from the book if I don't help him, straight into the fires of the pit."

"The entire world is doomed if the book has its way! Is your soul so precious that you would destroy the rest of creation to save it?"

"Gloria!"

Ruth's voice jerked her out of a fugue. She had only lost a second – Jamie and Aurelien hadn't moved, but her hands had returned to her typewriter keys.

The house shook under the onslaught of the wind. Winged shapes moved in the sky, spiraling down like bats.

Far larger than bats, Gloria realized, as they drew closer.

"The angels," Aurelien whispered.

The wind howled; the balcony doors burst open, flying outward. Glass panes shattered. A stack of pages lifted off the desk and flurried across the room.

A figure filled the opening, wings stretching beyond the door frame. Part bird, part beast, almost insectile. Just as Ruth had drawn it, cobbled together like some dreadful sculpture. Red storm-light flashed through the gaps and tatters in its wings. Its long, beaky maw opened on a hideous screech.

The shotgun answered. Gloria jerked back and watched, deafened, as Nora strode forward – the gun steady on her shoulder – and emptied the other barrel.

The creature fell backward and disappeared. Nora retreated from the window, pulling shells from her pocket. She caught Gloria's eye and gestured impatiently. *Keep going.*

Lightning flashed, searing crimson. By its glare, Gloria

saw a clawed limb reach over the edge of the balcony. Another followed, and the wounded monstrosity hauled itself over the ledge. One wing hung shredded and useless, and it limped as it advanced, but still it came.

Ruth shouted a warning. Nora looked up as the second shell slid home in the breech. The barrel rose – too slowly.

The creature ripped the shotgun out of her grip, sent it spinning into the darkness on the far side of the room. Its next strike caught her across the face. Nora spun beneath the force of the blow and went down in a heap.

Ruth screamed her name. She leapt forward but caught herself just inside the circle. The monstrous angel turned toward her, beak snapping. Its good wing eclipsed the lantern light. It swayed, balanced on taloned toes, scarcely a foot of space between its claws and Ruth.

Those claws flashed. Gloria's throat closed on a scream. But instead of raking Ruth's face, sparks flared from the boundary of the circle and the creature lurched back a step. It hissed like a steam engine but stayed where it was.

Jamie released Aurelien and leaned close to Gloria. "Don't stop," he urged. "This is our only chance."

Shock had cleared her head for a moment, but now the voice of the book built inside her again. Gloria fought to focus on Jamie's words instead. Her own words.

"This isn't over," Esther repeated. She picked up the book. Such an innocuous thing in her hand, that slim leather-bound volume. She opened it to the back, where blank pages remained. She offered me the book and her pen. "Stories don't truly end, do they? Write something else."

Rachel let go of my hand.

The seam in the sky gaped wider and light poured out like molten gold. Aurelien stared at that glow, his face slack.

"My brothers are there, waiting for me—"

"What if you could join them?" Gloria asked.

His eyes were wide with terror and awe, but at least they were his own again and not Maldefaunt's. For how long?

"I've failed them twice over. How could I face them again?" He shook his head.

"It's not too late," Gloria said, as much to herself as to the monk. "This can't be the end. We can still change things." She looked at Jamie. "We can't undo the past, but it's not too late to ask for forgiveness."

Ruth's breath – wet and ragged with sobs – hitched sharply. Nora was moving. The caretaker levered herself up on one arm, swaying as she rose to her knees. Blood glistened black on her face.

Whether the creature heard Nora move, or whether Ruth's startled glance gave her away, Gloria wasn't sure. It swiveled as the woman regained her feet, gathering itself for a strike.

This time, Nora was faster. She shoved the monster square in the wounded shoulder, driving it backward into the circle.

Sparks flared again, bluish-white and blinding. The creature shrieked and flailed as it tried to escape, but those sparks kindled to flame, and its leathery hide caught. Pale fire licked across its outstretched wing, consuming the torn membrane. Skin crumbled and bones cracked.

Less than a minute later, all that remained was a pile

of bones and flickering embers. The circle spit a few final sparks, then dimmed.

Sobbing, Ruth leapt across the boundary and flung her arms around Nora.

Aurelien looked from the fading circle to the sky, where the monstrous host still circled. "Forgiveness," he murmured.

"Redemption," Gloria said. "There's still a chance for it."

His face softened, eyes liquid. "After all my hubris, after all my failure, they still wait for me."

Another winged creature dove toward the balcony. With a heartbreaking cry, Aurelien ran to meet it, flinging himself into the air, into its embrace. The creature jerked back in surprise, great wings beating the air. Then, as though that were all it had been waiting for, it lifted higher. The monk clung to its neck as it rose toward the burning sky and vanished into the light.

Gloria blinked, her vision blurring. Tears spilled down her cheeks. For an instant, the terrible pressure eased, and her thoughts were her own again.

Thunder spoke, very close. Rain struck the roof like stones. Gloria didn't have to look to know what color that rain would be.

"Hurry!" Jamie shouted over the roar.

Ruth released Nora and took up her paints again. Her brush moved frantically across the canvas, framing the storm with dark lines.

I took the book and the pen. I had read to the end, and now the story lived inside me and I within it. We were bound together, the book and I. It was true – stories didn't end, no matter where the pages stopped. If the story didn't end, neither could I. And if I couldn't end, neither could the story.

I set pen to paper and began to write.

"It's working," Jamie said, wonder in his voice.

"Jamie!" Ruth turned, stepping to the side so they could see her painting. A door framed the raging red storm. A portal into the sky.

Jamie looked at Gloria, his eyes wide and black. "Thank you. Thank you for this. But the work isn't over."

"It isn't over," she said, her throat tight.

The wind gusted again; one of the lamps went out. An inhuman screech rose beyond the balcony.

Jamie held out a hand – his palm had healed. He touched Gloria's shoulder, and for an instant, she felt the weight and warmth of his grip. Then he turned toward the painting and the waiting door.

The door opened, and I stepped inside. I heard Esther's whispered benediction. Rachel called my name as it closed behind me. Then nothing. Nothing but me and the story.

One step, then another, and Jamie reached the canvas. He stretched out, and the door opened. Ruth called his name as he stepped through, her voice cracking.

"No story truly ends," Gloria spoke against the fury of the storm.

The door opened, and he was gone.

The breach in the sky stretched wider, blinding bright. Thunder roared, shaking the house to its foundation. Rachel threw her arms around Esther. They clutched each other, trembling, waiting for the end.

After a moment, Gloria realized the end had yet to

manifest. She opened her eyes, shaking her head to dislodge a strand of Ruth's hair from her face. She didn't remember standing up.

Ruth released Gloria and reached out to take Nora's hand. The three of them stood in front of the shattered windows, staring at the sky.

The wind subsided to a steady breeze. The red clouds faded, losing their color until they were only dull gray thunderheads. With a groan, those clouds opened, and a cold, clean rain fell over Arkham.

CHAPTER 9

This time, fire consumed the pages. Gloria sat on the hearth – her hands gray with ash, the thin, pungent smoke of burnt paper tickling her nostrils – and fed them one by one into the flames.

Jamie's notes, Jamie's writing, her own revisions and additions. It had the makings of one of the best books she might ever write, not to mention leaving Jamie with a legacy beyond that of a minor poet who died too soon. She pretended it was only the smoke that made her eyes water.

"Are you sure?" Ruth had asked when they collected the papers. "So much work went into this. So much pain. To destroy it…"

"It's too dangerous. Even with our page sealed, to call any attention to *The Book of Endings* is too much of a risk. Besides, I have all the inspiration I need right now."

Ruth sat beside her, passing over the next sheaf of pages as each one burned. Her own sketches were included in the stacks, all the illustrations she had done for Jamie. The paintings she had cut from their canvases; Nora promised to see them destroyed in the next brush-burning. Only one had been spared – the painting of Gloria at her typewriter, poised against the wave of darkness.

"What about… the page itself?" Ruth asked, as the pile of papers dwindled. That, they knew, would not burn. It was currently sealed in a tan manila envelope, between the pages of the heaviest dictionary they could find in the house.

Gloria frowned, pressing her tongue against her teeth. They couldn't destroy it, couldn't let it loose, and had no convenient cellar in which to wall it up. What did one do with dangerous materials?

"Ah," she said. "I have an idea. I just need to make a phone call or two."

The next afternoon was cool and gray again, the sun a brighter disk behind the high vault of clouds. These clouds, however, were already thinning on the horizon.

Ruth and Gloria paused on the steps of Orne Library, watching the sky. "We might see stars for a change," Ruth said, fishing a cigarette out of her handbag. "I'm not sure if that's a comfort or not."

"Neither am I," Gloria admitted. "Either way, I hope to sleep tonight."

Behind them, high in the recesses of the Ruggles Rare Book Room at the Orne Library, the single page of *The Book of Endings* lay locked in a glass case, buried beneath a dusty stack of tomes the librarian had assured them hadn't been taken out in years. Gloria had used all her newly acquired pull with Jamie's uncle, Charles Emerson, to arrange an introduction with one of Miskatonic University's librarians.

Between Emerson's donations to many New England libraries, and this particular librarian's fondness for weird fiction, they had managed to finagle a favor.

It wasn't safe. Nowhere they could hide the page would be truly safe, but this should keep it out of sight for some time. For the rest, they had to trust Jamie.

On the way to Miskatonic, Gloria had asked the cab driver to swing past the bookshop. This time, her imagination had proved correct: the shop was closed, the sign gone from the window. Maldefaunt had vanished, loose in the world, awaiting another opportunity to spread his contagion. Gloria had the lingering feeling that this wasn't the last they would hear of him.

Ruth struck a match and lit her coffin nail. A pale ribbon of smoke unwound from her nostrils as she exhaled. "What will you do now? Keep writing the same stories?"

Gloria had spent much of the day considering exactly that.

"Yes and no," she said at last. "My stories have always contained the things I've seen – the horrors that lie behind the cracks of the world. But now I know those horrors can be fought. I think it's time to change the tone of my work. If anything I can write will let someone like me, someone like Jamie, know they're not alone, then I owe them that. And if a story can give anyone hope, I owe them that as well." She owed Jamie that much and more, but that wasn't a debt that could be repaid, only paid forward to help others.

"What about you?" she asked as they started down the cobbled walkway. Red and gold leaves drifted on the breeze, and beams of sunlight dappled the lawns. "Are you going back to Mr Wiggins?"

"I don't think I can do that now. I have friends in London – the ones who taught me about ghosts and other things. They offered to teach me more, years ago, but I was more interested in my career. Now, though, I believe I'll take them up on that offer. Nora might come with me."

She shot Gloria a sidelong glance. "You could join us."

"I could," Gloria mused aloud. The idea felt good in her mind. "I might. But first I need to go back to New York. I have a novel to write."

INVESTIGATOR ORIGINS

From the Arkham Horror Archives

Jenny Barnes, the Dilettante

By Annie VanderMeer

I held my breath when I walked in the room, expecting the worst – things broken and overturned, blood on the walls. I was surprised to find it almost orderly, with only trace signs that items had been tampered with. The bed was made, but looked like it had been pawed over as someone searched for things hidden under it. Clothes in the drawers had been shifted, but not thrown about. It evoked the kind of eeriness that itches at your mind, like the temperature in the room when it is just below comfortable, or a note in a song that sends shivers down your back.

I found them in the desk drawer. A pen had been left uncapped, something Izzie would never do, even at her most disorganized. My letters. I had been writing her for years, but these three were on the top. A chill seized me when I touched them, as I knew which ones they were.

Dearest Izzie,

Greetings from the sticks! You would not believe where I am, darling. I am sorry it has been so long since I last wrote. I imagine this post will also take a dreadfully long time to get to you, but please know I have been thinking of you. You know I am not the short-tempered sort, but this journey has certainly whittled me down to sharper edges.

When last I wrote you, I was about to head to a fête on the Dynamic at the port of Palermo – a bit rustic, certainly; you will remember how scandalized everyone was back home that I chose to visit Sicily and not Venice! – and while I imagine it would have been a bit small for your taste, it was such a charming craft, all strung with lights. It glowed like an ember in the darkness! Wine flowed, and everyone was so gleeful. It was easy to get caught up in the excitement and the bounty of the evening.

While there, I could not help but notice an older man whose excitement that evening seemed rather strained, as though on a table set with blazing candles, one taper was guttering in its wax and struggling to remain lit. I thought myself brave to engage this curious creature in conversation, and lo and behold the man was Professor Lucius Angstrom, a scholar and anthropologist of some note! It seemed he had little taste for parties, but he sought funding for a potential archaeological dig at a promising site at the Susa Valley, near Turin, and had gone to a wealthy relation to seek it. The poor man hardly knew what he was in for – he had boarded the Dynamic at Marseilles, thinking himself a guest for merely a single party. I daresay the man had nearly been shanghaied, finding himself not in the north of Italy, but in the far south instead.

Pardon me for seeming as though I am mocking the poor fellow. His situation was rather humorous, but the pained look on his face and the nature of our shared interest in the anthropological moved me to inquire further about the dig site in question. His face bloomed with life, and I daresay he was nearly a different man! He went on and on about the curiousness of the location, how rich merely a single survey had been. That such a great find existed in a place so well trafficked was a wonder, he said, and he felt a dire need to act quickly, lest someone else take credit for the find. I inquired briefly why indeed this was the case, and at this his fire seemed to dim again. He mentioned, in a low and stuttering way, as a child might if caught in a lie, that although there were multiple cathedrals and abbeys in the area, there seemed to be a local superstition surrounding that particular site; it was viewed as a place both curious and potentially dangerous. But again, the flush returned to his cheeks, and he dismissed the notion as modern Christian thought seeking to paint all pagan activities with a brush of evil. Such superstitious claims were wholly unsubstantiated, he said.

I will admit here that I did not guard my enthusiasm or my tolerance for alcohol as well as ordinarily I might have – the servers were like lithe ghosts – and I let myself fall fully into the fascinating dreams of a truly vast, undiscovered dig. Visions of wondrous items danced across my mind, and as the darkness of late night threatened to snuff out the lights of the ship and send everyone stumbling home, I promised the good professor that the dig would indeed happen, and I should be quite happy to fund it. Thus you may have already received confused letters from our cousins Angelique and Jean Paul, curious as to why I have not joined them in Paris yet – blame good wine and an overabundance of ambition on my part. The worst of it was this: I demanded to be a part of the dig as well, and Angstrom was only too delighted to comply! I wish I could wholly blame the wine, but I think you know me far too well for that!

So it was that upon the following morning, I found myself meeting with the good professor at what seemed to me an intolerably early hour, speedily scratching out a cheque for expenses, and facing the cumbersome situation of having to put together some kind of baggage appropriate for an expedition of this nature. The professor was aghast at my insistence on bringing along my typewriter, but after I made it abundantly clear that either it went with me to the dig or there would be no dig at all, he (wisely) relented.

While I set in order the remainder of my affairs, the good professor set forth immediately to Turin, to go about meeting with his students and preparing the dig. I followed thereafter in what can only be described as a comedy of errors. It was a wonder I did eventually make my way to the Susa Valley.

Such beauty! It is difficult to describe this place to you, Izzie; it seems as though it is both in the middle of everything and on the edge of the world. There are deep valleys and scrubby trees, wide pastures, and the towering white-capped spires of the Alps in the distance. I was so enamored of the wild and winding beauty of the place that I hardly minded how bumpy the ride was along the road – a road so ancient it dates back to Roman days! It is so silly how we once thought our own house so old, and yet just today I rode along a path placed by hands thousands of years dead. The night seems to weigh so heavily here – it reminds me of the darkness around that boat in Palermo, but without the blaze of lights to stave off the gloom.

The farmer who met me at the station was kind enough to drop me at the only local inn, a rustic little place called L'ultima Lanterna, and I gratefully arranged myself a room for the night. I had just finished a delicious agnolotti when I asked the proprietor if he had any contact with a dig in the area, and if I might contact Professor Angstrom to let him know I had arrived. Izzie, you would have been shocked to see the change in the man's demeanor. I knew I did not have the best command of the dialect, but knowing both French and Italian, I had thought I could puzzle it out. I imagined I had offended him somehow. I opened my mouth to apologize, but he told me brusquely that it was a shame so refined a lady would be in the

company of such – I think he called them scoundrels or
pirates. Nevertheless, he said he would send one of his
workers to the dig in the morning, to let them know I
had arrived.

I thanked him for his kindness, but he put up a hand
to stop me and said in broken English, "That place is bad.
Bad place. Maledetto. I leave alone. Others? Maybe not."
I tried to thank him, but he moved away and refused to
speak to me again for the rest of the night. I thought I saw
others around me look suspicious and move away, but I
was tired, so I might remember it improperly. At any rate,
what can one say about rustic superstition? It is charming
when it is about things like putting out saucers of milk for
the fairies, but watch out when a calf is born deformed or
an ewe's milk turns sour, and it seems everything might be
an ill omen. I had to remind myself that overabundance
of wine or not, I did choose to come out here, and I better
well make the best of it!

That said, my dear sister, I will end things here. The
light of this lantern is getting low, and the professor is
supposed to meet me sometime tomorrow, I would
imagine. I shall send you a letter from the dig site and
let you know what wonders we have found. Now I go to
dream of that, and put the silly worries of ill omens and
superstitions far behind me. Much love to you!

Warmest Regards,
Jenny

I did not know how to read signs like that then – it
was the first time, and the way I had been raised had put

me in the permanent state of mind that I "knew better." Knew better than to let someone tell me I should not go somewhere, or that something did not bode well. I was certain the things that had happened on the way there were mere inconveniences that made for a good letter, not any kind of warning. I simply would not have listened to the signs and warnings, not back then. I wonder if they were laid out not to dissuade me from that path, but to warn me against future ones. My mind is now one that thinks about things like that, but back then it would have been as impossible as breathing underwater.

I picked up the next letter. Things were not that bad. Yet.

Dearest Izzie,

Things have been busy. The dig site is a rough place to live, but I am getting used to it – I will admit I wish I had not come here, if only because early on I felt myself almost more an obstacle than an aid to the situation. When I met with Professor Angstrom at the inn, he assured me things were going well, and I had the expectation of arriving at a well-organized camp. Then, when we finally came to our destination, I found things in a state of half-disarray, with boxes of tools only partly unpacked, research tents half set up, and the workers' rest area hardly more than a threadbare bit of tarp. My shock was apparent, as the professor was quick to explain that the disarray was due to the fact that it seemed every single patch of land had yielded some valuable find – shards of pottery, figurines, heads of weapons – and thus every time they dug into the ground and attempted to make camp, some discovery had forced them to move things again.

As the professor spoke, I confess I felt a slight stirring of unease. I remember being so charmed by how taken he was with the thrill of discovery back on the good ship Dynamic, how much it lit his face with delight; now it seemed that light was something out of control, a bonfire that could consume him. I said that it was all well and good to take valuables out of the ground, but it made no sense if they were then put where the elements would destroy them. That seemed to snap him out of his reverie, and he sheepishly conceded my point. I asked if he had anyone on his staff who had more experience dealing with the outdoors, who perhaps had been a veteran of the Great War and knew how to make camp properly. To my great relief, the driver, a student of his named Peter van Rijn, replied that he did, and Angstrom gave him the responsibility of being camp overseer. Thankfully the man proved capable, and within short order, proper tents were erected for the staff and workers.

Since then, things have been a whirlwind of activity, and although occasionally I have been enlisted to help clean off this or that item, it unfortunately seems that most of the time my best use is to stay well out of the way. The dig site expands at what seems a constant rate. Although the local villagers still want nothing to do with us, Professor Angstrom has been able to recruit plenty of hardy workers from Turin, especially ones who disagree with the Fascists and have been forced out of work. Sadly, this has put us more at odds with the locals, who have begun to refuse to sell enough goods to keep the camp running smoothly. Although both the professor and Mr van Rijn objected to my suggestion that I be allowed to go hunting to supplement our food supplies, after I returned from an outing with three brace of ducks, the pair swiftly became enthusiastic about my success.

In my spare time, I have hiked the wild valleys and visited multiple magnificent abbeys and cathedrals in the region. After I asked a monk at one of them about the area where the dig is, he crossed himself and began uttering a prayer of protection, and would not speak to me further. Such it is with anyone local. It has become such a source of frustration for me that once, I am ashamed to admit, I sought out a local scholar with an affinity for drink and plied him with some local wines until he gave me some sparse bits of lore about the area. I had learned from Professor Angstrom that ancient Roman records mentioned a group of barbarians who lived there. They had battled tooth and nail to prevent an invasion of their territory, and were said to have fought to the last. The local added his own bit of legend to the story: those members of the tribe who were not killed in battle built a massive ceremonial pyre, and they leapt onto it together rather than be taken as Roman slaves. Rather ghastly and in keeping with the kind of grim poetry that legends of that time have, but what the local added was that every time anyone had attempted to settle there, something had gone wrong – murders, disappearances, and the like. When I pointed out these were as likely to have occurred anywhere else in the valley, the man simply snorted, said something rude in the local dialect, and refused to speak to me further.

There have been darker moments at the camp as well, and I daresay that individually these events would seem like silly pranks, but together they fill me with the greatest feeling of unease. Strange things, like objects going missing, or broken tools. One morning, we all awoke to find the area had been trampled all around by something with hooves, although no shepherds here keep goats or would drive them near our camp if they did. No one had heard nor seen anything during the night. Once, after I had shot a wild boar and we had our cook field dress it, we had buried the offal in a sack. The following morning, we found the bloodstained sack next to a fire, in which the guts had apparently been burned – the residue was as fresh as if the offal had been set aflame an hour previous. Again no one had seen anything. No one has been hurt and nothing valuable has been stolen, but these events have been taking their toll on the workers. Some have left and doubtlessly talked to the locals, who are even more wary of us than before. Workers who have stayed have done so either from need or because the professor has invested in many casks of the strong local liquor called grappa, a crude way to raise morale.

There is a bright note, however! For all the pallor of this place and the low level of dread, Professor Angstrom has been working at a near frenzy, and under Mr van Rijn's careful supervision, the team has been uncovering an incredible number of artifacts, piled in layer after layer. The other day, we came upon a rather remarkable discovery not far from the center of camp: a barrow, dug into the earth and propped with massive stones. (Mr van Rijn said the stones were likely chiseled out of a far-off hill and dragged for miles before they were fitted into place – imagine that!) The professor was gleeful at the find, saying it was very likely the burial place of a high-ranking member of their society. It was half-collapsed, and so eager was he to explore the inside that he set every member of the team to digging out the entrance. This is the strangest thing, but once the entryway was halfway cleared, I volunteered to go inside myself and investigate! Mr van Rijn protested, saying it was unsafe, but I was smaller than anyone else and could easily fit, and the professor consented. While the other members of the team worked on clearing out the entrance further, I went in with a lantern to examine the interior.

It was extraordinary! Awfully musty and dirty, to be sure – I wrapped a spare shirt around my face and hair, and still, it was hardly enough – but it was truly remarkable to be the first one in such a place in countless years. I carefully made note of various semi-intact vases and bits of pottery, but then noticed suddenly there was a looming statue in a corner. I looked closer, and saw with disquiet it was a man looking menacing and leering, with rough features – and further still, I noticed that not only was he naked, but someone had cheekily snapped his manhood right off!

Oh, Izzie, I am a mature woman, but I admit something about that made me blush terribly and look away, as though with shame! But when I did so, the light *of my lantern caught a small glint of something lying on the dirt floor, and I leaned in for a closer look. I picked up the object and brushed it off, and found that it was the most interesting thing: a small medallion no taller than my pinky finger, probably of bronze, and so unusually heavy! To be sure, I do not claim a full archaeologist's knowledge of such things, but it seems far more intricate than I would expect jewelry to be from such folk. On its face is a man – crafted with such familiarity I could swear I have seen him in the village nearby – and on the reverse, some kind of spiral pattern. All but the edges are covered with a fine verdigris. It captured my attention so wholly I started with shock when the workers called out that they had cleared the entrance for others. Without quite knowing why, I simply pocketed the medallion, and I continued in assisting with the dig.*

I know you will probably think less of me for this, but forgive me – I did not mention the medallion to either Professor Angstrom (who I doubt would even care, obsessed as he is with what is yet to be found) or Mr van Rijn. I have already sent a letter to a talented jeweler I know in Marseilles with a sketch and a description of the medallion, and a request to make a copy – if he does a proper job, I have told myself I shall return the original and be content with the facsimile.

Another night here draws to a close, and so does this letter. I hope it finds you well, dear Izzie. Think well of your foolish sister out here on her odd quest.

Warm Regards,

Jenny

Last letter, dated two months later. The situation had gone downhill much faster than that, but it took time to even begin to put things into words. I had to type, because I remember every time I tried to write something by hand, the letters quivered. It was easy to tell myself I was just putting off writing until I found a new typewriter. I learned more quickly than anything how easy it was to lie to myself, and how much I hated it.

Isabelle,

I am so sorry it has taken me so long to write. I know you have probably heard from Jean Paul and Angelique that I am in Marseilles, but doubtless they are surprised and offended that I have leased my own apartment rather than stay with them. They are very polite, but I do not think I can make them understand. I do not even know how much I can tell you, or understand myself.

The dig is gone and Professor Angstrom is dead, and I barely escaped with my own life. That is the short version of it, but in the long one there is so much I can hardly describe it. I have written this letter over and over in my head since the night it happened. This is the seventh time I have tried to type out the first page, and I do not know if I can even finish this one. But I shall try, Izzie, for your sake and mine.

I hope my last letters got to you all right. If they did, you will remember I mentioned the growing agitation of the professor, the wariness of the locals, and the strange things that had been occurring. It was a combination that was not stable. Finally, things came to a head in the worst of ways.

While I had been doing my best to supply the camp with what food I could hunt, the workers had been growing increasingly upset with the reluctance of the locals to sell to us. The locals had heard of the strange occurrences at the dig site and took them as evidence that the place was cursed, while the workers blamed the locals for the incidents. That night, a group of workers stole the truck from Mr van Rijn, broke into the stocks of the local inn, and made off with some of its goods. When they returned, van Rijn was furious and fired them on the spot – but they were too drunk and numerous to force out of the camp, and we resolved to leave the matter until morning, when we planned to and pay the owners of the inn for the damages.

We never had the chance to apologize. Some locals had seen the crime and recognized the truck, and their resentment ripened into rage – they organized an angry mob and set upon us in the night, determined to drive us out. I woke to yelling and ran outside to see them tearing down tents, shattering our artifacts, and breaking our digging tools. Some carried torches, others lanterns, but all I saw in the darkness of that fateful night seemed to me like the shrieking faces of demons.

Suddenly there was a shot – the chilling report of a pistol – and one of them fell, in his death just an angry but innocent man. Eyes turned to the source: Professor Angstrom, wielding a pistol and holding a torch. "Back!" he screamed, "These treasures will never be for you!" and he hurled the torch into the center of the excavation pit, where moments ago workers had been celebrating – and into which a keg of grappa had been moved.

The fire that leapt into the air seemed to snarl like a living thing, and all hell broke loose. The professor continued to shoot, and men fell – workers and locals attacked each other in a frenzy, and I stood transfixed at the sight, until Mr van Rijn roughly grabbed my arm, startling me out of my reverie, and yelled that we had to go. In a daze, I seized only what I could carry – including the strange medallion, which I had taken to wearing around my neck – and joined him and the few students Angstrom had brought with him. We piled onto the old truck and tore away into the night. The last I saw of Angstrom was a vision of him in the night, laughing – and throwing himself onto the pyre that the excavation pit had become.

We few made our way back to Turin with little more than the clothes on our backs, and whatever scant objects we were able to save from the dig. Mr van Rijn brought me along to testify before the authorities, and I knew it was only my status as a citizen of wealth that kept all of us from jail. We were told in no uncertain terms that the authorities did not want to hear any more of the situation, that lives had already been lost and the camp had been burned to the ground, and the place in question would be declared a "restricted area" by the government. Some items from the dig were confiscated, but to my great relief, within two days we were all cleared to go – with the strong advisement that *we should leave Italy in a hurry. We counted ourselves lucky and did so. I bid an exhausted farewell to van Rijn when we were safely across the border (via boat to Marseilles – as none of us wanted to go anywhere near the Susa Valley again), and though he made some overtures to stay in touch, I found myself too traumatized to want anything more to do with him, even if he doubtlessly was as shaken by the experience as I.*

I have spent the time since in this apartment, pacing and trying to make sense of it all. One of my few visits out has been to the jeweler I mentioned in the previous letter; his work on the replica medallion was exquisite, and I have had him send it along to you. Somehow, holding onto the original makes me feel a connection with the one I know is headed to your hands, and it gives me a sense of peace. I cannot really explain it, but I find myself in that position rather a lot lately.

Forgive me if I do not return home right away. I am grateful to be alive, and while part of me would like nothing more than to run out, bury myself in beautiful and expensive things, and eat and drink to gladly celebrate that fact, I cannot stop thinking about what I have been through. I have seen quiet folk become monsters, and felt dread and terror so deeply I sensed my heart was ready to escape my body. It is not easy to evade those kinds of feelings, or to forget them, any more than it is for those who have seen the horror of war to put their nightmares outside of their minds for good. I have to find a meaning in what I have been through. In the

*meantime, think of me, and I hope that medallion finds
you well and safe. I love you, sister.*

> *Yours,*
> *Jenny*

The final passage and the paragraph just before it, the
one about the medallion, were underlined as if by a hand
tightening on the pen. Someone had been reading my
letters to Izzie – but why? What importance did these
marks hold? Why had her room been ransacked? And
where was Izzie now?

I wish I had written more about the medallion, had left
myself more clues. I remember too much about the tragedy
of how the dig ended, and not that much else.

I have learned a great many things since that night,
however, and the first of those is that I am no good at
giving up.

Roland Banks, the Fed

By Graeme Davis

Rivertown sat brooding in the autumn mist. Beneath their gambrel roofs, ancient houses squatted and dreamed of bygone days. Some dreamed of sleek merchants, bewigged and gaitered, taking up silver-topped canes and setting forth to see the tall ships come in and make them richer still. Some dreamed of bright parlors and brighter conversation: of intrigue, scandal, and matchmaking over tea and cake. A few dreamed of other things: of bright knives and dark blood, of screams and chanting, of pungent incense and scorching flesh.

None of the houses seemed to notice the man in the trench coat and fedora who walked the dark and cobbled streets with collar turned up and brim pulled down. He seemed somehow less real than the ancient and moldering piles: a shadow from the future, projected onto the mist like an image in a crystal ball.

If he sensed the dreaming heart of Rivertown, the man gave no sign. He passed by a stone-walled graveyard, ignoring the moss-covered tombstones as completely as they ignored him. The old church dreamed of rousing sermons and resounding anathemas; of witches condemned and unbelievers chastised; of births, deaths, and marriages stretching back two centuries and more. The man passed it by without a glance.

Down a dark and tree-shadowed lane, set in the low bluff that fronted the turbid river at the edge of French Hill, the Black Cave did not dream. The cave never dreamed: rather, it was the thing dreamed of. A more sensitive soul than Agent Roland Banks might have recalled, consciously or otherwise, past nightmares of pitch-black, twisting mazes; might have paid heed to the local legends of strange noises and unexplained disappearances; and might have quailed at the thought of entering the broad, yawning mouth. But the Bureau of Investigation did not recruit sensitive souls, and Roland Banks was no dreamer.

Spook stories were a smuggler's tactic from time immemorial: local legends remembered, amended – even created, with deep but bogus antiquity – to keep superstitious locals away. The stories of the Black Cave were not the first examples that Banks had heard in his career with the Bureau. Even without the lurid tales, the cave's position would have been enough to demand investigation.

Black Cave was the perfect spot for bootleggers to store contraband liquor brought up the Miskatonic River from offshore rendezvous with Canadian ships.

His keen ears caught a soft footfall deeper in the cave. Banks drew his .38 with his right hand while he pulled the flashlight from his coat pocket with his left. He did not press the switch, but held the light at the ready. There was no sense in giving away his position until he knew how many people he was dealing with. He stepped cautiously into the cave mouth, hugging the right-hand wall.

A muffled thud and a familiar curse made him smile.

"Murph?" he hissed. "Is that you?" The shuffling ceased abruptly.

"Who's asking?"

"It's Banks. What are you doing here?"

A huge, dark-haired man emerged from the gloom, pointing a big, black .45 with one hand and holding a handkerchief to his head with the other. His face looked like granite in the half-light of the cave entrance. Tom Murphy well deserved the nickname "Mountain."

"Hit your head?" Banks asked.

"No, you dope, I'm powdering my noggin for my big close-up," the big man growled. "What do you think?" He lowered the handkerchief and examined it with narrowed eyes. Finding no blood, he stuffed it back into his pocket. Neither man lowered his gun, although neither seemed particularly inclined to start shooting. "Who sent you? The Bureau? Agency? Blackwood?"

"None of them," Banks answered. "I came to see the scenic grottoes. They're quite famous, you know."

"Fine," said Murphy, "I'll start. Blackwood case – missing kid, last seen near the river. I found signs of a struggle lower down, and a trail leading up here."

"How many sets of tracks?"

Murphy shrugged. "Do I look like Daniel Boone?" he said. Banks shook his head sadly.

"And the Blackwood Detective Agency told you to steam in anywhere without knowing what you're up against? I thought I'd taught them better than that."

"Hey, I never said I was a gumshoe. They offered me the job and I took it. I guess their pet G-man is busy moonlighting someplace else." He gave Banks a significant look. "Such as, whatever you're doing here, which you carefully told me nothing about."

"All right, Mister Big Nose," said Banks, "I'm looking for smugglers. Happy now?"

Murphy responded with a grimace. "Why'd you Feds have to go spoiling everyone's fun all the time?"

"We're just mean-spirited by nature," said Banks. "We hate to see other people being happy."

"You know what?" said Murphy. "I believe you."

"So we're both going into the cave?" said Banks.

"Looks that way," said Murphy.

"And we're not going to get in each other's way."

"I won't if you won't."

"All right, then." Banks lowered his .38 and switched on his flashlight. "Let's go."

The rich, loamy smell of the cave filled Banks's nostrils, speaking of damp and life. It was overlaid with sharper smells – smoke and urine among them – that spoke of human visitors. The arc of the flashlight revealed debris left behind by the drifters and vagrants who sometimes went there to get out of the weather – and, it was rumored, for other, darker purposes.

Above clusters of broken bottles and kicked-over fires, the walls were scratched and painted with strange, writhing symbols and lines of gibberish that looked almost like writing. A large triple spiral had been drawn on the ceiling with what looked like candle soot. His stomach slid sideways with a feeling like seasickness, and he looked away quickly.

They pressed deeper into the cave, following the tracks on the sandy floor. Boots and shoes of all sizes – even a dainty pair of women's pumps – had trodden a path that was hard to miss.

Reaching a fork, they paused. A charnel breeze blew from the passage to their left; the floor was solid rock now, with no footprints to guide them. Murphy nodded in that direction with his eyebrows raised. His gun was drawn now; it looked like a toy in his massive fist. Banks shrugged and followed the big man into the darkness. They made their way down a narrow and winding passage to a cave-in that choked the tunnel completely. The foul breeze blew through the crevice between the fallen rocks; glimmers of light, of a color Banks could not precisely name, trickled through here and there.

Looking down, Banks saw a pool of silvery liquid seeping out from under the rocks. It seemed to sense their presence and flowed eagerly toward their feet, causing Banks to step back hurriedly, pulling Murphy with him.

As they took another passageway, he noticed the walls of the passage sweating silver here and there, as though the tunnel had tasted them and begun to salivate.

Banks's mind peopled the shifting shadows with more knife-wielding maniacs and with enemies far more monstrous, which is, perhaps, why the bats came as a shock. He could not hear their voices, but the sudden storm of wings, and the hundred tiny breezes as they passed by, left him gasping. Murphy climbed to his feet, casting a huge and misshapen shadow in the light of Banks's fallen flashlight. At least it was still working. Banks stooped to pick it up.

Banks opened his mouth to speak, but Murphy silenced him with a gesture. "Hear that?" he whispered.

For a few moments, Banks heard nothing. Then, through some whim of the cave's air currents, he heard it. At first the sound was indistinct, the voice of something small and afraid, but it was impossible to tell whether it was human or animal. Then it rose to a scream, and took the form of a word: "Mommy!"

The two men exchanged a glance and then set off down the passage. The echoing passages and shifting air currents distorted the voice, making it impossible to tell where it was coming from, but they followed as best they could through the labyrinth. Deeper into the cave, there was none of the foul debris of chance vagrants, but the bizarre carvings and daubings on the walls became more frequent. They passed a series of dizzying spirals, and one word that was readable: "Azathoth."

It was utterly unfamiliar, yet Banks shuddered when he read it.

They walked on, and a deep chanting became audible beneath the whimpers and cries of a frightened child.

"Doesn't sound like your bootleggers."

"No," Banks agreed, "it doesn't."

"How many of them, do you reckon?"

"I only hear one chanting. There could be others."

Murphy nodded gravely.

The child's voice had subsided into sobs, but they were close enough now to hear the quieter sounds. The chant continued, and threaded in and out of its unpredictable rhythm came the sound of a flute or pipe of some kind, equally random and toneless.

Banks had heard such piping before. He squeezed his eyes shut and shook his head to block out the memory.

When Banks opened his eyes again, Murphy was checking the slide on his .45. Setting his flashlight carefully on the ground, Banks flipped out the cylinder of his .38; it was fully loaded and rotated freely. He snapped it back into place.

When Murphy nodded his readiness, Banks turned off his flashlight so it would not give them away. The sudden blackness struck him almost like a blow: without sight, the chanting and piping seemed to grow louder, closer. Banks heard Murphy's breathing beside him, as loud as a bull in a byre. The big man was standing as still as Banks was.

Somewhere at the back of his mind, Banks knew that it was pointless to wait for his eyes to adjust to the darkness, but he waited all the same. Then, incredibly, he became aware of a dim, greenish phosphorescence somewhere ahead. At first he thought that his eyes were deceiving him, as sometimes happens in complete, subterranean darkness. He blinked, but the dull smudge of light – or at least, of lesser darkness – was still there, and he could almost make out the side of the passage in dim variations of shadow.

"You see that?" he breathed.

"Green?" asked Murphy. "Yeah. What is it?"

"Beats me. Seems to be where we want to go, though. You ready?"

"Okay." Murphy shifted on his feet, but Banks reached out to stop him.

"Me first," he said. "And Murphy?"

"What?"

"If you have to shoot, shoot around me, not through me."

"Make sure you keep low, then. What side do you like your hair parted on?"

"You're a riot. Come on."

Banks moved forward on the balls of his feet, as softly as a cat. Behind him, the larger man's footsteps sounded as loud as the marching of a drill squad, but the chanting and piping continued without a break. Whoever was there, they were too busy to hear the two men coming.

The dull green glow became almost bright as they advanced. It streamed from a fissure in the side of the passage, casting enough light for Banks to see Murphy's face twitch as the terrified child called for his mother once more. Stopping the big man with a gesture, Banks crept up to the fissure and risked a glance around it. When he swung back to face Murphy, the G-man's eyes were wide and his mouth was wide with terror. He edged back to the big man.

"One man," he whispered, his voice thick and hoarse. "You take him, I'll grab the kid." His jaw worked soundlessly for a moment. "And don't look at the piping thing."

Ignoring Murphy's questioning look, Banks raised his .38 and swung around the corner.

NORMAN WITHERS, THE ASTRONOMER

By AP Klosky

The Miskatonic University Science building was awash with light and laughter. Bow tie-clad servers carried trays of shrimp puffs and flutes of sparkling cider, gliding elegantly between the tuxedoed bourgeois of Arkham, Massachusetts. To any outside eyes, the dedication celebration for Miskatonic's new Gerald Warren Astronomical Observatory was a marvelous soirée.

Professor Norman Withers looked on from his table. A snarl of disdain was barely visible beneath his voluminous beard.

So many people. So loud. I hate these pompous affairs. He sipped slowly from an almost-full flute of sparkling cider. So

*much money and time, wasted. Norman tugged at his black
bow tie; despite his old-money upbringing, he had always seen
himself as being much more suited to the laboratory than the
social club.*

He had not wanted to attend the ceremony in the first
place. These soirées were cloying affairs. The reek of cigar
smoke and bourbon, of pungent perfume and burning
candles, made his eyes water. Bernadine would have
called him a "fogey" by this point. Back when she was at
the university, she had always tried to tear him away from
the lab. "Come with me, Professor," she used to taunt him.
"Your eyes will go crossy, staring at those books all night
long. Let us go look at the stars."

Picking up his flute of cider, Norman walked slowly to
the bank of windows along the east wall. The jazz ensemble
hired for the soirée romped through an upbeat tune as he
passed by. Norman grimaced nevertheless; the clarinetist
was a half-step off and the discordant harmony echoed
through the high halls.

Norman looked out the bank of windows. The streetlights
of Miskatonic made it difficult for his old eyes to pick out
stars, but he knew they were there. At this time of year?
Sirius, Castor and Pollux, Capella. All there, but just out
of view.

Just like Bernadine. Gone.

A familiar tinkling silenced the chamber. At the far end
of the room, President James Erwin softly rapped his fork
against a champagne flute. Beside him stood the luminaries
of the Miskatonic River Valley. As the crowd's chatter
diminished to an impressed silence, Norman followed suit,

idly thumbing his champagne flute as he prepared for the imminent speech.

Waiters and staff silently slipped to the shadows, and the lights seemed to envelop President Erwin in a halo of radiance. Raising his glass, Erwin spoke over the applause of the enraptured attendees:

"Thank you," he began. The din finally died down. "Thank you for coming this evening. We are here tonight in celebration of a great achievement – one that will facilitate a limitless number of great achievements to come. Your generosity has provided Miskatonic University with the finest in astronomical and meteorological equipment, and a facility custom built to house these new machines. Our professors and our researchers will have the best ability fathomable to reach into the stars and find new vistas.

"We stand, my friends, on the edge of a new age. Our new telescope has allowed us to discover new planets – entirely new worlds, never before seen by human eyes. And the best of our discoveries are yet to come. The depths of space will be ours to plumb, in the name of knowledge and progress."

Erwin's broad smile glinted bright and confident in the hall. *His enthusiasm*, Norman thought, *sure is infectious. He's got the oldest money in Arkham eating out of his hand.* Erwin continued:

"One of our university's oldest slogans has been, from the Latin: *lux in obscuro sumus*. 'We are the light in the dark.' The equipment you have so generously donated, the funds that you have so beneficently provided, will allow Miskatonic to stand as that light in the darkness, bringing illumination to the shadow enshrouding outer space.

Today, we watch the stars move and the comets twinkle in far-off galaxies. Tomorrow, could we not reach into the skies ourselves, sending explorers to far-off planets? I say, it is our next and greatest step!"

Erwin smiled that broad smile – a smile well practiced in schmoozing donors at events such as this one. "Tonight, we raise our glasses not just to your generosity. Tonight, we raise our glasses to the future, and what future promises your contributions will bring to our world. On behalf of Miskatonic University – on behalf of the discoveries your donations will fund – I thank you!"

Donors, waiters, musicians, and more raised their glasses, alternating delicate sips with near thunderous applause. Norman sipped as well, though his eyes radiated his skepticism. *Do not get me wrong, President Erwin: I appreciate the new equipment. I think, perhaps, however, you are just a touch too optimistic about what may be truly out there.*

Norman set down his champagne flute, still mostly full. The side stairs – the stairs leading up to the new laboratory: his laboratory – seemed to beckon. Glancing once around the room, Norman excused himself and climbed the stairs.

The lab was near silent, outside of Norman's own footsteps. The scent of still-drying paint, applied only a few days prior, filled his nostrils. The hum of gleaming new devices droned softly in the background.

Norman's gaze flicked to the shadowed corners of the laboratory, still tidy and new. Letting out a sigh, he slid off his jacket, placing it over the back of an office chair.

The data from his latest experiment lay beside Norman's

desk, transcribed by one of his graduate students. He picked up the sheaf of papers covered with numbers and coordinates. To anyone else, the Byzantine scrawl would be meaningless. To a man of Norman Withers's staggering intellect, the numbers read as easily as a well-worn dime novel.

Yes, President Erwin. Far too optimistic.

Norman slumped down in his chair. The stars were still missing. Six of them, in fact. An entire star cluster, beyond Aldebaran, was simply gone. Whole stars had winked out like snuffed candles.

The numbers did not lie. Data was incapable of falsehood: a rare truth in a universe far too enamored of equivocation.

What more? There were...anomalies. Gaps in the stars; far distant objects present one moment, but nowhere to be found upon later observation. Even the few data points collected thus far revealed this strangeness.

There could be only one conclusion. Something is traveling there. Something is moving between the stars.

The sudden slam of a door broke Norman from his reverie. Fumbling, he shoved the folio into a folder in his desk.

"Professor Withers...Norman?" A familiar voice called. The slick smile of President Erwin seemed to shimmer in the dim light.

Norman stuttered a response, "President Erwin? Yes, I am... I am here. Just checking up on some of the work I had my students putting together. The new measurements have been most promising."

Erwin sauntered over. His tie was loosened, though he seemed just as formal and practiced as earlier. He clasped a hand on Norman's shoulder, "Norman, the party is out there. Take a night off, my friend. The stars can wait for an evening while we celebrate. Tonight is a triumph for your entire department."

Norman gazed longingly at his desk drawer. Missing stars. Things sailing through the void of space. A mystery beyond comprehension. Creatures that walked through angles unimaginable. Could he possibly stop his work? Even for a night?

Norman shook his head. "I am sorry, James, but I am on the cusp of something big." Something terrifying, but he could not say that. Not even James would believe him if he said the end of the world was coming. He needed proof, but even then, what would proof do in the face of annihilation?

Proof would be a start, at least. And then, just maybe, someone else could devise a way to avert the apocalypse.

Silas Marsh, the Sailor

By Jason Marker

"On deck there," cried the lookout from the foretop. "Land fine on the port beam!" The brig *Eileen Marie* rounded Cape Ann, heading north toward her home port of Portsmouth, New Hampshire, under a full press of sail. Returning from a six-month cruise with ports of call in the Bahamas, Panama, and South America, the ship's forty crew members were eager to be ashore among their friends and loved ones. Her captain – a stolid and thickly bearded middle-aged Portuguese sailor named Cristóvão Ingrande – stood at the wheel and stared at the distant, haze-shrouded cape with satisfaction.

"Mr Marsh," called the captain in his thick Iberian accent. "Go aloft with your glass and tell me how the bay looks."

Silas Marsh, the ship's first mate, had already been eyeing the distant cape through an old achromatic spyglass from the ship's waist. At the captain's order, he swung into the mainmast shrouds and ran up to the top with his glass slung around his neck like a man walking up the stairs in his home. Marsh was a big man with a sailor's broad shoulders; powerful arms; and lean, muscular frame. He had been at sea for more than a decade, since he was a boy. Through natural aptitude and hard work, he'd risen through the ranks from volunteer to able seaman to this lofty pinnacle as the first mate of a well-run and well-respected trading vessel. Marsh had served aboard all manner of ships, from tugs and scows to whalers and huge, steam-powered merchant vessels. He'd even done a turn as a very young ordinary seaman aboard a Merchant Marine vessel carrying supplies during the Great War. The ports of call painted on his battered old sea chest read like a travel guide to the world's tropical paradises: Kingston, Freeport, Valparaíso, Buenaventura.

"Shove over, Hansen," Marsh said to the maintop lookout as he came over the rail via the futtock shrouds and dropped into the pile of sails and cordage stored there. The young man shuffled over. Marsh trained his glass on the cape, seeing the Thacher Island Twin Lights clear in the late afternoon sun. He swept the bay and saw the usual maritime traffic from Rockport and Essex. He called down to his captain, reporting on traffic and conditions, and then returned to his glass. Far to the north, just at the limit of his glass's power, he saw the ruined seawall and tumbledown docks of his accursed hometown.

"Innsmouth," he muttered.

"Innsmouth, Mr Marsh?" asked the young lookout.

"Yes, Hansen, Innsmouth." Marsh sighed and clapped his glass shut.

"Have you ever been?"

"Aye, I have. I grew up there, you know."

"I've never been there, but I've heard dark rumors about it. What's it like? Is it as bad as they say?"

There was no answer, and an uneasy silence settled over the foretop. They sat there, Silas and his eager interlocutor, on the folded sails looking out toward ruined Innsmouth. The silence was relieved somewhat by the cries of distant seabirds and the sounds of the crew below them putting the ship about.

What could he say about his ancestral home that Hansen would believe? Where to even start? How could he express to Hansen, a mere child born in another land, the awfulness of Innsmouth?

Could he tell Hansen about how Obed Marsh brought both treasure and an awful curse back from the South Sea islands? About how that ancient and cunning sailor, a distant relative of Silas's on his father's side, had founded a secret society called the Esoteric Order of Dagon, which supplanted both Freemasonry and all established churches in the old city? How could he explain Devil Reef and the terrible creatures that capered on it under the new moon? What about the great, mysterious plague of 1846 that had carried off many of the town's inhabitants and the scions of its greatest families? Could he relay the horror inherent in the rumors that it hadn't been a plague at all, but something otherworldly and unspeakable? What would Hansen say to the fact that Silas's ancestor had brought the devil into the city and hell followed closely after?

Silas was born a poor and distant relation of the most important man in a dead city. His family had been rich in land – they lived in a rambling Georgian relic inherited from the Marsh side of the family – but had possessed little actual money. His days were spent playing in the weedy yard or staring out at the sea through the clouded windows of the rooftop cupola, and his nights were filled with terror as he listened to the furtive scuttling of misshapen shadows creeping between tumbledown mansions in the darkness. It was a difficult life, and Silas ran away to sea before he was fourteen years old, mostly in an effort to escape the crushing loneliness and sense of dread that had filled his childhood. He'd had few friends as a child, and one by one, those had disappeared or grown distant and sullen, as Innsmouth people often do.

In his mind's eye, the city's dilapidated, slumping skyline blurred at the edges, softened by memory: the rundown square; the empty, boarded-up commercial buildings slowly crumbling into nothing; the gaping hole in the tower atop city hall, where a fine clock had once told the time. He remembered the ramshackle waterfront that ran along the silted-up harbor with its overpowering stench of rotten fish and its desolate slips, their ships broken up or sunk long ago. There was always a feeling of being watched, of countless staring, watery eyes surveying the cracked pavements and oily sea from the decrepit businesses and rotten warehouses.

When he left, all those years ago, Silas swore that he

would never return. Now, strange rumors about his family and their fortunes were calling him reluctantly back to the city of his birth. Was it as bad as rumor said? No, it was far worse, but he had neither the strength nor the inclination to discuss it further with his young shipmate. He shifted as if to stand and clapped Hansen on the shoulder.

Breaking the silence, he said, "Perhaps not as bad as some say, but it's still a very unpleasant place. It's old, lonely, and poorly cared for. The town is a shadow of what it once was: the town square is in shambles, and most of the neighborhoods are full of boarded-up or collapsed homes. Most people left it long ago after the shipping and fishing dried up, and the old families that remain are, well, peculiar. The harbor is awkward and largely silted up nowadays, and its entry is guarded by Devil Reef that's dangerous even at spring tide. When I was a boy, there were parts of town where I could linger for hours without ever seeing another living soul. It's a strange place, Hansen, and one that I have few fond memories of. But never mind that, shipmate." Silas forced a smile. "We'll be in Portsmouth by tomorrow morning with our pockets full of money and all the pleasures of home laid out for us."

CAROLYN FERN, THE PSYCHOLOGIST

By Mallory O'Meara

Green New England woodland flew past, but the picturesque scene could not dispel the memory of blood. Dr Carolyn Fern's pale forehead leaned against the window of the passenger car as it rocked gently, but she found no comfort in the rhythm of the locomotive.

The train from her home in Providence barreled toward storied Arkham. The wheels beneath her bumped and turned while she mulled over the grisly case that sent her north.

When Malachi was first admitted, it was difficult for Carolyn to reconcile the hysterical patient in his record with the quiet young man before her. He answered all her questions thoughtfully and thoroughly while pushing his dark, unkempt hair out of his eyes.

She was only six months into her residency at Providence Sanatorium, but her expertise in hypnosis was already gaining a positive reputation in Rhode Island's psychiatric community. When Malachi was brought to her, it was with the hope that she could extract information from his sleeping mind that his waking one would not yield. But by the time he ended up slouched on the leather couch in her small office, he was cooperative and calm.

"Just being away from Arkham seemed to do the trick, is that right?" She smiled at him kindly. He nodded slowly in return.

"I suppose so, Dr Fern."

"But you are still suffering from intense nightmares, or bad memories?"

"Well, doctor, those are two things I've got a bit of trouble keeping straight."

She smiled again.

"Malachi, let us see what we can do about that."

Carolyn had him recline and lean into the cushions of the couch. When he was relaxed, she asked him to close his eyes and breathe deeply and evenly. He opened one eye and smiled sheepishly before following her instructions. He counted backward until he fell into the placid hypnotic state that Carolyn waited for.

"Malachi, can you hear me?"

He exhaled. "Yes."

"Malachi, can you tell me your last name?"

"No. It has been removed."

Carolyn frowned. "Who removed your last name, Malachi?"

He was silent. His forehead began to shine with sweat.

"Malachi, tell me: what happened when your last name was removed?"

"Shadow figures stood above me and blood dripped from their fingertips. They held long, curved blades. I felt their chanting deep in my chest." Malachi's hands trembled as he described nightmarish scenes to her.

Over the coming weeks, they repeated these sessions several times. He was always able to give vivid descriptions, but he could never distinguish whether they had actually happened. During their last session together, he finally told her more.

Malachi lay on the couch. He was more jittery than usual, and it took two attempts to bring him into the hypnotic state.

"Malachi, can you hear me?"

"Yes."

"Malachi, who removed your last name?"

A single tear ran down his cheek.

"The Darkness that Watches."

That night, Malachi was discovered dead in his hospital bed. A strangely curved knife was embedded in his heart. Even now, in the overcrowded heat of the train car, the thought chilled her.

The massive building of the sanatorium was only a short walk from the train station through Arkham's bustling downtown. Its peaked brick bulk squatted behind a wicked wrought-iron fence. It was a building meant to intimidate and contain.

Carolyn was surprised to discover a warm and inviting

reception lounge inside. Overstuffed chairs gathered around beautiful antique tables. Large windows let in bright sunlight.

"Dr Fern, I presume?"

A trim, older man stood in the lounge with his hands clasped behind his back. A sharp-featured nurse stood by his side. Carolyn approached them, offering a handshake.

"Pleased to meet you. You must be Dr Mintz."

"Indeed! Welcome to Arkham Sanatorium." He bowed and gestured to his companion. "And this is Nurse Heather, my assistant." The nurse offered a thin smile.

"An impressive building you have here," Carolyn remarked. "Thank you for accommodating me."

"Honestly, it is my pleasure. When I heard that you were visiting us to acquire some records, I volunteered to help. I have been eager to meet you. You see, I have been doing a lot of work on dreams myself, and I hear your hypnotic talents are extraordinary." Dr Mintz opened a door at the end of the lounge. "I was wondering if you might be interested in collaborating on a research project of mine. Before we get you those records, I would love to show you my work."

Carolyn nodded. Dr Mintz smiled back widely.

"Wonderful! Please, follow me."

The pleasant atmosphere of the reception area disappeared as soon as Dr Mintz shut the thick iron door behind them. The temperature dropped to a clammy chill, and a foul, sharp stench hung in the air. As they walked through the meandering stone halls of the sanatorium, Carolyn began to feel uneasy. It seemed like it would be very easy to get lost.

Dank air drifted out of some of the darker hallways. Carolyn asked, "Do some of these passageways lead underground?"

Nurse Heather nodded. "It's a very old building, doctor."

"Surely you do not keep patients down there?" Carolyn peered at the moist walls. Dr Mintz and Nurse Heather exchanged a look.

"That is where we are headed," replied Dr Mintz. "We find it is the best place for our more… shall we say… troubled residents. My patients."

Descending a cramped staircase to a dim hallway, Carolyn heard an anguished howling. The echoes of the scream ricocheted off the stone walls. A dull pounding thudded across the floor. She shot Dr Mintz a questioning look.

"This is where our patients with the highest level of disturbance both live and receive treatment. What you are hearing are the howls of a man known as 'the wolfman.'"

"Because of all that baying?" Carolyn asked.

"Because he is a cannibal." Nurse Heather answered. Carolyn blanched.

Dr Mintz gave Carolyn a reassuring smile. "My work on dreams is still in the experimental stages; therefore, I am only allowed to use the sanatorium's most extreme cases as subjects, those deemed incurable by ordinary methods."

They made their way down the hall. Moans, cries, and knocks against the stone echoed as they passed room after room. Finally, they reached a crooked wooden door. Nurse Heather held it open for the two doctors and ushered them within.

Beyond the door lay a long, low room. A threadbare couch outfitted with leather restraints stood next to a curious machine. Dr Mintz stepped next to the machine and waved his hand in a flourish over its mess of wires and attachments. "This is my dream enhancer. Once a patient is sedated and restrained on the couch, I connect the wires to a metal cap, which is placed on top of the head. Electrical pulses applied to a deeply sleeping patient, combined with an injection of Muscimol, intensify dreams."

Carolyn leaned in to inspect the machine. She noticed deep gouges that marred the sides of the couch and dark stains that spotted the upholstery.

"Would this not cause them extreme distress?"

Dr Mintz nodded eagerly. "Exactly right, Dr Fern! Many of them begin to speak and cry out. My theory is that this may cause them to reveal the contents of their dreams, and perhaps the root of their mental distress."

Carolyn stepped back, scowling. Dr Mintz, that sounds similar to torture."

Dr Mintz grinned. "These people are already deeply disturbed. If I can harness that to help find the cause of their nightmares, it is worth it. That is where I am interested in your hypnotic method, doctor. I feel that a patient under hypnosis would be more forthcoming with useful details when attached to my dream enhancer."

Carolyn nodded politely. "Well, it certainly seems like an interesting theory. Unfortunately, I am very busy on my current case. Maybe some other time." Or perhaps maybe never.

"I see. Nurse Heather will show you out, then."

"What about the records I asked for?" Carolyn asked as Nurse Heather opened the door.

"The nurse will retrieve them for you. Good day." Dr Mintz waved her away as the nurse shut the door.

She sighed and stuffed the stack of papers back inside the crisp envelope. She had spent the evening reading through the paperwork Nurse Heather had given her, and the notes she had taken were scant. Instead of Malachi's case file, there was only a copy of the reports from his physical exams.

The only item of interest was one peculiar note from the night he was discovered. He had vomited profusely upon arrival, and the contents of his stomach consisted primarily of undigested clumps of a plant colloquially called "witchweed," a rare flower only known to grow on Hangman's Hill. The concierge at Carolyn's hotel informed her in a whisper that Hangman's Hill lay to the west of Arkham's Merchant District and was infamous as the site of strange legends.

Carolyn knew before reading exactly what the flower looked like: small, pointed blossoms that were such a dark blue they were nearly black. Malachi had described them to her many times while he recalled his nightmares.

She finished reading the reports with more questions than answers. Who had dumped Malachi's unconscious body at the edge of Arkham? What did they do to him that night?

Carolyn returned unannounced to Arkham Sanatorium the next morning.

"Good morning! I am looking for copies of the records of a certain patient named Malachi."

The young man behind the reception desk gave her a comically disappointed look.

"Doctor, I apologize. Those records were lost."

Carolyn had anticipated this. She smiled warmly at him and passed an envelope across the desk. "I'd be happy to take a look myself while you look through this for me."

His eyes widened as he looked inside the envelope. It was filled with money. He cleared his throat and looked around. "I think I can help you, doctor."

He slipped the bribe into his pocket as he stepped out of the room. A few minutes later, he returned to sit at the desk. The door was left open behind him. Carolyn hurried through. He looked up at her nervously. "I pulled his folder out."

Carolyn stepped into a cramped records room. Along one of the walls, a folder stuck out conspicuously. She tugged it free and quickly scanned through it. A small, handwritten note was pinned to the top.

Brought in with Donovan Loucks. See file.

She frantically scanned the rows of records until she came to the "L" section and found the folder.

Arkham Sanatorium Admissions Report: Patient comatose and covered in shallow lacerations in what appears to be a ritualistic pattern. Orne Library card under the name Donovan Loucks found in jacket pocket, assumed to be patient's.

Day 5 –

Patient still uncooperative. Screams and raves nonsense unconsciously about a "darkness that watches."

"He recently escaped from here."

Carolyn started. The man behind the desk stood next to her. He lowered his voice.

"It is an ongoing investigation, so please read quickly."

Carolyn nodded. It seemed that this man had escaped from Arkham Sanatorium a few days before Malachi's murder. She felt close to some sinister secret, something Malachi was murdered to protect.

When she opened the door to her hotel room that afternoon, thoughts and theories about Malachi's death consumed her mind. She murmured to herself aloud: "If his records were 'lost' on purpo–"

She froze as the door swung open.

A small, dark-blue flower lay on her pillow.

DEXTER DRAKE, THE MAGICIAN

By Mallory O'Meara

"Now, keep your eye on it, closely." Dexter Drake flipped the golden coin smoothly across his knuckles. Back and forth, back and forth it went. The young waitress grinned at him. Dexter opened both hands wide. The coin was gone. "See? You looked away! Now it's disappeared."

The waitress laughed and refilled his coffee. The diner bustled with the chaos of morning customers. "What's a fancy sir like yourself doing here in Arkham?" she asked.

"Here to find the magic shop, of course." Dexter smiled at her and ran a hand through his black hair. "Say, you wouldn't be able to give me directions there, would you, doll?"

"Sure," she said, "you'll have to walk Uptown. The shop you're looking for isn't far from the hospital, you know – St Mary's? Big place, easy to find."

"All right. Thanks, miss." He winked at her.

As she walked away to attend to other diners, the small scruffy head of a little boy peered over the edge of Dexter's booth. "Is that real magic?" the boy whispered.

Dexter's face darkened as he turned to look the child in the eye. "Trust me, kid: you don't want to see real magic."

Dexter's first terrifying glimpse of "real magic" came right after the Great War, while he was still in the service. The men of his company rarely got leave, so when they did, they took full advantage of it. Quaffing tankards of beer and drunkenly capering through towns in das Rheinland was what Dexter looked forward to most during the hard weeks on the road. He loved to explore the ancient cobbled streets, so different from those of his young country back home.

One warm spring night, Dexter and his friends had the good fortune of getting leave during a seasonal festival in a nearby town. Gleefully inebriated, they wandered through the revelries. Peddlers hawked their strange wares in barking voices. Steaming carts of food bumped over the cobblestones. The hair ribbons of beautiful dancers shone under the streetlights.

It was late in the evening when they came upon a shoddy street magician performing small tricks for passersby and decided to stop and watch. The man's clothes were in tatters, and his greasy hair swung as he made various items disappear into thin air. Dexter's friends clapped enthusiastically, hooting and hollering at the magician.

"That was good, but I think Dexter's better. Show us some real magic!" yelled Roger. Ed chimed in, "Yeah, give the man a show!"

The crowd went quiet and turned to face the Americans. The magician stopped his tricks and took a step back, eying their uniforms.

"Soldiers, eh?" The magician scowled. His English was heavily accented as he issued a low warning: "You should not be here. Leave, now."

"Do ya wanna rethink what you just said there? Or have we got ourselves a resister, boys?" Roger smirked, rolling up his sleeves. Some of the women in the crowd began to shoo their children home, while the local men pressed in closer, something between fear and anger in their eyes. Ed puffed himself up and stood looming behind Roger.

The magician began to chant in an unknown tongue. Dexter started to reach out to Roger, but something about the magician's eyes stopped him.

"The hell is this?" Roger balked.

Ed teased, "Watch out, I think he's casting a spell on you!" The soldiers started to laugh, but their joviality shriveled up and died as the magician's voice grew louder and the shadows seemed to move around them. The air on the street thickened as the magician's voice thundered, his voice now unnaturally deep.

Black tendrils of night began to swirl around the magician's head, and his eyes gleamed. The chanting grew louder. Roger took a step back, bumping into Ed, and they exchanged a worried look. The tendrils absorbed the beams of streetlight, as if the darkness was feeding on the glow. A peal of thunder boomed from the dark, clear sky, and the Americans bolted. The magician's mad laughter followed them into the dark, like a far-off thunderstorm rumbling through the hills.

None of his friends would speak about that night, claiming not to remember the encounter. Roger and Ed chalked up Dexter's unease to the effects of overindulgence. But Dexter could not forget the things he heard and saw that night. How many times had he bolted up in bed, reeling from a nightmare cut short by a crash of thunder? The magician's eyes had followed him back to America, where he'd sometimes whirl around to see some passerby staring at him from across the street with the same look.

Dexter looked over his shoulder before opening the door to Ye Olde Magick Shoppe, where the soft chime of a bell greeted his entrance. Inside, the shop was dim and dusty and smelled of stale frankincense. The shelves groaned with the weight of curious items of all shapes and sizes. Glass bottles with dark liquids, their corks crumbling away, crowded a low table. So many of the magic shops he'd visited in his search across the country were gaudy and garish, touting a great quantity of "magic supplies" that typically amounted to nothing more than colored candles and bright silk scarves. This one felt the most like the chanting from his nightmares, although he wasn't sure whether that was a good thing.

Dexter picked up a short dagger from a cushion resting on one of the shelves. Runes etched the fuller of the blade, and dark stains spotted the leather of the scabbard, like blood. As he tried to decipher the symbols, they began to blur in his vision, as though they were transposing themselves over each other, swapping back and forth and–

"–help you, mister?"

Dexter jumped and nearly dropped the blade. An old woman stood beside him, shapeless under a number of moth-eaten shawls. She gently took the dagger from his hands. "I'm Miriam Beecher."

He gave her an embarrassed smile. "Dexter Drake, ma'am. Do you own this place?"

Miriam set the dagger back down on the cushion. "I do. Are you looking for something?" She took a step back to examine him. "Wait just a moment – Drake? The famous magician?"

Dexter bowed with a flourish.

She scowled at him and held up one gnarled finger. "This isn't the kind of place for magic tricks." She paused and peered at him intently, then closed her eyes. A moment later, she reopened them, rubbing her brow. "But you aren't looking for magic tricks, are you?"

He shook his head. "You're right, Miss Beecher. On stage, I perform the sort of cheap illusions that entertain people. But I'm not looking for tricks." He paused, and continued more quietly, "I'm searching for the truth. Real magic. Word around is this is the shop for it."

She narrowed her eyes, pressing her lips flat against each other. "Sometimes the truth is best left hidden."

Ever since his encounter with the magician in das Rheinland, Dexter had wanted answers, and he'd found his first clue while still in Europe. The post-war turmoil across the continent meant ancient families were fleeing to different countries. Collections that had been secret for centuries were suddenly being sold, the estates that held them left open.

One night at the *taverne*, Dexter had found himself seated with the old servants of Château-Sancillé. Over several beers, they had told tales of midnight gatherings, strange shadows, and disappearances. Dexter had foolishly decided to visit the manor to find out more.

The château itself had looked innocuous: rows of windows and white wooden symmetry rose above the surrounding greenery. Although the gardens had overtaken the courtyards in the wake of the owners' departure, nothing else had seemed out of the ordinary.

He stepped across the threshold into the musty, still air inside. Dust motes caught the last rays of light that shone through the windows. He hadn't believed that the house's malevolent reputation could have scared off potential looters, but now that he was inside, he understood.

The beautiful furnishings around him contrasted with the deep sense of unease ringing in his blood. Instead of the expected scents of wood polish and dust, the château smelled like an old butcher shop. The air was dank and had a coppery undercurrent, as if it were laced with something unwholesome.

After a few minutes, he finally came upon the house's library. It was an enviable collection, tomes stacked on beautiful mahogany shelving from floor to ceiling. Dexter took his time searching through the titles. He had only a passing grasp of French, but the books did not seem to be arranged in any particular order.

Along one shelf was a small gap, the wood stained and warped. He reached his hand tentatively inside, feeling a scrap of paper, some of its edges burnt and flaking. Dexter pulled it out and examined it closely. Latin inscriptions and illustrations of centipede-like tendrils crawled across the page, like those shadows had done that night. He shivered.

Far beneath the floorboards, there was a *thump*. Dexter felt the strong vibration through the soles of his shoes. He carefully wrapped the scrap of paper in a handkerchief and stowed it inside a jacket pocket. The *thump* came again. After a frantic look around, Dexter fled.

A rare book expert in Paris examined the scrap for him, although she had refused to touch it. Her hands were covered in thin linen gloves as she handled the paper carefully. After a few minutes of intense scrutiny and a sharp intake of breath, she told him it was a piece of a dreaded book titled the *Necronomicon*, a Latin edition from the fifteenth century that had been published in Germany. The expert implored Dexter to burn it.

He refused. He wanted to find the rest of the book.

Dexter leaned against the counter and matched Miriam's intense gaze. "Years ago, I saw something. Something I've been trying to explain ever since. I've gathered all the books on magic I can find, trying to make sense of it. Some of the spells I've found, they–"

Miriam grabbed his wrist and interrupted him. Her long, yellowed nails dug into his skin. "You should not dabble in things you do not fully understand, Mr Drake."

He pulled his wrist free from her grasp, not expecting such strength from so old a woman.

"And there are things no one should understand," she whispered, her voice rasping across her dry, cracked lips.

"Things like this?" Dexter slid the scrap of the *Necronomicon* out of one of the pockets of his suit jacket and pushed it across the counter toward her. She recoiled as if scalded. "Where did you get this?" she hissed.

"I found it in the library of an abandoned estate. I want to buy the rest of the book it came from," he said and leaned forward eagerly. "I think it holds the key to what I am trying to understand."

Her eyes narrowed at him. "The key?" she asked. "This is a dark path you walk, Mr Drake. I will not sell you this book," she said, shaking her head slowly.

He looked around at the run-down building, the threadbare carpeting, the worm-eaten shelving. "I've got money, Beecher. Enough money for you to fix up this dump. Or open a better shop. Or whatever you want. Name your price."

Miriam backed away. "I will not sell you this book, Dexter Drake. You should leave this shop, leave Arkham. It is a dangerous place for the likes of you," she said sternly. "Go now, for your own sake, and for the safety of your kin."

She turned and disappeared through a moldy curtain behind the counter. Dexter scowled. He slammed the door on the way out, his hands shaking. What if the old woman was right? It might be safer to abandon this quest. Maybe he should burn the scrap – burn the whole collection of ancient books and papers he had collected.

Dexter recalled the dark tendrils swirling around the

magician's head. He imagined those tendrils spreading across a city, consuming all the light that they found.

He had seen proof of evil in the world. If he had a chance of fighting it, he needed to understand it, and Miriam had confirmed that Arkham was the place to do so.

Gloria Goldberg, the Author

By Annie VanderMeer

Her hands didn't seem to be part of her as she opened the doors to the diner – shaking, pale, strange, like they were a million miles away – but Gloria did the best she could to appear composed. She tried every little trick she normally used to calm herself before performing a reading: a small little closed-mouth laugh, quiet enough that only she could hear it, to burn off nervous energy. A deep sigh, imagining a feather resting on her lips, then lifting and dancing away on the air. Measured steps to the clean golden counter, counting them in her head, a number to be sorted and discarded. Sitting down on the stool felt intensely solid to her, as if she were a ship docking at a harbor. Her smile became more genuine.

The sky fell open like a deluge of rainwater splitting apart wet newspaper. Something from space – not outer space, but a space, a place beyond – pulled itself through the gap like pus spurting from a wound, hideous and rank and, and, and, and–

Gloria winced despite herself. Earlier, that vision had been so strong it had literally knocked her over on her way out of the bookstore. People had come to her asking if she needed their help, but she saw them as corpses, as though visions of their dead faces had been laid on top of their live ones: a mimicry of film, a mockery of life. She'd stammered that she'd just tripped and was fine, had fled faster than she'd meant to, and headed here – here, where she had often sought solace, sliding into one of the plush red booths with a pile of books, ordering a cup of coffee, and reading. This was a place where she could sit, reflect, and distance herself from her problems. She could tell just how shaken she was tonight by the fact that she'd steered herself to the counter, not a booth – all the better to be closer to humanity, to try to shake the dread that still clung to her.

She'd been trying to hold the vision at arm's length, as doctors had once suggested: to pin down what she saw with similes, using writers' tricks to draw circles around what she beheld, just as she always had when the visions came to her. She trapped them, these indescribable things: branded them with names, gassed them with intentions, pinned them down with descriptions. She made the horrors her own, after a fashion. Ultimately, she spun them into her tales, made them not nightmares but fictions, stories to titillate and spook. They'd made her a comfortable living, despite their ghastly nature, but she'd never confided her visions to anyone – not to her two children, now grown and living their own lives in Boston and Philadelphia; not to her fans and admirers; not even to her late husband, Benjamin, who had passed away due to a heart attack a few years back. She'd meant to tell him, someday…but he'd gone to his grave believing her occasional sudden stumbles and wide-eyed gasps were simple attacks of vertigo. *But this one was so much worse–*

"What can I get you, Mrs Goldberg?" A familiar voice snapped her out of her reverie, and Gloria smiled at the speaker before she could even fix upon a face, a reflex from shaking out of so many visions before. The proprietress, Velma, had gently touched her hand, and Gloria patted it reassuringly.

"Just some coffee, thank you."

"You had a reading tonight, didn't you, hon?"

Gloria took comfort in the mundane sounds of Velma giving the already-gleaming counter a courtesy wipe down before setting down a white ceramic mug and filling it with coffee.

"Land sakes, but I couldn't do with getting up in front of people and telling them a story. I think my knees'd turn to jelly right on the spot! Just cream, right, Mrs Goldberg?"

"Right." Gloria's smile at the friendly middle-aged woman was genuine. "If I were making that story up on the spot, dear, I'd be just as scared as you. Lucky for me, I write them down, so I know exactly what I'm going to say! But you – I wouldn't be able to do what you do for half a week, bustling around, remembering everything just so. I don't know when you get time to rest!"

Velma laughed and flipped the towel to rest on her shoulder. "Oh, it ain't all bad. Why, Oliver Thomas is taking me to see the new play coming into town soon, something about a king or some such. Sounds like just the kind of thing to put on my glad rags for!"

Velma turned to get the cream from the opposite counter, which was set against the gleaming, metal-backed wall, and suddenly Gloria's breath caught in her throat. Through the service window in the chrome wilderness of the kitchen beyond was a figure – clad in silken robes once regal and golden, now stained and ragged – staring at Velma with a frightening intensity. The figure, unaware, turned back to Gloria, and the author's seized breath changed to a choking cough of fright. The rotting figure had only sockets where her eyes should be, shrouded with tiny ochre veils.

"Dear me, are you all right, hon?"

Gloria blinked. More of the vision. It's not going away; it's getting worse.

"Oh, fine–" Gloria affected a second cough, "–just caught a bit of tumult down my windpipe."

Velma laughed gaily, and Gloria glanced back through the service window, but the golden figure was gone as if it had never been. Which is probably true.

"A 'tumult'! Land sakes, don't you just turn a phrase," Velma chuckled. "Don't you bother spending your ten-dollar words on the likes of the folks here, honey; it's pearls before swine, I'm afraid."

"Who you callin' swine, huh?" a new, male voice demanded in mock outrage. Velma laughed again, moving over to pat the arm of a gentleman just sitting down at the right side of the counter.

"Don't you sass me, Sheriff Engle! You may be the law out on the streets, but in my establishment, I'm the boss!"

The laughter of the two let Gloria's mind calm for a moment. She counted the parfait glasses on the shelf and idly read the tickets tacked above the service window. Feeling steadier, she carefully took the cream and poured it into her coffee. A half second later, the white liquid bloomed through the dark, curling sweetly like–

–the explosion that rocked the ground beneath her, collapsing buildings like they were children's toys, flame that–

–cream in coffee. Only that. A simple stirring of her spoon, and the vision faded, replaced by the pleasantly murky, tan coffee. She sipped the bitter brew, tried to relax once more, and returned to taking in the small details of the room around her.

Velma's Diner wasn't big, but it was clean and well-minded, walled with simple stained wood and bright with hanging dome lights that cast a warm, bright glow. Well-loved glasses gleamed and metal appliances shone on the counter, evidence of Velma's inability to stand still without cleaning or polishing something. Turning her head, Gloria noticed that nobody was in the booths at this hour except, for one man who sat facing away from her with an *Arkham Advertiser* and a half-eaten muffin. The valise on the seat opposite him suggested he was a traveling salesman, probably from a nearby town like Kingsport, having one last bite before heading back out on the lonely road. He turned a page of the newspaper he was reading and idly scratched the back of his neck ...

No. Under his palm suddenly yawned a foreign tear, a mouth – no, a gill, like a giant fish, opening and flapping wetly like a bass in a boat, thrashing and gasping for air.

This isn't. It isn't real. It isn't stopping.

"Cherry, right, hon?"

The sheriff laughed. "Don't you make me say it twice, Velma; you know I can't refuse it baked fresh!"

The top of the glass pie stand clattered on the counter. The knife left the pie, red-smeared and sticky. The pie oozed on the plate, hideously crimson. And one cherry slowly rolled out of the crust and onto the plate like viscera, the cherries now not blood or offal but suckers on a great mess of limbs, octopodal and writhing, reaching out–

–as the limbs reached from the shattered sky, from that being – whose visage was madness itself–

"Oh! Dear me, are you all right? Did you slip?"

The vision had changed, burned away by a sudden radiance. Gloria blinked, dazzled, at the shape before her. Where the figure in yellow glaring from the kitchen had exuded corruption and decay, this one glowed with power and promise, glittering with an aura of magnificence that her visions had never shown her before. Gloria gaped, and passed a hand over her eyes–

And saw again that it was only the waitress Agnes, kind and concerned, kneeling beside her where she'd fallen onto the floor, sweet and lovely and tired. The younger woman helped Gloria to her feet, and the author tried without success to sense in her that strength and wondrous presence she'd detected before.

"Thank you," Gloria said slowly, willing herself to search in her handbag for the proper change. "I'm so sorry, but I believe I have a nasty summer cold coming on. I'll just be heading home."

"Don't mind the payment, Mrs Goldberg, really," Velma piped up apologetically, waving her dishtowel like a lady might a hankie. "It's just a cup of coffee! I couldn't bear it if you somehow came to harm in my own diner!"

If what I saw was true, it won't matter where we are.

"Oh, that's too kind of you, Velma. I promise I'll pay you double the next time I'm in."

Velma gave some kind of response she barely registered, which the author returned with a nod, and again Gloria felt ten miles away from herself as she exited the diner and scurried down the street toward home.

For the first time in my visions I saw something that made me feel… hope. Like the kind I put in my stories. Gloria didn't smile, but a knot inside her chest seemed to loosen a little. *I wouldn't mind something like that being real.*

ABOUT THE AUTHORS

JENNIFER BROZEK is an award winning author, editor, and tie-in writer. *A Secret Guide to Fighting Elder Gods*, *Never Let Me Sleep*, and *The Last Days of Salton Academy* were finalists for the Bram Stoker Award. She was awarded the Scribe Award for best tie-in Young Adult novel for *BattleTech: The Nellus Academy Incident*. *Grants Pass* won an Australian Shadows Award for best edited publication. A Hugo finalist for Short Form Editor and a finalist for the British Fantasy Award, Jennifer is an active member of SFWA, HWA, and IAMTW. She keeps a tight writing and editing schedule and credits her husband Jeff with being the best sounding board ever.

jenniferbrozek.com
twitter.com/jenniferbrozek

RICHARD LEE BYERS is the author of fifty horror and fantasy books including *This Sword for Hire* and *Blind God's Bluff*, novels for Marvel's *Legends of Asgard*, *Forgotten Realms*, and the Impostor series. He's also written scores of short stories, some collected in *The Things That Crawl* and *The Hep Cats of Ulthar*, scripted a graphic novel, and contributed content on tabletop and electronic games. A resident of the Tampa Bay area, he's an RPG enthusiast and a frequent program participant at Florida conventions, Dragon Con, and Gen Con.

twitter.com/rleebyers

AMANDA DOWNUM was born in Virginia, and has since spent time in Indonesia, Micronesia, Missouri, and Arizona, with brief layovers in California and Colorado. She lives in Austin with her partner and their snake, and can be found haunting absinthe bars, goth clubs, and other liminal spaces. Her hobbies used to include cooking hearts and rock climbing, but now most of her time is devoted to studying Mortuary Science. Her day job sometimes lets her dress as a giant worm.

amandadownum.com
twitter.com/stillsostrange

ANNIE VANDERMEER is a writer, game/narrative designer, founder of the Tiamat Collective, and general madwoman. She enjoys cooking, plants, video games, and crafting haunting tales of eldritch horror. She lives in Seattle with her significant other and the tenuous alliance of their three cats.

tiamatcollective.com
twitter.com/murderblonde

GRAEME DAVIS discovered the Cthulhu Mythos in 1982 after picking up an imported first edition of Chaosium's *Call of Cthulhu* RPG. He helped develop *Warhammer Fantasy Roleplay* and *Vampire: The Masquerade*, and he has written Cthulhu Mythos gaming material for several publishers. He is also the author of a *Dungeons & Dragons* novel and several published short stories.

graemedavis.wordpress.com
twitter.com/graemejdavis

A P KLOSKY is a Dayton-based freelance writer, editor, and game designer, having worked on projects from companies including Fantasy Flight Games, Cubicle 7 Entertainment, Pinnacle Entertainment Group, Fainting Goat Games, and more. As Owner/Chief Executive of Blackfall Press, Klosky wrote and produced the award-winning *Cold Steel Wardens: Roleplaying in the Iron Age of Comics*. In addition to roleplaying and board games, Klosky enjoys cooking, reading, writing restaurant reviews on Yelp, and spending time with his wife and daughter. He is, and always will be, a Pittsburgher.

blackfallpress.com
twitter.com/blackfallpress

JASON MARKER has written for numerous gaming worlds, including *Arkham Horror*, *Legend of the Five Rings*, *Star Wars: Edge of Empire*, and *Robotech*. He is currently the editor in chief of a large motorcycle news and lifestyle website.

MALLORY O'MEARA is the award-winning and bestselling historian and writer of *The Lady from the Black Lagoon* and *Girly Drinks*. Every week, she co-hosts the literary podcast Reading Glasses. She lives in the mountains near Los Angeles with her two cats, where she is working on her next nonfiction book. Bourbon is her drink of choice.

malloryomeara.com
twitter.com/malloryomeara

ARKHAM HORROR™

Fresh eldritch terrors coming soon...

Deep in the Amazon jungle, the boundaries between intrepid adventurers, dreamers, and deranged fanatics blur inside a web of terror.

A daring actress and a barnstorming pilot team up to investigate a disappearance, but must instead save the world from supernatural disaster.

ARKHAM HORROR™

Riveting pulp adventure as unknowable horrors threaten to tear our reality apart.

Something monstrous has risen from the depths beneath Arkham, Miskatonic University is plagued with missing students and maddening litanies, and a charismatic surrealist's art opens doorways to unspeakable places.

A movie director captures unnameable horrors while making his masterpiece, and an international thief stumbles onto a necrophagic conspiracy.

WORLD EXPANDING FICTION

Do you have them all?

ARKHAM HORROR
- ☐ *Wrath of N'kai* by Josh Reynolds
- ☐ *The Last Ritual* by S A Sidor
- ☐ *Mask of Silver* by Rosemary Jones
- ☐ *Litany of Dreams* by Ari Marmell
- ☐ *The Devourer Below* ed Charlotte Llewelyn-Wells
- ☐ *Dark Origins, The Collected Novellas Vol 1*
- ☐ *Cult of the Spider Queen* by S A Sidor
- ☑ *Grim Investigations, The Collected Novellas Vol 2*
- ☐ *The Deadly Grimoire* by Rosemary Jones
  (coming soon)

DESCENT
- ☐ *The Doom of Fallowhearth* by Robbie MacNiven
- ☐ *The Shield of Daqan* by David Guymer
- ☐ *The Gates of Thelgrim* by Robbie MacNiven
- ☐ *Zachareth* by Robbie MacNiven *(coming soon)*

KEYFORGE
- ☐ *Tales from the Crucible* ed Charlotte Llewelyn-Wells
- ☐ *The Qubit Zirconium* by M Darusha Wehm

LEGEND OF THE FIVE RINGS
- ☐ *Curse of Honor* by David Annandale
- ☐ *Poison River* by Josh Reynolds
- ☐ *The Night Parade of 100 Demons*
  by Marie Brennan
- ☐ *Death's Kiss* by Josh Reynolds
- ☐ *The Great Clans of Rokugan, The Collected Novellas Vol 1*
- ☐ *To Chart the Clouds* by Evan Dicken

PANDEMIC
- ☐ *Patient Zero* by Amanda Bridgeman

TERRAFORMING MARS
- ☐ *In the Shadow of Deimos* by Jane Killick

TWILIGHT IMPERIUM
- ☐ *The Fractured Void* by Tim Pratt
- ☐ *The Necropolis Empire* by Tim Pratt
- ☐ *The Veiled Masters* by Tim Pratt *(coming soon)*

ZOMBICIDE
- ☐ *Last Resort* by Josh Reynolds
- ☐ *Planet Havoc* by Tim Waggoner *(coming soon)*